What readers say about *Condemned to Freedom*:

What's so refreshing about John DeFrank's book is its originality. It's different. It's full of academic mischief. And some of the characters are just devilishly fun to follow.

As a screenwriter, I am constantly reminded that the reader had better want to turn the page, or else it's on to the next script. The character, Randori, is a rebel with an education who pulls you into his world of risk. But he's a hero with flaws. In today's motion picture world, it would be easy to latch onto him from the get-go. ... Once you begin to read this one, the story will grip you and head for the deep!

—Brian Kreider
Executive Director, Pennsylvania Historic Dramas
The Blue Eyed Six, What Would Mister Hershey Say?
Writer/Director/Producer – CNN, TNT, NFL Films

I rarely read current fiction, much of it being intellectually flabby. *Condemned to Freedom* has none of that. It flexes twists and turns of plot, gripping situations of intense social and educational impact, while relentlessly pelting with John DeFrank's indefatigable wit. My highest compliment: I read every page.

—Thomas DeAngelis
School Board President, Bishop McDevitt (Harrisburg, PA) and Parent

Condemned to Freedom provides a capsule of many of my experiences as a thirty-eight year secondary educator. The mystery weaves drama and suspense through some of the perils of public schools. Counselor Randori, a knight in shining armor, peppers the story with satire and humor, common weapons of wise educators. A very clever and insightful account of a "behind the scenes" view of public education.

—Frank Kuhn
Retired School Counselor and Coach

To Marilyn –
Best wishes to a first grade teacher.
Joh

CONDEMNED TO FREEDOM

A Novel

By

John DeFrank

BookLocker.com, Inc.
2010

ACKNOWLEDGEMENTS

First things first: to my family. Thanks and love to my wonderful wife Jamie for her unflagging support and assistance as I worked though potholes and plot holes. Jamie reads everything decent that comes down the pike, and her insights into what is believable and what is intriguing versus what is "garbonia" helped me more than she can know. She also endured and understood the *vacant stare*, symbolic of what passed for thought as I was either piecing together the puzzle of the mystery or wondering what kind of person attends a funeral because he wants to admire the casket. Laura, my beautiful daughter, who is more literate and intelligent than I can ever hope to be, read and proofread *Condemned*, and offered her keen insight into what literature ought to look like. Brian, my son number one, lightened the atmosphere with his sense of humor and beautiful guitar playing. And finally, Ethan, my youngest, my marvelous distraction, pulled me away from monomaniacal drudgery to play board games and catch baseball.

Captain Pat O'Rourke of the Derry Township (PA) Police was kind enough to listen to my story and inform me on investigative techniques, police procedures, and drug investigations. Bob Peebles, an officer with the Cornwall Borough (PA) Police, offered insight into the workings of a small rural department and the Drug Abuse Resistance Education (DARE) program. Trooper Joe Bressi of the Pennsylvania State Police helped me refine Nick Neidrich's identity. Any procedural or factual errors in the book are the result of the story-telling license I took and not the advice and consultation of these fine officers.

Sensei Guy and Rhonda Speicher, my Moo Duk Kwan instructors: thank you for seeing me through my martial arts education and training and putting up with my inability to raise a kick above the waist.

Alice Knutsen proofread the final copy of my manuscript and offered a sharp perspective that helped me smooth the final rough edges of the story. My original 180,000-word manuscript/monster was proofread/endured by Jackie Scacco, my administrative assistant.

Guinea pigs I asked to read the story included Larry Killian, a great pupil services director, psychologist, boss, and friend; Leigh Kuhn, a reading specialist and colleague from back in the old Catholic School days; Susan Rodgers, my sister-in-law, an elementary school teacher; Traci Paioletti, a family friend and good neighbor; and

MaryBeth Evanko, godmother to Ethan and Jamie's best friend. MaryBeth deserves special recognition for her amazing cookies and brownies, the glucose of which fueled my synapses.

To Dr. Barbara Pavan, Committee Chairperson for my doctoral dissertation, professor of Educational Administration at Temple University, and published author. Her comment that I ought to consider writing professionally gave me the confidence to undertake this project.

Finally, to anyone I forgot to mention, please accept my apology in advance. Be sure to let me know about my omission, so I can include you in the acknowledgements of the sequel.

Thanks and blessings.

John

FOREWORD

I met John DeFrank several years ago when I was working at the Pennsylvania Department of Education and was responsible for overseeing and administering six hundred Alternative Education Programs statewide. John was involved with setting up a new program at his school with an outside provider and wanted to ensure the best for the students. I had always respected his philosophy on how to help needy students. In his words they were "not bad kids, but hurting pups" and with guidance and supportive services, much like a mother with her pups, they could be nurtured and learn to be strong and self-sufficient. He believed in strong mental health and behavioral health care, with a large dose of character education, more than discipline and punishment. He was a champion for his students.

His book *Condemned to Freedom* exemplifies the good fight he has always fought and never tired of, yet within it bleeds perhaps a bit of the exasperation I know he feels at those in charge and of the status quo in education. The very special education laws that protect the weak and needy sometimes cover for the corrupt and immoral. *Condemned to Freedom* is a murder mystery but interwoven within these pages is John's own ideology of personal responsibility and the mission we must all share in living as role models for our youth and for our own souls.

Although *Condemned to Freedom* is a work of fiction, the lessons of life are there for the reader to unfold as John has threaded them within the characters and their actions. His Freedom County represents all the small towns that are troubled by the changes that they see: disappearing moral standards, drugs, local corruption, and murder within their own communities.

I don't believe that John feels he can erase all the evils of the world for these kids, but I do believe he would change the way we all deal with evil: by rising above it, and standing strong to our own convictions, whatever the consequences. Schools do not own the epidemic of violence, nor can they cure social-economic status or social injustice. What can be done is for each of us to commit to the morals and values we know to be true and just.

One of my favorite parts of the book is when "Doc" Randori, the counselor, talks about a parable written by Yuzan in the *Budo*

Shoshinshu to explain what real honor means to him. In the parable, a man entrusted his neighbor with a hundred gold pieces for safekeeping before he left on a journey. For security, no one, not even the man's own family, was to know of this arrangement. On the journey, the man was killed. ... Doc continues:

> Of course, it would've been dishonorable to keep the gold. But even in returning it to the man's family, we can judge the neighbor's personal level of honor. The lowest level would be to desire to keep the gold, but return it only out of fear of being caught. The next level would be to consider keeping it, but then realize that would be wrong and, feeling guilty, return it. The highest level of honor would be to return the gold without question or thought.

Recently, I took a "strength survey" for a leadership position. One of the questions dealt with stealing if there were no way you would be caught, and no one else would ever know. I hesitated for a moment. Years ago I would have answered very quickly but something in me has become weak. I thought of the great leaders of the past and present, and of those I know who would never think of doing such a thing, and of my parents who would be ashamed of me. Yet, the question said, "If there was no way you would be caught and no one else would ever know." That is where real character comes into play, doesn't it? John's book is about the level of honor in all of us.

Nancy A. Avolese, former Pennsylvania State Coordinator for Alternative Education and Founder of *The Center for Innovation Education Solutions, LLC*

This book is dedicated to American school teachers and counselors.

MAJOR CHARACTERS*
(Arranged in some semblance of order)

POLICE:

Ed Knepp – Sergeant, Newcastle Borough Police
Nick Neidrich – Trooper, Pennsylvania State Police
Harley Snitz – Chief of Police, Newcastle Borough

FREEDOM CONSOLIDATED SCHOOL DISTRICT PERSONNEL:

Cat Blanchard – Assistant High School Principal
Virgil Davis – Assistant High School Principal/Athletic Director
Leroy Dubcek – School Psychologist
Tammy Eboli – Teachers Association President/Department Chair
Kass Marburg – High School Principal
Meryl Morgan – School District Director of Secondary Education
Phil Olson – School District Director of Elementary Education
Brian "Doc" Randori – High School Counselor/Coordinator of Pupil
    Services
Kerry Wyatt – School District Director of Pupil Services

TEENAGERS:

Justin Frederickson – Student, Freedom Con High School
Paul Roberge – Student, Freedom Con High School
Brad Prusster – Student, Freedom Con High School

Three-year-old memo Sgt. Ed Knepp had hidden in his private logbook:

CONFIDENTIAL
FROM: Dr. Robert Samson
TO: Phil Olson, Kass Marburg
RE: District Restructuring

Phil and Kass: You are the only staff to get this notice. Destroy this memo when you finish reading it, and do not discuss it with anyone.

Effective next year, I am changing the organizational structure of the district to a Site-Based Management (SBM) model. What does this mean to you? In the past, principals answered to their division Director:
    Middle School and High School principals reported to
        Meryl Morgan, Director of Secondary Education;
    Elementary principals reported to
        you, Phil, as Director of Elementary Education;
    Pupil Services personnel reported to
        Kerry Wyatt, Director of Pupil Services.

Under SBM, principals will have autonomy over their buildings. The Directors will support the principals and coordinate efforts, but they will have no supervisory control. All administrative staff will report directly to me, and I will have final say over all district matters.

Phil, your elementary division will continue to operate the same as always. However, these changes will curtail the opposition I face from Meryl Morgan and Kerry Wyatt and allow all administrators and district staff to align their loyalties with my goals. You might ask where the School Board stands with regard to these changes: I have been assured that the Board will not oppose any decisions I make.

One final note, I will eliminate Doc Randori's position of Assistant Director of Pupil Services. Unfortunately, I cannot legally terminate his employment, but I will demote him to high school counselor. He will continue with some quasi-administrative duties for Wyatt and Morgan, but you, Kass, will share oversight of him, and I encourage you to monitor his performance and document all breaches of professionalism.

Man is condemned to be free because, once thrown into the world, he is responsible for everything he does.

—Jean-Paul Sartre

Big Bob Samson should have appreciated the last evening of his life: the soft requiem of a dove in a nearby hemlock, the heady incense of honeysuckle and mulberry on the sultry summer breeze, the blood-red sunset flowing along the western horizon. Instead, Samson raised his arms, turned his face to the sky, and thought of himself.

He was the chosen one, the man the Freedom Consolidated School District had depended on to resurrect its football program, and later the man who brought glory to the District as its superintendent. The community took pride in its football and education traditions, and Samson took credit for both. He was the creator; Freedom was his world.

Having emerged from the air-conditioned sepulcher of the District Office for the first time in twelve hours, Samson strode toward the steps, moving with the bearing and confidence of an ex-United States Marine. He was proud to count himself among that elite group, contending that there are no *ex*-Marines—*semper fidelis* means *always* faithful. They break recruits to the core before absorbing them into the Corps. In most, the Marines develop character, but if the core is rotten, it twists into caricature. Sometimes it is difficult to tell the difference.

Samson's football record spoke for itself. His arbitrary leadership style and questionable knowledge were balanced by supreme self-confidence and, even his most grudging detractors had to admit, strong organizational skills. He also had been blessed with the greatest run of talent the county had ever seen and a coaching staff made up of excellent teachers and willing disciples. Through the years, the details blurred; mirages became reality and eventually mutated into the legend that was Big Bob Samson.

Success as a coach allowed Samson to circumvent the established route to administrative power. As a teacher, Samson lectured colleagues on how things ought to be, and would be if he were superintendent. He was the man with the plan: run a district as you run a military unit or a football team—with discipline, organization, and honor. He bypassed the dues-paying role of assistant principal to become the high school principal. Three years later, he vaulted over better-qualified superiors to be appointed district superintendent, further enhancing his stature in Pennsylvania educational circles.

Thus was his reputation built, and wherever Samson went he was treated with a reverence he had come to expect. Anyone who treated him with less than "proper respect" became a lifelong enemy. Most feared personal and professional retribution, but if it came down to it, Samson was prepared to "kick ass and take names." He followed a regimen of weightlifting and boxing that carved his frame into lean fighting trim. There were times he had challenged men to fight, but to his regret, those incidents never got past the verbal humiliation of his adversary. Secretly, he wished someone would physically attack him so he could inspire awe through retaliation.

Samson envisioned that someday a movie might be made of his life, and he often imagined his final scene. It would be grand and poignant, an occasion of pride and sorrow for those whose lives had been graced by his presence, all accompanied by a sound track of French horns in melancholic but heroic anthem.

His end, however, came with a tiny jingle of car keys that brought heavenly promise but served instead as his death knell. Bob Samson, "Big Bob" to admirers from afar and friends up close, *Doctor* Samson, as he insisted to everyone else, faced his last battle almost alone. He would have preferred it that way, because the scythe that cut through pride and flesh came as unappreciated as the sunset and the mourning dove and the scented breeze. In the end, Big Bob Samson knew the reaper and came to realize that death overcomes all myths incarnate. And, as the day faded to black, so did the life of a legend.

The Newcastle Borough Municipal Building stood hard against the southern ridge of the Freedom Valley. Originally named Iron Hall, it was a monument to rustic gentility; its walls were built with stone hauled from the nearby quarry, stone left as dregs by the miners who supplied the raw materials for the historic iron forge. Massive oak doors, hewn from the surrounding forest, were sturdy gatekeepers to the past; gleaming elongated windows reflected communal aspirations for the future. The fixtures, forged in the local furnace, were chevrons of respect held for this emblem of community.

When the iron ore played out, Iron Hall came to symbolize the local ironworkers themselves—dregs left behind for greater riches elsewhere. Strong and proud, but dregs, nonetheless. The sense of insular community was lost forever as the men went to work in the steel mill in the neighboring city of Freedom. Iron Hall, the only community center large enough to host the annual Fasnacht Day festival and every kind of bee imaginable, thus became the Municipal Building, and history was partitioned into borough offices and the police station. With the signature pride that natives of Pennsylvania Dutch country hold for their property, craftsmen's care was taken to preserve its architectural integrity.

Solid and traditional, apt descriptions for both the building and the law enforcement crew it housed. Chief Harley Snitz had headed the Newcastle Police for 31 years, due in large part to personal hallmarks of prudence and courtesy. That his prudence ran to stodginess, even downright stubbornness, only endeared him to his constituents, as those traits fell in line with community mores. So respected was Snitz that when smaller adjacent boroughs cut their departments in cost saving measures, their governing bodies gladly chipped in fair shares to have the Newcastle force patrol those municipalities. As a result, Snitz's crew had grown to more than twenty officers and support staff and ranged across a crescent running from Avalon on the eastern edge of Freedom City through Newcastle Borough in the south to Culver Pond in the southwest—the entire southern third of Freedom County.

In recent years, the emergence of drugs, with the inevitable thefts and assaults that followed, stretched the limits of Snitz's force, and the fact that people wanted their children to be regarded as children and only the pushers be brought to justice stretched the limits of his patience. The increasing problem made some citizens wonder if the Chief's time had passed. He wanted to handle drug investigations with his own unit, despite pressure to seek help from the Pennsylvania State Police.

Bob Samson's death was a different story. Snitz never had handled a murder investigation, so teaming with that esteemed outfit made sense. If he held any lingering doubts, the events of the weekend had convinced him. On Friday night, after Samson's wife reported him missing, activity was confined to Snitz's own department. Then, after the body was discovered on Saturday morning, news crews from Freedom and the nearby cities of Harrisburg, Lancaster, and York arrived to cover the accident that had befallen the local sports legend. Actually, "felled" would have been a better word, for it seemed that Samson had gone down like Achilles by what some thought to be his only weakness: reckless driving through the winding hills of southern Freedom County. By the time regional late news aired, the death of a beloved school superintendent and one of the most successful football coaches in mid-state history was the lead story. And through the miracle of television, Snitz's face, weathered by years and world-weary wisdom, had become familiar to central-Pennsylvanians.

The Chief shunned the public light, but he was thankful that the media still viewed Samson's death as accidental. His decision to enlist the help of the State Police was looked upon as an act of magnanimity and, yes, prudence that further endeared him to the citizenry. Truth be told, it was also a formality; they were already involved. A State Police crime scene team had discovered that the initial theory of the cause of Samson's death—a drive off a cliff and resultant drowning in the quarry—was wrong.

Still, Snitz did not appreciate being called to State Police barracks to organize the investigation. In his mind, Newcastle Borough was where the murder occurred; that was where the investigation ought to begin. Summoning his resolve, he insisted that their investigator travel to his turf so they could begin working on leads right away. To his surprise, the invitation was accepted without debate.

Standing at the picture window behind his desk, the Chief was as much taking respite in the view as he was watching for the trooper who was to become his partner when an unmarked cruiser roared into the lot. Snitz sipped coffee from a paper cup and shook his head in mild amusement as a tall man in civilian clothes unfolded out of the vehicle.

Why do police go to so much trouble making their cars inconspicuous that they actually stand out? Who would buy a car like that? Then there was the officer himself. This was certainly the investigator Snitz had been waiting for. It was too muggy for a jacket, unless a person was concealing something, like a sidearm. Any lingering doubts about the man's identity were snuffed when the Chief noticed the crew cut—the planar perfection of which would have done the Carrier Enterprise proud—and white athletic socks, peeking out over black soft-soled shoes, spit-shined neon signs that advertised *cop*. Snitz's first impression, sense of style notwithstanding: if ever there were a recruiting poster for the Pennsylvania State Police, this man should be the model. As the trooper moved forward, his jacket flapped open to reveal a black T-shirt straining against a coiled steel torso that matched a stern face of chiseled obsidian.

As Snitz left his office to welcome the investigator, he passed Phyllis Utz, his dispatcher, and Ed Knepp, his second-in-command. The two were sharing donuts and complaints about the intrusion of an outsider onto their turf. Aware that even under the best of circumstances the locals were reserved toward newcomers, the Chief said, "He's here; make him feel welcome." And then, more as an order than a request: "Please."

His flinty glare had barely sparked when the trooper entered, craning his neck to take in the surroundings before leveling his gaze on the three people staring up at him. The deputy and the dispatcher remained motionless, except for jaws engaged in slow, thoughtful mastication. The Chief smiled and stepped forward, extending his hand.

"Harley Snitz, welcome to Newcastle."

"Chief." A small crease etched upward at the corners of the state policeman's mouth. "Trooper Neidrich. I'll be heading up the investigation from our end."

Snitz made introductions. His face flushed when Knepp gave a wary nod and Utz's face squeezed into something that came across like the reaction to a gas pain.

If Neidrich noted their disapproval, he gave no sign. "Beautiful building you have here, Chief. Sorry if I offended you by asking you to come to my office, but I've learned to trust the security at our barracks."

"I surely understand." Snitz stared at Knepp, whose own eyes were downcast, gazing over his imposing epigastrial horizon that put the donut box on the desk in partial eclipse.

"Let's go to my office Trooper Neidrich. … Coffee? Donut?"

Again, Neidrich's lips made an almost imperceptible curve into what might have been a smile. "Coffee's good." Patting his midsection, he added, "But no donut, thanks. And please call me Nick."

The weight lifted from Snitz's chest. Years of police work had honed his ability to judge people, and so, despite the trooper's somber presence, he felt he was going to like the young man. At times, the State Police acted as though they were a superior breed, firm in the belief that they underwent more grueling and sophisticated training and upheld a loftier mission than local lawmen. Snitz, for his part, had always held himself as a model to the community and believed that fitness and integrity were essential to the profession. The trooper seemed to treat the Chief as a peer.

Snitz shot a sidelong glance at Knepp to see if Neidrich's words had made an impression. The sergeant hefted the donut box like a football under one arm so he could eat with his free hand as he shuffled down the hall.

"I'm new to the area," Neidrich said. "What kind of support can we count on?"

"The city cops will be there if we need them. They have enough business of their own, though. The DA's a lame duck, he'll be happy to leave us alone."

"Good," Neidrich said. "Any suspects come to mind?"

"Most folks loved Bob Samson."

"Let's keep respect for the dead out of this." The trooper's words nipped at the heels of Snitz's.

The curt admonition shook the Chief into professional mode. "How do we know for sure he was murdered?"

Neidrich's features softened and the almost-smile reappeared. "Guess I'd better explain." As quickly as his expression had relaxed, it hardened again. His eyes paused on Snitz before honing in on Knepp. "I want to emphasize, though, the longer people think the death was an accident, the better off we'll be."

"We'll keep mum; won't we, Ed?" Snitz said, a slight threat in the undertone.

After watching Knepp bob his head in vigorous assent and mime the movement of a key turning on his lips, Neidrich continued. "Samson was dead before he went over the cliff. There was no water in the lungs, so he wasn't knocked unconscious by the impact, then drowned. Impact wounds came post mortem. His seat belt wasn't buckled, but the air bag went off. Then there's the fact that –"

Knepp interrupted. "Wait a minute. Bob always wore his seatbelt. I've ridden with him in that Mercedes; man, he tooled!"

"Interesting," Neidrich said. "Trajectory from the cliff-edge to where the car settled in the water indicates he wasn't moving fast enough to have been out of control."

Snitz winced. It would be pointless to tell Knepp he should have chided his hero for being reckless; his sergeant never had the guts to stand up to Samson. "If he always wore a seatbelt except on Friday …" the Chief scrubbed his chin with the palm of his hand, "that might support a scenario that he was helped off the cliff."

Neidrich started to speak, but Knepp broke in again. "What's that have to do with the price of bologna in Lebanon?"

Snitz exhaled a deep, slow breath. "You see, Ed, either the murderer didn't realize Dr. Samson always wore his belt, or he wanted the plunge to maximize body damage, or both."

"True," Neidrich said, "and some of the injuries can't be explained by his dive. In fact, some were obviously the result of an assault."

Knepp broke into raucous laughter punctuated by a scowl. "You're saying he was beat up? Nobody could handle Big Bob Samson. No one in the county." He looked to Snitz for support, but found only a disapproving frown.

"Ed's exaggerating, but it would take a tough man to handle Dr. Samson, I dare say. What kind of injuries are you talking about?"

Neidrich leaned forward, elbows on knees, and clasped his hands. Snitz noticed fingers like old tree roots—the gnarled trophies of a hand-fighter—before the trooper's words pulled his mind back to the topic at hand.

"Wounds were inflicted by a tubular object about an inch in diameter. Black and gold paint flecks—highly shellacked, *japanned—*

were embedded in the wounds. Nothing in the car or the quarry matched up."

"The past year there's been quite a few muggings," Knepp said. "Has to do with drugs—getting money for drugs, I mean. I'd be for thinking we should check some of our usual drug suspects. Bet your bottom dollar Bob dinged them up a bit."

Snitz shook his head. "Most drug-related robberies have been purse-snatchings or car break-ins. Not many outright assaults, unless they were deals gone bad."

"Could've been a mugging," Neidrich said. "Wallet was rifled. But druggies probably would've left the body. Besides, this attack was efficient." Neidrich leaned even closer and spoke in a near-whisper.

"Here's the clincher, along with the blows, there was a single thrust of a sharp—very sharp—instrument up through the solar plexus. Straight-edged double blade."

After a moment of stunned silence, Knepp bolted upright. "Must've been two perps, maybe more. It'd take at least two people to kill Bob. Ain't, Harley?"

Ain't, Harley? — a shard of local argot, meant to elicit agreement. It would have made the hair on the Chief's neck stand on end if he were ever anything less than impeccably groomed. Whenever Knepp emitted the phrase, Snitz wanted to disagree, even if the attached assumption was correct. "No one is invincible, Ed."

Rather than acknowledge his boss's tempered response, Knepp continued. "And it would take two people to move him; he weighed a good two-twenty. But what I don't understand is why they'd move his body."

"I can think of two reasons off hand," Snitz said. "The killers wanted it to seem like an accident, or, more likely, the location of the attack could lead to their identities."

"That's my thought," Neidrich agreed. "So we need to backtrack his steps."

Knepp sat up. "I can help you with that. I know his hangouts."

"Good, we'll check those places right away."

"Have you established time of death?" Snitz asked.

"The body being in the water makes it tough to be exact. Security system has Samson coding out at 8:03. Sunset was 7:48—dusk, good cover for an attack."

"Bloody knuckles?" Knepp asked. "Skin under the nails? DNA?"

"Again, water's our enemy. We got some hair and fibers. Also, grass stains on his pants and gravel in the cuffs, which could've come from falling during the assault or the body being dragged. But there was no indication he fought back. Whoever it was got the drop on him, maybe someone he knew. Back to my original question, any suspects?"

"Dr. Samson made some enemies." The Chief scrubbed his chin again, and his face screwed into a pucker from the effort it took to say something negative about a person. "He had power. Sometimes he used it for good, sometimes for not so good. He went after folks who rubbed him the wrong way. Enough for someone to murder him? I don't know. Folks didn't mess with Dr. Samson, though. I'd figure someone to shoot him before taking him on close range."

"OK," Neidrich said, "Let's cross-reference people who had an ax to grind with those physically and emotionally capable of carrying out the job."

"I think two addicts ambushed him for drug money." Knepp rose to choreograph his hypothesis, playing three roles and embellishing his improvised skit with staccato commentary. "One perp holds a gun on him. The other perp takes his money. Bob takes the punks on. He disarms the one with the gun, but the other perp stabs him. Then the perp who had the gun picks it up and pistol-whips Bob after he's down. To get rid of the evidence, they take him to the quarry and send him off." Knepp bent over, palms on knees, puffing for breath. He mopped a sleeve across his brow and stuffed his shirt back in his pants, a futile effort because, as he squatted to retake his seat, his shirttails made another break for it. "Yep, it was druggies," he wheezed, nodding with conviction, having forgotten the integral point that Samson had suffered no defensive wounds.

Taking advantage of his sergeant's mental lapse, the Chief squinted and said, "That's an interesting scenario, Ed; I think you ought to follow up on it, especially since drug investigations are your specialty. You can be in charge of that prong of the investigation." Snitz glanced at Neidrich, who was staring at Knepp, impassive except for a furrowed brow. "Meanwhile, I'll work with Trooper Neidrich."

"Good to go that way," Neidrich said with a nod, understanding the Chief's intent. "Someone who knows the locals following both lines of investigation."

Wide-eyed, Knepp asked, "How many State Bulls can I have to help me?"

Neidrich started to respond, but Snitz cut in, speaking with slow-paced sagacity: "You should follow the drug lead alone. That way, when the truth about Dr. Samson's death breaks, and the State Police are concentrating on the personal grudge angle, we'll draw attention away from you. That way, you can operate with greater latitude." The Chief nodded, adding softly, reverentially, "A lone wolf."

Gazing off into the middle distance, Knepp said, "I like that."

Snitz turned to Neidrich and changed the subject. "As far as suspects, there have been rumors of affairs, but if they're true, he did a good job covering his tracks. He moonlighted business deals, too, real estate and such. Maybe someone felt cheated."

"That's where we'll start," Neidrich said.

Knepp had just inhaled a huge chug of coffee and almost choked in his eagerness to speak. "Don't forget the Freedom Con people. My sister-in-law, Lionda, is a secretary in the District Office, and she gives me the inside poop. Most school people loved Bob, but a few hated him. For the haters, start in Kerry Wyatt's office, where Lionda works. Wyatt's in charge of special education, counseling, psychology," Knepp gave a dismissive wave, "that stuff. Him and Meryl Morgan, she's the Director of Secondary Education; they didn't get along with Bob. They're eggheads. Wyatt's a bleeding-heart, always going on in that psychobabble. Morgan keeps coming up with ideas to fix things that aren't broken. Because of Bob, the District runs like a clock."

"You consider them suspects?"

"Wyatt's too old and Morgan's a woman." Knepp sneered. "Plus, they're chickens. But they're in tight with the guy who would do it for them: Doc Randori. He's Wyatt's hatchet man. No one likes him, and he doesn't like anyone right back."

"That doesn't make him a suspect," Snitz said. "Dr. Randori's an all right fellow."

"To you, maybe, but I've visited Lionda when Randori's there. Everyone will be joking around, then I'll walk in and the others keep going, but he just stares at me. He never talks about his personal life, and he doesn't socialize."

"Wanting privacy doesn't make him a murderer, Ed."

"It sure makes him suspicious. Besides, nobody hated Bob more than Randori."

Neidrich sat forward. "Tell me more."

"They had bad blood from back when Randori coached football at St. Thomas More. Bob coached there first, you see, and he had the best record ever at that school. Then Bob came over to Freedom Con. Randori followed Bob at Thomas More and never could fill his shoes. His Catholics played against us, and we whupped him every year."

"Come on, Ed, there's a little more to the story."

Knepp bent closer to Neidrich and lowered his voice. "Darn right there's more. According to Lionda and Theresa Wagner—that's Wyatt's other secretary—Randori was an administrator, Wyatt's assistant, until Bob demoted him to guidance counselor. Bet that cut his pride. Yep, if I was looking inside the District, that's where I'd start."

Neidrich studied Knepp's face. "Any suspects besides this Randori guy?"

"No one who had the motives and ability like Randori."

"How so?"

"Randori has a bad temper—and he's a karate expert. Ironic, isn't it?"

"Not ironic, Ed," Snitz said, "it's coincidental."

Swollen purple clouds kept the dawn at bay, muting the rectangular starkness of the Freedom Consolidated District Office. A crouching shadow took the steps in lithe strides then slipped through the glass entrance door and dissolved into the inky, tomb-like interior. Working toward the rear of the building, the intruder was swift and silent, a predatory cat—with each step, the outside edge of the foot touched the carpet then padded inward onto the ball and propelled the body forward.

Outside the Pupil Services Suite, the intruder surveyed the secretarial station, the buffer zone between the hallway and Kerry Wyatt's office. At the far end, a lamp cast a small cone of illumination for Theresa Wagner, one of Wyatt's two administrative assistants, who sat with earphones on, typing a recorded transcript. As usual, Wagner had been the first employee in the building. Soon, though, Kerry Wyatt and Lionda Knepp, the other assistant, would arrive.

Reaching Wagner's throat unnoticed would be difficult. The path was a treacherous route through unkempt stacks and random files strewn like autumn leaves across a forest floor, leaving narrow estuaries of carpet that led to Wyatt's office, the secretaries' desks, and the vault. The vault. It held the records of every student who had undergone psychological testing. The intruder froze in reflection.

A late-afternoon breeze pushes lace curtains aside, ushering slanted sunlight into the bedroom. Shadows dance along the wall and flutter on the ceiling, but neither gentle breeze nor warm sunlight brings solace to the little boy cringing beside the low, marble-topped dresser as he stares through a sliver of doorway into the hall. He wishes he could shut the door like a stage curtain and end the scene. There is no ending this scene, though; nothing a ten-year-old can do. It has to play out, and it will end. It has to end.

An anguished howl pierces the air: "All right! All right!" The hall light clicks on, and then silence, except for a quivering sob and the drone of airplane propellers in the high distance.

The light switch clicks again, and the boy screws his eyes shut as the banshee scream pierces the air. "I get it! ... You proved you could find me! ... You always find me!" The light clicks on and off, on and off, accelerating to strobe-like speed until the boy can stand it no longer; he claps his hands over his ears and opens his mouth in a silent scream as the frantic voice rings out, "Leave me alone! Please leave me alone!"

Footfalls trip down the steps. The front door opens and slams shut. Again, welcome silence. The boy opens his eyes and pivots to the window, parting the curtain so he can peek down onto the peaceful suburban scene. He looks up and down the street and holds his breath, hoping it is over.

Hope crashes down as his mother reappears in the middle of the street, arms aloft, face raised to the skies. Even the elms that line the street cannot muffle the piercing shrieks. "You win! ... I give up! ... You win!" She chants over and over, the supplicant falling to her knees and crossing herself. "God, make them stop!"

Neighbors peer through windows. Bolder ones step onto their porches to stare or exchange glances, repulsed yet transfixed by the horrid matinee.

The curtain dropped on the amber past, and wild eyes constricted to slits of grim determination. The intruder glanced up at the clock to see how long the reverie had lasted—seconds.

Bending at hips and knees, he snaked forward, a stare fixed upon his prey. One wrong move would incite a preemptive strike to cut off a scream. Reaching for Wagner's throat, the attacker snarled, "Who killed Bob Samson?"

The assistant's hands shot up, her chair flew back, and she let fly a haymaker. "I hate you, Randori!" she shrieked.

Leaning back as the telegraphed punch whizzed within inches of his nose, Doc Randori responded with a satisfied smirk, prompting a schizophrenic reaction as Wagner laughed despite herself while cocking her fist for another swing. Before she could launch it, the lights went on.

Kerry Wyatt, the Director of Pupil Services, entered and he surveyed the scene. His graying temples pulsed and bulldog jowls set, and he pointed an accusing finger at Wagner. "You!" he seethed. "The greatest educational philosopher since John Dewey has been lost to the world, and you try to decimate our ranks even further? What is wrong with you, woman?"

Riled and ready to rumble, Wagner shot back: "You call yourself a psychologist? Joking about Dr. Samson's death; you'll go to hell for that!"

Wyatt's feigned fury melted into a broad Cheshire Cat grin, and his glistening, coal black eyes gleamed at the sudden opportunity to confront moral indignation. "Is that right, Mother Theresa? As I recall, no one harassed Bob Samson more than you did."

Still struggling to regain her composure, the woman screeched, "He wasn't dead then!" Glancing past Wyatt, Wagner spotted Meryl Morgan entering the office. "Boy, am I glad to see you. Help me out here."

Most people were glad to see Morgan. The consummate administrator in demeanor and ability; at the same time, she was no one's idea of the classic schoolmarm: a mane of wavy raven tresses framed her face; dark eyes and lush lips competed for attention with a perfect olive complexion—a masterpiece set atop a pedestal of tortuous Mediterranean curves. Realizing that, to many, her beauty defined her, Morgan rarely let down her guard; it was only around Wyatt and Randori that she came close to relaxing.

She serpentined along the same route Randori had taken earlier. "You know, if a person got off on bureaucratic effluence, this place would be positively orgasmic." Morgan's words came curt and pointed. "Let me guess; Doc has been harassing Theresa again, and Kerry, in a weak attempt to add humor, has confirmed that even the most intelligent man will prove himself an imbecile if given half a chance."

"Meryl, I'm appalled," Randori said. "You, of all people, jumping to unwarranted conclusions. I was testing Theresa's reflexes. Then, when Kerry came in, we started discussing Bob's place in history."

"Better history than current events," Morgan said. "Hate to say it, but there it is."

"You too, Ms. Morgan?" Wagner said, gaping. "I thought if anyone had compassion it would be you."

Morgan trained a stern gaze on Wagner. "Bob Samson was no friend to the kids in this district, at least not the needy ones."

"Why help the *great unwashed*?" Randori said. "Their parents don't pull our strings. Freedom Con takes care of the country club set and the jocks."

Lionda Knepp, Wyatt's second administrative assistant, arrived in time to hear Randori's sardonic declaration. She tossed her purse on her desk and, without greeting or introduction, launched into a creditable imitation of Samson's booming basso: "We got to get rid of Randori. Who needs a counselor when we could hire another cheerleading coach for me to bang."

Morgan arched an eyebrow. "How counterintuitive is that?"

Wyatt and Randori smiled at Morgan's words. The previous year, Randori had begun using "counterintuitive" as a euphemism, synonymous with the World War II military acronyms SNAFU and FUBAR, but more covert. Whenever Samson and his administrative cronies arrived at one of their many faulty conclusions or unethical decisions, Morgan, Wyatt, or Randori would respond with something like, "Sorry, but that seems counterintuitive," and bring sub rosa relief to an otherwise frustrating experience.

Wyatt moved to the entrance of his conference room. "Now that Meryl is here, let's meet before things start hopping." As he closed the door, he said to no one and everyone, "And now that Lionda is here, she can accompany Theresa in a game of ring around the rosary over Bob's soul."

Inside, Wyatt pulled a chair away from the table as a gesture for Morgan to sit beside him, but she was already moving to a seat alongside Randori. "That headline in the *Chronicle*," she said: " 'A Legend in His Own Time.' Can you believe that? Then, the article—"

"Yeah, well I'm a rumor in my own time," Randori cut in. "What garbonia. And I'll pass on paying respects at the funeral if you don't mind."

Morgan laughed and gave a backhand slap at Randori's arm. "God, Doc, you wouldn't respect anyone who acted like a boss. You're lucky; you don't have to be political. Kerry and I are on the Cabinet; if we didn't show, people would notice." Her brows rose with a sudden new interest. "I wonder if Virgil will go to the funeral." She referred to Virgil Davis, an assistant principal/athletic director who was their main ally at the high school.

"Virgil will go," Wyatt said. "He and Bob were ex-servicemen and they coached football together. Virgil once told me that he always attends funerals of colleagues, even those he didn't like. It's a matter of respect for a comrade who fought a common foe. He sees him to the grave, and, as a symbolic send-off, tosses dirt on the casket. It's a custom the men in his unit started, and he's continued it ever since."

"Speaking of dirt," Morgan said, "Bob dealt him so much that I would think some tiny part of Virgil would be glad to be rid of him."

Wyatt shook his head. "To Virgil, it's a matter of honor. He told us there was only one exception to their custom, a soldier they were so prejudiced against that they ended their relationship with the man altogether."

"Virgil?" Morgan said, incredulous. "Prejudiced?"

"Hard to believe, I know. But you heard it, too, Doc; isn't that what he said?"

"Something like that, but I don't think he meant it the way it sounded; he just had too much to drink. I will be anxious to hear if Virge keeps up his custom, though." Randori pushed himself erect. "Can we talk about something else? I don't want to waste any more time on Bob Samson."

Wyatt nodded and heaved a deep sigh. "Well, now there's an opening at the top. Are you going to apply, Meryl? I'll support you."

"Me too," Randori said, grinning, "but that would probably hurt more than help. Besides, I'm worried that Phil Olson has his political ducks in a row." Olson, one of Bob Samson's protégés and the Director of Elementary Education, was Morgan's counterpart and equal on the organizational chart. "Phil knows what's near and dear to each board member, and he's kissed it passionately, proving once again that, at Freedom Con, platitudes trump philosophy."

"Meryl is best qualified," Wyatt said. He reached to touch Morgan's forearm, but her eyes shot a glare that made his hand recoil. "At the emergency Board Meeting last night they promised a fair and balanced selection process. Meryl will far outshine Phil."

When concentrating on a person, Randori resembled a predatory bird: piercing, close-set eyes; Roman nose; set jaw; hair brushed back into a tight ponytail—all elements that intensified the impression. As he examined the slight tumescence of the veins in Wyatt's neck, the counselor forced a disarming smile. " 'Fair and balanced,' I can't wait. Phil's the kind of guy that rises in this system. He says the right things to the right people, never makes waves. And, above all, he always chants the District mantra, 'We have to do what's right for kids,' even while he makes decisions that contradict it."

"Meryl got her position on merit," Wyatt said. "And I'd like to think I was qualified when they created this job for me."

Randori shook his head. "You guys are too close to the situation. Sure, you're the best qualified to do what you do, and, believe me, you make us all look good. But, neither of you is appreciated. Kerry, you run Pupil Services because no one else can or cares to, and it's your head on the block when things go wrong, which is inevitable. Meryl, you're like the first lady. You look good in the position—and Bob would've liked to see you in a few other positions, too."

"That's inappropriate," Wyatt snapped, "even by your standards!"

Morgan held a hand up to stave off Wyatt's defense of her honor. "It's all right, Kerry." She shot a hard sidelong glare at Randori. "This is why we keep Doc around: he's like a pet ape that throws shit at our rose-colored glasses."

Randori searched Morgan's eyes and saw the wounds his words made. "Look Meryl, if you wanted to be superintendent, you should've pandered to the country club set or picked up some board member's pet project. Instead, you focused on helping the neediest kids, which everyone thought was cute, but it wasn't politically savvy."

"Don't you think you're being just a little cynical?"

"Cynical, Meryl? Bob wanted you on the Cabinet so he could say, 'Look how enlightened I am, having a woman on board.' The way he set things up, though, the principals run the buildings and he ran the District, which leaves you and Kerry in a purgatory where you have all of the responsibility to make things work but none of the power to—"

"Stop," Morgan said. First anger, and then a fleeting sadness swept across her face.

"I'm sorry, Meryl," Randori said. "I didn't mean to—"

Morgan gripped the counselor's hand and rose to leave. "Shut up." Turning her back to the men, her voice softened. "Don't worry about it, Doc. It's one of the caustic realities of befriending a person who holds the human race in disdain."

Her verbal parting shot delayed her long enough to avoid a literal parting shot by way of a door to the face as Lionda Knepp burst in, eyes wide. "God, Meryl, I'm so sorry! I hate to barge in but, but—"

From the far reaches of the office came Theresa's disembodied voice. "Oh, for heaven's sake Lionda, spit it out."

"Bob Samson was killed!"

"I hear Harry Truman isn't doing too well, either," Randori said, grasping the opportunity to lighten the pall he had cast over Wyatt and Morgan.

"No, wiseass, I mean his death wasn't an accident. Ed just called. But please don't say anything to anyone. It's confidential."

"Not for long, I'd wager," Wyatt said. His dig at the Knepps' lack of discretion would have passed unappreciated except for Randori's quick glance.

"But he died in a car accident," Morgan said.

"Ed said some of the injuries were inconsistent with a car crash."

Randori smiled, but without humor. "Bob's car took a header a hundred feet into a quarry. Seems like a pretty wide array of hurts could occur."

Wyatt pressed for details. "What kind of injuries?"

"Ed didn't say."

"There goes my theory," Wyatt said with a resigned shake of the head. "I thought he was trying to see if his ego would fill the gorge."

Morgan frowned at Wyatt and prodded: "Did your brother-in-law say anything else?"

"Well, you know how the paper said he might've hit an unexpected curve? Dr. Samson grew up out there; he knew that road like the back of his hand. Then they thought, what with all the deer in those woods one might've run in front of him and he swerved. But there were no skid marks. Seems like he just drove real slow right into the quarry. Anyway, my source on the police force," Lionda said, almost giddy at having the opportunity to use the phrase, "thinks things are going to get interesting. The State Police are in on it now."

Wyatt checked his watch as a signal for adjournment and flashed his Cheshire Cat smile. "Well, at least we won't lack for something to talk about at the wake."

Lionda rushed her boss. Wyatt backpedaled into his office, slamming the door in her face, but the buzz-saw shrillness of her voice cut through to reach his ears. "Don't you dare! Everything I told you is confidential police business." Her last words, "Do you hear me?" rose near the range of canine-only reception.

Randori patted the secretary's arm and smiled with reassurance. "Don't worry, Lionda, we won't let them take Ed's bullets away again."

The smothering stretch of humidity had lifted, unveiling the vivid hues of Nature's late-summer peak, and sunshine burnished the day, emblazoning it in soul remembrance. Before Nick Neidrich and Harley Snitz entered the District Office, the Chief gave a wistful glance to he sky. "Isn't this the way it always is? The past four days, we've been hoofing around the county in the most gosh-awful heat wave of the summer. Now here's a nice day, and we'll be stuck inside."

"We had to cover that turf," Neidrich said, sticking to business. "Seems everyone outside the District admired Samson, or at least said they did. When I learned how much his family stood to inherit, I was sure we'd at least catch a nibble."

"Odd couple, Dr. Samson and Sarah. She's good Mennonite stock from over in Mohnton. All those folks you met at their house were family."

"Nice people. I felt bad asking about Samson's will."

"They understood. No surprise, Sarah moving home with her sister and putting the real estate on the market with the profits going to her church. And the kids split the stock portfolio—not that either one needs it. They're doing OK for themselves."

"So, there goes the financial motive."

"I wouldn't suspect either one, anyway," Snitz said, pursing his lips in certainty. "I've known Bonnie and Robby since they were tykes. Great kids. They've got that Dutch work ethic and values. That's Sarah's doing."

"It struck me that no one in the family thinks ill enough of anyone to offer up suspects. That wasn't the case with Samson's friends, though; they all implied we ought to be looking at people he worked with."

Snitz scratched his temple. "Some did a lot more than imply."

Neidrich held the door, allowing Snitz to lead the way into the District Office. The receptionist, who was on the phone, smiled and waved them past.

They entered the Pupil Services Suite and Snitz stopped at the first desk. "Trooper Neidrich, this is Ed's sister-in-law, Lionda."

"Nice to meet you," the woman said, offering a hand while keeping a leery eye on the Chief. So, you guys are here to find out if

Kerry did in Dr. Samson?" Snitz started to speak, but Lionda trampled his words. "Well, you'll have to wait your turn. Kerry's on the phone with our lawyers; we've got another special ed hearing."

Theresa Wagner took off her headphones and, without waiting for introductions, chimed in, "It's getting so every family that doesn't like their kid's special ed plan wants to sue us instead of just work things out."

Lionda added, "I'd like to get my hands on the pencil-necked lawyer geeks that wrote these special ed laws. They're killing us."

Theresa interrupted again. "They think we'd like nothing better than to deprive some poor child of an education."

Neidrich held up his hands to stem the emotional tide, but the secretaries' passions escalated, one feeding the other in a mad tag-team. "I'm sure they don't—"

"The heck they don't," Theresa said, standing now, with one hand on her hip and the other pointing at Neidrich. "You have no idea—"

Wyatt appeared in his doorway and raised his voice above the din. "Back into your wicker baskets, you two. When I want you, I'll play a flute." He heaved an exasperated sigh and invited the lawmen into his office.

Before they sat, Snitz made introductions and added, "I guess you know we're looking into the possibility that someone had a hand in Dr. Samson's death."

Wyatt smiled as he shook Neidrich's hand. "Yes, nothing stays secret for long around Freedom—especially when Ed and Lionda are involved."

Snitz blinked and dipped his chin. "We need to look into some things, Mr. Wyatt. Can you think of anyone who hated Dr. Samson enough to want him out of the way?"

A wide grin spread across Wyatt's face. "Questions like that will hardly narrow things down. Bob had no dearth of detractors, and I may have been chief among them." Turning serious, he leaned forward, propping his elbows on the desk. "The question is more than who wanted him out of the way; it's who would follow through … with violence?"

"You're the psychologist," Snitz said, more in deference than as a challenge.

Wyatt's eyes held a mischievous glint. "Fair enough, I'll hypothesize. If he were poisoned, I'd say it was the Food Services Director; if he died of boredom, I'd suspect one of our fellow administrators; and if ruptured eardrums resulting in a cerebral hemorrhage did him in, just look outside this door for two banshees."

"Mr. Wyatt, be serious," Snitz said. "Your name has been mentioned."

"Me?" Wyatt laughed. "I was home that evening quaffing a bottle of mediocre Chardonnay to dull the pain of an equally ordinary movie Doc Randori recommended."

"When was the last time you saw Samson? Neidrich asked.

"That day. We had an unsatisfying meeting in which the agenda took a back seat to his self-promotion—typical. I was subjected to a philosophical diatribe along the lines of a filibuster until 6:00. Luckily, he had a later meeting."

"What did you do afterward?"

"I picked up a tuna sub with provolone from Sorrentino's—that was why the Chardonnay. Around 7:00, I started watching the movie. After that, I read and went to bed. I had to get up early to drive to New York to visit my daughter."

"Sorry I have to ask you this, but can anyone vouch for your whereabouts?"

Wyatt waved off the Chief's concern. "You're just doing your job, Harley." He pressed his fingertips together and tapped them to his lips as he stared into the middle distance. "I did talk to Meryl Morgan on the phone. She called near the end of the movie—9:00, maybe—wanting to know how my meeting with Bob went." His eyes sparkled. "Another thought just struck. I can prove my story is true. Perhaps you could dust the DVD for mayonnaise-smeared fingerprints. Then, using radiocarbon dating—"

"It doesn't seem to bother you that Dr. Samson is dead," Neidrich interrupted. "What was your problem with him?"

"The truth?" Wyatt's stare darkened and his jowls dropped into a forbidding frown. "I had the same problem anyone who wasn't one of his lapdogs had. As a man, he was a thug who wanted to prove he was more than that by getting a doctorate and dressing well. Professionally, he was a classic example of a man who rises to the top through politics and sheer testosterone. That's not uncommon in this business, but it had its impact on my programs. For a while, the only thing I had to fight was neglect, but then taxpayer pressure—and therefore school board pressure—came because of the costs of a growing district and giveaways to the union."

Neidrich continued to handle the questioning. "What kind of giveaways?"

"I believe you would call it 'the farm.' For a hard-liner who had community support, Bob unaccountably gave a number of concessions in the last negotiations. In the end, to offset some of the costs, he cut my budget, moaning about—how did he put it? —'The bottomless money pit of Pupil Services.' "

"Bet that was hard to take," Neidrich said, affecting a sympathetic tone.

"It certainly was, especially these days, when the school has to fill the parental role for an ever-increasing number of children. That responsibility falls directly on Pupil Services. But, what is it they say about fighting city hall? The Board backed Bob. So, it was the four of us against the District."

"Four of you?"

"Meryl Morgan, Doc Randori, and Virgil Davis joined me in the good fight." For Neidrich's benefit, Wyatt added, "The battle went beyond Pupil Services into Curriculum and Instruction—Meryl's area. At the risk of sounding self-righteous, it was a fundamental battle between doing what is best for students versus doing what is politically expedient. We're somewhat idealistic, but around here idealism is impractical." He paused to let his words set. "How's that for a profound observation?"

Snitz broke in. "From what I gather the disagreements became bitter at times."

Wyatt smiled and nodded. "It's a good thing Bob realized he needed Meryl and me to get things done. Forgive my arrogance, but his weaknesses were our areas of expertise, and those areas pretty much span the educational spectrum. That doesn't mean he gave up control, though. Make no mistake, Bob ran everything."

"Where does Dr. Randori fit in?" Neidrich asked.

"Doc is a counselor, so he helps both Meryl and me through his job coordinating the Counseling Department. Plus, he handles special education for me at the high school."

Snitz said, "If you and Ms. Morgan have no power, how can he get things done?"

"Doc's not an administrator; he's in the Association, so he can use guerrilla tactics, which Meryl and I can't get away with—union members can complain about other union members, but it's not a true labor grievance. Plus, Doc reads people well." Wyatt paused and narrowed his eyes, reconsidering. "That's an understatement. He has an uncanny sense of what's going on in people's minds. That helps him avoid some problems, but when there's a problem he can't avoid, he's relentless in dealing with it. Doc can handle a war of attrition because, to the District establishment, he's an outsider—no friends, no ties."

Snitz took advantage of the opening. "Would Randori get into a 'war of attrition' with Dr. Samson?"

Wyatt looked askance at Snitz. "I'm unclear what you mean by that, Harley. If you mean professionally, Bob had all the power, and Doc knew that. He wasn't in awe, though; he didn't even pretend to be. But murder? Doc has too much integrity for that."

"What caused the bad blood between them?" Neidrich asked.

"Bob had to have people under his thumb, and Doc rebels when someone asserts power over him. In that way, Doc shows some traits of Oppositional Defiant Disorder."

"Aren't folks like that prone to violence?" Snitz asked.

"Only on occasion." Wyatt said. "Doc's ODD, if that is the case, manifests differently. He becomes cold, withdraws. Unfortunately, that's where his integrity works against him because it's usually obvious to the person he's reacting to."

Neidrich said, "In other words, he bottles up his anger. Unhealthy, isn't it? I've found individuals like that sometimes blow."

Wyatt tilted his chin upward. "Interesting insight, but one should avoid long-distance psychoanalysis." As Neidrich stiffened and his jaw set, warmth softened Wyatt's words. "You should know that Doc has appropriate outlets for stress. He's devoted to his children, and he has his martial arts."

Snitz took another tack. "Ed says Dr. Randori acts suspicious when Ed is around."

"Which proves my point. Doc doesn't like Ed. As I understand it, Ed played football for Bob and later became his bodyguard at games during the time that Doc and Bob coached against each other." Wyatt paused for Snitz's nodding confirmation. "I don't know if Ed started the rumor, but he definitely passed along that Doc rewarded his players with drugs for winning games. An unsubstantiated claim, but Ed's position with the police brought credibility to the story. If you know anything about Doc, you know that he would neither forgive nor forget something like that."

"Ed was young," Snitz said. "Dr. Randori shouldn't hold a grudge all this time."

Wyatt chuckled. "Ed still tells the story, Harley. He's lucky it's just a grudge and not a vendetta."

Neidrich and Snitz had time to kill before their meeting with Meryl Morgan, so they decided to enjoy the day. As they stood on the steps in front of the District Office, Snitz started to speak, but a peek at Neidrich cut him short. The younger man's face turned up to the brilliant cerulean sky, and he was smiling, an impression more than an expression, but a smile, nonetheless, from deep within. It was such a rarity that the Chief forgot whatever it was he was about to say. When they first met, Snitz believed that Neidrich was simply a no-nonsense cop. Then, as days passed, he saw sorrow loom in the corner of the trooper's every expression. But here, for the first time, from some emotional abyss rose a radiance that melted the hoar of gloom. The Chief smiled to himself and walked in silence, hoping whatever it was that had brought Neidrich happiness would gain a foothold in his heart.

For Snitz, it had been the most exhilarating week in a career that had crept almost unnoticed into a comfortable, monotonous twilight. A twinge of guilt tugged at him for enjoying his job so much as a result of a man's death, but that lasted only as long as it took to return to his appreciation of the moment. Chief Harley Snitz had been thrust to the forefront of the biggest murder investigation in the history of Freedom County. Every morning he woke with the anticipation of unraveling more of the puzzle, of working with a colleague who was professional and intelligent, of having a job that was … exciting.

Snitz led the way to a spot where wooden benches and a picnic table dotted a clearing amid a small grove of trees. At lunchtime on pleasant days the District Office staff found respite there, gazing across the road at a tranquil pasture before reluctantly returning to their sterile fluorescent hive.

As he and Neidrich sat, the Chief's thoughts turned to their interview with Kerry Wyatt. It had been interesting, but he had to mine his memory for useful nuggets, part of an overall ambivalence he often felt after talking to the man. Although he enjoyed being around one so intelligent and engaging, he always left thinking the Snitz family must have crawled struggling out of the shallow end of the gene pool. He believed Neidrich felt the same way, judging by the testiness his colleague betrayed as Wyatt admonished him about the use of "long-distance psychoanalysis."

"So, what do you think?" Snitz asked, his zeal to move on with the case overcoming his desire to allow Neidrich a daydream.

"Not much."

"I mean about Mr. Wyatt?"

"I'm not sure I like him, but I don't necessarily think he's a suspect."

"Don't let him bother you. He makes lots of folks uncomfortable, but he doesn't mean any harm."

"Was it that evident?"

"Just a feeling. Imagine what it must be like to be his boss and realize that an underling is smarter than you could ever hope to be. To a man as proud as Dr. Samson, that could be a real problem. That's probably why he gave Mr. Wyatt so much guff."

"Wyatt was right; you can't psychoanalyze a person you haven't met, especially if you don't have all the information. I studied psychology in college; I know that, but it hit my pride anyway." Snitz's bewildered frown begged further explanation. "I always felt like I had to be more scholarly than everyone else. Would you have guessed that I was in National Honor Society in high school? Or that I was class salutatorian? Look at me. Big lug, ex-jock, black; I couldn't possibly be intelligent. Right?"

In truth, Snitz's initial impression was that Neidrich seemed more scuffler than scholar. He evaded the trooper's incisive stare.

"I've often felt the same way," a voice said.

Startled, both officers looked up to see a figure, backlit by the sun, a man slightly shorter than Neidrich but built along similar lines, given a few pounds.

"Dr. Randori," Snitz said, squinting. "Where did you come from?"

"Up there," Randori said, pointing to a door on the west side of the high school. "I saw you and thought I'd say hello. Kerry just called; I'm on my way to see him."

Neidrich's eyes tracked to the high school, then to the District Office. The grove fell on a direct route if one avoided paved walkways. He stood and extended his hand. "I'm Trooper Nick Neidrich."

"Brian Randori. Sorry, I couldn't help overhearing. Throughout my doctoral program I thought people saw me as a jock." Randori let out a one-syllable chuckle. "My Western PA language patterns didn't help."

"I noticed," Neidrich said. "When you said 'up there' it came out, *up air.*"

Randori rubbed his jaw and smiled crookedly. "Yeah, anyway, as far as overcoming the academic misconceptions, I can identify with you. The hardest part was not being black anymore."

Neidrich's smiled vaguely. "Come again?"

"Never mind. It was supposed to be a joke, but it didn't come out as funny as it sounded in my head before I said it. OK, I'm not black, but then neither are you." He stared into Neidrich's eyes, and his grin dissolved into a disarming smile. "Right, 'Night Train?' You're really an Irish lad from South Bend."

"And now I'm a cop." Neidrich said, still measuring Randori.

The counselor cocked his head but remained locked in eye contact with the trooper. " 'Night Train' Neidrich, woe to the receiver invading your turf. There'd be two hits—you hitting him and him hitting the ground. I especially liked the clothesline number you used to bring out once a game." The counselor shifted his eyes to Snitz and motioned with his head back toward the trooper. "That's how he got his nickname, after Dick 'Night Train' Lane, the old Detroit Lions' defensive back. He'd bring that arm around like a club on an opponent's neck, and the guy went down like he was shot. Nick always got that fifteen-yard penalty, and then he'd get all remorseful, like his arm operated on some separate and evil intelligence."

Neidrich shook his head with contrition. "I don't know what got into me."

"That's it!" Randori laughed, nodded, and pointed. "You've still got the act down. But I knew the game you played. That fifteen-yarder was a small price to pay; for the rest of the game running backs went down easier, and receivers got alligator arms when they went over the middle. Man, I thought I'd be seeing you in the pros for years."

"Yeah, well, it's a long story."

Randori completed the thought: "And none of my business. So, now you're investigating Bob's murder. Yes, Ed told Lionda there was foul play. How unfortunate."

Randori's lack of sincerity made Neidrich's next question a reasonable one. "Mind telling us where you were the night of Dr. Samson's death?"

"Watching my kids. Lynn, my wife, works part-time, second shift at the Med Center. It was one of those nights."

"Can anyone vouch for you?" Neidrich asked.

"Yeah, my kids and my dog." Randori checked his watch. "I better get going."

Neidrich leveled a stare at the counselor. "We'll need to talk—you know?"

Randori turned away and saw a man exiting the District Office. "There's the guy you need to talk to." He called out, "Hey Virge, over here."

The man stopped and swiveled his head to see where the voice had come from, then wheeled to face the counselor. "Jesus Moses, Randori, some people work around here," he growled, approaching his friend and the officers in a rapid bow-legged shuffle. When he got near enough to use a normal speaking voice, he continued. "Our business office has more people than IBM, but now *I* have to do the athletic bank deposits because *they* can't spare anyone. And here you stand, killing time, soaking up the sun." It seemed as though his rant was finished, but, like embers catching a breeze, he flared up anew: "Where's your coffee cup?"

Randori ignored the tirade. "Virgil Davis, meet Nick Neidrich. He and Harley are looking into the Bobster's death. I was just telling them no one around here is so foul-tempered as to be considered a viable suspect."

"Yeah, yeah," Davis said, forcing a grin meant to pass as a smile as he reached to shake hands. "There was a Nick Neidrich that used to play for Notre Dame."

Neidrich lowered his eyes. "That'd be me."

"Man, I thought you were a sure shot pro."

"My sentiment exactly," Randori said. "Well, I'd love to hang out and gab, but unlike some people, I have bigger fish to fry than athletics and bank deposits."

Davis scowled. "Go gargle with razor blades, Randori."

The counselor wagged a finger at Davis as he back-pedaled away. "Nick, Harley, be sure to take a close look at this guy. I think he has anger issues."

Davis watched the counselor disappear into the building before musing, without a trace of irony: "Doesn't make a very good first impression, does he? Doc's a good man, though. A little unusual, but don't believe the things Ed told you."

"What makes you think Officer Knepp said anything?" Neidrich asked.

Davis shot an incredulous look from Neidrich to Snitz and back. "Come on, Ed hates Doc, and he's not shy about telling anyone who will listen. It all stems from his blind devotion to Bob Samson. Ed played for Bob, and Bob demanded that his disciples follow him without question or thought."

"That's part of a successful team," Neidrich said.

"As long as it pertains to football. When it comes to running a smear campaign against an opponent … In case no one told you, Bob was one mean bastard."

"Enough of a bastard that he deserved to die?" Neidrich said. "Where were you last Friday night?"

Davis let out an embarrassed laugh. "Believe it or not, I was Bob's friend." Both officers stared at him in silence, prompting him to add, "OK, I was at our football scrimmage up at Coal Mountain. I followed the team bus; we got there around 6:00, and I came back when they did. Got in around 11:00. A bunch of people can vouch for me."

Snitz patted Davis's arm. "I know you're in a hurry, Virgil; I'll call you. If you think of anything that might help, get in touch."

"Will do." Davis shook each officer's hand. "And let me know if you need any help talking to people at the high school."

As they watched Davis hustle to his car, Snitz said, "I don't buy either Virgil or Dr. Randori as a murderer, Nick."

"When I told Randori we need to talk, he changed the subject."

"I'm surprised he came by in the first place. He could've gone to the back door and avoided us altogether."

"How old are Randori's kids?"

"I'm not sure, elementary school age, maybe."

"So he'd probably put them to bed around 8:30, 9:00. His time would be unaccounted for until his wife got home at 11:30, or so."

The unexpected discussion with Randori and Davis made the lawmen overshoot their appointed time with Morgan. As they entered her office, she was on her way out.

"Harley, I thought you weren't coming. I was on my way to see Kerry."

"Sorry we're late, Ms. Morgan," Snitz said. Smiling shyly, he added, "It's tough coming in on a day like today."

"I can understand that," Morgan said matter-of-factly. She shifted her briefcase to her left hand and offered a handshake to Neidrich. Her grip was strong, her eye contact direct. The trooper's initial impression was that her beauty hid an uncommon will.

Morgan reversed direction and invited the men into her office. Rolling a chair away from her desk, she formed a triangle with them in the center of the room. The office was tidy and tasteful. A single table lamp brought warm ambiance to the forest green and mauve decor, which in turn complemented the cherry desk and chairs.

Morgan's attire was equally immaculate, blending professionalism and style in a seemingly intentional, but futile, effort to mute her femininity. She sat erect, legs crossed, hands palm down on the armrests of her chair. Upon later reflection, Neidrich would recall that her position had remained unchanged throughout the interview.

"You're here to discuss Dr. Samson's death, or murder I should say."

"Word spreads fast." Neidrich said. He had a hunch that niceties, such as complimenting Morgan's taste in furnishings or expressing appreciation that she took the time to speak to them, were unnecessary and might be construed as patronizing. He decided to be direct. "Do you mind telling us your whereabouts the night he died?"

"I was doing work at home."

"On a Friday night?"

"Friday doesn't matter to the work, Officer Neidrich. This is a busy time."

"Trooper Neidrich," he corrected. "Can anyone vouch for you?"

"My laptop."

"Sorry?"

"My computer. It logs the date and time of entries. I worked from around 7:30, after I ate supper, until I went to bed, probably around midnight."

"Dates and times can be manipulated, can't they?"

Pensive, Morgan looked off for a moment but quickly returned to direct eye contact. "Yes, I suppose. You're welcome to check it for tampering."

"It would show when you started a document but not how long you worked on it."

"Correct, but I worked on several. Start times are listed for each. I haven't worked on them since, so the times should be intact."

"You worked that whole time uninterrupted?" Snitz asked, shaking his head. "Whew, my brain would lock up."

A smile passed across Morgan's face. "It's the only way I can work. I did take a break to call Kerry Wyatt. He's inspirational, or, better put, thought-provoking."

"What time was that?" Snitz asked.

"Between 9:00 and 9:30, I think; I'm not certain, though."

"Wyatt's interesting," Neidrich said. "Dresses well for, forgive me, an educator."

"We're professionals; we ought to look professional. Kerry has excellent taste. And probably has more money than Bob had—real estate. He's liquidating, though, to move to Costa Rica when he retires next summer."

Neidrich cocked his head. "Unusual choice. When did he start planning that?"

"He visited a few years ago; now he goes back every year." After a moment, Morgan added, "You'd never guess it to look at him, but he's daring."

It seemed strange to Neidrich that she spoke fondly of Wyatt, but showed no regret about his impending retirement. "As superintendent, won't you miss him?"

"I will miss him. Whether or not I become superintendent is problematic."

"But you're the logical choice," Snitz said.

"Who said logic had anything to do with it?" Morgan said with a finality that discouraged further pursuit of the topic.

Neidrich said, "What did you think of Dr. Samson?"

"Not much."

"As a person or a professional?"

"Yes," Morgan responded, punctuating her curt reply with a one-sided smile.

"Was this just your belief or was it a general feeling?"

"Bob had his supporters, and there are those who owe their success, or rather their status, to him. Out in the schools, some staff had run-ins with him. Nothing worth killing him over. And he became popular with the rank and file after the last contract."

"What were the feelings for him here in the District Office?"

"Kerry and I had problems with him, but then you already knew that or you wouldn't have chosen us to interrogate."

Neidrich smiled. He liked Morgan; a faint aura of vulnerability shimmered through her surface stiffness. "Interview," he said.

"How's that?"

"This conversation is an interview. You seem like a person who is precise in the words you choose. Interrogations, to me anyway, are adversarial."

"Well, this doesn't seem adversarial."

"What about Dr. Randori? Has he ever spoken disparagingly about Dr. Samson?"

"Doc didn't like Bob, that's no secret. But dislike is a far shot from murder."

Snitz followed up. "But how much do you know about Dr. Randori? Everyone says he keeps folks at arm's length."

"I'm much the same. That's one of the reasons Doc likes me—I think he likes me, anyway. It's difficult to figure out why he chooses the sides he takes. For some reason, he's chosen to align with Kerry and me.

"So, you two would know him best."

"Better than most, but that's not saying much. Kerry once said that the bits Doc reveals about himself are—how did he put it? —'Morsels that promise a banquet never to be served.' Doc's come from hard times, I think, but that's more a sense I have than a conviction. I'm sorry, there just isn't much I can help you with. You might talk to Virgil Davis. He's known Doc for years."

Neidrich wasn't about to let Morgan off the hook so easily. Their morning at the District Office thus far had yielded some insight into personalities, but no leads. "There must have been things he's said that reveal his character."

"A lot of what Doc says and does is contradictory. For example, he loves the *Tao Te Ching*—the way of Nature—and *The Art of War*." Morgan smiled affectionately and looked off at some fond thought. "I don't know what that tells you, except that he's appealingly strange. And he'll quote Groucho and Karl Marx with equal enthusiasm."

"Eclectic," Neidrich deadpanned. "He's not respected by other administrators."

"Doc's against bureaucracies; any convention, in fact, that doesn't make sense to him. That drives most administrators, anyone who thinks he ought to be subservient, crazy. Now, to me, he's loyal."

"So you two are close ... relatively speaking," Neidrich said.

Morgan pursed her lips. For the first time, a blush-toned hesitation preceded her response. "Doc can show warmth, but just when you think you're close, you find a wall where you thought a relationship ought to be. Is it something he has no control over or does he do it on purpose? I don't know."

"Doesn't sound like he has the makings of a good administrator."

Morgan smirked. "You could say that."

Neidrich honed in, the better to catch the smallest nuance—body language, inflection in voice—that might reveal more than this reserved woman intended. "Are you saying in a nice way he's incompetent?"

Morgan's smile disappeared, and her tone became brusque. "Absolutely not. Doc's an iconoclast; to most organizations that's worse than incompetence. It doesn't take Kafka to figure that out. He's an excellent counselor, dedicated to his students, which is all you should ask of an educator. Administration is a different game. It's pitted with artificial socialization. Back-slapping, political schmoozing; that's not Doc."

"And his relationship with Dr. Samson?"

"Slash and burn. Bob thought it was a slap in the face when he eliminated Doc's position here in the District Office, but Doc wanted out of administration and away from Bob, where he could be more subversively defiant." Morgan face flushed again. "Which, I'm embarrassed to admit, Kerry and I have encouraged."

Snitz kneaded his chin thoughtfully. "Do you think Dr. Randori could have considered doing harm to Dr. Samson?"

" 'Considered?' I don't know what goes on in Doc's mind. You need to ask the right question. Do I think he did it? That answer is no."

"Is there anyone else you think we ought to check up on?"

Morgan shook her head. "It's hard to believe anyone I know could have committed murder."

Neidrich noticed Morgan sneaking a peek at her watch. He tapped Snitz's arm and stood up. "We're keeping Ms. Morgan from her job."

Morgan rose to escort the officers to the door. "If there's anything else—"

Neidrich stopped and turned. "Sorry to pull a Columbo on you, but when was the last time you saw Dr. Samson?"

For the first time, Morgan dropped her guard and let slip a small giggle. Quickly covering it with her hand, she said, "Oh, I'm sorry. It's just that your 'Columbo' line sounded just like something Doc would say." Regaining her stony facade, she answered the question: "I was in Harrisburg the day Bob died, so I guess the last time I saw him was the day before—Thursday."

"And you don't know who was the last to see him on Friday?"

"Didn't you talk to Shirley, his secretary?"

Snitz pulled a page of Samson's appointment book out of his breast pocket. "The last entry was Kerry Wyatt, but Sarah Samson said he called to tell her he had a later appointment, and Mr. Wyatt says he left after they met."

"I have no idea who it could've been." Morgan paused to grin. "Pardon my use of the local vernacular, but I'd be for thinking you ought to find out."

"Say, Meryl," Lionda said. She hiked her thumb toward Wyatt's conference room. "Kerry and Doc are plotting the overthrow of the District."

Theresa frowned. "You'd better get in there before they screw up the plan."

Morgan gave a polite, half-hearted smile but returned no eye contact as she headed to the conference room. Inside, Randori remained seated, fixing a stare on her from his customary location: facing the door.

Wyatt rose, beaming. "Meryl, join us. Doc and I were discussing my visit from Harley and the state policeman, Neidrich. They talked to you, too?"

Morgan returned Randori's gaze as she edged around the table, sitting beside Randori and across from Wyatt. "They asked a lot of questions about you, Doc."

Wyatt shrugged and cocked his head. "I don't know, Meryl, they seemed just as curious about us."

Randori said, "From the time we found out Bob was murdered, I figured they'd check me out. But you two? They're reaching."

"Is there anything you want to tell us, Doc?" Wyatt asked.

"I like you guys, but do you really think I'd admit it if I offed the Bobster?"

"Bob hated you calling him that," Morgan said, smiling. "That's why you couldn't have killed him; you enjoyed offending him too much." Turning her attention to Wyatt, her voice hardened. "And I can't believe you're even suggesting Doc might have killed Bob."

"I'm sorry, it was stupid of me. I guess I'm a little touchy. We have a problem, one that could land us in legal difficulties. You might know the student, Doc: Paul Roberge? Anything you can tell us?"

The counselor dipped his chin balefully. "His name has come up at Coordinating Council. Problems ever since middle school: class disruptions, insubordination, and he doesn't play nice with other children. Paul was held back a year in elementary school, so he's older than typical kids in his grade. We have reports that he's extorted money, instigated fights. Tough to pin anything on him, though, he either intimidates victims so they don't talk or makes sure it's his word against theirs. And, although Virge and I can't prove it—yet—he's using and selling drugs."

"What a sweetheart," Morgan said. "Why isn't he in alternative school?"

"He's building his resume, but like I said, the bad stuff we can't prove. The big thing is, his parents go beyond enabling; they outright save him." Contempt colored Randori's words. "You know the rote: other guys influence him, the school's out to get him—"

"Well, they're doing it again," Wyatt said, his voice rising as he cut Randori off. "They just had a private psychologist down in Essex County evaluate Paul."

"How is that bad?" Morgan asked. "If they can get him some help—"

Wyatt slammed his palm on the table. "Help to beat the system. I've crossed paths with this psychologist before. This charlatan has two specialties: slapping unwarranted 'Learning Disabled' labels on students so they can get extended time on the SATs, and helping wealthy parents get their problem children out of trouble."

Morgan and Randori exchanged glances, both taken aback by Wyatt's lapse in conversational decorum. As a psychologist himself, he was a trained listener, often going so far as to allow an unnerving pause after someone spoke, in case a telling afterthought was forthcoming. For him to interrupt two exchanges was unprecedented.

Wyatt picked up a letter and rattled it angrily. "This cover sheet accompanied the psych report; it says we've ignored the boy's significant learning disability. But that's not the best part." He scanned the letter. "Here it is: 'It is evident to this evaluator that Paul's behavior in school is the result of anxiety and frustration over the school's callous disregard for his learning needs.' "

Randori leaned back, "Whoa, what Paul needs is a motivational ass-kicking."

"The report addresses that, too. 'Paul's frustration has brought on a defeatist attitude that could easily be interpreted as a lack of academic motivation.' Amazingly, he's covered all the bases without getting any information from the school."

Morgan gave a dismissive wave. "Without that, his testing isn't even valid."

"Good luck winning a hearing with that argument," Randori said.

"That's why I'm going to have Leroy evaluate him, too" Wyatt said, referring to Leroy Dubcek, the high school psychologist. "But we have to consider this private eval."

Randori smiled. "All right, I *consider* it bullshit."

Morgan flicked an amused glance at the counselor. "I'm glad you find humor in this, Doc, I have a feeling Kerry didn't share this story merely for your entertainment."

"True," Wyatt said. "Would you mind getting together with Leroy? The clock is ticking, and I don't want to make any mistakes."

"You got it. But you know Leroy and I might have a difference of opinion, and since I don't have supervisory clout anymore, I can't make him do anything."

Morgan arched a brow. "And then there's Tammy Eboli, the union—uh, excuse me, Association—president. She'll be looking for any slip-up by you."

"Leroy and Tammy are flexible," Randori said, pausing for effect as his colleagues frowned in disbelief. "They can smile to your face while they're stabbing you in the back. And you know neither one will have qualms about reporting me to the principal. Are you two going to back me against Kass Marburg?"

"Kerry and I are with you," Morgan said, "but you know it has to be discreet."

Through grimly pursed lips, Wyatt said, "Kass doesn't take kindly to anyone interfering with his high school. He especially doesn't like you, because Bob didn't."

Morgan added, "And Leroy's done such a good job convincing everyone of his unparalleled expertise that he's become Kass's go-to man for special education."

Randori brushed his fingernails in a light backhand fashion across his cheek. "In the immortal words of Sessue Hayakawa: 'Be happy in your work.'"

"Just remember," Morgan said, you're here to build bridges, not destroy them."

Bewilderment washed over Wyatt's face, and Morgan's eyes twinkled with mischief "I love digging to see how deep your cultural gaps go, Kerry. Although, I suppose we should cut you a break. You know a lot about things no one else does but nothing about stuff most of us take for granted."

"Thank you, Meryl," Wyatt cut in, his eyes sliding from Morgan to Randori before settling on her hand, which rested absently on the counselor's forearm. Glancing at his watch, he rose and moved to the door, a signal that the meeting had ended. "I tolerate these excursions in trivia because they keep your minds occupied with something relatively harmless, but I have neither the time nor the inclination to dip my toes into the stream of consciousness in which you bumpkins wade."

Randori took on a pout of mock contrition, but as Wyatt turned his back, he and Morgan stood and faced each other with identical expressions—eyes wide and mouths forming tight Os—chastised children mocking their strict father behind his back. As the director opened the door to usher Morgan and Randori out, they snapped back to innocent sobriety in the face of Wyatt's stony stare.

"*Bridge on the River Kwai*," Randori said.

Wyatt shook his head. "Sorry?"

"That's the movie Meryl and I were talking about. You ought to check it out. You'd be amazed at the things you can pick up."

Doc Randori lived in the Village of Darby, west of Newcastle Borough, a half-hour drive between farmers' fields that butted up against the southern ridge of the valley. It was a pleasant drive, and Nick Neidrich used the time to clear his mind and prepare to question the suspect. Interesting person, Randori: friendly, but reputedly antisocial, soft-spoken, yet having a way of eliciting loyalty in some and fierce enmity in others. People who disliked the counselor were quick to suspect him as a murderer, but Harley Snitz gave those allegations little credence, maintaining that the individual character of each accuser was itself suspect. Contradictions clouded Neidrich's mind, and by the time he swung onto the oak-lined street where Randori lived, he had to recheck the address in his notebook.

He pulled into a slot in front of a modest brick rancher and unfolded out of his car, turning full circle, surveying the neighborhood. Cape Cods and ranch homes stood abreast, each one guarded by trim shrubbery and manicured lawns. New-mown grass scented the air. As he entered the walkway leading to Randori's front door, his attention was drawn to the hipped roof where two squirrels skittered along the slopes in a manic game of tag before leaping onto a nearby branch with acrobatic ease. Neidrich pressed the doorbell but heard nothing. As he moved to ring again, a voice came from behind.

"Doesn't work."

Startled, the trooper swung around to see Randori, five feet away, spinning a pair of pruning shears in his left hand. "That's the second time you appeared out of nowhere," Neidrich said, not amused.

"I didn't mean to startle you. Now, scaring Kerry's secretary—*that* I enjoy. All warfare is based on deception, Nick, and those little squirrels create a big diversion."

"Are we at war?"

Randori flashed a friendly smile. "There's coffee inside." He spun the shears on his finger again, gunslinger-style, and jammed them into the pocket of his khakis. "Come in and meet Lynn."

They wound their way in silence toward the rear of the home and the kitchen where they found Lynn Randori hovering over a sheet cake with a tube of frosting in her hand. A fine dusting of flour and confectioners sugar covered every surface, including the woman herself. Small bowls of colored paste were strewn in disarray across the counter top; a mixer, splattered with a rainbow of streaks representing the contents of the smaller bowls, sat in the corner.

"Nick, this is Lynn, the Jackson Pollock of pastry."

Randori's wife swung around in surprise, her face going ashen. "Jeez, Brian, I didn't hear you coming."

"He's good at that," Neidrich said, offering a handshake. "Trooper Nick Neidrich. State Police."

Lynn wiped her palm on the leg of her jeans and shot a puzzled frown at her husband before clasping Neidrich's hand. "Uh, hello, Trooper Neidrich."

Neidrich focused on the girl-next-door attractiveness of Randori's wife. She was short and athletic; her close-cropped black hair complemented dark, almond eyes reminiscent of an angel from a Byzantine religious fresco and which, at the moment, betrayed rising apprehension.

To set her at ease Neidrich forced a smile. "You're the first person I've heard use your husband's given name."

The tension radiating from Lynn abated slightly. "The first year we dated, I thought his name was 'Coach.' That's all anyone ever called him." Suddenly aware of the mess she had made of the kitchen, she added, "Sorry about the way the place looks."

"No, I'm sorry. I should have called first."

The men exchanged glances. Maintaining a flinty stare, Randori's amiable words belied his expression. "Lynn's a terrific baker. And a talented artist." He dusted off a sketch lying on the island. "Check the ferret she drew. She's making a ferret cake."

Lynn punched her husband's chest, sending billows of flour dust rising from her sleeve "It's not a ferret cake; it's a carrot cake. And it's a squirrel. See the bushy tail?"

"It needs to be bushier," Randori said, a smile finally softening his features.

Neidrich saw that Randori's teasing was wearing thin on his wife. "Why a squirrel, if I may ask?"

"It's our dog, Holly's, birthday," the counselor said, as if that explained everything. Turning to his wife, he got to the point of Neidrich's visit. "Nick is talking to people who didn't hold the Bobster up as a major deity."

"Your husband's not a suspect," Neidrich added, feeling a white lie did no harm.

Lynn patted her chest and blew a small sigh. "Well, I'm sure Brian won't mind getting out of yard work. But be warned, you talk to him at your peril."

"Why's that?"

"You'll see," Lynn said, sphinx-like.

Randori handed a mug of coffee to the trooper and said, "Follow me," leading the way to the sunroom adjoining the kitchen.

"You sure you want to talk here? Your wife might hear us."

Veering off into his own context, Randori said, "There hasn't been any music worth listening to since the '70s—except jazz, of course." He punched a button on his CD player, and it picked up in the middle of Steely Dan's *Caves of Altamira*. With a tortuous wrench, he brought the conversation back on course. "Lynn knows me too well to be worried. She also knows from my coaching days to be skeptical of what's in the media. Speaking of which, hasn't anyone caught onto your football background?"

"That was a long time ago," Neidrich said with finality.

"You sound just like Brian: what's past is past." Lynn entered, balancing a carafe on a serving tray. "For an old history teacher— emphasis on the 'old'—he shuts off the past so much that sometimes I think he has something to hide."

Randori flashed another iron glance at his wife, who was spared because she was looking at Neidrich, but, like the flash of a camera, it left an indelible impression on the investigator. Before he could reflect on its meaning, the counselor's dry smile reappeared. "My past may be lengthy, but it's inconsequential. Nick, on the other hand, was among the finest sons who ever shook down the thunder at Notre Dame. We are in the presence of the one and only 'Night Train' Neidrich."

"I'm impressed. If Brian says you were good, you must have been very good. He tosses compliments around like they're manhole covers." She placed the tray on the table within reach of both men. "Here's more coffee and some pear cheesecake, Brian's favorite. He'd eat pears every day if I let him."

"Typical Lynn," Randori said. "She's been feeding me like this ever since she found out about the school employees' death benefit."

Lynn let slip an impish grin and raised an eyebrow. "And when he keels over, I'll collect enough dough to open my own bakery."

Neidrich took a small bite of the confection and rolled his eyes. "Sounds like a plan. I'll be your best customer."

"So, I can knock him off and get away with it? Deal!"

"Lynn, please don't go on like this. Trooper Neidrich's time is at a premium."

Randori's wife shook her head and cast a hooded stare at Neidrich. "It seems like Brian likes you, so he'll find something you two have in common and go off on it. You have to build a dam on his infamous stream of consciousness; otherwise, you'll never get your job done." Leaving, she stopped in the doorway and turned, her voice taking on an ominous tone. "And beware of philosophizing. Just beware."

No problem letting a suspect take me along the garden path, Neidrich thought. *Someone talks enough he'll plant evidence against himself along the way.* He watched Randori's wife retreat out of earshot then said, "When your wife mentioned your past, you danced away pretty good."

"Lynn comes from a good, God-fearing family. My background is a little different. Kind of like the *Addams Family* without the laugh track."

"Do you always joke when things get personal?"

"I want Lynn to be at ease. Wives worry. Doesn't yours, you being a cop?"

Neidrich's eyes dropped to the wedding ring he had never gotten around to removing. "Mary, my wife, passed away a few years ago."

Randori blinked then dipped his head in an attempt to recapture the trooper's eyes. His voice turned mellifluous, hypnotic. "You're still hurting."

"I'm getting over it."

"Don't block it or it will never go away, but don't wallow in it, either. Embrace your pain, then you can deal with it."

A creased brow cut across Neidrich's stoic presence as Randori leaned closer and continued in smooth but insistent tones. "There are no shortcuts through grief. The greater the love, the greater the memories ... the greater the pain. So, the pain is good. It symbolizes how much she means to you. If it lingers too long, though, it begins to kill everything around it. You have to let your heart heal, Nick. Mary will always be with you—in your memories, in your heart. The memories, the love, become her legacy."

"I feel like I'm being disloyal if I let go."

"You're disloyal if you don't," Randori pressed, "unless, of course, Mary would have wanted you miserable the rest of your life." He tilted his head and offered a sympathetic smile. His point made, he went on. "You have kids?"

"Two, like you. My dad's retired; he lives with me and helps out." Neidrich realized that Randori had taken him off on a tangent, an unproductive one. A wary glint returned to his eyes. "Ms. Morgan told me you're a good counselor; I can see why. You roped me in pretty good there, but my personal life isn't important right now."

"It's more important than anything else we'll talk about."

Not taking the bait, Neidrich said, "You told us you were here with your kids the night Samson died. How hard would it be to sneak out while they were asleep and take a jaunt into Freedom County?"

Neidrich felt Randori's eyes drill deep into his mind and heart. "Let me say one last thing. Your kids deserve a happy dad, one who lives in the present with them."

Neidrich was torn. He had his job to do, and he did not want to open a wound that had festered for four years. At the same time, Randori's words had struck the unsettling chord of truth. In the end, he decided he would have to ruminate on the counselor's words in private—or did duty simply win out? "Answer my question."

"Would you leave your kids alone while they were asleep? Imagine the terror a child would feel, waking up at night to find no one at home. Our kids have to be able to trust us one hundred percent of the time."

The counselor still hadn't answered the question—avoidance is a mark of guilt. "Did you leave your house that night?"

Randori smiled knowingly and nodded. "No."

"You nod but say 'no.' Which one is it?"

"No. And no one stopped by or called."

"What did you do that night from, say, 7:30 until 11:00?"

"After the kids went to bed, I watched some TV, then did my forms and stretched."

"Forms?"

"*Katas*—martial arts." Randori squinted, assessing Neidrich. "You're not sure. Katas are choreographed series of punches, kicks, and blocks that develop discipline and concentration—the body, mind, spirit number—to me, the primary aspects of the art."

Neidrich seized the opening. "You're a black belt, an expert in karate, from what I hear. That sport would train you to inflict heavy damage on someone."

"The black belt is just the end of the beginning. I'm no longer a novice, but I have a long way to go before I'm truly accomplished. My first art is Moo Duk Kwan, which is Korean; karate is a catchall term, but strictly speaking, it refers to Japanese styles. And martial arts aren't about fighting, they're about not fighting."

"Still, if push came to shove, you are trained in combat, hand-to-hand as well as weapons. A lot of schools teach the use of exotic weapons."

"Exotic? Just tools adapted to meet need. Peasants in feudal Japan converted farm implements to weapons, to protect themselves."

"Why would they need to do that?"

"Some of the warlords were thugs. Their samurai, bound by honor, had to do their bidding, and sometimes that bidding took the form of brutal oppression." Randori shook his head with regret. "Samurai honor called for unquestioning loyalty to their lord. That's the part of 'honor' I disagree with. If the samurai had read Sun Tzu, the great Chinese warrior, they would know that the general may disobey the sovereign if the sovereign's dictates will lead to defeat."

"Your cause and effect relationship is loose. You're not talking about defeat; you're talking about fulfilling your commitment to honor and loyalty."

Randori grinned. "Ah, but if in following loyalty you sacrifice your honor, you've lost your soul. I would submit that the oppression of any group is dishonorable and will eventually lead to the defeat of the powerful. Some words keep ringing in my ears: 'We shall overcome.' "

Neidrich chuckled. "Boy, Lynn was right. You laid as good a philosophical trap as any of my profs at Notre Dame—and you got me off on another tangent. Do you work with any martial arts weapons?"

"For a while I worked with *nunchakus*—nunchucks—but they took time away from my personal development. Besides, the word *karate* translates to 'empty hand.' "

"Do you own a set of nunchucks?"

"Sure, hang on." Randori went to a rosewood cabinet in the corner of the sunroom. After fishing around for a few seconds, he located them. Cradling the nunchucks palms up in an almost ceremonial manner, he approached Neidrich.

A blunt instrument had struck Samson—so brutally that black and gold paint chips were embedded in his skull. Neidrich had recalled weapons demonstrations during his training at the Academy. The nunchucks used had been *japanned*—lacquered glossy black—with gold trim. Here was Randori, holding an almost identical pair. The trooper stood, poised to defend himself.

Randori stopped just out of arm's reach. "Good, Nick, always be ready; that's what I tell Lynn and the kids. When she gets out of work at midnight and has to walk to her car, or when she leaves a mall, she's looking for keys and checking her packages; she's not being watchful. Muggers are cowards; they look for the weak and the unready. I like to think I'm a little above that. Besides, these won't do much harm. Look."

Neidrich gripped the nunchucks; his fingers sunk into dense black foam rubber covering a solid shaft, and only the gold dragons were painted. "What's this?"

"I tried wooden ones; the self-inflicted shots to the head and groin convinced me these would be better for my health. Besides, Lynn doesn't want weapons in the house."

"Not even knives?"

"Kitchen knives. You're welcome to search the place."

Neidrich waved off the offer, then a notion struck. "Who knows you have these?"

"People at my old dojo." Randori looked off in memory. "Wait, I took them to school once: last spring when we opened our on-campus alternative school. We had the kids learning karate for their phys ed requirement, and Kerry wanted me to do a demonstration. I didn't like the idea—showing off—but Kerry can be convincing."

"Who was at the demonstration?"

"Kerry, Virgil, the program director, the teachers, and the students. Why's that?"

Neidrich saw the wheels turning in Randori's mind and figured the man was making deductions of his own. "Just a point of interest." He made a mental note to check out the people who had attended the demonstration and the members at the martial arts school, then changed the subject. "You and Samson had a bad history."

Randori flicked his fingernails across his jaw and considered the trooper's face like an archaeologist studying a projectile point. " 'Bad history,' good name for a rock group." A glower from Neidrich prompted, "Sorry. Bob thought he was a warrior, so he acted the way he thought a warrior would. A lot of people bought it. I never did."

"Can I infer from what you're saying that you see yourself as a warrior?"

"Someone else would have to make that call. If I say I'm a warrior, the response itself puts the lie to the statement. A warrior never says what he is; he just is."

Neidrich smiled. "From what I gather, humility wasn't Samson's strong suit."

"His strong suits were all negative. He took himself way too seriously."

"He was a Marine veteran."

"Yeah, I'll give him credit for that. Man, I could never give myself over to that discipline."

"He did have the respect of a lot of people."

"Don't confuse respect and fear. A person can't demand respect, only command it. You can't grab it any more than you can grab the river. If you deserve it, respect flows to you. Only the arrogant or the weak and insecure demand respect. It may seem trite in this day and age, but Bob Samson had no honor." The counselor looked down, abashed. "I probably shouldn't have brought it up; I sound self-righteous."

The suspect was on another tangent, but Neidrich thought this one might lead to greater insight into Randori's character. Besides, he was intrigued by the topic. Honor had been an important concept throughout his life. His father had shown it in the military, and Neidrich honed his own at Notre Dame and at the State Police Academy, but the term was used only on formal occasions and in ceremonial settings. "*Honor* is a word we avoid anymore, isn't it?"

Randori eyes took on a determined glint. "Yes, and it's a shame; the lack of honor is *the* major problem we have to deal with."

An overstatement? "What's your definition of honor?"

"I don't think you can define it; it's transcendent."

"So, how do you decide if a person is honorable—intuition?"

"You can observe: does a person take responsibility for his—or her—actions? But it also involves intent: I don't know a person's innermost thoughts ..." Randori cocked his head and studied Neidrich. "But yeah, I do go with gut feelings—mea culpa."

Neidrich stared at Randori, his silence affirming the inadequacy of the counselor's definition. He had opened this can of worms, and now he had to explain himself.

The counselor heaved a sigh. "OK, here goes. This won't be a great definition, but it's the best I can do off the top of my head. There's a parable written by Yuzan in the *Budo Shoshinshu:* A man was about to go on a journey. Before leaving, he entrusted his neighbor with a hundred gold pieces for safekeeping. For security, no one, not even the man's own family, was to know of this arrangement. If he died, the neighbor was to give the gold to the man's wife and children. On the journey, the man was indeed killed, so the neighbor had to make a decision. Of course, it would've been dishonorable to keep the gold. But even in returning it to the man's family, we can judge the neighbor's personal level of honor. The lowest level would be to desire to keep the gold, but return it only out of fear of being caught. The next level would be to consider keeping it, but then realize that would be wrong and, feeling guilty, return it. The highest level of honor would be to return the gold without question or thought."

"That's pretty good. There have been times I've questioned suspects, and they said the reason they didn't do the crime was that they'd be afraid of getting caught."

"Yeah, I don't think it's a big step for a person like that to take the dishonorable path. Just opportunity."

Neidrich leaned forward, captivated by the concept. "You could apply that story to any misbehavior. Like a car salesman who has to choose between being honest and gouging a customer for an extra thousand dollars."

After momentary consideration, Randori added, "You could apply it to business across the board."

Pursing his lips, the trooper squinted and pointed at the counselor. "Politics."

"Shit," Randori said, "you trumped me."

Both men let slip clipped chuckles. Once escaped, though, the combination of easy conversation and the sudden crack in the dam of pent up tension surrounding the murder investigation lifted the heavy atmosphere, prolonging the laughter.

Lynn Randori appeared in the doorway. "Brian, did you spike the coffee?"

"No, I'd be afraid I'd get caught."

The timing of the response coaxed a choking hoot from the trooper. He couldn't remember the last time he genuinely enjoyed himself, and he didn't know why it had occurred on this occasion, but Randori returned a smile of appreciation.

Having been left out of the joke, Lynn ignored it and held up a cake that looked like a framed picture. "It's finished," she said, tilting it as much as she dared for the men to see. "What do you think?"

"Is it leaning against a tree?" Randori asked.

"That's its tail. It's bushy," Lynn said, her patience dwindling.

"It looks great," Neidrich said, defusing the situation. "You really are an artist."

"Thank you." Lynn turned to her husband. "I'm glad someone has taste around here. Speaking of which, guess who's not going to taste this cake, Brian Randori?"

Randori winced. "It is a fantastic cake, Lynn. Hey, I've got an idea. I'll get the dishes for you."

"Too late," she said, waving her husband off.

Neidrich placed his mug on the table and rose from the divan. "I should go."

Turning to Randori's wife, he said, "You have a beautiful home here."

"Thanks." Her next statement, "Come back soon," began with enthusiasm but trailed off as she realized that a return visit might mean trouble.

Randori reinforced his wife's words, but with a marked absence of enthusiasm and inflection: "Yes, by all means, come back soon." He followed that with an equally flat, "Maybe stay for cocktails and dinner. We truly enjoyed your visit."

Lynn blushed. "Stop being a—"

"Wise ass? Is that the term of endearment you were searching for, dear?"

Lynn's jaw set, "You're welcome back anytime. Bring your family, too."

"Great," Randori said, "a social event. Nothing I like better."

"God, you're a stiff," Lynn said. She turned to Neidrich. "Brian says he's not sociable, but let him run into an acquaintance somewhere, and he'll talk until the person starts making up lame excuses just to get away." Acting out the scenario, her eyes darted around as she stammered, "I have to go, uh, help my mother build a cedar chest."

"It's called overcompensation," Neidrich said. "Like the tangents he gets people off on. Socially, he's uncomfortable, so he says the first thing that comes to mind, no matter how inane, boring, or inappropriate."

"Our daughter, Lizzie, calls him the 'anti-social butterfly.' "

"You two about done? I'd like to get back to my yard work."

Lynn checked her watch. "Gosh, I have to pick up the kids at karate." She grabbed her car keys and accompanied the men to the door. Crossing the threshold, she stopped and said, "It was a pleasure meeting you, Trooper Neidrich."

"Nick," Neidrich found himself blurting. "You can call me Nick."

"Well, Nick, let me tell you, I'm impressed with your understanding of people. You've just met Brian, but you really have him pegged. ... 'Overcompensation.' " She chuckled, heading for the car. "Very astute."

Neidrich and Randori stood, facing each other on the sidewalk with the trooper squinting into the sun. The counselor smiled and shifted to the left. "Making your adversary face the sun may be good in battle, but not in conversation."

"More Sun Tzu," Neidrich said.

"You do know *The Art of War*. Very good. It would help in your job."

"Yes, but how could those ideas be important to an educator?"

"You'd be amazed how many people undermine our efforts to help kids, either through their own ego or because they want to protect their turf. Then there are the families. On one end are the negligent and abusive parents; on the other are the ones who enforce the notion that their kids can do no wrong. And every year those groups grow, pinching us in the middle. I'm sure you fight the same battles."

"True, but it seems pretty good around here, though; nice, conservative area."

"It is—the whole Freedom Valley is great in a thousand ways—but it's not Nirvana. No place is, anymore. Freedom City does its best, but the feds and the state have strapped social services, so poor kids are more at-risk than ever. Plus, drug dealers and gang leaders are moving in on them. Meanwhile, Brad and Tippy Angloshit and their friends have parked their upward-mobiles in the suburbs. To self-actualize, they have to climb the corporate ladder, so both work full-time, and they expect the schools to do the parenting for them, but in reality their kids are raising themselves."

"These are hardworking people you're talking about," Neidrich said, frowning. "They get an education, they're industrious, and sometimes they have to relocate if they want promotions. Don't you think you're being a little paranoid?"

Randori's eyes flared, and it took a long moment for the embers to cool before he responded, "You're defending the materialist morality? What garbonia. Promotions that bring more money and power, but at what cost? They move around more than gypsies on a java jive. Dad works sixty hours a week, commutes a couple more. Mom works full-time, too, so they can keep their Escalade gassed up and give their kids everything except what they want—attention—and what they need—stability and consistency."

"God, you're depressing."

"I've been told that."

"I hope you're going to give me an answer to these problems before I leave."

Randori's eyes twinkled, setting off a wry smile. "It's simple, really. We have to be examples to our kids, teach them life is more than money and instant gratification."

"You know, you're right," Neidrich said, his jaw set. "When you think if it, that goes for all adults. It fries me when I hear some jillionaire jock or rock idol claim he's not a role model; he's either naïve or rationalizing."

"Yeah, they claim their behavior or their performances don't influence kids. They're right as far as well-balanced kids go, but at-risk, alienated kids are absolutely drawn to anti-social examples. People like that are cancers on the marrow of society."

Randori's last words were glib, but hooded eyes and menacing undertone seemed to leave unsaid, "and they should be surgically excised." A lingering shade chilled the trooper's spine, reminding him of the potential danger of being sucked in by the suspect's surface affability. As he came to this understanding, it also brought the realization that the counselor was studying his face, divining his thoughts. Summoning composure, Neidrich said, "I like your choice of words. For what it's worth, I agree."

"What you think is worth a lot."

Neidrich cast a wary eye on Randori. "You've complimented me more than once today. And Lynn said that you seem to like me. Explain something; all I've heard is how aloof you are, but I've found you to be friendly, to me and, this morning, to Harley."

"Oh, Harley, he's great."

"You've known him for awhile. You don't know anything about me."

"Let's see, you graduated from Notre Dame, so you're intelligent; you were the captain of the team, so you're a leader who was respected by his peers and coaches; you became a state cop, so you have a sense of justice; and you're black."

"What does my being black have to do with anything?"

"It intensifies the achievement. Plus, this morning when I made that crack about not being black anymore, I watched your reaction— direct observation of behavior; not outward appearances, preconceived notions, or expectations—and I saw self-confidence rooted in personal achievement, not thin-skinned false pride that masks low self-esteem. You're not some China doll that'll break with a little chip at your ancestry. All of these things tell me you probably had a good upbringing, too."

"You sound like Sherlock Holmes with your deductions."

"I think I could've been a fair detective if I'd gone that way."

"And maybe all your compliments amount to a bunch of manipulative –"

"Garbonia." Randori finished the sentence, laughing. "The word I would choose is garbonia. But it's not, Nick; I'm just being honest. Look, you and I don't have to do lunch or go out for beers. I'm not a socializer, but I do have a sense for people. You—and Harley—are the good guys. I don't think you'll railroad me."

A smile skipped across Neidrich's face, leaving as abruptly as it had arrived. "OK, you did your analysis. Try this on for size: You went to Hamilton College, so you're among the best and brightest. Taking what I know of that school with what I'm learning about you tells me that you're a true liberal artist, an independent thinker who won't be influenced by propaganda—*garbonia*, if you will. You're probably as secure in dialogue with a brilliant professor as you are in the solitude of your own mind."

During the trooper's analysis, Randori stared at the ground, raising his head only when Neidrich stopped. "It seems like you just described someone a lot better than I am, Nick, but if it leads you to believe I'm innocent I'll buy it."

"So, who do you think killed Dr. Samson?"

"All I know is it wasn't me. I wouldn't want to harsh my karma. You questioned anyone who has a better alibi than I do?"

Neidrich hesitated, not wanting to discuss a case with a suspect, but he reconsidered, believing it would do no harm as long as he limited the information to that which the counselor could find out on his own. It might even promote trust, and trust could lead to a slip-up if Randori were, in fact, the killer. "Not really. Your friends are in about the same boat as you are."

"What friends? You mean Kerry and Meryl? I can see Meryl not having an alibi. She was probably at home doing paperwork. Which is a shame, because a woman like that should be out having the time of her life. Problem is, her career is her life. But Kerry? He's a social guy."

Neidrich chuckled. "You're right about Ms. Morgan—in every respect. But Mr. Wyatt was home, too. He had to get up early on Saturday to visit his daughter in New York. Ms. Morgan vouched for him. They spoke on the phone."

Randori's eyes narrowed, and he looked off, mulling the information. "Interesting, so it's only the phone call that makes their alibis better than mine."

"Right, but people seem to agree that your motives are the strongest, that you have the physical capability, and that you're the most suspicious character."

"I've had to deal with that most of my life; I'm used to it."

Randori extended his hand, and Neidrich surprised himself by smiling as he clasped it. Initially, he had followed Randori's lead, acting friendly to bring down his guard, but he found himself starting to like the man. He had to be careful, though; Randori was charming, but so was Ted Bundy, even as he was committing the most heinous crimes. And then there was the counselor's adherence to the Sun Tzu teaching that the general may disobey the sovereign if the sovereign's dictates will lead to defeat. Did Randori see himself as a general at the front and Samson as an oppressive sovereign? Could he believe that righteous disobedience justified a surgical excision?

Mingling scents of books and desks and paper, of cleanser and polish invaded Randori's nose and, in strange enchantment, worked their way to his heart, triggering remorse at the loss of summer freedom and apprehension of renewed tasks. Kerry Wyatt would have called it a *Pavlovian Response*; the coach in Randori identified it as *butterflies*— butterflies floating on the bouquet of a new school year.

He detoured to Leroy Dubcek's office before heading to the Counseling Center. By Dubcek's choice, the office was tucked in an isolated hallway, separate from the rest of the department. He said it gave him the privacy needed for testing, but Randori believed the psychologist wanted to establish that he was different, special—above the counselors. He found a *Testing: Privacy Please* sign dangling from the handle. As he turned to leave, he saw Dubcek walking toward him, balancing a cup of tea.

The psychologist glanced up, his eyes widening at the sight of Randori. Knitting a patch of gravity onto his forehead, he said, "Isn't it terrible, Dr. Samson's death?"

"How do you think the Steelers are going to do this year?"

The psychologist's head jerked. Randori's question had stitched yet another furrow in his brow. "I have no idea. You know I don't follow sports."

"Well, I don't follow obituaries. The sign says you're testing."

"Oh, sorry," Dubcek said, his expression softening, a relative term as the psychologist's typical facial cast was one of utmost seriousness. "I put that up so no one interrupts me. It's only the beginning of the school year, but I'm already falling behind. I really need my own secretary."

"And I need a Starbucks kiosk outside my office. I'd prefer it inside, but confidentiality would be a bear."

If Dubcek shared in the humor he gave no sign, but Randori indulged in a private smile as he pushed the door open and stepped aside for his colleague to enter. Inside, he watched Dubcek gently lift his trouser legs to sit before he himself pulled up a chair.

Dubcek sipped his tea. "You're here about Paul Roberge."

"We'd like you to test him."

"Do we have a signed *Permission to Evaluate*? It is illegal to test without that."

It irked Randori when Dubcek stated the obvious as though it were his own private knowledge reserve. To distract and entertain himself, he shifted his eyes to the psychologist's bulletin board. Randori found bulletin boards—and bookshelves and walls—interesting, believing that they provided a map of an individual. His chief entertainment came from determining whether they reflected a true depiction of their owner or the image the person wished to project. Dubcek's board included a *Meditation for the Overworked*; a list of the most stressful occupations, with "Psychologist" highlighted at number six; the admonition, laminated for posterity: "Don't give so much of yourself to others that there is nothing left for you"; and finally, the legal criteria for the classification of *Serious Emotional Disturbance*. With the exception of the SED criteria, all of Dubcek's postings were more convenient to a visitor's view than his own.

"The parents signed off. I thought Kerry told you the clock's ticking on this."

"You know I always respect timelines. I will evaluate Paul and arrive at my own conclusions. I've already reviewed his cumulative folder, the counselor's anecdotal notes, and his discipline file. On the surface, I don't see a learning disability. Quite possibly, though, his learning problems stem from an emotional disturbance."

Randori tented his arms and tapped his fingertips. "You're concluding that from a paper trail? Have you met the kid?"

The psychologist's face soured. "It's my job to know the troubled students."

"Troubled? Paul's not afflicted; he's a carrier."

"Now who is prejudging?" Dubcek shot the French cuffs under his tailored suit and sat erect, a satisfied smirk punctuating his retort. When Randori responded with a smile, Dubcek turned serious again. "I first learned of him last year when he was referred to the SAP Team for possible drug abuse. I was his case manager."

"So, following SAP procedures, you contacted his parents?"

"No, after interviewing him, I saw no signs of a drug problem."

"I'm not sure I agree; the general belief is that he is involved."

"I avoid general beliefs; I rely instead on years of education and experience. My considered conclusion is that he is dysthymic—he is depressed and has been for a while."

"Depression?" Randori looked at Dubcek with new interest and concern. "Why? He seems more like a Conduct Disorder—a Socially Maladjusted kid. With that and drug involvement to boot, you'll get a false positive for emotional disturbance."

Dubcek's defensive traits were as obvious as the hair rising on a cat's back. He leaned back, folded his arms, crossed his legs, and buried his chin in his chest. His face twisted into an acerbic pucker as he peered over the top of his bifocals. "Paul may indeed externalize; however, his acting out could be his efforts to gain control over his life and the hopelessness and frustration he feels in his classes."

Randori did not want the boy to be found eligible for special education services. He was convinced his assessment of Roberge's behavior was accurate, but he also wanted to avoid forcing events, knowing that force often brings about the opposite reaction to that which is intended. Aware of Dubcek's abiding desire to get in the last word, the counselor allowed that vanity.

As expected, Dubcek changed the subject. "I was talking with Tammy Eboli; she questioned your qualifications to run the department. Why does she hate you so? Did she make advances that you rejected? You know what they say, 'Hell hath no fury...' "

"I don't know what her problem is. Why she doesn't worry about her department, why she feels she has to meddle in—" Randori bit off further comment. He respected Eboli as a teacher, although he thought she was insecure—a weakness Dubcek could exploit by passing Randori's words along to her. "But you know what? I still kind of like her. She's just doing her job."

"And that job is Association president," Dubcek said, pressing his criticism. "Tammy is an excellent teacher—just ask her—but she wants it all: power, control."

Unwilling to take Dubcek's provocative bait and give him more verbal fodder than he already had, Randori rose and opened the door. "It's disappointing that problems have already started with Tammy. I was hoping this year would go better."

"I'll keep my antenna up," Dubcek added with a self-conscious smile. "You know you can count on me."

The focal point of Harley Snitz's office was the picture window that hung behind his office desk. Natural light seemed to emanate from the glass itself, casting a celestial aura around his frame and bathing the room in warm sepia tones interrupted only by his shadow that flowed across the desk top and cascaded onto the hardwood floor. Though Snitz had no reason to be pleased with the progress on the case, a beatific smile softened his creased features as he took in the panorama before him. The clear air splashed the canvas in paint-by-number hues, drawing a sharp demarcation between platinum cumulus clouds, bright blue sky, and emerald horizon. Even starker was the contrast between the brilliant outdoor vista and the drab interior upon which the Chief had turned his back.

"I can't imagine working in an office without windows. And I definitely couldn't work at a job where I'd be inside all day."

"Me neither," Neidrich said, surveying the office. Any thought that went into Snitz's office decor emphasized comfort over beauty, an island of sameness in a world changing too fast. Thick walls enclosed tall casements, windowsills deep enough to be used as extra seats if the room were to become crowded. Walls and ceiling were tan, although Neidrich suspected the original color had been several shades lighter. A cracked ochre patina of ancient varnish encrusted broad oak chair rails and molding, both floor and crown. The floor itself was a matching phalanx of six-inch-wide boards, its high-traffic area so worn that the surface grain resembled isobars on a topographic map. Water-stained black-and-white pictures of local miners and buildings hung off-kilter alongside blow-up maps of Freedom County and Newcastle Borough. Chairs that seemed as old as the Chief himself fanned around his oak desk.

Neidrich had settled into a leather chair in front of the Chief's desk. He usually shunned the impersonal cool firmness of leather; this chair, though, was much like Snitz himself—broken in, mellowed, gracious. It was Neidrich's favorite chair.

"Ms. Morgan's office is nice," Snitz said, half-turning. "She's a class act." He nodded with conviction. "She's—what's the word I want?—dignified."

"You think she'd protect Randori out of loyalty?"

Snitz finally turned his back to the window and his jaw stiffened—
as it did whenever his attention was pulled away from his landscape.
The window vacations didn't bother Neidrich, though, because they
brought the Chief rehoned mental acuity.

"Protect him from a murder rap? Never. She has too much
integrity."

"Did she defend him as staunchly as you'd expect?"

"No. I'd say she stuck up more for Mr. Wyatt." Snitz held up a
finger, suppressing a premature extrapolation. "Some say she and Mr.
Wyatt have a thing going, though, so I'd be for thinking that's the
reason."

"It just seems she's precise in everything she says. … Oh hell, I'm
reaching. It's not good when a murder investigation goes on too long;
trails get cold."

"It'll take as long as it takes. We're covering the bases. We even
looked into the women Dr. Samson's friends told us about. All old
news; all had alibis. Your people are checking the alternative school
folks and the membership, past and present, of the local martial arts
schools to see if anyone had a problem with Dr. Samson."

"He told his wife he had a meeting. There's something, someone
we're missing."

Snitz shook his head. "You had a crew comb the District Office
and the parking lot. My guess is he was forced into his car and taken
somewhere, then killed."

"Or enticed into the car by someone he knew and either trusted or
didn't fear."

Snitz opened a drawer and produced two oranges. He offered one
to Neidrich, and the two men worked on their fruit in silence. The Chief
used a penknife to start, then took a spoon and separated the rind from
the fruit. Neidrich bit the top of the orange, then ripped at it with his
thumb. His gnarled fingers were clumsy instruments, and he grimaced
as he glanced from Snitz's pristine orb to the pulpy mess in his own
hand. Reaching into the drawer again, the Chief handed the trooper a
paper towel and a moist wipe. "I bought these for you; I know you like
oranges, but when you have fingers like kielbasa, maybe your methods
need changing."

Neidrich's brow constricted. "An apt metaphor for my handling of
this case."

Neidrich and Snitz were already seated in Virgil Davis's office when he entered, slamming the door behind him. Davis, who at the moment had irons in both athletic director and assistant principal fires, yanked the chair away from his desk in mock anger. "I resent being questioned like a common suspect. Are you profiling me?"

"Your profile's just fine," Snitz said, "except maybe those sideburns. What are you talking about, 'profiling'? "

"You know damn well what I'm talking about. Check out the veteran. About the only worse profile I could have would be if I were a black vet."

"No," Neidrich deadpanned, "it's just the white ones that are crazy."

"Why Trooper Neidrich," Davis said, "that was almost funny."

"It was funny," Snitz said.

"It wasn't Richard Pryor funny," Davis said. "Martin Lawrence, at best."

Neidrich scowled. "I could run you in for that."

"Try it. They'd have to get another athletic director; games would be cancelled, refs wouldn't get paid. What do you think is more important, athletics or your piddling murder investigation?"

Snitz smiled. "I wouldn't bet my life on the difference."

"Damn, this room is cold." Davis said, leaping out of his seat. "If I don't get some coffee, I'm liable to confess to something just to get the hell out. Want some?"

Neidrich nodded, but Snitz shook his head as his mouth puckered in a sour smile. Davis shot a knowing grin at the Chief.

"Interesting how few people around here even attempt to show sorrow over Samson's death."

"Is that why you've been so somber all this time, out of respect for the dead?" With no response forthcoming, Snitz continued, "Dr. Samson didn't bring out sympathy. Still, you'd think Virgil would have some, especially since they were close at one time."

"Womb to tomb," Davis said, trying to kick the door closed while balancing a cup in each hand as both investigators watched with detached amusement. "Out of respect, I threw dirt on his casket to see him off. Life goes on, though." He studied the cups intently, but as he stepped around his desk coffee overlapped, splashing onto the floor. "I hope this stuff doesn't eat through to the concrete. This is new carpet."

"The trick is to not watch the cups," Snitz said. "Trust your balance."

"You sound like Doc," Davis said. "The Zen of coffee transport."

Snitz watched Neidrich sip then grimace. "Now you know why I bring my own."

Davis lifted his cup in a toast, took a long haul, smacked his lips, and winked. "It's an acquired taste, like scotch. So, what's up fellas, didn't my alibi check out?"

"Yes and no," Snitz said. "The people you mentioned said they saw you at the scrimmage, but they couldn't vouch for the time."

"I did see our coaches afterward. Besides, Coal Mountain is a forty-minute drive. You saying I drove up there, showed face, drove back, killed Bob, then drove up there again? I can tell you details of the scrimmage."

"Which you could've seen later on video," Neidrich said. "Look, you're OK—for now, anyway. We're here because we need help."

Snitz nodded. "We're stuck. We can account for Dr. Samson up until 6:00, when Mr. Wyatt left him. But that's where the trail ends."

"I've already told you all I know. In all honesty, Bob and I hadn't been close in a while; the last time we talked at any length was last spring. He could've found a new hangout. Everyone around here knew his face, though, and the way his death has been publicized anyone who saw him would have reported it by now."

"That's what we were thinking," Snitz said.

"So ... he probably had a late appointment, or he just did paperwork. One thing I'll give Bob, he liked to be prepared. He always said, 'Take care of the little things and the big things will take care of themselves.' If he met with anyone, it had to be business, what with the opening in-service coming up on Monday."

"Who wants to do business that late on a Friday, in August?" Neidrich asked. "I'd think people would want to wring out all the free time they can before school starts."

"Things pick up in August. People want to be ready for the kids."

"So, who do you think he might've met with?" Snitz asked.

"My guess would be a school board member or the business manager."

Neidrich shook his head. "We checked the board members, and the business guy left around 4:00 for a family camping trip in Wellsboro—three hours away. We checked the other administrators, too."

"Even Phil Olson? He never made a move without Bob's approval."

"Olson left early. He and his wife went to a wedding in Virginia that weekend. He was quick to volunteer Dr. Randori as a suspect, though."

"Dipshit," Davis muttered. He scratched his temple and fixed his eyes on his coffee cup. "Back when Bob was coaching, at the beginning of the year he'd meet with the staff to map out the whole season, but his biggest concerns were the most immediate. He'd want that first day to go without a hitch, believed it set the tone for the season."

"What happens on the first day?"

"In the morning, there's a meeting for all District employees. It's a big thing, presented jointly by the administration and the Association."

Neidrich sat up. "You think he might want to iron out details with the leader of the teachers' union? Any conflict between those two?"

"Oh, plenty, but everyone conflicts at one time or another with Tammy Eboli."

"Is it possible he met with this Eboli woman?"

Davis paused, weighing the thought. "They weren't getting along, so I think Bob would've gone out of his way to avoid Tammy. Still, it might be worth talking to her."

"Can you set it up?" Snitz asked.

"Right away." Davis phoned his secretary and asked her to call for Eboli. He frowned at the woman's response then hung up. "Tammy took a personal day."

"You know where she is?" Snitz asked.

"For a personal day, teachers don't have to tell us. I'll get her phone number and address for you. I think you're wasting your time, though; as much of a pain in the ass as she is, I don't think she's capable of murder. Tammy's a lover, not a fighter."

Neidrich cocked his head. "Conclusion based on assumption, or experience?"

Davis winked and pointed. "You're getting better. Next time, tell both sides of your mouth to smile."

THE MARCH OF TIMES

Harley Snitz watched Nick Neidrich sidestep people and furniture on his resolute approach and yearned for the days when he moved with such easy agility. When the trooper entered, Snitz got straight to business. "Good news. Ms. Eboli can meet with us at 9:00; she said she'd give us a half-hour."

Neidrich checked his watch. "We've got time. Let's take a ride so I can get the lay of the land."

The Chief leapt up and snagged his hat in one motion. "I know just the place."

Neidrich drove as Snitz directed him into the Southern Mountains—foothills to the trooper, who was raised on the Allegheny Plateau. Tooling along back roads, he handled curves with an ease that was too casual for the Chief, whose face drew into the rictus of a man pretending to enjoy his first roller coaster ride; his hands gripped the seat, and he leg-pressed an imaginary brake on the floorboard. A glance at Snitz and Neidrich got the message. He eased up on the gas, and a simultaneous sigh of relief came from the passenger seat as they continued at a casual pace along the winding, weathered blacktop.

With the exception of the Culver Pond area, the ridge was undeveloped. Dense woodlands abruptly began with the rise in elevation and ran the southern spine of the valley. On both sides of the road, trees pushed close to the edge, their lush branches interlaced in prayer for eternal summer.

Snitz pointed to a gravel road leading to a ranger observation tower at the highest point on the ridge. After negotiating sharp bends and axle-busting potholes, Neidrich parked on a stretch of crushed brush and packed clay at the base of the tower.

Climbing the steep flights, between puffs for air, the Chief said, "I come here when I want to think. You can see for miles, put things in perspective."

When he reached the top platform, Neidrich craned his neck in all directions. To the west, steam clouds rose from the cooling towers at Three Mile Island, hidden over the horizon. To the north, Freedom City and its suburbs spread like a coffee stain on the lovely pastoral canvas. The trooper's gaze, like that of most who climbed the tower, settled on the south and east, into Essex County, the heart of Pennsylvania Dutch land. Harvesters moved in lazy silence, shaving wavy ribbons of tan and gold across rolling farmland that basked in warm sunlight and morning dew, earth tones replacing green, with autumn coming on. Silos, barns, and farmhouses, simple yet immaculate structures, dotted the landscape. It was a timeless scene. Had he been able to view the Amish country beyond, Neidrich could have erased almost all vestiges of modern life.

Where dirt roads once blended into the surroundings, two charcoal macadam lightning bolts wrenched treacherously along property lines on a meandering yet inevitable path toward market in Lancaster. Neidrich's mind jerked away from his lush imagining of an enchanted past to a stark realization of modern life—those roads brought a threat more jolting than their black intrusion on the bucolic scene; farmers' lifelines, they were also harbingers of the end of a way of life. Farther to the south than his eyes could reach, suburbs pushed ever closer and someday soon would be in view. Families, who had tilled the land for decades, now tired of their backbreaking work to eke out a living, one by one succumbed to the financial temptations of the developers. Soon, the valley would no longer be beholden to the sun and the rain but to the dollar.

Winds of change already were blowing from east and west, carried along the Pennsylvania Turnpike, hidden below the wooded slope to the south. Vagabond professionals, seeking the pot of gold and a safe, peaceful place to raise their children came to the end of the rainbow, only to commute to work in cities thirty, forty, fifty miles away. At the same time, the idyllic land they had discovered was consumed by their very presence, the fields giving way, not to neighborhoods where folks live and commune, but rather to those pods of civilization known as developments, tracts where people exist as friendly strangers. And rootless progeny of absentee parents supplanted the corn, children who, in their unconscious search for meaning in the vacuum, find only pastimes. Without the land to bind them, without the family to guide them, some drift toward destinies no one wants.

But then, Neidrich thought, two hundred years ago one of the true natives of the land may have stood as he now stood—perhaps on the same ridge—watching dirt roads deliver wagons full of settlers, seeing the forests disappear, pondering the end of a way of life. What would some descendent standing on the same spot two hundred years from now reflect upon and look forward to?

Neidrich stared, mesmerized, as Snitz's voice broke his trance. "Nick? Are you OK?"

"Just thinking about something Randori and I were talking about."

The Chief shivered as a chill breeze brushed the back of his neck. Glancing over his shoulder, he saw a shadow spreading over the valley. "I think we're in for some bad weather."

Neidrich nodded. "Looks that way."

The skies opened as the cruiser left the gravel road. Pinpoints at first, little more than mist, but by the time Neidrich turned onto the blue highway leading to the high school, giant balls of rain splattered his windshield and his wipers flipped madly, trying to keep the road visible.

"What do we have, Harley?"

Interpreting Neidrich's verbal shorthand, Snitz said, "Tammy Eboli, leader of the teachers' union. Pretty fair teacher, as I understand, but, well, she seems like a hard case. Kass said she gave him guff about meeting with us; wanted to make it a union issue."

"How can that be?"

"Heaven knows. Kass insisted on setting up the interviews, so we wouldn't disrupt school operations. He's the boss; I thought, works for him, works for me. Up to now, we haven't had problems, and we've already talked to, what, a couple dozen people. But Ms. Eboli, she didn't want to meet with us before school because she had to get ready for class, couldn't stay after because she teaches some adult ed class. She's supposed to have a duty-free lunch, so that was no good, and her prep period is supposed to be for preparing for class."

"Sounds like she doesn't want to talk to us at all."

"She suggested fifteen minutes at the end of the day this after, but Kass told her we needed more time."

" 'This after,' I love it. When I first moved here people would say that, and I'd say, 'This after what? This after supper? This after I take a nap?' "

"Everyone knows it means this afternoon." Snitz shot a wry smile. "You call yourself a detective?"

"Not lately," Neidrich said.

The cruiser tooled over a slight rise, and the Freedom Consolidated campus sprawled before them. Hurrying as much because they were late as to avoid the downpour, the officers weaved through the administrative office to the conference room.

Entering, they found Tammy Eboli already seated, correcting papers. When she saw Snitz and Neidrich, she rose and stood arms akimbo, her stance suggesting either haughtiness or an invitation for the men to check her out, a task easily taken on. Eboli was in her early thirties, a blush-tan picture of lean athletic grace. Toe-pinching spiked heels dramatized her height and the length of her legs, which disappeared at the hem of a form-fitting skirt. She wore a matching tailored business jacket that emphasized the dramatic inward curve of her waistline. After standing to meet the men, her only movement was to toss her luxuriant honey-blonde tresses back off her shoulder. "You know this isn't a good time."

Neidrich forced himself to stare into the deep blue pools of her eyes. "Mr. Marburg said you didn't want to meet with us."

"Kass gets confused. I said I'd meet with you, but when the building principal sets it up during school hours, it has contractual implications."

"Are you saying that if we had called you directly it would've been no problem?"

"There's always a problem if we meet during work hours because when I'm here I'm a teacher and a member of the Association."

"So you'd prefer we meet at your home."

"No, I don't want police cars in front of my house."

Neidrich cast a sidelong glance at Snitz and proceeded to the meat of his interview. He had decided to assume that Eboli met with Samson on August 26. His gaze fixed on the teacher's face. "I understand you were the last person to see Dr. Samson alive." Opening with that question provided the opportunity to catch Eboli off-guard; if wrong, he could always back off, insisting he had bad information.

The teacher was unshaken. "Evidently not, judging by what happened."

"What time did your meeting take place?" Snitz asked.

"We started at 6:15; I left at 7:30."

"You're certain of the times?"

"Definite. I had a workout class scheduled at the gym at 8:00 and I was there until after 10:00. You can check."

Snitz frowned. "Why didn't you come forward to tell us about your meeting?"

"Because I don't have any information that can help you. It was just bad timing."

"Bad judgment, too," Snitz said. "You should have contacted us."

Eboli tossed her hair at Snitz's reprimand. "Well, here we are. Ask away."

"Wasn't that a little late to be meeting on a Friday? In the summer?"

"Dr. Samson is—was—a busy man, Chief Snitz, and I teach business courses at Essex College and yoga and spin classes at my gym. We tried to meet earlier in the week, but it didn't work out."

"Long meeting," Neidrich said.

"Not really, we had a lot to—" Eboli nodded and smiled but with no congeniality attached. "Oh, I get it, you're implying something else was going on."

"Was there?"

"No!" Her eyes flared then softened, along with her tone. "We went out to dinner a few times, but that was last year. To me, they were business meetings. He had a different agenda—he wanted to get into my pants." Eboli held up her hand. "Before you ask, nothing ever came of it. I didn't know if he was a letch or he wanted to influence contract negotiations. Either way, it was no-go for me."

"You did get a good contract last time around," Snitz said.

"True. I told Dr. Samson that if my rejection of him reflected in any way on the collective bargaining process, I'd file an unfair labor practice claim and consider a sexual harassment suit. His wife would find out, and he'd get his golden image tarnished."

"That threat alone could force him to favor you in negotiations," Snitz said. "That's pretty close to blackmail, isn't it?"

"You're forgetting; he started the whole thing. You wanted to know why our meeting lasted so long. We had a lot to discuss." Eboli ticked two agenda items on immaculately finished nails. "We finalized plans for the opening-day teacher in-service, then we sketched out the entire year. After Dr. Samson got over the fact that he wasn't going to nail me, he developed some respect. But it was difficult; cooperation like we had doesn't come easily, especially when we had separate goals; or I should say separate agendas to reach common goals?"

Eboli's response was insufficient to Snitz. "What did you discuss, specifically?"

"Potential areas of conflict. When I was elected, I vowed to smooth relations with administration while still advocating for teachers. The record shows I was successful."

Snitz pressed. "What did you talk about?"

"It's inappropriate for me to discuss issues that may never arise. We just set the tone for how we were going to work together this year."

The Chief leaned forward and lightly clapped his palms on the table in a small venting of frustration. "There's nothing you can tell us? We need you to be specific."

"Am I a suspect? What would my motive be?"

Noting Eboli's agitation, Neidrich intervened. "We just want to know if Dr. Samson said anything that might help us."

"We talked about Doc Randori, the curriculum leader for the special education and counseling departments—if *leader* is the word you want. He creates friction, tries to give everyone orders, but he doesn't have the knowledge, so no one respects him."

"I don't understand," Snitz said. "Why can't he give orders if he's the department supervisor? And how did he become supervisor if he doesn't have the knowledge?"

"He's not a *supervisor*; he's a *curriculum leader*." The difference eluded the lawmen, so Eboli elaborated. "A curriculum leader can give direction, but he can't issue directives. Randori has no administrative authority, and as far as I'm concerned, he has no moral authority, either. He's a liar and a coward. The only reason he's in the position is that he's Kerry Wyatt's puppet."

Snitz needed further clarification. "Why would a person want to be a curriculum leader if he has no authority?"

"Because he's obsessed with power."

Neidrich glanced at Snitz and saw that he, too, grasped Eboli's contradiction. The momentary silence gave the trooper the opportunity to segue. "We're getting off track."

"No we're not. As soon as I heard Bob's death was suspicious, I thought, there's a no-brainer: pick up Randori. You have motivation. Those two never got along. Randori was always badmouthing Bob, and when Bob recognized Randori was a lousy administrator, he demoted him. That was something an egomaniac like Randori couldn't take. You know, of course, he blew up on Bob only a week before he killed him."

Snitz cocked his head. "How's that?"

"No one told you? Kerry Wyatt informed Randori that Bob was going to cut the karate program at our alternative school. He said there weren't enough funds, and, besides, it was tough to justify teaching violent kids to fight better." Eboli smirked. "I think Bob just wanted to piss Randori off, though. So, Randori confronted him, demanded to know how Bob and his cronies could afford national conferences, electronic organizers, and other gadgets when the money could've been spent on kids. Then he asked how Bob could justify driving around in a Mercedes on the District dime."

"The District is paying for that car?" Snitz asked.

"The lease deal was part of his contract that was never made public."

"I bet that cooked Dr. Samson's cojones." Snitz's face reddened. "Excuse me, made him angry."

"Bob said it was none of Randori's business how funds are spent; furthermore, he was going to fire him for insubordination. That's where I got involved."

"How so?" Neidrich asked.

"Last Friday, Bob said he wanted me to support his getting rid of Randori. I told him Randori asked some good questions, questions I wanted answers to, as well."

Snitz scratched behind his ear. "You defended Dr. Randori?"

"Look, Randori's a jerk, but right is right. District money should be invested in kids. It's just unfortunate for Bob that he crossed the wrong guy. Now, do you have the evidence you need?"

"Evidence," Neidrich said, "I don't know. But it is interesting."

Snitz said, "You worked on District business the whole time that night?"

A sharp glance prefaced Eboli's response. "What else would there be?"

"I don't understand why he didn't list your meeting on his calendar."

"You'd have to ask his secretary."

The Chief arched a brow. "Did you leave together?"

"No," Eboli snapped.

"Any old boyfriends object to your seeing Dr. Samson way back— when was it?"

"No. And he hasn't made any moves on me since last spring."

Neidrich broke in. "No need to get defensive, Ms. Eboli. We're just piecing together the events of that night."

"I can't help you there. And for the record, I wasn't being defensive; I just don't like loaded questions and innuendo. You sound like an administrator."

"Did he say if he had any appointments after he met with you?"

"No, he said he had to wrap some things up. My guess is he was going home. He was a good family man." Eboli rolled her eyes. "Most of the time."

Snitz took over again. "Did you see any other cars in the lot?"

"No, just mine and his. I noticed because, at first, I thought he stood me up. His car wasn't in his assigned space."

Neidrich glanced at Snitz, but the relevance of Eboli's statement was lost on him. Of course, it would be. The Chief knew none of the details of the State Police evidence sweep of the District Office and surroundings. "Where was it?"

"By the picnic table, where it's shady."

Eboli checked her watch, and Neidrich said, "Thanks, Ms. Eboli. We realize you're on a tight schedule, and we appreciate your cooperation." He slid his chair back. "Is it all right to meet again if there are any further questions?"

Following Neidrich's cue, Eboli rose and smiled, extending her hand. "Any time." She clasped his hand and held him captive in her doe-eyed gaze. "Just call."

As they left the office, the investigators ran into Virgil Davis. "Hey fellas, I see you caught up with Tammy. She's a treat, isn't she?" The ensuing silence suggested he change the subject. "We need extra security at the game Friday. Want to help?"

"Jim and I will be there," Snitz said. "Ed said he's busy, though. I can't believe he'd miss the game against City."

"I'll help," Neidrich said. He did want to see a football game, but he also hoped to get a handle on the school social atmosphere, to see if Ed's side of the investigation had any validity. He also wanted to catch Davis with his guard down. "No charge."

As usual, the officers reserved discussion until they were in the privacy of the car. Even then, they typically said little before collecting their thoughts. This time, though, Snitz was quick to ask, "Do you think she listens to herself when she talks?"

"She did contradict herself a few times. I think she hates Randori and can't separate from that. Look how his name came up; it was when we pushed her to be specific about what she and Samson discussed."

"Think she might be covering up what went on that night?"

"Maybe, but in her zeal to incriminate Randori she practically exculpated him."

Snitz grinned and winked. "I love it when you talk like a Notre Dame grad."

The ghost of a smile crossed Neidrich's face and he dropped his eyes, in contemplation as much as embarrassment. "At the same time, we can't dismiss what she said. The 'coward' part, that's just bile. Wyatt told us Randori is subversive, prone to guerrilla tactics. To a person as direct and, it seems, confrontational as Ms. Eboli, that could be interpreted as cowardice. But guerrilla tactics might be what Samson faced that night. Also, we know Randori wanted to get out of administration, so that negates her statement about his obsession with power. But anyone with any pride would be embarrassed about how the demotion might look to others. Especially if Samson bragged about it. Add to that their argument a week before the murder, and I can see how, in Tammy Eboli's eyes, Randori might be the killer."

"Speaking of eyes," Snitz said, his own eyes piercing into Neidrich's. "I saw how you and Ms. Eboli looked at each other. Don't go down that road, Nick."

"I don't know what you're talking about, Harley." Neidrich sneaked a peek into Snitz's unwavering stare. "Oh hell, yes I do. She's beautiful."

Snitz gritted his teeth. "You've been alone too long. That young woman's looks are clouding your mind." His words seethed and scalded like steam from a teapot. "She's the most hostile person we've questioned so far, but she bats those eyes and tickles your palm, and suddenly you forget all that."

Neidrich bristled, faltering through attempts to begin excuses before he heaved a sigh of resignation. "You're right; of course, you're right. But she could be right, too."

"You still think Dr. Randori is a suspect?"

"So far, our best and only one. I don't know, though; I can't get a fix on that guy. One thing is certain; he can arouse passionate dislike. By the way, you were hostile toward Ms. Eboli. I admire your nice way with people, but you pushed her."

Snitz clamped his lips, considering before answering. "I just wanted to pin down her recollections." Then, "Heck, I'm no better at excuses than you are. I heard she's a bit of a manhunter; I wanted to figure out her relationship with Dr. Samson. The way people talk, though, we'd have known if there was more—especially between those two."

Neidrich's eyes flashed with canny intelligence. "Did you notice at the beginning of the interview, she referred to 'Dr. Samson,' but when she was going off on Randori, she dropped her guard and started calling him 'Bob'?"

It was the game of the year in Freedom County: the two biggest schools, a backyard rivalry, the "haves" of Freedom Con versus the "have-nots" of Freedom City. The main parking lot was nearly full, and a queue of incoming cars stretched a quarter-mile down the road. Snitz waved to the fire policeman directing traffic, and the man in turn pointed them toward the reserved parking spaces.

After cutting the ignition, Neidrich made no move to leave the car. "Square one," he said. "After what Tammy Eboli told us, I had the forensics team comb the picnic area and the spot where Samson parked. No luck. There's good topsoil, and the grass is a treated rye blend. The stains on Samson's trousers were from dandelions and weeds, and the soil had high clay content. The gravel in his pants cuffs was a different grade than anything around the administrative lot. And no blood traces anywhere."

"So, Dr. Samson wasn't attacked around the District Office. Did your people find anything we can use?"

Neidrich's head took one slow, pendular swing. "The clay is common throughout the valley, and weeds are weeds. No herbicides or pesticides showed up. I had some hope for the gravel, but that particular grade is common."

"Dr. Samson didn't stop anywhere public," Snitz said, frowning, "and the area between the District Office and his home is farmland and woods. I don't know where to go from here."

"What's the area around the quarry like? Any places Samson might've stopped?"

"Just trails and spots where kids drink beer and make out."

"Just the same, let's have one of your men give my people a tour of that area."

"We'll get on it at daybreak," Snitz said, forcing a hopeful tone. "Were you able to get anything on Ms. Eboli?"

"Witnesses have her twenty miles away at her gym from 8:00 until 10:30—even later than she told us." Neidrich smiled, trying to build on Snitz's apparent buoyancy. "How's Ed's end going? Does he still think that he's working on the same case we are?"

"Doesn't seem like he's making much progress, but he's on a crusade. Even if he doesn't tie anything to the case, he can put a dent in the drug problem. I never thought I'd say this, but it helps that Ed's jaw flaps more than the flag at Fort McHenry; it'll keep some of the spotlight off us. Don't get me wrong; I love Ed like a son. And let's face it, as remote a possibility as his theory is, it's still a possibility, so it's not like I have him on a wild goose chase."

"Are you sure?"

Snitz let slip a small chuckle and his cheeks went red. "I don't know why I feel guilty. Ed does work well with kids. It's with adults he runs into trouble."

Neidrich welcomed the opportunity to talk about something other than the case. He liked spending downtime with the Chief—a man devoid of guile and pretense. Half turning in his seat, he asked, "Ed have kids of his own?"

"No, he and Molly have had problems there. They're saving up, trying to adopt."

"Nothing changes adults like having kids," Neidrich said, pausing before adding the qualifier, "Except for adults who haven't outgrown their own childhood."

"Ed will be a good dad. He'll live for that child. Molly, too." Snitz nodded with conviction. "They will."

"Trying to convince yourself or me?"

"Both, I guess. We don't need any more bad parents."

Neidrich studied the Chief's face. "For what it's worth, you convinced me."

Snitz's lips bowed up into a tight smile. "Back to Dr. Samson. Your people finished checking his private life?"

"Business dealings were on the up and up—straight real estate deals with a stock portfolio on the side. Most of his relationships outside work were golfing buddies, country club cronies. Samson had an entourage; they fed his ego and he slapped backs and bought drinks."

"He was a celebrity," Snitz agreed. "His dark side showed at work. But that's typical. If you're around a person just a bit, in a relaxed setting, all you really see is what's on the surface—his personality. It's when you're with someone a lot, especially in stressful situations, you see what that person is made of—his character."

"Or lack of it," Neidrich agreed. "I don't think Samson was a guy I would have respected a whole lot. So, maybe his murderer is a person with a strong belief system, someone idealistic, who stands for something. And whoever killed Samson is intelligent. It took planning and patience."

"I don't know. Stabbing someone doesn't exactly look like a car accident."

"Maybe our man didn't care and just used his weapon of choice." Neidrich raised his chin to emphasize his next point. "What do you think about the paint chips embedded in Samson's head? They're consistent with the finish on some martial arts weapons."

"Seems too convenient, like someone wants to lead us toward a martial artist."

"That's where I was headed; I just wanted to see if you're going the same way."

Snitz ran his fingers through his hair. "A stab like that makes for a bloody scene. Why would someone make such a mess then have to clean it up and move the body to the quarry so it looked like it happened there?"

"That quarry is isolated, and it would require strength to heft Samson into his car, drive there, then reposition him behind the wheel before sending him over."

"Fits better with two attackers," Snitz nodded.

"Possibly, but that would require two homicidal school people or one with an outside accomplice. Educators and murderers generally don't rub elbows socially."

The Chief patted Neidrich's shoulder. "There's not much evidence, we don't have witnesses, and my brain's getting foggy. I'm for thinking there's nowhere to go but up. Let's go watch some football."

Inside the stadium, Neidrich scanned the stands. When his eyes fell on the playing field, a rush of animal awareness, a vestige of the primitive mind, surged on a tide of adrenaline and engulfed the trooper in a maelstrom of sensations. Conditioned by year after year of autumn weekends spent hitting and getting hit, a chill rose like a vapor from an organic wellspring; his neck tingled and a shiver rippled his skin, the visceral response of the champion to the arena.

"Nick? Say Nick." Snitz's voice parted the mists of Neidrich's consciousness. Smiling in response to the younger man's beaming face, the Chief clapped the trooper's shoulder and pointed. "Over there."

Davis and Randori stood twenty yards away, their backs to the investigators, arms identically propped atop a four-foot chain-link fence that encircled the track surrounding the football field. They were engrossed in the Freedom Con pre-game warm-ups.

As he and Snitz approached the educators, Neidrich announced their presence. "I see the SWAT team is here early."

Randori turned and smiled. "Virge hasn't been home all day." He gestured toward Davis, who was togged in a rumpled olive twill suit. "He never goes home."

"Hey, if I did, all I'd think about is everything that could go wrong here."

"The anal-retentive athletic director," Randori said. "Virge maps out his procedures every year before the season starts, then he updates it for every game, depending on weather conditions, continental drift, avian migratory patterns—"

"Yeah," Davis said, "and Mr. Improv here operates totally from the gut. Then if something goes wrong, he says, 'No big deal, we'll do better next time.' No wonder you sucked as an administrator, Randori; to you, intuition equates to advanced planning."

"Better than being counterintuitive."

The counselor's inside insult brought a prompt response from Davis. "I'm counterintuitive? Your intuition is counterintuitive."

"That's why you two make such a nice couple," Snitz broke in. "You complete each other. Where do you want us, Virgil?"

"You and Nick can circulate. I have rent-a-cops stationed at each end of the stands and behind the end zone areas of the field. Cat—Cat

Blanchard, Nick, our other assistant principal—will be in the home stands. If there's trouble, it'll probably be right here. This is where kids gather. Some just socialize; others make connections for beer or drugs or just look for trouble. Doc will be here with the AD from City."

"Where will the principal be?" Neidrich asked.

Davis shot a crooked grin at Randori. "Kass will be in the stands watching the game. He doesn't get his hands dirty."

Neidrich raised his chin toward Davis. "Mind if I tag along with you?"

"Got to move double-time," Davis warned, already stepping away. "Let's go."

Following Davis was an eye-opening experience. First, they went to the press box where the athletic director dropped off game programs for reporters. He tested the scoreboard control panel for the third time that day. From his pocket, he produced an extra camera battery, insisting the cameraman take it, even after the man opened his case to display two spares. Moving down through the stands to the field, Davis reminded the leader of the chain gang—the group that managed the first down markers—to coordinate efforts with the referees. Then, he tracked down the band director to make sure both schools knew when to perform. Next, Davis headed for the locker rooms; first, the officials' dressing room to hand each referee a check, then to the team rooms to drop off stacks of game programs and give the Freedom City head coach the key to the visitors' locker room. Neidrich, in deference to Davis's duties, decided to forego any peripatetic conversation except for small talk about the details of an athletic director's job.

As they walked back through the main gate, Davis said, "I have a couple more stops, then we can go to my office and talk. You do want to talk to me, right? I can't think of any other reason you'd want to follow me around."

"Right," Neidrich admitted. "I'm learning a lot, though. Back when I played, I thought the game just happened."

Davis's eyes twinkled, precursors to a Santaclausian guffaw. "So did I." He bellied up to the concession stand, ordered two coffees and handed one to Neidrich. Next, he led the way to the ticket booth where his game manager zipped and locked two security bags and handed them to him. Patting the bags with finality, Davis said, "All right, my business is under control; now we can take care of yours."

They trekked back toward the school in silence broken only by brief exchanges about the weather and football. Both men knew that the meatier conversation had to wait until they were behind closed doors. Within minutes, they were at Davis's office. Before closing the door, he scanned the administrative complex and backed inside. The athletic director waved the trooper to a chair and slumped into his own.

Neidrich surveyed the office: Freedom Con championship team pictures lined the walls like a phalanx, and individual student photographs were tacked up in slapdash fashion, but there were no Davis family photos. "Any pictures of your wife and kids?"

After a long swig of coffee, Davis said, "I don't have any kids. We—Lois, my wife, and I—figured it wouldn't be fair to them, me working the hours I do. And Lois, well, it just wouldn't have worked." Distracted, Davis patted his coat pockets until he found his pack of cigarettes. Lighting up, he leaned back, closed his eyes, and expelled a gray cloud toward the ceiling. "That's better. I've been at it since six this morning."

"I thought this was a 'smoke-free campus.' "

"It is," Davis answered offhandedly as he searched his desk drawers. "That's why I didn't light up outside where someone could see me. ... Ah, there it is." He pulled an ashtray from beneath a stack of game contracts. "I keep saying I'm going to quit. You think those patches work?"

"I don't know. I never smoked." Pointing to a picture of a young man in a football uniform, Neidrich recognized the face but little else. "Nice mullet."

Chuckling, Davis said, "More hair, less me. I didn't smoke back then. I picked up the habit in the service. Now I smoke for weight control." Davis laughed, patting a belly that was noticeably absent in the photograph. Then he repeated, "Picked up the habit. Funny how we pick up a cigarette habit but become addicted to other drugs?" The athletic director shrugged, inhaled deeply, and blew a stream of smoke toward the ceiling. "But you want to talk about something—or rather someone—else. Doc, he's your main suspect, right? Followed by me."

"I did want to get your take on Dr. Samson's untimely demise."

"*Smert' za vorotami ne zhdet.*"

"Say again?"

Davis rocked forward and grinned, cold eyes dampening any hint of humor. "It's an old Russian saying: 'Death keeps no calendar.' There's no such thing as an 'untimely demise.' "

"You learned Russian in the Army?"

Davis nodded. "Some Farsi, too. And you want to know if I killed anyone, because you're looking to find someone capable of doing the grisly deed. Well, when duty called I answered." Davis pulled a pen out of his shirt pocket and began to scrawl on a notepad. "Mostly, I scouted enemy positions, listened in on communications."

"So, you got close to enemy lines."

"Lines were kind of fuzzy. I had to be airlifted out once. 'Tight sit.' …Tight situation." Davis tore the note he had been writing from the pad and handed it to Neidrich. "Here's my old CO's contact info."

"Service toughened you. You haven't been grief-stricken over Samson's death."

"Bob and I had the old love/hate thing going. I coached for him, and he recommended me to be head coach when he got the high school principal job. I was his handpicked AD. As far as I know, he always spoke highly of me. That's the upside."

"The downside?"

Davis paused and took a final long drag on his cigarette, stubbed it out, and fieldstripped it into the ashtray. All the while, he leaned forward, staring at his hands, his grimace reflecting thoughts exhumed from an unhallowed grave in a dark corner of his mind. Pulling out another cigarette, he tamped the end against his knuckle. Finally looking up, he measured his interrogator eye-to-eye. His expression had changed almost imperceptibly, metamorphosing into what Neidrich called a "game face"—the facial cast coaches want to see on players before a game—controlled aggression. Neidrich knew a real game face from a phony one; Davis was a player to be reckoned with.

"Bob used people." Looking off, the athletic director reconsidered his words. "No, it was more than that. I don't want to sound melodramatic, but Bob got off on enslaving people. He did it with football players, friends, women—especially women, the more vulnerable the better." Davis's eyes brightened. "Wait a minute." He ripped a sheet of paper off a note pad, scratched out several names, and shoved the scrap across his desk toward Neidrich. "These women have good reasons to hate Bob."

Neidrich glanced at the paper. "We got these names already. You're sure there's no one else. How about Tammy Eboli?"

"Tammy? No way. The superintendent and the union head? Too high-risk."

"Indulge me for a second. Suppose Eboli and Samson did have an affair, then an old—or a new—boyfriend of hers decided to eliminate the competition."

"I knew Bob better than anyone did, and you met Tammy, right? I'd be very surprised if they hooked up; you can't have two alpha dogs in a relationship. Bob would get you to do something for him, but he'd never allow himself to be indebted to you. Instead, he'd treat you like dirt so you knew you were still under his thumb."

Neidrich was aware of at least one instance in which Samson had placed himself in debt to Eboli, but he accepted Davis's assessment for the time being and moved on. "Samson recommended you to succeed him as head coach."

"Yeah, but he left the cupboard bare; twenty-some seniors had graduated. The league was strong. We won three games, which I consider an achievement. Still, everybody said, 'Bob would've made that team a contender.' So he got the last laugh."

"How do you figure? He's dead."

"Well, he's a legend, and I was a head coach for two years." Davis paused, allowing his eyes to drive his bitterness home. "Then, after Bob became superintendent, I applied for the high school principal job. He didn't even give me an interview; instead, he brought Kass over from the middle school. OK, that happens. So, I applied for the middle school job Kass vacated, but they gave it to a 28-year-old who'd been in the district one year and done nothing to distinguish himself.

"Bob said I was too valuable as assistant principal and athletic director; I had to be a team player. I'll tell you, if Doc wasn't here for me to vent to—" Davis gagged on the bile his memories had dredged up. "He says I should go back to teaching and regular hours, says I don't owe the District anything."

"I guess you'd have to make up the pay somehow."

"Heh, I wouldn't lose significant pay; in fact, hour-for-hour I'd make more."

Neidrich frowned. "Sounds like Randori's giving you good advice then."

"Then who'd do this job?" Davis waited for an answer. With none forthcoming, he added, "Doc says that's not my problem. God, I'd love to be able to think that way."

"Sounds like your loyalty isn't reciprocated by the District."

"A couple years ago, Bob had the staff watch this video called *Whales Tales*. It's about a whale-watch business up in Cape Cod and the great attitude its employees have. The workers say they have a choice of the attitude they bring to work. It can be positive or negative; it's up to each individual."

"Sounds great," Neidrich said, intrigued. "Be good for a football team."

Davis snapped his fingers and pointed at the trooper. "That's exactly what I said. I was feeling pretty good about Freedom Con afterward. Even Doc, wet blanket that he can be, said he'd use the video if he were still coaching. But then he brought me back to earth right quick. He said the moral of the story from our administration's point of view is: if you have a bad attitude, it's on you; it's not their fault. So, be a happy, mindless little zombie, no matter how they treat you or how much shit they pile on you."

Freedom Con's system bred sickness; Neidrich saw how a staff member could become alienated, and by extension he realized that Davis had a motive to do Samson in, although he believed the man's values ran toward duty and loyalty, not homicide. But it was time to talk about his prime suspect. "So that's how Randori thinks?"

"I believe the clichéd term is 'outside the box.' " Davis field-stripped another cigarette into the ashtray and rolled his thumbs and fingers together to rub off the remaining tobacco. "That's why I admired him as a football coach. His teams were hell to prepare for. He has no respect for conventional wisdom. He questions everything. That's why he pisses bosses off so much."

"What was Randori's problem with Samson?"

"The problem was mutual. When Bob was coaching here, he wanted to schedule a patsy for the first game, to get our team's confidence up. Doc's team, St. Thomas More, brought local rivalry, but, like a lot of private schools, it had fallen on hard times through decreasing enrollment. We had more students in one graduating class than they had in the whole school. Historically, though, they had a winning tradition, so it was perfect scheduling; when we trounced them, it would mean something to our kids." Davis chuckled. "It was a good idea; should've worked. And it did—to an extent. It was Bob's best team ever and it was Doc's first year as a head coach.

"Here's the sit: the game is on our field; Doc's boys come out, all thirty-some of them, we have over sixty and outweigh them twenty pounds a man—Doc loves those odds, calls it 'the Alamo number.' As usual, his guys are silent as the grave while ours are psyched up, whooping and hollering."

"Were the Catholic High kids scared?"

"No, it's a Doc theory. He believes silence is strength. Never talk to an opponent. He thinks hollering is actually detrimental; it sends potential energy and aggression into the air. The only time you should shout is right at the moment of impact with an opponent; it focuses your energy into the collision.

"It works, too; I can attest to that. Our kids were jawing between every play. At first. As the game goes on, though, it gets eerie. When Doc's kids are on offense, they break the huddle in silence, but at the snap of the ball, their whole line shouts in unison as they hit our kids. Even their ball carriers shout when they're about to be hit. Then on defense, their kids are all over the field; eleven guys, all trying to get in on every tackle. 'Get to the ball as fast as you can and arrive in a bad mood.'

"Long story a little bit shorter, it ended up being our closest game of the year, and they beat us statistically in just about every category. The only reason we won was Bob had the referees in his hip pocket. We jumped ahead 13 to 0, but Catholic High was leading at the half, 14 to 13. In the third quarter, we went ahead again, but Doc's bandits were in great shape. In the fourth quarter, our kids were sucking wind and Catholic High was picking up steam. They scored again, making it 24-21, us. That's when the refs took over. Back then, schools contracted officials for home games; Bob had approval for ours. That night, the father of one of our players was the head referee. We got the ball with three minutes left, and that clock didn't stop for anything. Doc called time outs and the ref ignored him; someone would go out of bounds, and the clock kept ticking. Then, with seconds left, everyone in the stadium thinks we're going to run out the clock, which is what I intend. Bob has other ideas. He takes over the play calling from me, has us set up in a running formation but calls a play-action pass—we fake the run and throw a bomb."

Neidrich stared wide-eyed. "What a classless move. So, you catch Randori's defense with their pants down and score a meaningless touchdown."

"Thank God, no. The receiver was open, but the pass was overthrown."

"What did Randori do?"

Davis hesitated. "You have to understand, this was years ago."

"What happened?" Neidrich insisted.

"After the game, Bob wants to shake hands, but Doc goes after him. Ed Knepp—he was Bob's bodyguard at games—steps in and threatens to arrest Doc."

"Randori's a violent guy."

"Like I said, it was a long time ago. I might've done the same thing if I were in Doc's shoes and in my twenties. How about you?"

"But Samson's supposedly the greatest coach in the history of the county."

"I could name a half dozen coaches as good or better than Bob, including Doc."

"Including yourself?"

Davis sat back, measuring the question. "Not to brag, but I believe so."

"So how was it Samson hired Randori to work here?"

"It wasn't his choice. Bob was the high school principal at the time. The superintendent respected Bob's accomplishments but didn't allow him too much influence." Davis checked his watch. "Hey, we'd better get back to the game. It'll be past halftime." He yanked two tissues out of a box and pressed one flat on the desktop. After dumping remnants of his cigarettes onto one, he used the other to wipe the ashtray then wadded them up and stuffed them in his pocket. He pulled out an aerosol can and sprayed pine-scented freshener around the room. Sniffing the air, he said, "What do you think?"

"It smells like someone's Christmas tree is on fire," Neidrich deadpanned.

Davis dropped his jaw in mock-surprise and then pushed up on his chin, making a show of having to close it manually. "Much better. Not quite funny, but you're trying."

"One can only try. Tell me, do you think Randori could have killed Samson?"

"Could have? Doc has the intelligence and the will to find a way to win just about any battle. The question is, did he? I just don't picture Doc as a murderer."

"Funny thing," Neidrich said, "how often we run someone in for homicide and a friend says, 'I never pictured him a murderer.' "

Neidrich and Davis strolled across the parking lot, each savoring the fragrant autumn night. The athletic director tried to peek at the scoreboard, but the angle was too sharp. Pointing to the horde of students in colored uniforms hovering around the concession stand, he observed, "It is the third quarter. The band kids are on break."

His eyes widened. "Shit!" Davis broke into a jog, then a run. Pulling out the walkie-talkie, he heaved a breathless shout, "Security! Home south—grass near stands!"

Neidrich's loping strides kept pace with Davis's churning legs. "What's up?"

"Fight," Davis said through labored breaths, pointing with the antenna of the walkie-talkie.

At first, Neidrich saw only an undefined throng, then the picture came into focus: a group off to the left, each individual facing a central point, others sprinting toward the core like debris sucked into a black hole, causing it to swell by the second. Fans on the edge of the home stands peered over the side rail, straining toward something more compelling than the game. By the time Neidrich and Davis reached the action they had to wade through a packed clot of humanity. Craning necks and standing tiptoe, spectators jostled and jockeyed for a better view. The trooper lost track of the athletic director as the mass took on a life of its own—a shifting maze, the path of least resistance for one became an impenetrable wall to another. Near the center, Neidrich's height allowed him to see the action before he could do anything about it.

The crowd ended a respectful ten feet from the core. There, two groups of boys squared off, as ethnic slurs and threats rose above the din. At ground zero stood Randori and the City athletic director, back to back, each facing one faction of combatants, forcing a standoff. Neidrich hoped they would keep talking; the longer they talked, the less likely fighting would erupt. Drawing his badge, he decided the best way to quell the disturbance was to announce his identity.

Too late. The largest boy in one group charged forward. With his right hand, he swung a chain that seemed destined for Randori's head. Grasping the chain-wielding hand with both of his own, the counselor pulled and turned counterclockwise, using the boy's momentum to careen into a tight orbit, the centrifugal force of which extended the chain straight out. After a three-quarter turn, Randori abruptly stopped, pushed his assailant's arm downward arc then quickly lifted it and ducked underneath as he reversed himself clockwise, yanking the arm up and back. The move brought Randori and his attacker back-to-back, their right shoulder blades pressed together, the boy's arm, chain and all, wrenched over and behind his shoulder, his elbow straining toward the sky. As Randori pulled down on his hand, the boy arched backwards, grimacing, and the chain dangled harmlessly down the counselor's chest. Kneeling slowly to one knee, Randori arched the boy's body backward onto the ground.

"Break it up!" Davis shouted as he and Neidrich emerged from the crowd, spurring the troublemakers in both gangs to melt into the dispersing crowd. The only ones left were two uniformed boys, members of the Freedom City band who had been in the middle of the fracas. They stood placid, not resisting, as the City athletic director held each by an arm.

The atmosphere, electric just seconds before, had evaporated, leaving a chill vacuum that dampened Neidrich's adrenaline, bringing a violent shiver of relief. His gaze returned to the counselor, still kneeling over his attacker, whose flannel shirt had flipped up, exposing an imposing girth. The action had taken mere seconds, movements so effortless they passed unrecognized by the throng. They had not escaped Neidrich, though, and it told him everything he felt he needed to know about Randori.

Harley Snitz arrived and approached Davis. Security people milled around, asking each other if anyone knew what had happened. "Chief Snitz and I will take care of this," Davis told them. "Get back to your positions. I don't want any more excitement."

On the ground, the boy spluttered through clenched teeth. "Dude, wait till my dad finds out. He's gonna kick your ass. Let go of my arm."

Randori smiled and responded softly, "If you relax, I will."

The boy gave one last tug of resistance before heaving a sigh of resignation, and the tension in his arm subsided. Randori helped him to his feet, and Davis dusted him off, saying, "Is your dad here, Justin?"

Reconsidering his threat, the boy said, "My dad doesn't have to know. Don't call him—please."

Davis ignored his plea, instructing the game manager to have Billy Frederickson paged before turning his attention to the boy. "Now, what was this was all about?"

"Look at them," Justin said, jabbing a finger at the band members.

Randori flashed a wry grin. "You don't appreciate Sousa?"

Justin frowned, perplexed. "They're Rickins; they were talking to our women."

"Who was with you?" Snitz asked.

"Nobody."

Snitz looked up to see Ed Knepp, hand on holster, hustling through the main gate toward them. "Ed, you're off tonight."

"I heard on the scanner there was trouble."

Neidrich and Snitz exchanged glances. "It's over, Ed; we're wrapping things up," the Chief said. He turned to the counselor. "What's your take on this, Dr. Randori?"

"The City band kids were leaving the concession stand. Justin was with some guys—the Avalon crew, I think; I recognized Zack Boyer and one of the Wenners. They started shoving the boys from the band. Some City guys jumped in to defend the band kids; by the time we got there, nobody was buying our act."

Knepp broke in. "You're saying our kids started it, and the City kids are innocent victims? Man, that's typical; you always take the side of the City kids—or the Catholic kids. Don't you realize who signs your paycheck?"

Randori leveled a flinty stare at the sergeant, causing Neidrich to intervene. "Justin admitted as much. He said the trouble started because the boys were Hispanic."

Knepp persisted. "Notice Randori never mentioned the City kids were Hispanic. He probably doesn't mind them shipping in drugs and gangsters from New York."

"This isn't getting us anywhere, Ed," Snitz said with hard finality.

As if in punctuation, Justin's father, Billy Frederickson, arrived. A larger version of his son down to the flannel shirt and work boots, he checked the guilty expression on his son's face and gritted his teeth. "What did he do this time, Harley?"

Snitz deferred to Davis. "A little scuffle with some City kids. Looks like Justin and his friends started it."

"What friends?" Billy Frederickson asked.

"Well, that's part of the problem," Snitz said. "Justin's had a memory lapse, but Dr. Randori recognized some of them."

"Dad, Randori hit me and tried to break my arm."

Justin's father took a menacing step forward. "Is that true, Mr. Davis?"

Neidrich flashed his badge in the elder Frederickson's face. "I'm Trooper Neidrich. Justin charged the boys, swinging his chain. If he'd hit anyone, we'd be talking aggravated assault, maybe inciting a riot. Dr. Randori disarmed him."

" 'Disarmed' me? He almost broke it. And I want my chain back."

"Throw him in jail," Billy Frederickson said.

"Dad!"

"If you won't cooperate, you should go to jail." The elder Frederickson pointed to the playing field. "I told you, you want to be a tough guy, go out for football. And I told you to leave that chain at home."

"I use it so I don't lose my wallet. Same as you, Dad."

"School rules say no chains on wallets, Justin," Davis intervened. "You just showed us why that's a good policy. And a football game is a school function. I'll give the chain to your dad, and it's up to him if you get it back."

"Now, how about those names," the elder Frederickson demanded.

"He'll kill me."

"Who's this 'he' you're talking about, Justin?" Davis demanded.

"I mean they'll kill me."

"Nobody will know you told us," Davis said. "There were enough witnesses; we can say we got the names from someone else. For the weapon, you're looking at a ten-day out-of-school suspension and possible expulsion. If you cooperate, I'll talk to Mr. Marburg, maybe make it an in-school suspension and leave it at that."

"Talk to them, boy," Billy said. "I bet I can guess most of them."

Justin glanced at each adult, his eyes finally resting on his father. Looking down, he said, "Kyle Weaver, Zack Boyer, Brad Prusster, and Judd and Jeremy Wenner."

"This doesn't sound like something you guys cooked up on your own," Davis said. He knew those boys, all from Avalon, had a pack mentality, but they usually required one leader to get things going.

Within the group, only Brad Prusster commanded that kind of respect, but he was a good kid.

Fixing his eyes ahead, Justin clamped his lips and stood motionless until the loudspeaker above emitted a piercing blare, startling him. Billy moved in on his son. "Damn, you made me miss the end of the game. Let's have it, who else was with you?" The boy flinched, raising his arm in a defensive reaction, but he still refused to talk.

Davis, wanting to bring the episode to a close, said, "Sorry, Billy, we'll have to go with the ten days out of school and let Mr. Marburg decide on an expulsion hearing."

Justin glanced into his father's eyes. What the boy found there must have been more fearsome than the wrath of his friends. "Marcus Wyncoat."

"Marcus? From Culver Pond?" Snitz said, incredulous.

Randori leaned into Neidrich, whispering, "It doesn't fit. Avalon kids go from blue-collar to dirt-poor; Culver Pond has two basic types: rich high-achieving kids and rich slackers like Marcus, but he's weak, passive. Unless –"

Davis spoke before Randori could complete his thought. "Paul Roberge."

Justin blanched. "You didn't hear that from me."

"No problem, Justin," Davis said with a smile. "You can go now— if it's all right with Chief Snitz, that is."

The Chief nodded, and Billy Frederickson squeezed his son's arm and led him away. When they were out of earshot, Snitz beckoned Davis and sidled up to Randori and Neidrich. "I don't like this: the Avalon Boys linked up with Paul Roberge."

"You got that right," Randori agreed, "but I didn't see him."

"He's good at letting others do his dirty work while he lies low," Davis said.

Snitz squinted. "Why pick on band kids, though? What's the point?"

"Maybe just to test his influence," Davis said. "I'll be the first to admit I don't know how that boy's mind works."

Ed Knepp, eavesdropping from the side, intervened. "Just punks. Say Harley, I have a couple things to do before I go home. Mind if I come in a little late tomorrow?"

"OK, but if you're working, keep track of your hours." In afterthought, Snitz added, "And tomorrow, catch me up on your case. We'll go over your logbook."

Davis turned to Randori. "What do you think?"

"I think the only case Ed's working on involves twist-off caps."

Knepp wheeled and moved on Randori. The Chief sprung between them, pressing his hands to his deputy's chest. The veins in Knepp's temples popped, and a rush of crimson blossomed on his face. His hand gripped his holstered sidearm. "Give me a reason!" Knepp threatened, nearing uncontrolled rage. "I'll pistol-whip you within an inch of your life."

Randori's eyes deadened.

The ten-year-old boy gazes through a haze at his sobbing mother as she tries to pick up the telephone, but before she can spin the rotary dial even once, the boy's father rips it out of her hand. "You're not calling anyone. It's bad enough the whole town thinks you're crazy." With pleading eyes, the mother blurts in anguished gasps, "The planes! ... The cars! I can't even go to the bathroom in peace!"

"That's it!" the father yells, his eyes flaring. "I'm calling the state hospital!"

The mother bares her teeth, and her eyes widen in revelation. "You want me out of the way so you can drink and whore whenever you want!" For the first time, the mother acknowledges her son's presence. Her fury smoldering, she tilts an imaginary bottle to her lips, pretending to guzzle. "That's your father, Brian." She points a condemning finger, as her voice rises to a shrill siren. "That's your father!"

The father raises the receiver to strike his wife. The boy rushes him, trying to push him away, but his father sloughs him off, knocking him to the floor, and moves toward his wife. The boy wraps his arms around his father's ankle, clasping it with all his strength. For the first time, the father's rage turns on his son. He makes an awkward half-turn, almost falling, and cocks his free leg. Before the boy can react, a shoe sinks into his ribcage with the sickening crunch of torn cartilage and cracked bone. The boy loosens his grip and writhes in pain, hugging his throbbing chest.

His mother uses the distraction to dart into the bathroom and lock the door. From her sanctuary, she cackles in triumph at her successful escape.

The father pounds on the door, the sound lost amid his wife's celebratory whoops. His hands drop to his side, fists balling in futility, veins popping. Turning, he stands over his son and lashes out with another kick. Before the boy can move his hands from his chest to protect himself, the foot plunges into his cheek and nose. The light of a million stars bursts and then sinks into the black void.

Randori dropped his right leg back and turned to the side, shifting his weight to his rear foot. He raised his left hand vaguely and brought his right hand up to chest height.

Knepp thrust a finger over Snitz's shoulder. "Yeah, you better be afraid. And from now on, you call me Sergeant Knepp."

"Binomial nomenclature," Randori said, looking off to ponder the concept, an angelic smile spreading across his face. "I like it—great for species identification."

Knepp frowned, bewildered. Before he understood, or even if he remained in the dark but suspected he had been insulted, Snitz gripped his shoulders. "Get going, Ed."

The deputy backed away, speechless, but still pointing and rattling his head in a series of menacing nods. As a final gesture of pride, he raised his chin, threw his chest forward and shoulders back, and wheeled toward the main gate.

"Jeez, Doc," Davis said. "That guy hates you so as it is; why do you antagonize him?" Randori's responding smile made Davis chuckle. "When I asked what you thought, I meant, about Roberge being with the Avalon Boys."

Randori looked out across the still-jammed parking lot to the string of lights that flowed, like iridescent molasses, up the road and into the night. "I don't know, Virge."

Davis cocked his head, puzzled at Randori's rare reticence. Then he followed the counselor's stare. "Yeah, I guess I don't know either." Brightening, he said, "Hey, you want to chaperone the post-game dance? Free soda! I need help; all I've got is Cat."

"Thanks a lot, Virgil," Cat Blanchard said from behind Davis. She had remained in the home stands until they cleared, and her arrival had unfortunate timing for Davis. "Don't you trust me?"

"No ... I mean, yes, of course I trust you," Davis stammered. "I just—"

"You just feel it's better to keep the little woman out of harm's way. I'm an assistant principal, too, you know."

"Yeah, Virge," Randori said, "as enticing as you make chaperoning sound, I think you need to give Cat a chance to make her bones."

Blanchard shot a narrow glance at Randori, but then another sight captured her attention—Nick Neidrich. Her suspicious pout melted to a demure smile.

Randori grinned. "Say Nick, have you met Cat Blanchard?"

Neidrich's face mirrored Blanchard's. "I've seen you in the offices, but we haven't met. Nick Neidrich," he said, extending his hand.

Blanchard clasped it, and she gazed up at him; her lips parted, a momentary pause before she spoke. "Nice to meet you, Nick."

Randori turned to Davis and whispered, "And at the dance hall, Tony and Maria set eyes on each other for the first time."

Davis affixed a, *What in the hell are you talking about?* stare on the counselor, but before he could pursue the matter, a voice broke in. "What's this, a meeting of the minds?" Kass Marburg, resplendent in the latest fall fashions and a stadium blanket draped over one arm, said as he passed by. I'd say everything came off without a hitch tonight. I'm heading home to bed." He moved on, waving over his shoulder.

Davis called after him, "Who won the game?"

Nick Neidrich maneuvered his sedan along the tortuous route leading into the hills embracing Culver Pond. It pained him physically to withhold testing the car's reinforced shocks on every twist and dip, but to do so would pain Snitz's nervous system. As it was, his partner seemed distracted. "What's up, Harley?"

"Farmcove. It just depresses me, is all. That's it, up ahead."

Neidrich followed the Chief's glance toward the psychiatric hospital. A brick main building loomed in the middle of a clearing, flanked by smaller structures, the sum of which resembled a singularly unimaginative apartment complex. Farmcove was a nonprofit facility originally established to treat adults, with a small wing for children. Until the early 1980s, there was only the main building, and that was half its present size. The drastic cutback of funding for the state hospital system combined with the skyrocketing rate of mental disorders among youth fed Farmcove's explosive growth.

As Neidrich and Snitz exited the car, a Freedom Area Transit bus, the letters *FAT* emblazoned on its side, pulled to the curb ahead. Despite their haste, the officers stopped to allow passengers to board. It was difficult differentiating between visitors and outpatients. No one engaged in conversation; most walked with heads bowed, avoiding eye contact. The lone exception was a woman, twisted and gaunt from the ravages of hard life, whose glazed black-hole eyes, gateways to a cold void where a soul once existed, scanned the trooper up and down, her lips parted in a ravenous leer.

After the passengers boarded, the Chief started to move on but stopped as his partner remained frozen in revulsion at the woman's brazen attention. "Not so long ago she could've had any man," Snitz whispered. "Crystal meth."

"Huh?" said the dumbfounded trooper.

Snitz changed the subject. "It's a good thing they don't call it Freedom Area *Rapid* Transit," he said, pointing to the acronym on the side of the bus and waving off the blue fumes emitted by the departing vehicle. The Chief's quip shook the trooper into a delayed reaction chuckle as they entered the hospital.

While the Chief announced their presence, Neidrich surveyed the reception area, taking in the calculated calm of the decor. Couches and chairs upholstered in muted blues and greens matched carpeting that seemed to flow into walls dotted with prints of spring landscapes and religious iconography. At the far end, beside stairs leading to the second floor, a waterfall trickled into a pool.

Snitz led Neidrich through a passage that wrapped behind the waterfall and brought them to Dr. Melvin Kaminsky's office where they found the psychiatrist talking to his administrative assistant. Neidrich had expected a stiff professional—aloof air and condescending tone—a concern allayed immediately when Kaminsky stepped forward to greet them. He had welcoming eyes and a beaming smile that spread across his round face and through his salt-and-pepper beard. Although he wore a tie, he was dressed for comfort in corduroy pants and tattersall shirt.

After shaking Neidrich's hand, Kaminsky turned abreast of Snitz and gently clasped his arm, leading him into his office. Although he spoke softly, his face betrayed the suppressed glee of a child anticipating his birthday. "Haven't seen you lately, Harley, but you've been a little busy, I guess."

"Sorry we're late, Mel."

"Not a problem; I can always find something to do." Kaminsky called back over his shoulder. "Leslie, please hold calls unless there's an emergency. And I could use a soda, how about you guys?"

Snitz smiled and Neidrich said, "Pop sounds good to me."

"Soda *pop*, please, Leslie," Kaminsky called to his secretary before closing the door and offering seats to the investigators. "Western PA?"

Neidrich answered with a polite nod then got directly to business. "We need to ask about people you know in the Freedom Con School District."

Kaminsky rubbed his hands together and beamed. "I was hoping you would. I could sink my teeth into a good murder mystery."

"The mystery, if we can speak confidentially, is that we have several suspects with no particularly good motives."

"This whole conversation is confidential," Kaminsky said, his smile dropping for the first time. He leaned back and tented his forearms, propping his chin on his fingers. "You want me to get inside the head of some people?"

Snitz looked to Neidrich to continue, but the trooper waved him on with a palm-up gesture. "Before we mention suspects, Mel, does anyone jump to mind?"

"No, I was acquainted with Bob Samson, though, professionally. Interesting man, controversial." Neidrich raised his eyebrows, leaving a question implied. Dr. Kaminsky explained. "When I started out here, I wanted to get mental health services to kids who qualify for Medical Assistance. I had a meeting with the county superintendents and pupil services directors to figure out the best way to deliver services. Kerry Wyatt saw the possibilities of enhancing Emotional Support in schools, so we set up a satellite clinic at Avalon Elementary School."

"That was Mr. Wyatt's idea?" Snitz asked. "The newspaper tipped its hat to Dr. Samson for that. He got some community service award, too, if I remember."

"Exactly. Funny thing, though, when I presented the idea to the superintendents, Bob saw no application to the schools. In the end, the superintendents deferred to the Pupil Services directors, and Kerry Wyatt jumped at the opportunity. I warned him that his boss wasn't too keen on the idea, but Kerry said to leave it up to him.

"Long story short, he convinced Bob that mental health treatment in the schools might cut Pupil Services costs." The glee returned to Kaminsky's face. "Kerry, of course, just used that as a selling point. Typically, if a mental health service is offered, demand soon exceeds the available service—cases come out of the woodwork. Anyway, Bob must have seen the public relations possibilities, because he called the newspaper, got TV coverage. So, although Kerry had the idea and did all the work, Bob came across as the guru, and he graciously accepted the accolades."

Snitz cocked his head to one side. "Didn't that frost Mr. Wyatt's turnips?"

"Kerry knows how the game is played. Schools are like any organization; bosses get credit for ideas their underlings come up with because if things fall apart they'll certainly get the blame. Bob was just more eager than most to take credit for someone else's efforts."

"So you don't think that was sufficient motivation for murder?" Neidrich said.

"Not unless you're grasping at straws. Given the right circumstances, many individuals are capable of extreme violence, but it would require a threat to all Kerry holds near and dear for him to even consider it. Don't you have any better suspects?"

Snitz squinted. "Are you sure no one came to mind when you learned Dr. Samson was murdered?"

"No one I suspect." Kaminsky leaned forward and his voice took on a conspiratorial tone. "But I do have some ideas."

Neidrich waited for Kaminsky to begin, but the psychiatrist leaned back again and toed his chair from side to side on its swivel, silent behind an indulgent grin.

"Well?" Snitz finally said.

"I was just letting the suspense build," Kaminsky said through a pleased snort. He picked up a pencil, and rolled it between his fingers, idly regarding it as he spoke. "This is stuff you guys probably already thought of. First, I don't believe the murder is related to drugs." Kaminsky looked up at the officers; his expansive smile reappeared. "Yes, Ed has already seen me, asking about drug users we've had through treatment, maybe some disgruntled kid who got expelled. Ed's off base, I think. Most addicts take the money and run, and they target easy marks. Murders involving drugs usually have to do with rivalries, money owed, or someone getting shortchanged on product. They don't take the trouble to move the body. Yes, I know that, too. Besides, I bet you could pinpoint most violent drug-related acts to a small area on the North Side. No, I think there was a personal reason behind it. I'm thinking crime of passion. Had Bob stolen anyone's wife or girlfriend lately?"

Snitz shook his head. "Dead ends so far."

"The fact that he was killed first, then his body moved … I could be wrong, but aren't bodies usually moved for a reason? Any disgruntled District employees?"

Snitz nodded. "Several, but we can't tie anyone to evidence so far. That's why we're looking for psychological predispositions."

"I guess you've also looked at relatives—even spouses—of those District people who didn't like Bob. Probably took two people, don't you think? I mean, it could've been one, but it fits neater with two."

Snitz raised an eyebrow. "Just how much did Ed tell you, Mel?"

Another giggle. "Most I just pieced together from what I read. Ed gave me a little, but it seems like you've pretty much kept him in the dark?" The sparkle in the psychiatrist's eye flickered, and then brightened. "Good move."

Neidrich shifted impatiently. "Seems like you aren't going to volunteer names of anyone you might suspect."

"It wouldn't be prudent. Sometimes the title of 'psychiatrist' gives my observations more weight than they deserve."

"Then, talk about Virgil Davis," Neidrich pushed.

"You doing some profiling based on the fact that Virgil is an Army vet?"

"Something like that."

"I would've thought a black police officer would avoid profiling."

"What some call profiling, I see as instinct based on training and experience."

Kaminsky scratched his stubbled chin, pondering the trooper's assertion. "Hmm, OK," he said with a shade of doubt. He peered into Neidrich's eyes for an exaggerated moment. "I guess I can buy that. In this case, it's understandable. Passed over for promotions, slightly paranoid; it all fits, to a certain degree."

Neidrich's eyes sharpened. "Davis is paranoid?"

"I use the term loosely, not clinically. And I see no Post-Traumatic Stress. Unfortunately, that has unfairly cast a shadow on people's perception of our veterans. No, Virgil dealt with the war well, probably because he was in Army Intelligence—more intrigue than live combat, although he was probably in his share of hairy situations. He's certainly cynical, though. Going from cynicism to paranoia is a short hop for some, and if any place can breed that, it's Freedom Con—political maneuvering, backstabbing, arbitrary moves by administration."

"How does Davis's paranoia exhibit?" Neidrich said, sitting back, poised to take notes.

"It's no one big thing. He doesn't trust people, not even his friend Doc Randori. We've been at meetings where Doc made comments that had nothing to do with him. Later, Virgil asked if I thought Doc could be trusted, but there was nothing Doc said that could have been interpreted as untrustworthy. Doc has always supported Virgil.

"Anyway, those feelings have rubbed off on—or maybe been reinforced by—Virgil's wife, Lois. I met her at a Safe Schools dinner, and she got in my ear about how the District screwed her husband, how he ought to stay away from Doc, and so on."

"You think Virgil goes home and gives Lois daily doses of his suspicions," Snitz said, "and she swallows them?"

"Or vice versa. Lois is resentful, due in part to Virgil's job. Instead of addressing his workaholism, though, she blames everyone else."

Neidrich nodded in agreement. "And yet Davis's own loyalty to the District has gone unrewarded. It had to bother him that Samson held him down."

"I'm certain that's true, but before you jump to conclusions, remember, he's always been a good soldier—duty first, and never question decisions of superiors."

Snitz pressed for conclusion. "So you don't think Virgil killed Dr. Samson?"

"I'd have to say it's unlikely. But long periods of overwork create stress, even in the strongest people. Combine that with marital problems and the guilt that accompanies them; well, let's just say I'd check his alibi."

"How about Doc Randori?" Neidrich said.

"Ooh, interesting dude," Kaminsky said, a gleeful lilt in both voice and eyes. "You have motive?"

"He and Samson were hate at first sight, and it became worse over time."

"Any culminating event?"

Snitz jumped in. "They had a set-to a week before Samson died over the decision to cut the karate program at their alternative school."

"That would upset Doc, but I don't think it's murder-worthy, do you?"

"How about demotion," Snitz added, "and the humiliation that goes with it."

Kaminsky shook his head. "That was a while back." The psychiatrist pushed away from his desk and leaned back in his chair, tapping his lips. "On the other hand, looking at those two incidents in light of what I know about Doc ..."

Snitz cocked his head and frowned. "What, Mel?"

"Doc is a vigilant guy, not hyper-vigilant, mind you," Kaminsky paused for emphasis, "but *vigilant*."

"Explain, please."

"Doc is watchful. He makes it a point to be aware of what's going on around him. He's quick to judge, too, goes on gut instinct."

Kaminsky winked at Neidrich. "Kind of like Nick with his profiling. As long as his perceptions are reality-based and dealt with as such, it's OK. It's when someone overreacts to perceived slights—let me give you a for-instance: take a referee in a basketball game. Every call he makes is going to upset one portion of the fans; it goes with the territory. He has to block that out, focus on the game. When a ref can't do that—has 'rabbit ears'—he overreacts to taunts, criticism, starts to lose his objectivity as things get tense. That's kind of an operational definition of hyper-vigilance; only for hyper-vigilant people, it's not circumstantial but rather part of the way they do life. Doc doesn't go that far, from what I've seen. He follows a certain moral code to guide his judgments."

"His moral code is a private one," Neidrich interrupted. "Like a vigilante."

Kaminsky flip-flopped his hand. "Vigilant, vigilante, two sides of the same coin. And Doc is cunning. He's one who could let time pass to cool the trail; wait for his moment, then strike. I like Doc; I'd hate to think he'd do something like that. And there are plenty of reasons to believe he's innocent, but there are some psychological precursors to true antisocial behavior."

"Why do you believe he's innocent?" Snitz asked.

"Character," Kaminsky blurted, his answer nearly overlapping the question. "I consult for the District. Doc and I discuss the emotional support and alternative programs, and the kids in those classes. He has strong values, consistent, too. In the time I've worked with him, I haven't seen a chink in the armor."

Neidrich leveled a gaze on the psychiatrist. "You mentioned psychological precursors and the fact that he's too passionate."

"Doc's a true believer, but, as you say, he's loyal only to his values. He comes across as being self-righteous; I think he's too humble for that. It's tough to parse out. It's not egotism. I'd call it ..." Kaminsky winced in his effort to force the correct words from his mind to his lips, "an arrogance of ideas."

"How can a person be both humble and arrogant?" Neidrich asked.

"I believe Doc has low self-esteem, and I can't say for the life of me why that is. He shows interest in others, yet he seems embarrassed when he becomes the focal point of conversation. He's genuinely shy. Now, he'll give you a hundred plausible reasons for his behavior, and he seems affable on the surface—" Again, Kaminsky stopped in mid-thought. "I don't know much, if anything, about Doc's early years, but now that I'm saying this out loud, it could be Reactive Attachment Disorder."

"I'm not sure I know what that is," Neidrich said.

"Before I go on, a caution: I wouldn't hang my hat on RAD."

"But what is it?" Neidrich insisted. "What brings it on; how does it manifest?"

"It can come about when the initial caregiving for a child is pathologically lacking, when there is disregard for comfort, affection—the basic needs. Like when there is little or no emotional bonding between mother and child in the very early developmental stages. It usually occurs when the mother is afflicted with alcoholism, drug addiction, or significant mental illness. For the child, it exhibits as inappropriate social interaction."

"Well, that's not Dr. Randori," Snitz said. "He can be downright charming."

"Oh, RADs can be that way. Over years, they develop coping mechanisms, or they have selective bonding from the start. In extreme cases, a person can be excessively inhibited or hyper-vigilant, but they can also be contradictory in social interactions. Doc mixes approach and avoidance behaviors. In other words, you feel comfortable around him sometimes; other times, he seems cold and distant. Plus, I've seen him in some forced social situations where he's inhibited, yet aware of everything going on."

Neidrich said, "Sociopaths share some of those tendencies."

"I suppose there would be some intersection between the two in extreme cases of Reactive Attachment, though I don't see it with Doc. He can empathize, really empathize—which a sociopath can't—and his gut instinct about people is dead on. And yet, when it comes to reacting viscerally, emotionally, to the trauma of others … I'm guessing here, but I think he faced some sink or swim situation when he was young; instead of going under, he used adversity to get stronger. So, there's a basic sensitivity for others who have had it rough, but it's more identifying with them than having true feeling for them. And he has absolutely no patience with people who've had it pretty good but treat others badly or act as though they have certain entitlements."

Neidrich nodded with assurance. "People like Samson."

TUESDAY, SEPTEMBER 13, 10:36 AM
EQUAL OPPORTUNITY BASTARD

Phil Olson's second Cabinet meeting as acting superintendent had just ended, and Kerry Wyatt waited for Meryl Morgan in his conference room for their customary debriefing—in Wyatt's words, playing "ain't it awful." On this morning, Wyatt had a more pressing concern than criticizing Olson, an easy target; he wanted Morgan to vent her frustration and anger over being denied the superintendency after Samson's death. She deserved the job, and Wyatt had fully expected it would be hers. But Morgan was a mystery. Even more than Randori, she kept her personal life private, and she concealed her feelings, as well. As a psychologist, Wyatt was accustomed to people being guarded in his presence, wary of conclusions he might draw. Morgan, however, was that way toward everyone. She had endured a divorce, and no one knew until she stopped wearing her wedding ring and returned to using her maiden name.

Some things shouldn't be held inside. Meryl should trust me, talk to me.

The previous winter, Morgan's administrative assistant had asked to meet privately with Wyatt. The woman's agitation, and her insistence that only he could help, induced him to grant her request. She made Wyatt promise to keep the meeting confidential for fear that someone might find out and fire her. It was obvious to Wyatt: the only *someone* it could have been was Samson.

When they met, the secretary revealed that Samson had been making sexual overtures toward her boss, advances that had reached the level where Morgan became uncharacteristically anxious whenever he entered her office. The most recent incident had spurred the woman to seek Wyatt's help: Samson had started by feigning tenderness, professing a respect for Morgan that had grown to admiration. She responded by saying she was flattered but believed professional relationships should remain platonic. Samson called her on that, claiming the superintendent of the district in which Morgan previously worked had revealed that her administrative advancement there was due to sexual favors she had provided the man. Reminding Morgan that he was in a position to make or break her career, and was prepared to do either, Samson added that she could work the same deal with him.

The secretary could not hear her boss's response, but an angry Samson soon left the office.

Wyatt had done his best to hide his revulsion. And what of Morgan, could she have sold herself at the price of advancement? Her ambitions were real. Knowing his friend, though, Wyatt concluded that the accusation was so absurd it had to be an invention of her former boss or of Samson himself.

He told the secretary to keep him informed but left unaddressed the truth that he had no idea how to proceed. In that moment, though, Wyatt admitted to himself that he loved Morgan. That epiphany made him distrust his own objectivity, so he decided to discuss the matter with Randori, the man he trusted most to develop a covert plan and carry it out with dispassionate efficiency. Randori's initial response— pounding his fists on the conference table and snarling, "I'm going to kill that bastard!"—made Wyatt question the wisdom of that decision. The counselor regained his composure, though, and suggested the strategy Wyatt ultimately employed.

Wyatt brought the issue up at a Cabinet meeting, where Samson would have to act in his official capacity. Speaking in veiled terms, and using real details from a supposedly secret affair between two staff members, he said that a female employee was being sexually harassed. He observed that the District policy regarding sexual harassment was nebulous and, therefore, unenforceable. As Samson's advisor, Wyatt recommended an announcement that such behavior was cause for suspension and, should the victim file charges, might result in the loss of professional credentials and civil action. Samson insisted that an innocent flirtation could have been blown out of proportion; he did not want to get the entire staff in an uproar over nothing. Expecting that rejoinder, Wyatt argued that avoidance of the issue put Samson and the District in jeopardy; furthermore, he—Wyatt—had been charged by the Board to propose staff welfare policies. His neglect of the issue had been a personal oversight, Wyatt admitted with appropriate regret, but he intended to rectify that at the next Board meeting. Samson was left with no choice but to accede to Wyatt's plan.

At its February meeting, the Board had appointed a committee to tighten the policy on sexual harassment. More important to Wyatt, Morgan's secretary reported that Samson's advances on her boss had ceased.

By May, a policy on sexual harassment had yet to be finalized, but Samson's nature again oozed to the surface. At a Cabinet meeting, during a discussion about administrative changes spurred by the retirement of one of the administrators, the subject of Morgan's professional future had arisen. Through a harsh laugh, Samson said, "Meryl will get her next promotion the same way she got her last one. ... Right, Meryl?" A lascivious glance left no doubt as to his insinuation. Stunned, Morgan excused herself, exiting the room with slow, but pained, dignity. Wyatt knew any comment he might make would betray his knowledge of Samson's prior harassment. It also crossed his mind that his silence was perhaps the product of cowardice, a notion that had dogged him ever since. Tucking that recollection into his reserve of humiliation, Wyatt self-consciously erased vestiges of embarrassment from his face as his friend entered. He need not have been concerned, as Morgan's thoughts were elsewhere.

"I'm up to here with speculation about Doc's involvement in Bob's death."

"Yes," Wyatt said, projecting his voice for the benefit of Theresa and Lionda, "I wish you two would stop accosting visitors about the Quandary at the Quarry."

He closed the door and held a chair for Morgan. Sitting beside her, he clasped her hand and forced himself to look her in the eye. "Before we get started, I've been meaning to talk to you for a while, but with all that has happened I ... " Wyatt had thought he was prepared to broach the topic, but he began to stammer. "At that Cabinet meeting ... when Bob ... and now, with Phil, I should have talked to the Board ... "

Morgan stiffened and withdrew her hand. "You did more than I could have expected. Just drop it, all right?"

A shriek pierced the walls of Wyatt's conference room. He rushed to the door and opened it to find Theresa Wagner winding up for a swing at Randori. Normally, Wyatt welcomed the distraction presented by their childish antics, but the disruption had washed out the inroads he was trying to make into Morgan's psyche and, he hoped, her heart. Still, his administrative assistant and the counselor had interrupted the embarrassment of the moment, and for that he was grateful.

"Doggone it, Randori, knock off that ninja crap. You nearly scared the pants off me!"

Wyatt rolled his eyes in faux-bliss. " 'Nearly' just isn't enough."

Wagner made a rapid gunslinger's turn and aimed a menacing finger at her boss. "Are you looking to test your new sexual harassment policy, buster?"

"You're right, Theresa," Wyatt said, abashed. "I'm so sorry."

"And just what's that supposed to mean," she challenged, sidling forward, as if to escalate the sparring from a verbal to a physical level.

"Not to put too fine a point on it," Randori said, his exaggerated conciliatory tone straining credulity, "but I think it means Kerry is apologizing."

As the blood vessels on Theresa's forehead engorged, Randori ambled into the conference room. Wyatt shut the door and said, "For a counselor, you have a real knack for inflaming situations."

Morgan smiled and tapped the chair beside her. "Join us, Doc. We were about to discuss my curriculum initiatives for the high school."

"Oh man," Randori said, "you're doing a Don Quixote number there boss, and Kass Marburg is one big freaking windmill."

Morgan gave a sly half-smile. "Kass *is* The Impossible Dweeb."

Wyatt joined the exchange, confronting Randori with a curled lip that belied the benign façade of his smile. "The quixotic profile fits you better than Meryl. She can certainly stand up to Kass."

"Agreed," Randori said, his eyes deadening, "but last time I checked, site-based management ruled around here—Kass's building, Kass's call, and he doesn't like any ideas that aren't his own. So, short of sending him off to join his idol in Valhalla—"

"So we just let the kids in the lower sections fall through the cracks?" Morgan said, her eyes sabers of resolve. "I won't do it."

Randori parried Morgan's glance with a conspiratorial grin. "I'm with you, Meryl. As things stand, the high school promotes a social-class sorting system that makes the Old South look like Hooters at happy hour. But a frontal assault," the counselor adopted a momentary twang, "ain't gonna work. Instead, train a few teachers and let them spread the word. I know some who love to sneak things in under Kass's nose. He'll never figure it out until it's too late. Darwin, not Lenin—that's the key."

"We need fundamental change," Wyatt scolded. "Your way will take years."

Morgan shifted to face the counselor and laid a hand on his arm. "The river wearing away the stone, right? We talked about doing that with the drug education and social values lessons."

"Are you two having meetings behind my back?" Wyatt asked with a trace of humor. " 'Social values' with the drug lessons? You'd better be careful."

Randori's eyes narrowed, and they locked onto Wyatt's. "The alternative is to separate values from drug use—hell, from all negative behavior. Too many people already do that. They'll tell you that every behavior outside the norm is a legitimate disorder, and that every disorder has an equal and opposite drug treatment. There are more drugs floating around Farmcove than there are at a Dave Matthews concert. But kids aren't getting better, because we've only masked the symptoms. Meanwhile, we teach them that it's OK to depend on drugs to manage behavior, and it's OK to act crazy, as long as their particular brand of craziness has a label. Then, we're surprised when some kid blows and tries to force-feed us a shrapnel-chip cookie."

He stopped abruptly; with an uneasy smile, he rose to leave, brushing his hand across Morgan's shoulder as he passed behind her. "If the taxpayers knew we spent time talking this philosophical garbonia, they'd demand a rebate. How's that for irony?"

Morgan clamped onto the counselor's arm. "Are you all right?"

Keeping his back to her, Randori chuckled. "Yeah, I have to do the Margaret Mead number on Paul Roberge." He gently pulled his arm away as he reached for the doorknob. "Not that it's necessary. I know how that kid thinks—and feels."

Ed Knepp, or "Officer Ed," as the children knew him, loved teaching DARE, the Drug Abuse Resistance Education program he had introduced to Freedom Con. It was the only opportunity his job afforded to act in a preventive way. He delivered lessons to fifth grade students, but more, he taught them to make informed decisions and helped them learn refusal skills that could transfer to other aspects of their lives. His work had its greatest payoff when the kids were in middle school and early high school. It was then that forces came together that put young people most at risk, as the peer group and neighborhood competed with the family for their hearts and minds.

The child's mind is a garden that requires nurturing, or the weeds and pestilence of society will choke off growth. As it enters adolescence, the critical mind is not yet ready to face the world beyond the family; it searches for identity in bold but fitful steps, wanting to be grown up yet armed with neither the life experience nor the intellectual sophistication to carry it off. Orexis, the inclination toward emotion and desire over reason, will never be stronger than it is in those years. Long-held belief systems shaken, risk-taking drives emergent—the seeds of self-destruction find fertile soil in this season. If kids make it to their junior year in high school without succumbing to the pressures of sex, drugs, and rock 'n' roll, chances are they will make it.

Officer Ed had little formal education beyond high school, but he knew from experience all this was true. Every elementary school child looked Knepp in the eye and swore he or she would never drink or use drugs. Then, years later when he busted keg parties or ran a kid in for selling a dime of marijuana, teenage eyes averted when challenged by his. Did they remember oaths taken years before, now broken? Or were they simply embarrassed because they knew what he stood for? Officer Ed didn't care why they looked away, or down; it only mattered that they were contrite. The eyes that concerned him were the ones that faced his, unrepentant. Fortunately, they were rare, allowing Knepp to concentrate on his front line victories. *If DARE helps just one kid*, his self-talk began; it kept him positive, kept him going strong.

Knepp could spot at-risk children by their eyes—distant, shrouded in sadness, older than the faces that housed them. Brandon Prusster had those eyes. In the few weeks he had known the boy, Knepp developed a special fondness for him, one of the brightest, kindest children he had ever met, proof that those qualities are not mere chips of genetic programming but resilient traces of the human spirit. How long they could survive in this child was yet to be seen. For Brandon Prusster was a child of Avalon.

The oldest suburb of Freedom, Avalon was a working-class neighborhood located just outside the eastern city line. It had risen to serve as convenient housing for steelworkers, and, in exchange for a leisurely walk to work, the mill delivered a corrosive, ruddy mist, carried on the prevailing westerlies, that draped Avalon like a widow's veil. Once the vibrant backbone of the community, the steel mill had become a hulking cadaver, but its specter still clung to the buildings and minds of Avalon, haunting even those who never knew it.

Brandon's grandfather, Ronnie, was part of the last generation to work in the mill. He started shortly after his girlfriend, Barb, had become pregnant. It was a time when a boy could drop out of high school and still be assured a job with respectable pay and benefits. Ronnie's father, a foreman, got him a slot on the graveyard shift, and the young man thought he was set for life. He and Barb bought a wood-frame home in Avalon near both sets of parents and moved in just as their son, Bolt, was born.

Ronnie's pastime was drinking. Realizing, though, that he would lose his job if caught with alcohol on his breath, he never drank before work. He even broke away from the Avalon Boys, whose sole requisites for membership were the willingness to hang out on the streets, drink beer, and fight. Barb was happy, thinking that her man was taking fatherhood seriously. In lieu of beer, though, Ronnie had taken up marijuana.

To entrench his job security, Ronnie became a strong union man. Soon after he became vested, he began to badger his father about a day shift position so he could go about the business of doing what came naturally to an Avalon Boy. It took almost two years, but an opening came and Ronnie slipped into it.

Two years later, contract negotiations were on the horizon, and the union believed a big increase in pay was a sure shot. What could management do, bring in new workers? Scabs would be in for a serious beating and the union workers, particularly the Avalon Boys, would be enthusiastic in its administration. Some of the local men who had risen to management—known as "white hats" because of the signature hard hats they wore in the mill—warned that the Pittsburgh bosses would never give in to the steep demands. Competition from Japanese steel, as well as the development of other alloys and plastics, had cut into profits. The union leadership advised its former line-mates to "remember where you came from" and stay out of it.

Pittsburgh made a final offer, a slight increase in pay in exchange for greater employee contribution toward benefits. The union could accept it or face the closing of the mill. At that announcement, jubilation arose on the streets of Avalon. To have made such a declaration, management must be desperate. Victory was in sight; all the union needed to do was turn up the pressure another notch. They went on strike.

The next day management closed the plant. Freedom City government and Chamber of Commerce had been caught as flatfooted as the steelworkers. No one had considered, much less prepared for, the worst-case scenario. As was true in many steel towns, over the years the company had shut out other industries that might compete for workers. Overnight, the local economy plummeted. Even as area businesses tried to absorb the workforce, unemployment became the highest of any county in Pennsylvania. The largest department store overhired and temporary work services moved into high gear, but good jobs were at a premium, and no business paid the wages to which the steelworkers had become accustomed.

Afflicted by a lack of education and a work ethic muddled by a growing dependence on alcohol and drugs, Ronnie had been unwilling to work at the low-paying general labor jobs for which he was qualified and was unqualified for jobs that required interpersonal and critical thinking skills, prime requisites to most employers. To make ends meet, Barb, who had been an excellent business student at Freedom Con and earned her diploma at the Adult Education Center, landed a secretarial job at the hospital while Ronnie stayed home with little Bolt, waiting for something good to happen. By that time, Ronnie no longer hid his drug use from Barb. He had begun to develop a potent crop of marijuana in the attic of their home.

Thanks to Ronnie's green thumb and Barb's work ethic, their financial footing stabilized over the next few years. Then, a surprise came along in the person of a second son—Brad. The birth was difficult, and Barb's extended maternity leave forced Ronnie to supplement his income. He expanded his marijuana crop to the basement and garage, a development that brought about neighborhood jokes that Avalonians never had to buy pot; they could just sniff the air around the Prusster house. Furthermore, through his drug trade Ronnie had made connections that supplied him with cocaine, connections that were willing to add another layer of insulation between themselves and the police. The cocaine money more than replaced the lost mill income. Had she desired, Barb could have stayed home to make certain Bolt got off to school and Brad would be well cared for. But she hated the dangers inherent in drug trafficking, and thought that if she advanced her own career Ronnie could seek legitimate work.

Barb asked her mother to look after little Brad during the day, leaving Ronnie responsible for Bolt. Ronnie's job kept him out late, and when he finally arose in the morning, he often found Bolt still asleep. Instead of waking the boy and driving him to school, Ronnie opted to get high with Bolt—smoke marijuana, that is; Ronnie felt it would be irresponsible to give his son cocaine. He did, however, get Bolt to sell pot at school and keep some of the profits, the Prusster version of an allowance.

Ronnie's drug use broke the unwritten law of dealers: don't sample your own goods. His daily intake of cocaine and marijuana knocked down with beer chasers forced Bolt to take an ever-increasing role in his father's business.

Around that time, an even greater threat to the family business crept into the community. In an effort to stimulate growth, the Freedom city fathers accepted federal funds to build low-income housing developments on the northern edge of town. In exchange for the dollars that flowed in, Freedom had to advertise the availability of this cheap housing in the major metropolitan centers of the Northeast. Families from the poorest areas of New York City and Philadelphia flooded the area looking for a new start and a safe environment for their children. Strangely, everyone forgot that these immigrants were moving to a town that offered limited employment opportunities. Freedom County thus became a Mecca of cheap housing and easy Welfare. And, unfortunately for the many families looking for a new start in a quaint, safe environment, the existence they had hoped to escape transplanted itself through the infusion of the few who brought with them big city problems, including drugs.

These newcomers, many of whom were Latinos, or *Rickins* in the parlance of the locals, faced hostile greetings from Avalonians, who saw them as competition for scarce jobs. Ronnie Prusster's dislike was more focused—the Hispanic drug dealers created competition for a market he thought was rightfully his. Further, he contended that they dragged down the standard of living—an interesting argument, considering the source. Despite his increasing drug dependence and attendant addled perception, though, Ronnie was considered a successful entrepreneur and street guru, and thus had profound influence on the newest generation of Avalon Boys. If Ronnie was the mind, Bolt had become the body. He uncovered the names of competing drug dealers and led sorties into the developments. Bolt and his friends considered the opportunity to beat up on any Latino a perquisite of the mission.

The Freedom City Police considered pickup trucks and SUVs filled with Avalon Boys an unwelcome infestation. Prior to this, they felt fortunate that Avalon fell outside their jurisdiction and that its denizens had contented themselves with intramural head-busting. The city police already had their hands full on the North Side, and now they had to deal with what they thought were ethnically motivated attacks. That belief had been accepted as fact until Harley Snitz got involved. The Chief had been gathering evidence against the Prussters. When he shared his information with the city police, an operation began that led to Ronnie's arrest.

With that, school took a back seat for Bolt, but Barb knew that a diploma held the only hope for her son to get a decent job and, better yet, get out of Avalon. Gone were the days when a young person with no marketable skills could drop out of high school and walk into an assembly line job with good pay and benefits. The modern assembly line was the fast-food industry, and it is difficult to support the American Dream on the minimum wage. Barb decided to ask an old friend, Virgil Davis, what could be done. Davis told her Bolt had missed so much school that it would be difficult to meet graduation requirements. Reluctant to aid a reputed drug dealer yet seeing the desperation in Barb's eyes, Davis agreed to help, but Bolt never gave him a chance. Already eighteen years old, he had made up his mind: he had to take over his father's operation or lose control to the North Side dealers. Besides, he was about to follow in his father's footsteps another way. He was soon to become a father.

That summer, Brandon Prusster was born, and Bolt brought stability to the family drug trade through a natural business sense, ambition, and ruthlessness. Having lost the home garden in the raid, Bolt arranged to grow potent strains of marijuana in-between cornrows on a local farm and in makeshift hothouses in rural homes—a Mephistophelean deal for farmers trying to fend off voracious developers. The cocaine trade, the riskier but more lucrative part of the business, was easier to maintain. Freedom natives who resented the Latino drug dealers remained loyal to the Avalon connection. For the three years Ronnie Prusster was in prison, Bolt grew the business.

Ronnie, meanwhile, spent most of his time working on a Ph.D. in drug trafficking.

The most important thing he learned, though, was that he missed his wife. Barb had been faithful in his absence, but she let him know that she resented what Bolt had become. Assuming the responsibility required of a father and grandfather, Ronnie promised that their younger son, Brad, would follow a different path and that their grandson Brandon would never even find out about the business. He kept his word. As Brad moved into his junior year, he was a solid "B" student in the college prep track—frontierland for an Avalon boy—and Brandon, by that time a fifth grader, had even greater potential, competing on a level with gifted students.

Yes, Officer Ed reserved a special place in his heart for Brandon Prusster. He wished he could take the little boy home with him, keep him off the streets of Avalon. His own inability to have children was his biggest regret in a marriage that had survived rough times due to his alcohol problem. Molly had seen him through that, and it was buried deep in his past, under the dusts of Avalon. But out of the silence in their home echoed a constant reminder that he had let Molly down in the one area that counted most to both of them. He blamed it on his drinking; Molly tried to reassure him that it was no shame to bear low sperm count. In strong competition with his regret was his resentment that people like the Prussters—people who had no right being parents in the first place—were so fertile. He feared that it was only a matter of time until Brandon's sweet innocence would turn rancid.

Brandon participated little in class, but when he did his words had meaning. The lesson on this day was straightforward information on drugs, and throughout Brandon had been quiet. But Knepp knew those sad eyes absorbed everything. The discussion shifted to heroin, and the youngsters, eager to show their knowledge, volunteered that it is an opiate and extremely addictive with a high relapse rate.

It was then that one of Brandon's classmates, Gwen Perry, said with finality, "I don't know how anyone with half a brain could get started on heroin. No way I'd stick a needle in my arm." Adding an oral exclamation point, she said, "Yuck-o!"

"You don't have to stick a needle in your arm," a small voice replied.

All eyes turned toward Brandon, and silence fell until Gwen slung her arm over the back of her seat and said, "Oh Brandon, I know they put it anywhere: between their toes, under their tongue; I don't care if they stick it up their butt. Don't be so technical."

In the ensuing laughter, Knepp strained to hear Brandon's chilling response. Eyes downcast, he said, "You can just snort it or smoke it."

Officer Ed stared at the boy. He had not yet shared that information in class, and, thankfully, local incidents involving that form of the drug had been few. The class ended, and Knepp asked the teacher if he could talk to Brandon. As they left the room, he put his hand on the boy's shoulder and asked, "Where to, Champ?"

"How about the playground?"

"Sounds good." No classes had recess at that time, so they would have privacy.

Knepp was surprised when Brandon headed for the swings; many fifth graders were beyond that. He sat on a swing beside the boy and rocked idly, toeing the ground and gathering his thoughts. Casting surreptitious glances, he watched Brandon pump his swing higher and higher. A small smile crept onto the boy's face as the cool breeze brushed his hair. "Mrs. Walters tells me you're one of her best students." This brought no response from the boy. Knepp noticed, though, that the smile had left Brandon's face. "What are you thinking about, Champ?"

"I don't want Gwen to be mad at me. She's my friend."

"I don't think she'll be mad. Gwen's a good kid. Besides, some things you'll know and do better than her; some things she'll know and do better than you."

"The only thing I'm better at is math. She's even better than I am at soccer."

"That's ironic," Knepp said.

"It's not ironic, Officer Ed, it's deplorable."

Knepp laughed. "You're a bright kid, Brandon. The big difference between a lot of kids is self-confidence. If you didn't hold yourself back, you'd be right there with her. Take the DARE class, you're capable of making as good a decision as any kid. And your knowledge is amazing. How did you know heroin could be snorted or smoked?"

Brandon stopped pumping the swing. When it lost momentum, he dragged his feet, bringing it to a complete stop. For the first time since they left the classroom, the little boy turned his sad eyes to Knepp, sizing him up. *This is where the covert curriculum of the DARE program comes in. Will this kid trust a cop enough to talk?*

"I heard my Uncle Brad and my dad talking about it."

TUESDAY SEPTEMBER 20, 10:30 AM   A WHIFF OF WEED

The decibel level of the late-bell was nearly sufficient to vaporize earwax. Staring down the deserted hallway at the tall, lean boy, the teacher thought, in all his years of teaching he had never seen a student so bold. Other teachers had closed their doors and begun class; still, the boy shuffled slowly, his hooded eyes riveted on the teacher's until the teacher blinked. Worse, he looked down. Paul Roberge's mouth curved upward, lending a vulpine cast to his stark, handsome features.

While they had been locked in their wordless struggle for dominance, the teacher noticed that Roberge's eyes seemed bloodshot, and as the boy brushed past, he smelled a faint, sweet aroma reminiscent of autumn days of his childhood when his father raked leaves and burned them curbside.

Roberge sauntered to his seat amid approving grins and hand slaps—the hero, again unscathed by so much as a word for his tardiness. The teacher chose to ignore this gradual loss of face among these "hoodlums" that he likened to sniveling toadies whose only strength or identity lived in the pale reflection of their leader.

On this day, the teacher was distracted by the immediate problem: should he address the suspected marijuana use, and, if so, how could he do it, yet remain anonymous? He was a teacher, not a cop; this was the administration's problem. Roberge was a rarity—a kid from a wealthy family in a general level class. Wealth brings influence, and influence lands a teacher's butt in a sling if the wrong people are crossed. In the end, he decided to take attendance; then, under the pretext of looking for one of the absent students, he sent a note in a sealed envelope to the office.

The attendance secretary took the note to the administrative assistant, who read it and delivered it to her boss, Kass Marburg. His office door was open, so she thought it was all right to disturb him even though he was talking with a board member. Marburg glanced at the note and forwarded it to an assistant principal, adding that he was in conference and did not want to be disturbed. Before the woman closed the door, she heard Marburg laugh and say, "So, we were all playing so bad we decided to chuck the back nine and head out to the dirt-track."

The secretary rounded a corner and peeked into Cat Blanchard's office to find her in the thick of an imbroglio between two girls who had decided they did not like the looks of each other. Judging from the multiple facial piercings of one and the purple and orange hair of the other, neither thesis could be rejected at face value.

That left Virgil Davis.

Virgil Davis was that endangered specimen—the career assistant principal. Most treat the job as the entry-level administrative position it is, where dues are paid before moving, determined, up the administrative ladder or, disillusioned, back to the classroom. The job brings with it the highest stress and the lowest esteem of any school position. Davis resented the many teen-oriented movies in which the assistant principal is depicted as the spawn of some bizarre mating of Elmer Fudd and Cruella de Vil. His job required diplomacy, judgment, and an understanding of child development. Like the school counselors, a planned workday was a fantasy. Problem solving skills, the ability to think on one's feet, and the will to act decisively were critical attributes. The assistant principal was in the middle of everything, and Davis's only regret was that, in reality, he was more of a disciplinarian than an educational leader. Any conflict among students and teachers had the potential to reach his door, and Davis backed down from none. His top priority was to have an orderly but unoppressive atmosphere; the latter quality, though, was up to the individual who caused the problem.

Over the years, Davis grew to know the students in the lower academic ranges. These were the disaffected kids: the ones for whom school held no relevance and who learned daily that they were equally irrelevant to the school. Virgil Davis and Doc Randori were their champions in the building, as were Kerry Wyatt and Meryl Morgan from the District Office. Although students sometimes thought them harsh, the educators were trying to instill self-respect and independence through personal and social responsibility.

Davis had seen many students succeed when a caring teacher, counselor, or coach, through hard work and patience, became involved in their lives, but it was getting to the point where there were more damaged children than even the most dedicated staff could serve. Every year, more and more of these young people fell in the throes of mental illness, substance abuse, crime, violence, and neglect. As much as these blights lashed at their souls, they became accepted parts of life, crowns of thorns donned along with backpacks every day. All too often the one safe haven that the school should have been became a microcosm of the failure they faced in the evenings, the nights, and in the early morning hours when these children lay alone, reflecting upon, or repressing, their innermost horrors. In the abyss, they meet the Paul Roberges of the world, whose siren song drags them, unaware, to damnation. Poised to lift them with life and hope, but also with reality, are the Virgil Davises.

Davis grabbed an envelope out of his desk and hustled out the door to fetch Cat Blanchard for some on-the-job training. He entered her office without knocking and met with a look of frustration. Blanchard was getting nowhere with her two frequent fliers. Having neither the time nor the inclination to deal with them, Davis entered the fray. "You girls are in this office way too often. Ms. Blanchard and I have business to take care of, so we need your cooperation. Promise you'll stay away from each other until we can arrange a peer mediation."

The rainbow-haired girl replied, "No way. If I see her, I'll kick her ass."

Sensing more bravado than true threat, Davis looked her in the eyes and smiled. "That would be your decision. You're responsible for your behavior and you're in total control of it. If you make the wrong choice, there will be consequences, and with your discipline records, you'll end up in alternative school for sure. I have confidence you won't let that happen. Now, what do you want to do?"

The girls looked down, refusing to respond.

Davis pressed, "I really need to hear an answer from both of you."

Glowering, the rainbow she-warrior said, "I won't start anything if she doesn't."

"Me, too."

"You need to agree that you won't fight no matter what." Davis gritted his teeth. "You can and you will find a peaceful resolution." Davis's demand initially met with hostile stares, but under his stern gaze they softened to assenting nods. When he saw that, he flashed a smile. "Good. Two more things: one, I'll let the language slide just this once; two, none of your friends best decide to take up the banner, because if anything happens to either of you because of some interested third parties, I'll consider it gang-related."

"I can't control what my friends do," the human pincushion said, bristling.

"True, but you can influence them. The school expels kids who commit assault, and we file charges. And before you get any ideas about taking this to the streets, you should know that we cooperate with all police investigations. So, I have one question; is it worth it?" Getting grudging acquiescence, Davis concluded, "All right, you can get passes and head back to class. We'll set up a peer mediation for you two."

Davis watched the girls stomp off. He thought he heard an expletive, but he had made his point; further discussion would be anticlimactic and needlessly confrontational. Besides, time was burning.

Blanchard shook her head in admiration. "How long will it take until I can handle these things like you do, Virgil?"

"Take control from the start, Cat, but don't let your pride or emotions get involved. Teach them to take responsibility for their behavior. And always keep your promises. Anything more from either of them, and they're off to alt ed." Davis hitched his thumb toward the door. "Now we've got to roll."

Moving around her desk, Blanchard was swift and graceful. As a newcomer to administration, she was enthusiastic about her job and making a difference; as a veteran educator, though, she was not naive. After seven years as an English teacher, she had decided that her strong beliefs of how education ought to be necessitated a change of venue, extending her sphere of influence beyond the classroom.

Blanchard had been ready for change, anyway. She had married while in college, and for four years, she did triple duty as wife, housekeeper, and financier to put her husband through law school. He repaid his debt by having an affair with a colleague from his law firm. With few tears and no indecision, Blanchard threw him out and started a new life. She joined a gym, and as she forged her body into taut condition, her will followed. After several years of distinguished teaching, she earned her administrative certification, got the first job she applied for, and stepped chin-deep into an assistant principalship with the idealism of a twenty-year-old, secure in the conviction that one intelligent woman of action was capable of doing more for kids than a hundred bureaucrats and their legislation ever could.

Davis and Blanchard moved to Paul Roberge's locker. The Student Handbook stated that students must be present for locker searches; Davis had learned the hard way, though, when dealing with students whose parents are hostile, unproductive searches are bombs waiting to explode in an administrator's face. "Cat, the first thing we need to do is search the locker, and I want you as a witness."

"Shouldn't Paul be here with us?"

"Nah," Davis said nonchalantly, "we have just cause."

" 'Just cause?' "

"Just 'cause we think he's holding weed. Trust me, Cat; this kid is a user and a seller. If nothing is in there, we'll just have the nurse check him out; we won't even mention the locker search. That will make him overconfident. Then maybe he'll get careless, so if we search it in the future, we'll be more likely to catch him. If we do find something, we'll get his parents in and search it with them present."

As Davis used his master key to open the locker, Blanchard scanned both directions. "We can't lose our credentials over this, can we?"

"I don't think so," Davis said airily, distracted by the task at-hand. Finding nothing on the top shelf, he squatted to inspect the bottom section. "Tell you what, if something happens, you plead ignorance and I'll take the ... What's this?" Davis closed the locker and rose to his feet. "Let's roll."

Turning to head up the hallway, they spotted a student at the end of the corridor, staring at them like a deer caught in headlights. It was the girl with rainbow hair. Davis realized she had been roaming the halls ever since she left Blanchard's office. He offered a broad smile. "I guess you had to walk around a while to cool off."

"Uh, yeah ... yeah, I was really mad. I couldn't concentrate if I was in class."

"Why don't you go to your counselor; see if you can talk this out."

"OK, Mr. Davis. Thanks, I'll do that." The girl wheeled and hustled off.

Blanchard's face turned crimson. "You think she saw we were in Paul's locker?"

"No, looking down the hall you can't tell whose locker is whose. Besides, when she saw us, her brain locked onto thinking up an excuse. Did you see her eyes?" Davis chuckled. "They looked like saucepans." Turning serious, he said, "Listen up. I don't think Roberge realizes what's in his locker. He's too smart to keep stuff there knowingly. But I don't want to take any chances in case he smells a rat and comes to check it out. So you stay here while I pick him up."

Paul Roberge ambled to a chair facing the door in Virgil Davis's office and slumped down. "What's the problem, Mr. D?" he asked, his voice and manner placid.

Equally tranquil, Davis said, "I'm wondering if you got high today, Paul."

The boy's eyes betrayed no guilt; his tone turned sarcastic. "Drugs, yeah right."

"Then you won't mind my having the nurse check you out."

Roberge sat forward, jamming a finger toward Davis's face. "Call my mother. Now! She's not at work; she'll be here in a minute!"

Davis smiled, his voice soft, friendly: "No problem." He picked up Roberge's emergency card and dialed a number. Handing the receiver to the boy, he said, "I want her here when we search your belongings, anyway."

Roberge complied. When his mother answered, he said in a brief, cold statement, "Mom, you've got to come to school. I'm in the office … again." He fell into a dead stare while the woman responded before snapping, "I'll tell you when you get here."

Davis called one of the administrative assistants and said, "Ms. Blanchard is in the four hundred hallway. Would you please ask her to join me? … And bring me Paul Roberge's sign-off sheet for the Student Handbook. … Thanks."

Davis reviewed Roberge's discipline file, then took the boy to the nurse, who checked his pulse and blood pressure, all the while engaging him in small talk about how he felt, whether he had been sick lately. The nurse concluded that, aside from bloodshot eyes and pupil dilation, there was no evidence of substance abuse. No surprise there, a nurse's check-up was most often a perfunctory exercise. It was difficult to accuse a student of drug use based on physical symptoms alone.

"What's with the red eyes?" Davis asked, flatly.

"I've got allergies?"

Mrs. Roberge entered the nurse's office before Davis could respond. Pinched and defensive, she offered no greeting. "What's going on? Paul, are you crying?"

Davis jumped on the opening. "Hello, Mrs. Roberge, you noticed the eyes, too?"

Before his mother could answer, Paul blurted, "I told him I have allergies, Mom."

Holding up his palm to stave off further conversation, the assistant principal said, "Let's go to my office. I'm sure you don't want other students listening in."

After a short, silent walk to Davis's office, they found Blanchard waiting for them. She offered a handshake, which Mrs. Roberge ignored, brushing past. Blanchard raised an eyebrow to Davis as she handed him a sheet of paper. "Dorrie wanted you to have this. I asked her to wait at the locker until we get there."

"Good thinking." Davis glanced at the paper and turned it around for Mrs. Roberge to see. "Here's the sheet you signed stating that you and Paul read and understand everything in the Student Handbook."

"Yes. So?"

"So, you read the drug policy. Mrs. Roberge, I have to be frank; have you considered the possibility that Paul's 'allergies' might be something else?"

"What are you trying to say?" she said, her voice teeming with bile.

"We think Paul might have gotten high this morning."

The boy lurched out of his seat. "You're—"

The woman placed a hand on her son's arm, cutting off his words. Her eyes narrowed to malicious slits. "False accusations can land you in a great deal of trouble, Mr. Davis."

Davis smiled and held up his hands to stem the aggression. "We're only concerned with helping students and having a safe, drug-free school. As a taxpayer and a parent, I'm sure you agree. Now, Paul needs to empty his pockets."

"He will do no such thing," Mrs. Roberge said, each word coming out as if it were its own sentence.

Davis remained calm. "If Paul has nothing to hide, there's no problem, but if he doesn't cooperate, we have to assume he's concealing something."

Paul looked his mother off. "It's OK, Mom." He stood and turned his pockets inside out, tossing the contents on the desk. Davis searched his backpack while Blanchard emptied his wallet. Except for eye drops, they found nothing suspicious.

"They're for his allergies," the woman said. "Paul, why didn't you use them?"

Davis sifted through the items on the desk. Glancing up, he saw the boy and his mother wearing identical disdainful expressions. "You two bear an incredible resemblance; you know that?"

"Can Paul get back to class soon? He's missing his studies."

"Just one more thing," Davis said, "a routine thing. We have to check his locker."

"No," the boy blurted. "You don't have 'probable cause.' "

"Good try, Paul, but that's a police term; we don't have their limitations. All we need is 'reasonable suspicion' and to have you with us when we search." Davis held the door. "So, it's best for everyone if we get it over with. Any problem with that?"

At the question, Mrs. Roberge's face shifted from naked scorn to trepidation. She stared at her son, waiting for some cue.

After a pause, the boy said, "Sure, but I expect an apology when this is over."

Davis told the boy to lead the way. As they walked, Mrs. Roberge scurried to keep up with her son while Davis and Blanchard trailed close behind, limiting the topics of conversation between mother and son.

They arrived at the locker, and Davis smiled at the administrative assistant. "Thanks, we'll take it from here."

"Open it, Paul," Blanchard said. Biting her lip, she looked up at Davis. He offered a quick wink and the slightest upturn at the corner of his mouth.

The boy spun through the combination then opened the locker and stepped aside. "Knock yourself out."

Davis repeated the order of his earlier search, moving from the top to the bottom while Mrs. Roberge looked on, her agitation growing by the moment. "Are you almost done? I don't want someone to see us and think Paul is in trouble."

The woman had barely gotten her words out when Davis said, "Paul, step back. Mrs. Roberge, take a look at this, please." At first, the boy stood his ground. Davis rose and demanded, "Move back to that wall!"

Davis gently took the mother's arm and ushered her to the locker. He squatted again, tugging the woman in for a closer look. He removed a pencil from his pocket and, using the eraser end, prodded some residue on the floor of the locker. "See? This clump looks like a cluster of marijuana, and over here are loose seeds."

Paul leapt forward, his eyes ringed with rage, "You planted that! I'll kill you!"

Blanchard quick-stepped between the onrushing boy and Davis, vulnerable as he squatted at the foot of the locker. Seeing that her son was about to shove Blanchard aside, Mrs. Roberge stood and commanded, "Paul, stop! Don't do anything stupid." She turned to Davis and smiled uneasily. "I'm sure there's some mistake."

"You realize you just threatened a school official," Blanchard said.

"Yeah, and—"

Before the boy could continue, his mother's voice rang in: "Paul didn't mean that. It was a natural reaction, considering the stress you've put him under."

"Mrs. Roberge, you watched me," Davis said, leveling sincere eyes on the woman. "You know this wasn't planted." He pulled the envelope out of his pocket and used the flap as a dustpan to collect the suspect substance. Rising, he continued, "Let's go to my office and talk."

On the way back to the office, the boy stared at Davis in coiled stillness. Inside, the Roberges refused seats, so the assistant principals remained standing as well. Davis said that, following procedure, he would turn the envelope over to the Newcastle police for examination. Meanwhile, Paul's mother was to take him home to begin a ten-day out-of-school suspension, pending the results of the drug testing. He added that, drugs aside, the threat alone warranted expulsion or placement in alternative education.

Throughout, Mrs. Roberge glared at Davis, prompting Blanchard to add, "You know, ma'am, things would be a lot better for Paul if some of the disgust you show for the school were redirected toward him."

The woman turned her fiery stare on Blanchard. Without speaking, she wrapped her arm around her son's shoulder and gestured toward the door.

"One more thing, Mrs. Roberge," Davis said. "You might want to take Paul to the hospital for a drug test. It would clear any lingering doubts you might have."

"Why would I do that? Paul told me he's clean, and I believe him."

"Then know this." Davis held up the envelope. "If the tests come back positive, you will cooperate with a drug assessment and follow-up counseling."

"He won't do it."

Davis pulled a copy of the Student Handbook out of his desk and handed it to Mrs. Roberge. "Page six will explain everything." He opened the door to close the conversation. "Thanks for coming in; the support of parents is important if we hope to keep our schools safe and drug-free." As he closed the door, he said to Blanchard, "Pleasant people."

"It doesn't get any better," Blanchard said.

"Yes, salt of the earth."

"No, it literally doesn't get better. Look who's coming."

Davis followed Blanchard's stare and gave a slow blink of resignation that his patience was to be tested further. "Great. Leroy Dubcek." Before the psychologist could knock, Davis opened the door. "Leroy. What can I do for you?"

"There was an incident of substance abuse this morning?"

Davis mustered an earnest expression. "The substance abuse was unsubstantiated, but there is substantial evidence of possession of an illegal substance."

One of Davis's small pleasures was tweaking Dubcek's serious demeanor. His current effort met the typical fate—dashed on the furrowed brow of grim piety.

"Who was the student?"

Davis knew the psychologist probably already had gotten at least part of the story from the nurse. "Paul Roberge. You didn't already know that?"

"I did hear something to that effect. Have you changed policy on this? Whenever a drug or alcohol abuse incident arises, protocol is that the Crisis Team must be called."

"You're misinformed, Leroy. The Crisis Team is called in high-risk cases where a student is a threat to himself or others. Other times, it's up to the judgment of the principal or counselor handling the situation."

Dubcek raised his chin and hiked himself to full height. "Oh, I disagree. These children are self-destructive and, therefore, potential suicides. They are crying for help, and if you probe deep enough you will find that out. Best practice demands a team approach. And that team must include a psychologist; only I have the expertise to evaluate these situations."

"Look, it was a simple drug bust. That's all."

"Did you know that I have been testing Paul? Kerry Wyatt and Doc Randori would want my input on any issues involving him."

"I've talked to Doc, and he and I are in agreement about how to handle Roberge."

"Doc Randori thinks too much like an administrator," Dubcek said, wagging his finger at Davis. "You must involve people with compassion in these situations."

Blanchard's eyes flared, and she entered the fray. "Are you saying administrators aren't compassionate?"

Dubcek's jaw went slack with the realization that he had revealed a long-held prejudice to the wrong audience. "Not at all," he stammered in an oral backpedal before regaining his composure. "It's just that assistant principals have to think of disciplinary consequences, proving that it is better to make team decisions."

"Leroy, it wasn't a crisis," Davis stated with finality as he opened the door. "It was disciplinary. You have a problem with that, talk to Kerry or Kass."

After Dubcek left, Blanchard pounded her fist on the desk. "I can't believe the arrogance of that man. Does he think he's the only person qualified to handle problems in this school?"

"Yes," Davis said.

WEDNESDAY, SEPTEMBER 21, 8:57 AM
THE UNBEARABLE ENLIGHTENMENT OF LEROY

Kass Marburg stared, fixated on his computer monitor, ignoring the knock at his office door. If someone wanted to find him, his desk was a good place to start. During an assembly or a pep rally while the assistant principals were working crowd control, amid the pandemonium of bus arrivals and departures, before homeroom period when students were free to mingle; almost any time in which the potential for student conflict was heightened it was a good bet he could be found at his computer. His usual explanation was that he was tinkering with the schedule or the budget.

Blanchard and Davis rarely had the opportunity to tinker, never early in the school day. From the time the first student arrived until the last student left for the day, the assistant principals had to deal with whatever problems arose. Davis sighed and twisted the knob. Jerking his head for Blanchard to follow, he strode to Marburg's desk to begin his report: "There was another fight at the bus dock this morning."

Marburg continued to stare at the screen. "I wish I could've been there."

"Two freshmen," Blanchard said before Marburg could follow up with the reason for his unavailability.

Davis grimaced and slowly shook his head. "Ninth graders aren't mature enough for high school. Another educational trend only half thought out."

Marburg swiveled his chair and dropped a baleful gaze on Davis. "You sound like Randori. Don't start my morning off with bullshit philosophy."

Davis searched for a touch of humor in Marburg's statement. Finding none, he said, "That's about it, Kass. You have anything for me? I've got to roll; lots to do."

"What happened with Roberge?" the principal asked with a tint of irritation. "I wanted to handle it myself, but I was in meeting with a Board member."

"It ended up on my desk," Davis said, his annoyance muffled by the awareness that he should not be brusque with his boss. "I took Cat along. Nurse checked him; his mother came in; we searched his belongings and locker."

"By the book," Marburg said.

"By the book," Davis echoed. He felt Blanchard's glance. "We couldn't prove anything by the symptoms, as usual, but I found a cluster of marijuana in his locker."

"Police tests confirmed that?"

"Yep. I explained potential consequences to Paul and his mom and encouraged her to take Paul for a drug test. Do you know if they went?"

"No, but they did get an attorney. They're saying you planted the drugs."

"But Virgil couldn't have," Blanchard said. "We were—"

Davis interrupted. "We were all right there. Cat and Mrs. Roberge witnessed."

"I wouldn't care if you did plant the stuff. I want that kid out of here. Set up an expulsion hearing."

"There's a minor glitch. Roberge is being evaluated for Special Ed."

Marburg raked his fingers through his hair. "Shit! Well, no point trying to reach Kerry. That man spends his life in meetings, and Randori's not a team player."

"I disagree, Kass," Davis said. "We should call Doc."

"Yeah, and we'll hear the history of marijuana in the Caribbean and more of his stoner Zen bullshit." As he spoke, Marburg picked up the phone and began to punch buttons. "I'm calling Leroy; he's doing Roberge's testing, right?"

Again, Davis felt Blanchard's glance. He stared ahead, deadpan, but made a mental note to talk to her about her reactions. Eye contact was unnecessary; he knew what she was thinking: the choice between Randori's mental flights and Dubcek's grandiose self-promotion was tantamount to choosing between lemonade and lemon juice.

Moments later, Dubcek arrived and seated himself at the conference table. Without waiting for anyone to solicit his views, he began: "Kass, this is a complicated case. An outside psychologist identified Paul with a Specific Learning Disability, but in my opinion he meets the criteria for Serious Emotional Disturbance."

Marburg frowned. "I have a problem with that, Leroy. It seems every time we have a student who acts up, you label him SED, and he ends up with more protection than if he had diplomatic immunity."

"That is a scary thought with that kid and those parents," Davis added.

Dubcek leaned back and folded his arms. "What is it you expect of me?"

"I expect to get Roberge into Alternative Ed for the rest of the school year," Marburg said. "Soon he'll turn 17; then maybe we'll get lucky and he'll drop out."

Dubcek crossed his legs and stared over the top of his bifocals. "Which would be convenient from an administrative standpoint, but it would be a gross injustice to Paul. He needs emotional support. His self-esteem is low enough already; to put him out of school would only alienate him and drive it lower."

"His self-esteem is fine," Davis said. "It's everyone else he has a low opinion of."

"What you see is bravado. Paul uses it to mask his pain."

"I'm feeling pain, too," Marburg said, "and it's in my ass. I want him out of the school population."

The psychologist raised his chin and his brow simultaneously, producing a haughty snort as a preamble to his statement: "I intend to ensure that his rights are observed. And if he is found in need of special services, he has the right to an education in the least restrictive environment. That would be in regular classes here in the high school—with academic and emotional support. If you want to check the law, call Kerry Wyatt or Doc Randori, but I'm certain I am correct." With that, Dubcek rose to leave, adding, "The alternative school is an inappropriate placement, ill-equipped to meet the needs of special education students."

"Wait a minute," Davis said, also standing, along with Marburg and Blanchard, so as not to give Dubcek the power advantage of looking down on the administrators. "Is Roberge identified yet? I don't think so."

"I am giving you my conclusions, which are usually accurate."

Marburg smiled; his voice became saccharine as he pressed the line of inquiry Davis had opened. "We have a 'Multidisciplinary Evaluation' meeting because a *team* makes that determination."

Davis followed up. "And that team includes an administrator, a teacher, and Dr. Randori, as well as you and the parents."

"That is true," the psychologist said, "and I would hope the administrator is Cat Blanchard; she would provide the administrative objectivity Paul deserves." Dubcek placed one hand on his hip and the other on his chest. "Furthermore, as the psychologist, I certainly hope my conclusions would carry some weight. After all, I am the only person in the building who can legally identify a student's disability."

If Blanchard felt that Dubcek was being patronizing or angling to take advantage of her inexperience, she concealed it beneath a flinty stare. "Input from the teachers and Dr. Randori's observation report have to be considered. The recommendations of the MDE team are just that—*team* decisions, not rubber stamps for your conclusions."

"It will be a team decision. However, I am also confident the teacher surveys will bear me out. And need I remind you that Dr. Randori is only a guidance counselor."

"Look, Leroy," Marburg said, appealing to reason, "if this kid gets the protection of special education law, we'll lose all control over him."

"So, this meeting is about getting me to go along with your plot to deny a child his rights just so you can have administrative leverage. Ethically, I abhor that."

"You refer to Paul as a child," Blanchard said. "By the time a kiddo gets to this level, he's a young man, responsible for his behavior."

"That responsibility is mitigated by his emotionality," Dubcek said, his finger wagging in rhythm with the emphasized syllables. "You need to be more enlightened."

Marburg stepped between Blanchard and Dubcek and thrust a finger into the psychologist's sternum. "Enlightened? We have a behavior code that ninety-five percent of the students follow with no trouble. Paul Roberge flaunts that system. He ruins the atmosphere for all the kids who come here to learn, and he's dangerous. He and his friends intimidate other students, they disrupt classes, and now we can prove there's also a drug involvement. I can go along with Conduct Disorder, maybe Oppositional Defiant Disorder, but not Serious Emotional Disturbance."

Dubcek sneered down at Marburg's finger, still poised inches away from his chest. Slowly raising his head, his calm voice belied the smoldering fury in his eyes. "Don't you ever lay a hand on me again." He turned on his heels and stalked out, slamming the door behind him.

After Dubcek left, Marburg seethed. "I want Kerry here. I don't trust Randori. Has he ever said anything to either of you about me?"

Davis ignored the question. "Listen Kass, Doc's on our side. He'll make sure Roberge's rights are upheld while still looking out for the welfare of all the students."

Blanchard embellished Davis's sentiment. "If you're caring at all it's difficult to hear about the hell some kids endure without coming to conclusions that will make their lives easier, but Paul Roberge doesn't fall into that category."

Marburg nodded in agreement with Blanchard as he began to press phone buttons. In moments, he was speaking into the receiver: "Theresa, is Kerry around?" ... "Is he ever there? I just want to know if he is scheduled to go to Paul Roberge's MDE" ... "Doesn't he know how important this is?" ... "I know I'd have to ask him that myself." ... "I know you're not his keeper." ... "Randori? I want Kerry there ... "Listen Theresa." ... "Theresa, just ask Kerry to call me. Better yet, have him call Virgil." ... "No, I can't be there; I have a building to run." ... "Of course it's important to me, but special education is Kerry's" ... "Theresa, I have to go." ... "I have to go." ... "Tell him to call Virgil." ... "All right—please."

Marburg hung up and buried his face in his hands. "I hate dealing with Pupil Services. Virgil, get together with Randori, then call the county alternative school."

"Doc's already contacted the alternative school. Maybe he can convince the Roberges that an alternative placement is in their son's best interest."

"Yeah, well, don't blow it, or I'll have both of your asses in a sling. Take that message to Randori."

Davis waited until he and Blanchard were in the hallway before saying more. "Come to my office while I call Doc."

Blanchard's eyes hooded, sharpening a skeptical stare, and her lips crooked into a tight grin. "You sure we can trust him?"

"What, you think he's going to kill somebody? ... Sorry, bad joke. Look, you don't know Doc very well; don't believe those rumors."

"I just can't warm to him. He seems, I don't know, snobbish."

"He's probably responding to your hostility."

"Hostility? Do you think I've been hostile toward him?"

"Not that I've noticed, and not that you realize, maybe." Davis stepped aside, allowing Blanchard to enter his office. When he turned to close his door, he saw Randori rounding the corner. "Well, speak of the devil and he shall appear. Doc, come here."

The counselor veered toward Davis's office, glancing over his shoulder as if checking to see if anyone was watching. "I'm in kind of a hurry, Virge."

Davis pointed to a sheet of paper in Randori's hand. "What do you have there?"

Randori sidled into Davis's office, and Blanchard took a wary step backward. The counselor watched her as Davis said, "Cat was wondering if we can trust you."

"Virgil!" she gasped, blanching.

Randori gave a slow nod. "You've heard of my penchant for homicide." With a wide grin, he said, "It's under control. ... Trust me."

"Knock it off, Doc," Davis said. "She doesn't know how to take you."

The counselor leveled a sober gaze on Blanchard. "She should judge for herself, not depend on someone else's opinion."

"The paper you're carrying," Davis said, holding out his hand. "May I see it?"

Randori hesitated before handing the paper over. "Are you sure you want to do this, Virge? Plausible deniability is a wonderful thing."

Davis offered no response; his attention was clamped onto the contents of the note. When he finished, he closed his office door and said, "I thought you were the one."

"I didn't read it myself," Randori said. "I'm merely delivering it for a friend."

"Yeah, your best and only friend—yourself." The assistant principal shook the paper in Randori's face. "You can get in real trouble for this, Doc."

"What is it?" Blanchard asked, moving closer to the men.

"Do you trust her, Doc, or will curiosity kill the Cat?"

A grin spread across Randori's face as he studied Blanchard's eyes. "Cat distrusted me long before someone did the community service number on Bob Samson." His words collided in her mind and reflected back through her eyes as the truth. "She seems like good people, though. Maybe if I trust her a little, she'll give a little back."

Blanchard read the note then raised her eyes in shock and newfound admiration. "You are the one," she said, echoing Davis.

"Don't get all *Matrix* on me," Randori said. "It's just an announcement."

Davis said, "Yeah, an announcement inviting faculty and staff to Kass's house for an ox roast on Sunday. You know, if he finds out it's you that's been putting up those phony announcements, you'll be the one, all right—the one who is crucified."

"What phony announcements?" Randori appeared simultaneously innocent and bewildered, the cumulative effect of which belied both.

"Don't you get all stupid on me," Davis said. "Like the one where Kass supposedly offered a big screen TV to the teacher with the best lesson plans."

Blanchard raised an eyebrow. "Or the one inviting female staff to Kass's office for interviews to be his homecoming date?" She stopped abruptly; her eyes and smile widened with dawning epiphany. "And I wonder who put the banner above the main doors on the first day of school: 'Fronti' something."

"*Fronti nulla fides,* " Davis said. "Kass thought it was pretty classy, putting up a Latin phrase to greet the students, until someone translated it for him: 'Don't trust appearances.' Juvenal wrote that."

"Well, I'm certainly glad you caught the delinquent," Randori said, his lips pursed in sincerity. "But I have no knowledge of these things. I lead a solitary, monastic life. Someone gave me a nickel and asked me to post it."

"Listen Doc, Kass is pissed about these. He's having people watch the bulletin board. And here you are carrying this thing right out in the open."

"Best way to hide something."

"God, you exasperate me," Davis growled. "What'll happen if Kass gets rid of you? Leroy will take over Pupil Services, that's what. And then where will we be? I hate to think about it." He crumpled the memo and threw it in the wastebasket. "Don't do that again, all right?"

"I won't," Randori said, eyes downcast.

His act of contrition was unconvincing; Davis emitted a low groan but got down to business. "Listen up, we need to talk about Paul Roberge. That MDE is coming up."

"I'm glad you busted him. Did you do a proper locker search to find that weed?"

"Fair enough, you got me back. So what do you think?"

"Too bad we don't have more on him with the drugs, because it's going to be tough to argue he's not emotionally disturbed. As it stands, you've got to try to keep those issues separate and deal with the drug situation before the MDE. Even then, you'll have trouble bringing this kid to justice, but we can use the drug bust as leverage for placement in the community alt ed or a special ed center in town. That way, we can keep him from contaminating the kids here at the high school."

"The Roberges have an attorney," Davis said.

"Sharks in the water? Then forget that."

"Why's that?" Blanchard asked.

"One: Leroy's psych report follows an independent eval done over the summer, and his recommends Emotional Support. Two: Leroy—if you know Leroy—will commingle the D&A and the mental health issues. He'll say if Paul is using it's because he's unconsciously self-medicating to deal with his emotional pain."

"Yeah?" Blanchard said warily. "So?"

"So, both psychological evaluations took place before you busted him. The interpretation of Special Ed law has been condensed into a neat little Hammurabian haiku: 'Once suspected, now protected.' Cute, huh?"

"That's not haiku," Blanchard said. "Haiku—"

Randori interrupted. "When you caught Roberge, the ten thousand Special Ed laws watched over him."

"The poet laureate of liberalism," Davis bristled.

"Don't shoot the UPS guy. Like a lot of laws, the original intent was good. Take a potential learning support kid, say, one who has a disability in reading comprehension. This hypothetical kid has average intelligence, but he's been failing, and people always assumed he just isn't bright. The law allows us to make accommodations right away— have tests read to him, for example—instead of waiting months for the process to unfold. It's only when unscrupulous people apply it—cases like this, for instance—that the law doesn't work. In fact, I don't think it even serves Paul's best interests. His family has to quit saving him, or he'll never be responsible." Randori paused, reconsidering his words. "What am I saying? He's probably a sociopath."

"I know I'm the new guy on the block," Blanchard said, "so forgive this stupid question, but what's the bottom line?"

A twisted smile meandered across Randori's mouth, a wry stream on the otherwise arid topography of his face. "There is an old saying, Cat: 'As far as special education goes, there are no stupid questions, just stupid answers.' But I'll give it a shot. Leroy will say that Paul is Seriously Emotionally Disturbed. Paul and his folks won't want to hear that at first. But when Leroy explains the perks—"

Blanchard frowned. "Perks?"

"Such as academic support to assist with his classes, which is what they wanted anyway, and an emotional support group to help make up for years of absentee parenting and deal with an attitude problem they refuse to acknowledge, let alone address. They'll jump at the chance."

"How does he get academic support if he's an Emotional Support kid?"

"The litmus tests for an Emotional Disturbance label are whether or not a kid's emotionality contributes to poor academic performance, and if it has occurred over an extended period of time. And time is a nebulous concept Leroy uses to his convenience; it can mean the time it takes to nuke a cup of coffee or back to the Pleistocene Age. I'd maintain that lack of motivation is Paul's problem. Of course, Leroy will counter that Paul isn't motivated because he's depressed.

"And here's the clincher: identified Special Education students have rights that limit the disciplinary consequences available to administration. Whenever one is suspended more than ten consecutive days or for an accumulated fifteen days, there has to be a

'Manifestation Determination' meeting to determine whether or not the behavior is a manifestation of his disability."

Blanchard shook her head in incomprehension. "And that means?"

"In crude terms, you have to prove his crazy behavior wasn't crazy, or it wasn't his particular brand of crazy, because if it was, that's normal behavior for a crazy person, and you can't expel an IEP kid for behaving the way he's expected to behave."

Blanchard stood slack-jawed. "That's ludicrous."

"I think that was the name of the attorney who came up with the concept. Now, there are exceptions for weapons, drug violations, and major violent incidents. But even then, you can only put him out for forty-five days, and then we have to re-evaluate him. Roberge is smart; he'll be the perfect angel during that time. So, he'll be back in our laps in no time." Randori shifted a sidelong glance at Davis and arched his brow. "And then there's that sticky hypothesis that Virgil was doing some gardening in the kid's locker."

"Bad thing," Davis said, ignoring Randori's jab, "is that Paul and his parents will interpret the law as an excuse for his behavior."

"And Leroy will be right with them," Randori added. "He thinks Torquemada wrote the Student Behavior Code after some Druid pissed him off. You realize, Cat, that Leroy's is the only enlightened path."

The assistant principals exchanged glances and laughed. Davis brought Randori in on the joke: "A little while ago we were told we weren't enlightened."

"You see?" Randori said, turning a palm up, Jack Benny style.

"OK," Blanchard said, "so what's our strategy—and cut the legalistic bullshit."

" 'Legalistic bullshit' is a redundancy," Randori shot back. "You can't cut it out because it's at the core of it all. And we'll be headed into a legalistic bullshitstorm if we're not careful."

Blanchard shook her head in disbelief. "My professor covered this in my school law class. If we have a disagreement between the family and the school, we go to mediation where we can iron things out peacefully."

The counselor's head swung like a doleful pendulum. "Either your prof wasn't getting enough oxygen in his ivory tower, or there's a heavy cloud cover up there. The Roberges got an independent psych eval because they don't trust us. They have an attorney. Our own psychologist backs them. Hell, they'll skip mediation and go right to a hearing. And we'll lose."

"But—"

"But nothing," Randori snapped. "We try to do our jobs according to laws that are so stacked against us that even when we care more about a kid than his family does, we can't win. When it comes to special education, the term 'justice is blind' becomes ironic. Or, what's more than ironic—moronic?"

"Are you saying you care more about Paul than his family does?"

For a fleeting moment, Randori's eyes flared and his jaw set. Then, his expression, and his tone, softened. "Enabling and saving aren't the same as caring; they make a kid feel entitled, like he's above the law. Doesn't it bother you that we've become a nation where some lady can sue the Pillsbury doughboy because bleached flour made her ninety pounds overweight and hypoglycemic, which made her depressed and caused her to pistol whip the supermarket bagboy because the kid didn't pack her barrel o' doughnuts in bubble-wrap?"

Davis enjoyed watching Blanchard's wide-eyed intake of Randori's diatribe, and so, he was taken aback when she blurted, "You know, you're right."

"I'm glad you two found common ground," Davis said. "Now that you can play nice, let me ask: What's the bottom line?"

"All due respect to Father Flanagan, but there is such a thing as a bad boy."

IF A FRIEND SPILLS IN THE WOODS

Paul Roberge opened his front door as the two girls who had rung the doorbell were backing off the stoop. They startled at the snick of the door latch, and Roberge flashed his most welcoming grin. "You here for my gathering?"

"Gathering?" asked the shorter girl, returning an uncertain smile. She and her friend looked past Roberge into the house. "I think we have the wrong address."

"I keep this side of the house dark, except the porch light, so it looks like nothing's going on. This is your first time here, uh …"

"Rachael," the girl offered, peering up at Roberge through limpid hazel eyes. "We go to 'City.' Candy said we could come."

The willowy blonde with Rachael spoke for the first time. "I'm Linda." Her eyes met Roberge's, but she quickly looked off to the side.

The boy stepped back and stole a glance at Rachael's dusky, athletic body. Her form-fitting jeans and sweater exposed a waistline that curved treacherously inward from her hips. "I'm Paul," he said. "This is my place." He turned aside to usher the girls' entrance. "I'll take you to Candy."

He led the girls on a winding path through darkened living and dining rooms. Voices and music increased from an indecipherable buzz to competitive chatter as they neared the rear of the cavernous Georgian home.

"Where are your parents?" Rachael said.

"Away for the weekend. They don't know about my gatherings." Leading them into the kitchen, he added, "I'll get you a drink."

"We can get our own," Rachael said.

For an instant, the boy's eyes hooded, but then he bashfully dropped his head. "I'm just trying to be a good host."

Linda offered a sympathetic pout. "What do you have?"

Roberge brightened. "Beer, wine, everything. For daring people, I have …" he cast a furtive glance around the room, leaned close, and stage-whispered, "soda."

Linda giggled. "I'll have a soda, diet if you have it."

"I hope you're really daring; I think it has caffeine."

Behind Roberge, a group clustered around a titanic boy who had a towel slung around his neck. He hunched over a cutting board, dividing a small pile of white powder into precise lines.

"Hey, Ace," Roberge said, "show Linda and Rachael why I gave you that name."

The mammoth turned and held up a playing card, the ace of hearts, he was using to divide lines of cocaine. He wiped his thumb and index finger along the edge of the card and rubbed them against his gums. "Want some?"

Rachael frowned. "No thanks."

"Too stuck up, bitch?" Ace snapped, his eyes blazing.

"Cut the 'roid rage, Ace," Roberge spat, facing up to the giant. "And take a shower before you come here. I have to burn candles to cut your stench."

As one, the others in the kitchen laughed, sycophantic hyenas indulging their host, and Ace backed off, stung by the verbal flaying. "Sorry, Paul."

Linda smiled at Roberge. "I'll do a line—if it's all right with you, Paul."

"Let her through," he said. His eyes scanned Linda's body as she bent her slender frame over the cutting board and pulled her hair behind her ears. Opening the refrigerator door, he fetched a can of cola and popped it open for her.

"Those were some big lines," she said, pinching her nose and accepting the can.

"That's why we call Ace 'lineman of the year,' " Roberge said. "It's sure not because of football."

"You'll be watching me on Sundays some day," Ace shot back.

Roberge ignored the boast. "Sure you don't want some, Rachael?"

"Not now, thanks. Where's Candy?"

"Follow me." Roberge lightly touched Linda's arm to lead her, with Rachael in tow, through the den where three boys played video games as several girls watched and swigged beer. They ended up in the sunroom and a musky cloud of marijuana smoke hung over a group seated at a coffee table.

Candy vaulted up from the table to join her friends. "Rachael! Linda!" she said, hugging each girl. "I'm glad you found the place.

Come, meet everyone." She clasped Rachael's hand and pulled her forward.

"Who's that over there?" Rachael asked, passively resisting Candy's tug and looking at a separate group of boys leaning against a windowsill on the far wall.

Roberge chuckled. "The two zombies that look like they're going to start drooling are Justin and Marcus. They've been partying since this afternoon."

Rachael lifted her chin toward the only clear-eyed person in the room. "The guy on the right."

"That's straight-arrow Brad." Roberge called to the boy, "Brad, over here."

"Paul!" Rachael said, embarrassed, as Brad pushed himself away from the window and ambled toward them.

"Relax, Rachael," Linda said. "He's hot."

"Rachael, Linda, this is Brad Prusster," Roberge said.

Brad glanced at Linda before locking onto Rachael's eyes. "I'm Brad."

"Yes, I know," Rachael said.

His face flushed in the awareness of his redundancy. "Yeah, I guess so."

"Well, I'm Rachael," she said with an open smile. "Pleased to meet you."

Justin Frederickson tore the pair's attention away from each other as he wobbled into a wide, unsteady stance and shuffled forward. "Hey Brad," he said in a dull slur, "You got a Rickin ripe for pickin'."

Justin's party partner, Marcus, let out a high-pitched giggle and hugged himself in glee. Roberge eye-checked Marcus, shutting him up, before addressing Justin: "Her name is Rachael, and she's with Brad. Be polite."

Justin staggered to Roberge's side and whispered loudly, "But you hate—"

Paul clamped a hand over Justin's mouth and squeezed his fleshy cheeks, making his eyes bulge as much as his drug and alcohol-induced stupor would allow. "Sorry, Rachael," he said, "Sometimes my friends don't have manners."

"Don't beat on him, Paul," Marcus Wyncoat's slushy voice yodeled from the corner. "Justin and me were just tuning up."

"I wouldn't hurt Justin," Roberge said, smiling even as he gripped his arm. "We're just going out back to talk."

Justin looked over his shoulder and beamed through gimlet eyes, "I'll be back before the train starts." Yanking his arm up and down, he howled, "Woooo-WOO!"

The teens at the table looked up. One boy, about to take a toke, said, "Get me ticket number two." Brad sprung forward and jammed his palm into the boy's smirking face, causing hot embers to cascade down the front of his shirt. Slapping at them, the boy spluttered, "Shit! This is silk! Don't you Avalon guys know how to chill?"

Roberge stopped at the door and turned, flashing a grin. "Gatherings are supposed to bring people together. Justin forgot that, don't you guys." He clapped his friend's back then shoved him out into the yard and disappeared through the doorway.

Brad's stare locked onto Roberge until Rachael's voice recaptured his attention. "You all right? What was that about?"

"Nothing. Sorry."

"Paul gets a lot of respect, doesn't he?" Linda said. "He's nice, too."

"Respect, yeah," Brad said. "I better check on them."

"I'll keep the guys away from Rachael till you get back," Candy said.

Rachael gave a shy smile. "I'll get a soda."

"I want a beer," Linda said.

"Get your own," Brad said. As he headed for the door, he wheeled and pointed for emphasis. "And hold on to them!"

"That was rude," Linda said. "Paul would've gotten our drinks for us."

Linda's words didn't register with Brad as he moved out the door and to the edge of the yard, peering into the woods until his eyes adjusted to the darkness. The indecipherable sizzle of Roberge's voice sifted through the trees, drawing his tentative steps into the brush as he zeroed in on their location, each step putting him closer to the danger of discovery. Finally, he could make out what was said, and he stepped behind a tree to listen.

"You got a big mouth, you know that, Justin?"

"You're always saying how you hate Rickins, Paul."

"Yeah, well, that particular Rickin was with Brad, and Brad's our friend."

"What do you care? Brad didn't set things up for you with Bolt."

"For once in your life, think past your next buzz. Brad's brother liked my ideas; he just doesn't trust me. If Brad realizes I'm his friend, maybe I'll get another chance."

"You're doing all right on your own."

"Doing all right and doing great are two different things. With Bolt's operation and my brains—"

"And your connections in Philly and at school."

"And guys like you, Justin. But you have to be loyal, do what I want. Do that and I'll always make sure you get product, and a cut of the profits."

"And women."

"Ass you'd never get on your own. But remember the only thing I ask."

"What, Paul?"

A loud slap made Brad jerk.

"Loyalty, you dumb piece of shit. You know what loyalty means? It means trust—I have to be able to trust you. Part of that is keeping your mouth shut."

"I keep my mouth shut."

"You didn't just a few minutes ago. Twice!"

"I didn't know I was saying anything wrong, Paul. We all hate Rickins."

"You don't have to like her to screw her. Wouldn't you like a piece of that—maybe tonight?"

A rush of rage radiated outward from the middle of Brad's chest. His neck and arms tensed and his fists balled. He stepped forward but stopped when Roberge went on.

"Your mouth is going to get you killed."

"Why, because I insulted some Puerto Rican slut?"

"No, because of things like the football game."

"What? I didn't say anything. Besides, you got me in trouble when you sent us after those Rickins."

"See what I mean? You can't even keep your mouth shut now."

"But it's just us here."

"That's right, it's just us. So, be honest. You gave them my name, didn't you?"

"No, hell no."

"I can't believe you're loyal to me if I can't trust you, Justin, and I can't trust you if you're not honest with me. And if you're not loyal to me, how can I be loyal to you?"

Silence fell as Justin unraveled Roberge's circuitous logic. He finally responded with a mournful plea, "Paul, believe me, I didn't tell anyone about you."

"One more chance. We can act like it never happened, but tell me the truth."

"Who told you? Mr. Davis would never … shit, it was Randori, wasn't it?"

"Yeah … Randori. Now, how about it, Justin?"

"They were going to expel me, Paul. My dad would've killed me." Justin broke into wracking sobs. "And I didn't tell them, the assholes guessed."

"But you confirmed it."

Dead quiet, broken only by Justin's pitiful gasps, then a barely audible, "I had to."

"Let's go back inside, Justin."

Brad tiptoed out of the thicket and sprinted across the lawn. He eased into the sunroom an instant before his friends emerged from the woods.

When they reached the yard, Roberge slung his arm around Justin's thick shoulders and pulled him close. "The talk we just had? It's our secret, right?"

"Believe me, Paul, I won't tell anyone."

"I believe you," Roberge said, flashing a grin as he held the sunroom door open for Justin to shuffle into the house. Roberge stared into the woods for a long moment. Still smiling, he nodded at some private truth before rejoining his gathering.

Back in the woods, a soft rustle in the underbrush hinted at an unknown presence. A dark figure moved from behind a tree, less than ten feet from the spot where Brad Prusster had hidden as he eavesdropped on Roberge and Frederickson. At first a phantom, the figure took several muffled steps in the direction of the yard. Just inside the copse, it came into focus as the silhouette of a man shrouded head to toe in black. Shadows from branches danced across his face, offering strobe-like glimpses of his features. As he stalked forward to the edge of the forest canopy, the glow from the sunroom cast a ghostly light on the face of Doc Randori.

SHEDDING INNOCENCE, SHREDDING INNOCENCE

Brad weaved through the sunroom and then the den, searching for Rachael. He finally found her at the kitchen table with her friends, staring up in bewilderment at Ace.

The behemoth loomed over Rachel, leering. "Tonight's my lucky seven."

Brad shoved past Ace and grabbed Rachael's hand. "She's with me."

Ace wheeled and cocked his fist. Recognizing Brad, he backed off, although his menacing glare remained. "You're lucky you're Bolt's brother."

Brad picked up Rachael's soda. Shooting a cold stare at Ace, he threw the can in the trash a split second before Rachael yanked her hand out of his grasp.

"I'm not with you—I'm not with anyone!"

"Come with me," Brad said. Singed by her glare, he leaned close and added in an imploring whisper, "Please. I'll explain."

Rachael warily rose, and Brad led her out of the kitchen, ignoring Ace's words that followed like wasps stinging the back of his neck, "What would big brother Bolt think about you doing a North Side *spiquita?*"

They moved in silence through the shadows to the front door. Opening it, Brad stepped aside and gently took Rachael's elbow. "Watch your step." Outside, he closed the door and laid his hands lightly on her shoulders, turning her so he could examine her eyes in the harsh porch light. "Do you feel all right?"

"Just glad to be out in the fresh air," Rachael said, fanning herself. "That smoke was getting to me. What's going on, Brad?"

He peeled a paint chip from the doorway and studied it. "I just wanted to get you away from Ace. He's an assho—a jerk. Sorry."

"Don't apologize," the girl said, smiling. "I've heard worse."

"Why did you come here tonight?"

"Something to do. Linda heard about this party from Candy, so we decided to come out after the game."

"Did City win tonight?"

Rachael laughed. "Do you care?"

"No." His eyes fell to the paint chip he was rolling between his fingers. "It was just something to say."

"She gave his arm a light chuck and smiled up at him. "Let's go for a walk."

They stepped gingerly down the steep driveway to the lane. Peeking out of the corner of his eye, Brad lost himself in Rachael's beauty and childlike wonder as she took in the wooded serenity of the affluent neighborhood.

"Nice out here, isn't it?" he said, drinking in her soft profile.

"It's so quiet. I love the trees. Not like New York, where I used to live. Someday, I want a house in Culver Pond."

"Not me. I want to get away from Freedom."

"Too many Rickins?"

"No," Brad said with more emphasis than he intended. Rachel's mischievous grin brought him relief. "No, too much trouble, not enough to do. I want to go to college."

"My parents are teachers. I think I might be one, too. What do your parents do?"

"My mom's a secretary, and my dad's ... unemployed." Brad felt a damp sheen on his brow and hoped the night breeze would erase the evidence of his white lie. "If we turn up ahead, we can go to the ranger tower. You can see all over."

"Sounds nice—better than that party, or gathering, or whatever it was."

"Gathering," Brad said, punctuating the word with sarcasm.

"It sounds so pretentious."

Brad chuckled. " 'Pretentious'—Justin and Ace probably never used that word; I bet they don't even know what it means. But they think they're better than you."

"But it does seem that way."

"It's worse. Paul calls it a gathering because he's bringing all these different groups together. But it's not him, you know. Well, it is his place and all, but if you look around, everyone is in their own cliques, anyway. It's only the drugs and other stuff, only after everyone gets high, that they mix."

"So, why do you go?"

"If I wasn't here, I'd be hanging around Avalon, drinking beer on a corner and talking the same crap every night. Besides, I have to watch out for Justin."

"That redneck is your friend?"

Brad let out a hollow, one-note laugh. "My best friend. Used to be, anyway. He's closer to Paul now."

"I don't see you with him, with either of them. What's the story with Paul?"

"We have to turn left here." He touched her arm again to alter her course.

They walked in silence, basking in the tranquility of the forest night. Brad led Rachael to the base of the tower. "I'll be behind you in case you slip."

"You just want to check out my butt, don't you?"

Brad's innocent eyebrow raise countered Rachael's impish grin, but as she stepped upward, her gentle sway was mesmerizing. They reached the top platform, and he watched her marvel at the silver quilt of moonlit landscape. The trek up the steep flights and the splendor of the moment left Brad breathless, both literally and figuratively. "Why are you alone tonight?"

"I'm not; I'm with Linda."

"You know what I mean. Is there a guy?"

Rachael locked onto Brad's eyes, and nodded. The simple gesture brought a pang that made him turn away. "We're through," she quickly added. "I just haven't been able to tell him yet. He used to be so nice, then he started hanging with these North Side guys; now he thinks he's a gangster. Pants all hanging off his ass, uh, butt."

Encouraged, Brad beamed into Rachael's eyes, taken by her shy embarrassment. "We're even."

She recovered and went into a parody, swiveling her head and bobbing side to side. "He's all pointing his fingers like he's got palsy and going with that rap-crap talk."

The gyrating imitation threw Rachael off balance, and Brad grasped her hips to right her. She stopped abruptly but didn't protest his touch. After a smoldering glance, Rachael dropped her head and continued her story. "The other day, he called me his 'bitch' to his friends." Her voice cracked. "It hurt, you know?"

"So, what's keeping you from breaking up with him?"

"I'm afraid that if he loses me, he'll go totally bad. He'll be just like them."

"That's why I stick with Justin."

Rachael gazed into Brad's eyes. "But what's to keep you from becoming like those guys back at the party?"

"Do you think I will?"

She tilted her head back, bringing her lips so close to his that he felt her warm whispered answer. "No."

Brad stared into the glistening pools of starlight reflected in Rachael's eyes. He pulled her close. She resisted for only a moment, but that moment brought the longing agony of the forever it took their lips to meet.

Rachael's hands slid up Brad's back, taking his shirt along, her own sweater rising as she stretched. Their bare torsos pressed together as they enfolded in a sweet, supple crush, and fever radiated from her body, rushing into his, arousing him. A soft moan as he pressed his hips forward in insistent ardor and his mouth explored hers.

Suddenly, she stopped, caught her breath, pressed against his chest, and said, "I can't. I mean, I've never—"

Brad lifted Rachael's chin and stared into her misting eyes. "Neither have I."

They fell still, minds and spirits lagging behind a decision their flesh already had made. Finally, sapped of the will to resist, they collapsed together in reckless surrender, fumbling, then tearing at clothing until they stood, swathed only in moonglow, drinking in each other's magnificence. Brad caressed Rachael's shoulders, then her breasts, his touch treasuring every curve. She reached out to him, and he felt he had never lived until that moment. Tears welled in his eyes as she enveloped him in a torrential convergence that swept their spirits out to the stars and flooded their souls. Too soon, the deluge passed, but they held their embrace as though release would cast the other adrift, and they caressed with lips and eyes until time and space returned to their idyllic citadel.

"We have to go," Rachael said. "It's late. I have to get home."

"I don't want to."

"Neither do I." She kissed him, one last, luxuriant kiss, then drew back, and a knowing smile spread across her face. As he grinned and leaned in to kiss her again, she dangled his boxers, like a closing curtain, between their faces. "Let's go," she said with a playful giggle.

They dressed and descended the steps, Brad leading the way. At the foot of the tower, he helped her to the clay plateau. She interlaced her fingers with his. "I'd like to come back here again sometime."

"Me, too."

"Maybe we'll actually take in the view next time," she said, tugging his arm.

They stepped onto the gravel road that ran the spine of the Southern Mountains, the touch of their hands the only communication that seemed right. Brad craned his neck, searching the shadows. "This is where we turn," he said, pointing to a spot where pavement abruptly began. "Do you think Linda missed us?"

"I doubt it. She had her eyes on Paul. He's her type; she likes dangerous guys."

"She picked the right one there." Brad picked up the pace. "Let's go."

"What's the hurry?"

"I thought you had to get home."

"Yeah, but a couple minutes more won't be a big thing."

"You never know."

Brad gripped Rachael's hand, speeding her along. When they turned onto the street where Roberge lived, he broke into a jog. She struggled to keep up, catching him as he strode up the steep driveway. Panting as much with anxiety as with the exertion of the last minutes, he stepped up to the door, turned the knob, and pushed it open.

Leading the way into the house, he peered through the darkness. As his eyes adjusted, he looked up and his fear was realized. A group of boys huddled outside the guest bedroom, exchanging excited whispers and laughter. Brad pushed through the mob.

"What the—?" said one of Ace's friends. "Wait your turn, Prusster."

"Brad, what's going on?" Rachael asked, her voice rising with apprehension.

He didn't answer. As he reached the bedroom door, it swung open and Ace's giant silhouette blocked the doorway.

The football player threw his fists triumphantly toward the ceiling. "SEVEN!" the queue of boys hollered in unison.

Brad brushed past Ace, rushing in, Rachael close behind. There, unconscious amid squalid stench and rumpled bedding was Linda, naked from the waist down.

"Linda!" Rachael shrieked, frozen in horror. "God, Linda!"

The clot of boys gaping into the room drew Brad's attention. Leaping forward, he slammed the door and locked it, shutting out their lurid protests. Rachael dropped to her knees, frantically sobbing and searching for Linda's clothing.

Brad returned to the bed and lifted Linda's head. "You OK?" The girl's eyes opened to slits and her lips parted in unintelligible mutterings.

He propped the girl up into a seated position, and Rachael tried to push underwear and pants over rag-doll legs, pausing only briefly to glare at him. Lifting Linda to her feet so Rachael could finish dressing her, Brad slung a limp arm over his shoulder while Rachael unlocked and opened the door. The group of boys had dispersed, retreating to the dark corners and crevices of the house. Rachael returned and wrapped Linda's other arm around her neck, as they sandwiched her, moving out of the room and the house.

No words passed between them as they stumbled down the driveway to Rachael's car. She opened a rear door and sat in the back seat as Brad draped Linda across her lap.

"Do you want me to drive?" he asked.

Rachael gave no answer as she pulled Linda's slumping body across the seat and exited through the far door. Brad opened the driver's side door, expecting Rachael to sit shotgun, but she rounded the front of the car and pushed past him.

"Let me go with you," he said. "I can stay with you till she's OK to go home."

Rachael turned the ignition and glowered up at him. "What was your job, straight-arrow Brad, get me out of the house so those pigs could drug my friend and screw her?" Before he could answer, Rachael jammed the car into gear and careened out of her parking space, leaving Brad standing alone on the road, watching her fade into the night.

Two pairs of glass doors at the high school's main entrance provided Randori's only window to the world, and he grasped every opportunity to view the farmlands in the distance. It sometimes crossed his mind as he left the catacombs of the Counseling Center that it was a planned tease, freedom just out of reach. Then he remembered to be thankful for small gifts. The way things were headed, schools would soon have to eschew aesthetics altogether and hunker back into secure bastions where both assailants and nature were held at bay. Randori shook off that grim possibility and entered the administrative office suite to find Davis and Blanchard awaiting him.

"We'd better hustle," Davis said. "Leroy will start the MDE without us."

A stern voice interrupted. "Hold up; I have something to say."

The three turned at the same time to see Kass Marburg approaching, clipboard in hand, accompanied by Tammy Eboli. Marburg was wearing his charcoal pinstriped suit, which meant one thing: he had to perform some critical function of the executive. Davis and Randori would have found it amusing in a "Look, Clark went into the phone booth but Superman came out" kind of way except that the suit loosed the megalomaniac, shifting Marburg into Lex Luthor mode. Davis had been holding the door, but one look at Marburg's face and he closed it and held his breath.

Neither Marburg nor Eboli offered greetings. Facing Randori, the principal looked down at his clipboard and read from a script: "Dr. Randori, Ms. Eboli is here as your Association representative. As of now, you are suspended from duty for assaulting a student. This is a serious breach of the public trust and your own professional code of ethics. Pending a disciplinary hearing, you will be suspended with pay. You may gather your belongings and leave the premises immediately."

Marburg's announcement caught the attention of a nearby secretary and several students. Davis bowed his head and Blanchard stood petrified in disbelief. Silence descended like a morning fog, clouding reality. Nowhere was the atmosphere more stifling than near Randori himself, as an abysmal no-man's-land seemed to open around him, and his eyes, dark embers, betrayed the fury harnessed within.

The thirteen-year-old boy, alone at the dining room table, stares blandly down at an equally bland TV dinner. He drops his fork and glances around, taking in the silence, before turning from the table to enter the gaping maw of the dark and empty living room. Moving around a hulking gray armchair, he heads into the hallway and stares at the telephone. A muffled scream jerks his head upward before he realizes the scream is in his mind. Dying rays of sunlight crawl across the windowsill on the upstairs landing and fall onto the boy's face, revealing the entombed vestiges of innocence. Squinting into the light, the boy makes his way up the stairs.

With slow determination, he twists the bedroom doorknob, enters, and moves to a small, marble-topped dresser near the window. Another muffled shriek brings a wince, and he looks out to the empty street. Seeing nothing, he turns to the dresser and the padlocked top drawer that mars its antique charm. His hand joggles the lock then runs along the cool marble surface of the top. Grasping the sides of the marble slab, he presses a knee against a dresser drawer, and gives a heave. The slab grinds forward until it totters on the front edge of the dresser. Sinews in the boy's arms strain as he lifts the slab, hauls it to the bed, and eases it onto the mattress.

Returning to the dresser, he studies three unfinished wooden slats that separate him from the contents of the drawer. Without warning, placid examination turns to violent action as the boy raises his fist and rains hammer blows on the center slat until it snaps clean. He examines the edge of his hand, pocked with splinters and bearing an inch-long gash near the base. Ignoring it, he pries the slat up and to the side, freeing it from the tenuous grip of the groove seating it to the side of the dresser.

Rivulets of sweat run into dead eyes, and the boy lifts the front of his shirt to wipe his face before reaching inside the drawer to extract a purple, velvet-covered jewelry case. He lifts the lid to find a Purple Heart, a Bronze Star, and military ribbons. He closes the case, carefully returning it to its original position. Removing the other half of the slat, he widens his search. His hand falls on a black enamel tube half hidden in the shadows. He blindly plucks a folding knife out of the drawer and presses a chrome button in the middle of the shaft. The blade springs forth, locking open with a definitive click. He lays the switchblade on the edge of the dresser.

Taking care to avoid the ragged edges of the remaining unfinished slats, the boy reaches to the rear of the drawer. Fishing around until he hears a heavy scrape of metal on wood, he slowly draws a black service pistol out into the open.

Davis raised his head and scowled at Marburg's choice of time and place to discipline Randori. Standard protocol, if not ethics, demanded that such confrontations take place in the privacy of an office with only a second administrator and a union representative present. If he had publicly disciplined any other teacher, Eboli would have slapped a grievance on him so fast his head would spin. But Davis knew the reasons behind the action: Eboli hated Randori, and Marburg didn't have the guts to face him in private. And, of course, there was added perquisite of humiliating the counselor.

Davis did not like the possibilities of what might come. "Jeez Kass," he said, "that was weeks ago. The only feedback we got was positive; even Justin's dad supported us."

Marburg broke free of Randori's stare. "This isn't open to debate. It's a directive from the superintendent." A tint of relief shaded the bold conviction the statement was meant to convey. That verbal backpedal was not lost on Tammy Eboli, as the polish of her professional demeanor faded to drab disappointment.

"We're on our way to an MDE," Davis protested.

"I'll take Dr. Randori's place at the meeting," Marburg said.

"But we need Doc's—"

"It's OK, Virge," the counselor said with a calming smile. He recast his dead-eyed gaze toward Marburg, measuring him. The principal looked away, trying to catch Eboli's eye, but she ignored him. Flashing a wicked smile at Davis, Randori turned to leave.

As Davis held the door for his friend, Marburg called after them: "I know you're the one who posted those announcements, Randori: the television, the homecoming date, the ox roast."

The counselor paused only a moment at the principal's words.

When Marburg and Davis entered Leroy Dubcek's office, the rest of the Multidisciplinary Evaluation Team—and then some—was already present. The psychologist sat at his desk and had jacked up his chair to a height where he looked down on the other participants. To his right sat Mr. and Mrs. Roberge, without their attorney. Then came two ringers, Claude Putty and Bertha Gordon, members of the Student Assistance Program. Davis realized that the MDE was scheduled during the time the SAP Team met, so Bertha, the assessor assigned to Freedom Con by the county Drug and Alcohol Commission, could attend.

Dubcek said, "I inadvertently left the SAP members names off the invitation letter, but they have information critical to this meeting."

Davis cursed himself for missing so many SAP meetings. It seemed that whenever he was absent Dubcek and his devotees abused their power in some way. He wondered what information they could have. "I didn't realize Paul had been on the SAP agenda this year. It's usually a good idea to get a kid's discipline file when you're working on a case, or at least tell me you're going to discuss him, so I can make it a point to be there."

"You are a standing member of the team," Dubcek said with a trace of indignation. "We assume you will be responsible and attend meetings."

"You know how busy Mr. Davis is," Marburg snapped. "You've never hesitated before to let us know when a SAP case was going to involve discipline."

Dubcek dropped his pen, which had been poised above his draft Evaluation Report, his way of implying exasperation at the holdup Davis had caused. "I don't think this is the appropriate time to discuss SAP procedures. Ms. Gordon has assessed Paul, and Mr. Putty has provided Paul's academics while he has been on suspension."

"Quick assessment, Bertha," Davis said. "We usually have to wait weeks. And if you followed protocol, you'll have reports from his classroom teachers."

Dubcek sat back and folded his arms. "Must I remind you that teacher reports to Student Assistance are confidential? If word got out that their input was discussed openly, few teachers would respond."

Marburg broke in. "But if that information was presented in summary form, it would preserve confidentiality. Or were you concerned how detrimental those reports would be to your argument that Paul deserves Emotional Support?"

Dubcek ignored the insinuation. "Mr. Putty will provide teacher input for the Evaluation Report. Now may I begin or should we wait for Dr. Randori?"

"He can't make it," Marburg said. "I'll represent the District."

Dubcek glanced at his fellow SAP members before making introductions. "I should explain that we usually do not invite students to MDE meetings, especially when we are discussing emotional factors. If we go to an IEP, Paul may join us." Dubcek picked up his pen again and shot the sleeves of his suit coat.

He opened by referring to a summary of the private evaluation and his own determination that Paul suffered from overriding emotional factors that interfered with his ability to learn. The Roberges' sad-eyed nods lent affirmation to his statement.

"As to information from the parents," he continued, "Mr. and Mrs. Roberge have felt frustrated with the school system since Paul was in seventh grade when they tried to get him academic help, but teachers and administration preferred to view him as a discipline problem."

"Hold on a minute," Marburg said, bolting erect in his seat. "I was the middle school principal when Paul was there. We met often about Paul's grades and behavior."

"We asked for help and advice," Paul's mother seethed. "Instead of educational strategies, we got lectures about how Paul had to pay attention and behave." She dabbed at her eye with a tissue. "And your answer every time was to suspend Paul. How was my son supposed to learn if he was never in school?"

"Your son was disrupting every class," Marburg shot back. "I couldn't count the complaints we got from parents of other students. We have to answer to all of our taxpayers."

Dubcek held his hands out, as if to stem the angry tide. "Mr. Marburg, you will have a chance for input when we enter information from the school." Turning his attention to the parents, he said, "You are saying, Mrs. Roberge, that Paul has had difficulty attending to task in his classes. That supports my findings that Paul's lack of focus is indicative of Attention-Deficit/Hyperactivity Disorder. I will talk more on that later. I will say, though, that all the research shows that punishment does nothing to remedy the situation and only serves to alienate the student."

Davis was about to defend the administration, but Marburg beat him to a response. "I thought you had a protocol to follow, Leroy. This is not a bully pulpit for you to attack the administration. And, isn't an AD/HD diagnosis a physician's call?"

"I hope we can keep this meeting on a professional level," Dubcek said with a haughty tilt of the chin. "Moving on, Paul has followed a normal developmental path and is in excellent health. Socially, he has positive relationships with age-appropriate peers and gets along well with adults, for the most part."

"Whoa," Davis said. "Paul threatened to kill me when I found his marijuana."

Mrs. Roberge shot to the edge of her seat. "He was stressed. You harassed him; you've been baiting Paul since he's been at the high school. You can thank your lucky stars that Mr. Dubcek talked us out of pressing charges against you."

"Yes," Dubcek nodded humbly, "I convinced the Roberges that animosity helped no one. We on Student Assistance felt that the MDE processes and ours were better paths. We are a non-threatening group that works in students' best interests."

Marburg's eyes narrowed. "For the record, Paul has had negative relationships with teachers and administrators throughout middle and high school. And, as far as peer relationships go, they may be strong, but they're with the wrong people."

Dubcek smiled as he turned to another page of his document and jotted a note. "Now, if I may continue. Educationally, any success Paul has enjoyed is due to concerned parents. Despite their best efforts, however, his grades began to drop in seventh grade. As you know, students afflicted with AD/HD are at great risk to have learning and emotional problems. Instead of making accommodations for him, teachers and administration simplistically judged Paul by his presenting behavior."

Paul's father finally spoke. He opened a folder he had been holding on his lap and produced several report cards. "Paul had a 'D+' average last year. I would say that's an accurate grade—for the school!"

Dubcek pursed his lips in earnest attention before continuing. "I will now proceed with the summary of my findings and interpretation of test results. For the sake of brevity, I will summarize: Over time, Paul's unresolved frustrations have driven him into clinical depression. He has exhibited destructive impulses at times, and emotionally tinged situations find him unable to deal with his feelings. In spite of this, he projects as sensitive and emotionally aware. There is evidence that he views himself as having the awareness and prerogatives of an adult. Mr. Putty completed a behavioral assessment, as did our SAP assessor. His observations find Paul's internalizing, or self-focusing, problems to be in the Clinical range, indicating serious emotional concerns. At the same time, they find him within the Normal range for externalizing, or antisocial, behaviors. Because of recent allegations of drug use, I asked Ms. Gordon to assess Paul. Her conclusions concur with mine: 'Paul is clinically depressed.' Dubcek smiled at the assessor. "Do you wish to add anything?"

"Yes," Gordon said, shifting in her chair and opening her clipboard. "My evaluation differs from Mr. Dubcek's in that it examines drug involvement. Paul denies the drugs found in the locker were his. I tend to believe him in light of the fact that he was open and honest throughout my assessment."

"Hold it right there," Davis said, hiking himself up. "If you're saying those drugs weren't his, you're implying they were planted."

The assessor remained placid as she splayed her fingers across her chest and continued in the same soft tones. "I would never make such an accusation. That is merely one of the possibilities. Paul admits many people know his locker combination.

"Now, if I may continue: Paul admits to occasional beer drinking and marijuana use at times of high stress. At these times, he is most vulnerable, as feelings of helplessness are present. He wants to be successful in school, but he feels powerless because it seems the administration and some teachers are out to get him. He then turns to chemicals in order to gain some control over his feelings. In other words, he unconsciously self-medicates to treat his depression. I, therefore, recommend no further disciplinary action. It is important that we help Paul, not punish him further. He does have good self-esteem, but like that of any teenager, it is fragile."

"Thank you," Dubcek said. "You nicely summed up my own conclusions."

Davis sat silent, wishing Randori were there to counter Dubcek's gambit logically. Much could be said about Roberge's behavior, but putting it in a special education context left Davis at a loss for words. It seemed more and more evident that Paul indeed qualified for emotional support. But Dubcek was moving on and Davis had to get his mind back to business.

"In peer relationships, Paul chooses friends who are clean. His parents report that some of the best students in the school call and visit him."

"How do you know that?" Marburg said, with a skeptical scuff on his words.

"Through statements Paul has made to both me and Ms. Gordon, who, I remind you, is also a psychologist. We have built-in checks in drug and psychological assessments that reveal when a student is being dishonest."

Marburg went into stentorian mode whenever he was caught off-guard or embarrassed at being outwitted. "You might as well use a crystal ball if you're going to make statements like that. Where are the reports from Paul's regular teachers? They'll answer a lot of questions." He had spoken to Roberge's teachers and was counting on their contribution to be damaging. This unanticipated end run by Dubcek, if permitted, would trump the case for the administration against Roberge. "Mr. Putty worked with Paul for one week. He's no substitute for six teachers."

"Through his SAP training he is a more astute observer when –"

The principal raised his voice, overriding Dubcek. "Your SAP team members go to three days of training and that makes them experts?"

Dubcek raised a finger to make a point, but reconsidered. He took a breath and sat back, pressing a self-indulgent smile onto his face. "I think we can disagree without becoming disagreeable. But I do have a protocol to follow."

A thought occurred to Davis: As long as Dubcek was stacking the deck, what was to prevent him from sneaking a peek at the cards, too? "I suppose you did the classroom observation, too."

"As a matter of fact, I did."

"That's Dr. Randori's job. You have to get input from a variety of sources. That's why it's called a *Multidisciplinary* Evaluation."

"I have found Dr. Randori to lack objectivity," Dubcek said through curled lips. "His observations are tainted by his personal feelings toward the student. I, on the other hand, am a psychologist, bound by impartiality. Now if I may continue—"

"No, you may not," Marburg interrupted, rising from his seat and pointed at Dubcek. "You have no information from the regular education teachers. This meeting is ending right now, and we're not going to reconvene until you get their input."

"And you have to enter Dr. Randori's observation into the record," Davis was quick to add. "You talk about objectivity, but you cherry-pick information to fit in with your predetermined conclusions and rig the rest of it to fill in the gaps. You don't care how much you damage the school or its students; all that matters is getting your way."

"That's not only unethical," Marburg said, "it's the kind of behavior that can cost you," the principal paused to level a stare on Gordon and Putty, "and any accomplices, your jobs and certification."

Having shocked Dubcek and his associates into silence, Marburg turned his attention to the Roberges. Scribbling on his legal tablet, he said, "I suggest you visit the county alternative school; its services can help Paul." He ripped a sheet out of the tablet. "Here's the number. This meeting will reconvene in a week. That will give Mr. Dubcek time to pull together the information he needs for a decent evaluation."

Mrs. Roberge looked to Dubcek, but the psychologist avoided eye contact, preferring to busy himself jotting notes into the Evaluation Report. The woman opened her mouth to speak when Marburg pre-empted her thought.

"Or we could just go straight to an expulsion hearing."

"Possibly," Paul's father stammered. "I mean, I guess we could at least visit."

"Very well," Dubcek said, although his face betrayed the belief that things were anything but very well. "We will reconvene in one week, if that works for everyone."

Dubcek asked the Roberges to stay after the meeting to review his testing results. When the room was clear, the psychologist checked the hallway and closed the door. "I just wanted an excuse to keep you here," he said. "Don't visit the alternative school."

Kass Marburg had reached a cloud nine high, augmented by just enough light lager to double-dot the "i" in euphoria. He had left work early for a round of golf, and it turned out to be the best he had ever played. Every year, his golf improved from spring through summer, and then, just as his game was getting good, autumn turned to winter and the weather forced a hiatus until the next spring, when he had to knock off the rust again. The cycle of life. But on this day, with September on the wane, autumn and Marburg's golf game were in early glory.

The day was nearly perfect and he wanted the feeling to last, so, despite having to get up for work the next day, it took little coaxing to get him to join his fellow golfers at the Miners Café for some beer and the best hamburgers in Freedom County. Marburg was a moderate drinker, but it was a day for celebration, and he became intoxicated, literally and figuratively.

Still, wanting to get to bed at a decent hour, he reluctantly bade goodbye to his friends and reeled off on a meandering route toward his car. The brisk night breeze brushed his hair and sent early fallen leaves hustling around his feet, giving him the sense that his body was merging with nature. He felt immortal.

Driving home, a melancholy pang burst his euphoric bubble: Kass Marburg's wonderful day was almost over. As he revisited all he had accomplished, though, his bliss returned. First, he had confronted Randori and put that bastard in his place for all to see, humbling, nay, humiliating him. And "karate boy" had been so fearful his eyes glazed over and he turned mute. After that came his artful handling of the MDE, proving that anything Randori could do he could do better. He grinned in recollection that he had dealt simultaneously with Leroy Dubcek and the Roberge problem that had made others quake in their boots.

He couldn't wait to tell Phil Olson. Perhaps the Acting Superintendent would demote Meryl Morgan to building administration and elevate Marburg into her position as Director of Secondary Education.

On this day, Kass Marburg confirmed that he was master of his building. To top it off, he had won enough friendly money playing golf to pay for his evening at the Miners Café and fulfill the winner's duty of buying a round of drinks. And, as he turned onto his secluded, tree-clustered cul-de-sac, he realized enough winnings remained to take his woman out to dinner at some romantic hideaway.

Yes, it had been a perfect day. It didn't get any better. Not for Kass Marburg.

As he wheeled into his driveway, the floodlight above his garage door did not turn on. He hoped it was just the bulb; the motion sensor cost more than the whole blasted thing was worth. Whatever it was, it could wait until tomorrow. Nothing was going to ruin his wonderful day.

Marburg cut his headlights and a sea of darkness engulfed him. The dense grove of maples surrounding his house afforded privacy, but most of their leaves had yet to give up the ghost, and their lush canopy swallowed the harvest moonlight. He opened the car door so the dome light would help him get his bearings as he flipped the trunk latch and edged to the rear to retrieve his golf clubs. Marburg considered leaving the door open to light his path until he could get inside the house and turn on the front porch light, but the beer had made him lazy.

Slamming the door, Marburg cast himself back into the inky night, and he had to feel his way to the front of the car until his vision adjusted to the darkness. Going more from memory than sight, he was inching past the garage when he heard glass crunch under his foot. Before he had time to consider how the glass got there, he heard leaves scurrying toward him. But there was no breeze; the dense grove blocked its flow.

Marburg started to turn toward the sound, but before he could fully react, a fist came from behind, ripping across the left side of his jaw, stunning him. The arm that followed wrapped across his mouth, smothering him, and a quick snap wrenched his head toward his left shoulder. He let out a muffled grunt as muscles and tendons strained their limits; his chin crushed against his clavicle. A voice said, "Trick or treat," and a keen chill cut across his exposed neck, allowing his head a dreadful freedom of movement. And Kass Marburg's wonderful day came to an end.

Harley Snitz hated early morning calls. They meant either trouble or a decision he had to make while cobwebs still draped his synapses. Fortunately, he got few of the former; unfortunately, he got too many of the latter. To avoid disturbing his family, he had gotten into the habit of waking early. Every morning at 4:45 he arose, did some light stretches and pushups, then went downstairs to start a pot of coffee. After that, he took the phone into the bathroom where he shaved and dressed—Snitz always showered the night before; he knew if he waited until morning, that was when the phone would ring. Finally, in uniform, he sat in the living room and read or worked on *New York Times* Sunday Crossword Puzzles until Aggie—Snitz's "first, last, and only love"—woke at 6:00 and they made breakfast together.

When the call came, Snitz picked up after the first ring. The night watch from the station didn't bother to apologize; he knew the Chief's routine. "We just got an anonymous call. Another car's in the quarry. Guy was pissing and moaning about us not doing our jobs. Figured I better call you right away. Ever since Big Bob went in, people have been pushing everything but the kitchen sink over the edge. Worst was the bastards that pushed the cow off. Think it's kids?"

"I haven't the foggiest," Snitz said with a dull edge he would have rather concealed. "Have you called Nick yet?"

"Just you. I figured you'd tell me what to do?"

"Thanks, I'll contact Nick," Snitz said. "Get a hold of Jim and tell him to meet me there. And tell him to cordon off the area, top and bottom, if he gets there first."

By the time Neidrich answered his phone, the Chief heard Aggie stirring in the kitchen. Snitz summarized the night watch's message and said, "I have a bad feeling on this one, Nick. Meet you there?" Snitz gently rehooked the receiver, but he hovered over the phone, staring into the middle distance.

A soft, pleasant voice interrupted his thoughts: "You want toast or something before you go?"

Snitz turned to find Aggie standing in the doorway. Her sweet smile warmed him, made him want more than anything to have breakfast with her and maybe go back to bed for a little while. He glanced away. "Thanks, but no, sweetheart. I'll pick up something along the way."

He was going to miss breakfast with Aggie; it was more than the break in routine that irked him. In the month since Samson's death, he had spent scant time with her. What bothered him most, though, was the sense of dread that accompanied the call. Since August, the quarry had been littered with all manner of debris: bicycles, badminton poles, old watermelons, young pumpkins, the cow, of course; someone with a well-honed sense of irony even threw in a kitchen sink. But only once before had a car gone in.

The rescue workers hooked the winch onto the car and began reeling it in. *The big ones sure are biting.* Snitz shivered with guilt for allowing the bizarre notion to enter his mind. It betrayed callousness, something he had always fought to avoid, particularly as his career entered its twilight. *Thoughts like those warn a fellow he just might've stayed on the job too long.*

That reflection lost in competition with another as Snitz realized he was taking in more information and handling things better than he had when they dredged up Samson. *Gain expertise, lose sensitivity—fair trade?* The homicide scene no longer made his mind race or blurred his perception. With that awareness came regret at the way he had handled the Samson crime scene before the State Police arrived. He had been the point man in a murder investigation. Folks were asking him what they should do, and darned if he knew. Even using his best judgment, he felt as if he and his men handled the crime scene like a bunch of rubes that had just found an unattended case of beer. Neidrich had told him he did just fine, but the Chief had a feeling that the trooper was being nice.

On this scene, Snitz was happy to allow the trooper to take control from the start. The entire area was cordoned off, and unauthorized trespassers were stopped and questioned before being ushered away. Molds and pictures were taken, gloves worn. Even the random freshly fallen branch was checked for threads, shreds, and blood. A State Police forensics team started going over the car before it was hauled up, before the body was extricated—Kass Marburg's body.

Neidrich huddled with the medical examiner as Snitz approached, taking care to sidestep the obstacle course of evidence markers. When he got within earshot, he picked up snippets of conversation: "Slashed throat" …"No accident." Neidrich noticed the Chief and said, "I need to talk to Harley. Stay put."

Neidrich touched Snitz's arm and motioned with his head toward their cars, halting only when they were a safe distance from invasive ears. Even then, he furtively scanned the area before speaking. "Let's move fast on this. I'll turn the scene over to my people. Can you have someone inform Marburg's family, then contact the school to find out if anyone knows where he was last night?"

"Kass lived alone, but I'll call Dorrie, his secretary. She's an old friend; if I tell her to keep mum, she will."

"For the time being, tell her Marburg was mugged. You mind lying to a friend?"

"I do, but it's probably best," Snitz said without conviction. He looked across the quarry to the bluff. "I will have to break the news to Kass's mom and dad."

"Can't you send one of your men?"

The Chief's face puckered with grim determination. "I need to do it, Nick. It's *my* job, not something I can lay on someone else."

After a quick consideration of the coarseness of Snitz's grit, Neidrich relented. "All right, but we have a lot to do, starting with a close look at Virgil Davis. Samson passed him over in favor of Marburg for the high school principal job. That could make for a grudge against both victims. Plus, his war experience would give him a whole different perspective on life and death."

"I look at it a little different," Snitz said. "I think Virgil values life more than most folks do because of that. He's really against violence now. Cripes, he's the one who started the Youth Violence Task Force in this county. And even though I don't think Dr. Randori is guilty either, something tells me he's more dangerous than Virgil."

"I trust your gut feelings on the people around—" Neidrich stopped mid-sentence as the Chief dropped his head and began rubbing his temples. "What is it, Harley?"

"A few minutes ago, I was thinking how much better I've gotten as an investigator since I started working with you, and here I am lapsing back into my old ways, letting my personal feelings cloud my objectivity."

Neidrich placed his hand on Snitz's shoulder. Smiling, he said, "Yeah? Well, maybe I treat everyone too much like a suspect. After I interviewed Randori, it was like I had a cloud over my head for days. For such an overall positive guy, he sure doesn't have much faith in human nature. What bothered me most is I realized I'm just as jaded as he is. You're not like that. After all your years as a cop, you still see people as being basically decent."

"Well, it keeps me from being a crackerjack cop."

"But it makes you a crackerjack human being. I'd rather be like you than like Randori." Neidrich looked off to some gloomy horizon. "Or me."

The Chief hoisted his chin. "When I put this uniform on, I need to be more like you. Now I'm doing that, and I'd be for thinking that maybe, just maybe, Dr. Randori and Virgil could've been in it together."

"Right. They have that 'us against the world' attitude, and they both feel a certain righteousness about how things ought to be." Neidrich speech took on a slow, pensive gait, as if he were fashioning a syllogism. "Righteousness grows out of honor; Davis has the honor of a soldier, and Randori has this weird kind of samurai honor. What if someone was so dishonorable as to lead the warriors to believe they had no recourse but violence? It's a small slip from righteousness to self-righteousness."

Snitz honed the point. "The difference between good intentions and bad."

The medical examiner's years of looking death in the eye gave his gaze an unwavering glint. "Possibly another Samson deal. Problem is, so many details about Dr. Samson's murder were leaked that I can't rule out a copycat. Both guys' faces were bashed; no paint chips this time, though. Both were finished off quick, and in both cases the knife was straight-edged, razor-sharp. This time, instead of a stab, like hara-kiri, there was a cut along the right side of the throat, severing the carotid artery. A dagger—which we know was used on Dr. Samson—is usually a stabbing instrument, although it can certainly cut crosswise, but in Kass's case we may be dealing with a different type of knife, and a different killer."

"Drawn from behind or slashed from the front?" Neidrich asked.

"Not sure yet. I do think Kass was killed somewhere else, and the body was transported here. So, there's a lot of blood somewhere; a cut like this, you'd get arterial spray like a garden hose. Some had to hit the perpetrator, his clothes. I'll be able to tell you more after I get Kass on the table."

"Let us know when you do." Neidrich turned to leave but stopped to add an afterthought. "Just one correction. My understanding is hara-kiri isn't a single thrust; it's more of a slash, a disembowelment."

The medical examiner frowned. "OK, if it's important I know that."

"It is," the trooper said. "There are already enough assumptions being made."

"I hear you. Look, I better get going if you and Harley want answers."

As the ME ambled off to get those answers from Marburg's body, Neidrich reflected on his words. Freedom was like any small town: it was easy to get information, hard to keep secrets, and impossible to stop rumors. He considered the problems inherent in working in an environment where lies and truths flowed freely and interlaced.

The reflection of sunlight off the windshield of the Chief's car prevented Neidrich from seeing inside the cab until he was almost at the door. Bending to speak, he bit off his words when he saw Snitz staring dumbly ahead, eyes unfocused, not so much as a twitch interrupting the dismal mask weighing down his face.

The trooper slid into the passenger seat, never taking his eyes off his partner, and let his hand fall gently on Snitz's shoulder. "You all right, Harley?"

Snitz's mouth gaped like a landed fish gasping for water; his lips parted, but no words came. Finally, in a raspy whisper he said, "Kass left school early yesterday for a round of golf. Dorrie gave me the names of some retired school people he usually played with."

Neidrich's frown deepened. "That's good news. Should be easy to piece his evening together."

Snitz's head dropped. "There's more." He lifted his cap and swept his forearm across his brow. "Before he left work yesterday, Kass suspended Dr. Randori for taking down Justin Frederickson at the football game. ... I just got word that Justin was found dead this morning, too."

Delivering the news of a loved one's death to family members had always been the worst part of Harley Snitz's job, but it was, nonetheless, his job—one he refused to delegate. He was good at it, though, because later when he attended the funerals—he always attended the funerals—family members thanked him for his sensitivity in their time of grief. Small solace. Adding to the burden, Snitz had grown up with Marburg's parents. He remembered none of the drive from the Marburg home to the station. A throbbing vise gripped his temples. Bowing his head to collect himself, his eyes fell on his badge. Every morning he stood in front of the mirror to pin it on his shirt, a private ceremony to remind himself of his mission. Most mornings, it seemed a weightless, impressed metal wafer, but now it was heavy, oppressive, almost more than he could bear; its hand of duty crushed the breath out of him.

Snitz entered the station; with each step, he made the conscious effort to level his emotions. He had to deal with them, but later. For now, he had to separate his personal feelings from his responsibility to the community. Passing the day dispatcher's desk, though, Snitz could not hide his feelings from Phyllis Utz, his long-time associate. "I hate this." That simple utterance seemed to exorcise the demon whose cloven hooves had been trampling his soul.

It helped that Jim, his youngest deputy, greeted him at his office door. Snitz smiled. The young officer's face—eagerness just beneath the professional surface—reminded him of another young officer from long ago. Since late August, Jim had quietly held down the fort and was, in effect, the acting chief while Snitz and Ed Knepp concentrated on their special assignments.

The deputy had been hard at work. "Marburg did play golf yesterday at the country club, then he went to the Miners Café with his usual crew: Killian, Hartman, Helsel. You know those guys—the worst any one of them would do is conveniently forget to count some golf strokes."

"Are we checking out their stories, anyway?"

Jim nodded. "Kass left them around 10:00 and headed home, or so they said."

"You doubt that?"

"No reason to. His clubs were still in the trunk when we fished the car out. Blood spray was on the bag but none on the clubs themselves, although he was blutzed pretty good on the face before or after he was stabbed."

"What do you make of that?"

"Quick guess, Kass was carrying the bag when he was attacked. Afterward, the killer threw the clubs in the trunk before taking the body to the quarry. Here's the big thing. Kass was ambushed outside his home. There's blood on the driveway, along with glass from the broken security light. Question is, why dump his body in the quarry?"

Snitz rose from his desk and trudged to his spot at the window. He always believed that when the panorama no longer transported him beyond his mundane concerns it would be time to retire. On this day, its charm was tested; the view seemed surreal, oddly out of place with the ugly events of the past month, and it was difficult to find peace, much less enlightenment. Turning away, he heaved a sigh, took one long, last pull of coffee, crushed the cup, and lobbed a shot at the wastebasket that caromed off the rim and spun to a stop in the middle of the floor. "I don't know."

Movement outside his office entered Snitz's peripheral vision. He glanced up to see Ed Knepp shuffling rapidly toward his office like a man who had something to say and was by-damn going to say it.

After fumbling with the knob the sergeant burst in, panting, and spluttered, "Justin Frederickson was found dead this morning."

"I know," Snitz said through forced calm. "You been on it?"

"He didn't wake up with his alarm," Knepp said between puffs for air. "That was nothing new, but when Billy went to check on him, he was clammy and bloated, hardly breathing, so Billy called me. I told him to call 911, and I beat feet over there. They rushed Justin to the hospital, but it was too late. We're waiting on the tox report, but I'm for guessing it was an OD."

"How's Billy doing?" Snitz asked.

"Bad. It wasn't the best time to ask questions. All I know is Justin was still grounded from that incident at the game; he was only allowed to hang out with Brad Prusster. But you know Billy works a second shift, so he can't enforce that."

"You'd best go over to the school and talk to Brad then." Snitz moved around his desk and gripped Knepp's biceps. "You took your own car this morning?"

Knepp frowned and took a wary tone. "Yeah, so?"

"You didn't have a radio or your cell phone. I have to tell you, last night was bad all around." Snitz gripped Knepp's arm tighter, as much to steady himself as to prepare his deputy for what he was about to say. "Kass Marburg was found in the quarry this morning. He's dead, Ed."

Knepp stutter-stepped backward and raised his hands as if to fend off the news. "How?" he groaned, barely above a whisper.

Snitz helped his deputy to a chair and hiked himself up on the edge of his desk, facing him. After filling him in he said, "This puts a new spin on the investigation."

"What spin? We all know Randori's the perp. You losing it or something?"

"It's something we have to consider, Ed," Jim said patiently. "Look at it a second. Whoever sent Samson into the quarry wanted to make it look like an accident—a bad cover, but a cover. But since the news media has picked up on it, everyone knows that." The young officer's gaze into Knepp's eyes intensified. Jim could have commented on the leaks to the media, but he kept to his point. "We have to ask, if it was the same killer, why would he repeat a scenario everyone knows is phony?"

"Maybe just to show us he could," Knepp said. He punctuated his statement by adding, "Duh! Randori might've kept his hands clean, getting druggies to help him. Don't forget, back when he was coaching at St. Thomas More, he supplied his players with drugs as a reward for winning games."

"I won't deal in rumors, Ed," Snitz snapped. "That one especially. I looked into that. Remember? Dr. Samson started it himself at the Miners Café. He was a good man in a lot of ways, but he couldn't stand to think someone might've been as good a coach as he was." The Chief stood and moved to his window. "Anyway, now you have Justin's death on top of your angle on the Samson investigation. You want help?"

"No," Knepp said, his voice clipped. "I mean, there could be a relationship between the two, but I think Justin was a straight OD."

Snitz eyes narrowed in an effort to bring his deputy's words into sharper focus. "OD? On what, cocaine?"

"Yup." Cocaine was no big news in Freedom County anymore. State and local police had been on top of it for decades, and, although it was still around, many of the local dealers had been busted, their pipelines to Reading and New York interrupted. The police patted themselves on the back for their efforts; Knepp himself had been among the self-congratulators until he had talked to little Brandon Prusster. He had forgotten that drug popularity flows in cycles: reduce the supply of one, and another rises in its place; ignore one, it resurfaces. "Horse"—heroin—hadn't reared its head since it was broken in the '70s. Knepp knew, once the cause of death was determined, he would have a small window of time before the State Police and others caught on and took matters out of his hands. *They think heroin is too big for a borough cop to handle, but I'll show them. Harley's always telling me to keep mum about a case; won't he be proud? And Harley won't be Chief forever. If I bust this heroin ring, heck, it might even shoo him off to retirement.* "Cocaine, that's what I think. And I better get back at it." After opening the door, he turned again to his colleagues. "I'm real sorry about Kass. Isn't it ironic? Kass, Billy Frederickson, and me all played on the same team for Big Bob."

"Sure is a coincidence," Jim corrected.

Knepp snapped his fingers, winked, and pointed at Jim. "An *ironic* coincidence," he persisted. "And there's another thing: Bob and Kass were killed exactly one month apart—August 26 and September 26. I'd be for thinking you better get Randori before October 26. You never know who's next." He repeated his Sinatra-like finger snapping, this time pointing at Snitz, before heading out of the station with more swagger than usual in his step.

Harley Snitz uncoiled out of his cruiser and headed into the high school. He was caught in the strange netherworld of contemplation: his body traveled through the physical world while his mind navigated through the magic-mirror world of reflection. This time he saw himself adrift in an unnerving time warp. Days ripped by, yet he had paged through a month in which progress seemed slow. He felt he should be taking in more information, and he should be making better use of the information already in his head. If only his mind worked like a computer, but then he remembered that the State Police computers were doing no better. Somehow, he knew that the answers he needed hid within the human heart, not in a hard drive. Pieces were missing, links that would tie everything together. The Chief just had to do the mental gymnastics, and he hoped, at his age, he still had the flexibility for the job.

The first thing Snitz noticed upon entering the school was the interest taken in his arrival. He felt the eyes, yet when he returned the glances, they quickly averted. Shrugging it off, he stopped at his friend's desk. "Thanks for your help, Dorrie. It's getting us off on a good foot."

The woman's eyes glistened with an incongruous blend of sorrow and steel, and they perched above a Mona Lisa smile that warned the Chief something was up. Dorrie rose, bringing her mouth close to his ear. Her whispered words brought goose bumps to his neck. "Harley, I know Kass is dead."

The Chief glanced around the reception area. "How did you hear?"

"You know the wrecker that pulled Kass's car out of the quarry? The driver's girlfriend is on our kitchen crew."

"I never could pull one over on you."

"Not even when you tried to be slick and started seeing Aggie behind my back."

Softness returned to her eyes, just as sweet as it was back in high school when she used to watch Harley get up from his desk to sharpened his pencil, back when he used to get up to sharpen his pencil so she would pay attention to him.

"Dorrie, you're lovely as ever."

She cupped her hand over her mouth and said, "Too late, you old fart. But then you're not here to see me anyway."

"I'd love to say I was, but there's a good woman who'd have my head. She doesn't mind me talking to Virgil Davis, though. He around?"

"In there with Mr. Wyatt. They're planning how they're going to deal with the fallout from these deaths."

"Deaths?"

"Come on, Harley," the administrative assistant said, pressing her palms against her cheeks. "Did I wear my stupid face to work today? Kass and Justin Frederickson."

Feeling guilty for misleading his friend, Snitz took her hand in both of his for a moment before turning away. He stopped at Davis's office door and glanced over his shoulder to find Dorrie watching him just as she did in the old school days; only now, concern etched deeper the furrows of the years. A grimace meant to pass as a smile was all he could muster before he turned again and peeked into Davis's office.

"Harley, come on in," Davis said solemnly, waving to a chair beside Wyatt.

"Is it all right? I know you're busy."

Wyatt patted his arm. "Please stay. I don't know how much information you can share, but part of our job is to dispel rumors."

"What do you have so far?" Snitz said with a wary sidelong glance.

"About Justin, mostly rumors we've heard from kids," Davis said. "Overdose?"

Snitz leaned forward. "Think you can get a line on where the rumors started?"

Davis gave a portentous nod to Wyatt. "Tough to trace rumors among students. They spread like wildfire. We'll try."

"I know Ed would appreciate anything you can dig up. He'll be stopping by to talk to some kids. Confidentially, it *might* have been an overdose, but that hasn't been confirmed. We'd like to check on his friends, especially if any are absent."

"We can do that," Davis said.

Snitz scrubbed his chin with his palm. "What do people know, or think they know, about Kass?"

"It's speculation," Davis said, "but the buzz is that Kass died a lot like Bob did."

"Doc's name has come up," Wyatt said, "especially from people who don't like him. Unfortunately, the timing couldn't be worse. Yesterday, Kass suspended him."

Snitz waited for more. He knew Wyatt well enough that it seemed odd for him to be without editorial comment, but all that followed was a tight-lipped frown. The longer the silence lasted, the more the weight of significance Marburg's suspension of Randori would carry, so he finally asked, "How did Dr. Randori respond?"

"Doc didn't say much—just kind of stared," Davis said, his physical response speaking more than his words. Absent was his typical direct communication, marked by piercing eye contact. Instead, Davis found an intense interest in the pen in his hand, twisting it as one might roll a cigarette. He added, "I should've defended him more."

"Don't let it bother you, Virgil," Wyatt said. "You see Harley, Doc and Virgil were to attend an important special education meeting. Kass and Phil Olson decided to suspend Doc without consulting me. It was critical that Doc or I be there; it was a very hostile family we were dealing with."

"I was surprised, though," Davis said, "Kass did a decent job at the meeting. He must've been feeling his oats after suspending Doc."

"Yes," Wyatt said, "but he did it through sheer bluster. He alienates people."

Davis chuckled. "I'll say. He alienated the family. *And* Leroy Dubcek."

"The psychologist?"

"Kass overruled Leroy at the meeting—Kass has been bucking Leroy a lot lately."

Snitz tried to maintain eye contact with Davis's riveting glare while making a mental note to check Dubcek out. "How so?"

"He broke up Leroy's little power game on the SAP and Crisis Teams. They had been overriding our disciplinary policy. Kass got fed up and ordered them to report to him on all their decisions. Leroy didn't listen so Kass had to kick his ass." Davis peered intently into Snitz's eyes. "Leroy takes it very personally when he doesn't get his way."

Wyatt shifted impatiently in his seat. "May I digress and conclude that we are dealing with yet another murder?"

"Possibly," Snitz said, tearing away from Davis's stare to note a brief brightening in Wyatt's eyes. "I guess I ought to ask each of you your whereabouts last night."

"I was here for a field hockey game after school," Davis said, "and last night we had a soccer game. Lois brought me some supper. She met me in my office and stayed with me while I did the game paperwork. I followed her home around 10:00."

"Exciting," Wyatt deadpanned.

Davis smirked. "I would've rather been at the opera, but my cape was at the cleaners with a mustard stain."

"Interestingly," Wyatt said, arching a brow, "I *was* at a performance—the Harrisburg Symphony."

"I assume there are folks who can verify that."

"Of course. I was with Meryl Morgan and another couple."

"Kerry, you dog!" Davis exulted, slamming both palms on his desk with rowdy joy, shattering the solemn pall that hung over the administrative offices. "A date with Meryl—fantastic! I was wondering when you two were going to get it on."

Wyatt blushed and shot a sneer at Davis on the second half of a double take before returning his attention to the Chief. "What Kass's death means as we counsel faculty and students is that, along with grief counseling, we will be dealing with the stress and fear associated with yet another murder."

"I better let you get back to your jobs," Snitz said, rising to leave.

Wyatt craned his neck toward the Chief. "Is there any reason we can't bring Doc back from suspension? We need all the counselors we can muster."

"If you two think Dr. Randori is OK to return to work, it's fine with me."

"Doc Randori is one of the finest men who's ever trod leather," Davis said, clucking his teeth and tilting his head in an emphatic diagonal nod.

Wyatt stared blankly at Davis before addressing Snitz. "I would add a similar sentiment if I had an equivalent command of the rural argot." He shifted his eyes to catch Davis's certain reaction. Upon receiving an appropriately indignant scowl, he continued, "Instead, I'll pass along something Doc once said to me: 'Winning a hundred times in a hundred battles is not the art of war; the art of war is to win without fighting.' "

Snitz nodded. "Sun Tzu."

Wyatt's eyes grew large, and he gave a respectful nod. "Why, I believe that is the source. I wouldn't have picked you as an aficionado of Eastern culture, Harley."

"I became one when Dr. Randori became a suspect. You realize that that quote came from *The Art of War* and that Sun Tzu was the preeminent guerrilla warrior of his time, around 2,000 years ago. His philosophy and tactics are still taught in military schools around the world. Mao Tse Tung lived by them, so did Ho Chi Minh." The Chief took a moment to bask in Wyatt's surprise. It was one of his rare guilty pleasures to watch people who had previously underestimated him come to the realization that there was more to Harley Snitz than met the eye. "You could say that both attacks—Dr. Samson's and Kass's—were won without fighting."

A brisk breeze whisked the driest leaves from the branches of the neighborhood oaks, rushing them into a playful zephyr around Nick Neidrich as he strode up Randori's walkway. Acorns popped under his shoes, and he craned his neck to allow his senses to take in the day. Out of the corner of his eye, he spotted Randori on the roof of his house, peering down at him from one of the hipped eaves that sloped to rain gutters on every side. The trooper shaded his eyes and called out, "Where's your fiddle?"

Randori chuckled and moved to the edge, dropping into a squat, a live gargoyle grinning down at the trooper. "You know, you don't have a bad sense of humor for a State Bull." He jerked his thumb toward the rear of the house. "Meet me around back."

Neidrich skirted the perimeter and searched upward, locating Randori above an attached garden shed. He watched the counselor step off the roof, take the steep slope of the shed in two steps, stoop, and in one nimble, silent movement spring onto a brick window ledge with his right foot and push off, landing in a soft crouch on the ground.

"You sure you don't have some mountain goat in your blood?"

"Don't tell Lynn I do that. It's a pain in the ass getting the ladder every time." Randori stripped off his work gloves and gripped Neidrich's hand. "I assume you're here on business."

"Yep," the trooper grunted, surveying the trees in Randori's yard as they headed toward the back door that led into the sunroom. "Those are pear trees, right? What's with you and pears?"

"I like them," Randori said with an inflection that deterred further inquiry.

Neidrich slumped on the sunroom divan as Randori punched a button on a small sound system and said, "Lynn's out shopping and won't be back till about 3:00, so we can get into whatever detail you want, but first, I'll get us some coffee." While the counselor was in the kitchen, Neidrich got into the flowing interplay of Pat Metheny's guitar and Lyle Mays' piano and the view of the sun-dappled backyard greenery. Occasional leaves fluttered down, tugged free of their moorings by the seemingly perpetual breeze that rambled through the branches of the hilltop yard. Transfixed by music seamlessly attuned to the setting, Neidrich felt his body sink into cushioned relaxation.

"Nice, huh," came a voice from behind, shattering the tranquility.

The trooper spun to alert, half rising. His startled reaction brought Randori to a sudden halt, causing coffee to lap up the sides of the mugs in his hands.

"Jeez, don't scare me like that," Randori said. "I almost wasted coffee."

"Don't sneak up behind me."

"Sorry, Nick," Randori said, offering a mug and sitting across from the trooper. "But this is full-blast Costa Rican. It must be cared for."

"Marburg put you on suspension yesterday. What was that about?"

"Suspension with pay." The counselor held up a finger to emphasize the distinction. "That's one thing the union ensured, although I think Tammy Eboli could have fought for me just a little. It's a bad rap. I supposedly roughed up a student." He jerked to attention. "That's right, you were there."

Neidrich nodded. "From what I saw, you went out of your way to avoid hurting the boy, especially since he attacked you with a chain. And it did seem like he attacked you, not the kids from Freedom City. Was it the angle I had, or what?"

"Hard to say. Some kids don't buy my act. Especially when I'm taking them into alternative ed. They see it as punishment rather than an opportunity to help themselves."

"Tangent."

Randori flicked his fingernails against his cheek and glanced off. "I don't know Justin other than to see him. I do know some of his friends, though. Racists, drug-involved—proverbial apples near the trunk, in many cases."

"Seems unfair, suspended for breaking up a fight. You used Aikido, right?"

Randori nodded. "With Moo Duk Kwan force is often met with force. Even blocks can bruise or disable."

"And with Aikido, you turn the attacker's momentum against him."

"Very good, Nick. To use the old hippie phrase, 'go with the flow.' Make no mistake, you can lay some serious hurt with Aikido, but it's also easier to avoid injury—to my opponent or to me. That's important; I don't heal as fast as I used to."

"I'm a strong believer in the martial arts. We had training at the Academy. That sneaky stuff you do—Ninjutsu?"

" Ninjutsu, the art of the assassin. I see where you're going."

"There aren't a whole lot of people training in that around here."

"No one I know of. And I'm not, either. I just read a little."

"That's not a good way to learn a martial art," Neidrich said. "Kind of like the man who defends himself in court."

"True. The only plus is, I do have formal training in another art so I can reason some things. But I'm in no way accomplished; that would be an insult to an expert."

More humility. "Why would a respectable family man study Ninjutsu?"

"I used to teach history."

Neidrich chuckled. "That was a crap answer."

"That 'sneaky stuff,' as you called it, isn't Ninjutsu; it comes from the running technique I learned to reduce the pounding on my legs after my knee operations."

"OK, but why read about Ninjutsu?" Neidrich pressed.

Randori leaned back and cocked his head, sizing up the trooper before he answered. "It's just good to be prepared. I don't want to come across as a militia type or some kind of extremist."

"Try me."

"A few years ago, I was talking to Son Wills, the superintendent at City. This was around the time the government was really getting into giving perks to the wealthy and big business at the expense of social services for people who can't get their REM going on the American Dream. Son said that the way things were going this country could polarize. And now it's worse than ever. Extremist talk jocks exploit the situation, widening the divisions, and they're the biggest hypocrites."

The counselor's voice was calm—too calm, because his eyes burned with fervor, which Neidrich found unnerving. Recently, he had gone to Randori's hometown to check into the suspect's background, and some of the details he had unearthed raised concern. Here was his opportunity to discover the depth of Randori's disturbance.

"How are they hypocrites?"

Randori seemed to sense Neidrich's intent, for he sat back and his eyes softened to match a benign, professorial tone. "People who take a stance on the fringe—far Left or far Right—have to spin information to fit their version of the truth. The very sins they condemn in their enemies, they have to excuse in their own, and vice versa."

"They do have their First Amendment right to free speech."

"They have the *right,* but where is their sense of *responsibility?* They pit American against American, under the banner of patriotism, of course, which is ironic, since they apply all the propaganda tricks of the Nazis.

"Some politicians are even worse. They claim to have vision, but most of them couldn't find their asses with ten lobbyists and a bipartisan panel. Plus, a lot of them were children of privilege; they've never known—really known—the other end of the socioeconomic spectrum, so they can't identify with it. To paraphrase Van 'the Man' Morrison: 'they're flyin' too high to see my point of view.' "

"What does all this have to do with you and martial arts?"

"You probably noticed that Freedom Con is a prime example of one system housing both *haves* and *have-nots.* Schools are a microcosm of society, and, like I said, society is becoming less and less civil. Look how street gangs are recruiting, growing, moving beyond the big cities into towns like Freedom. Hate groups are growing at the other end of the lunatic fringe—central PA is a hotbed of them, you know. And where will you and I end up? Right in the middle."

"Are you predicting a class war? A revolution?"

"Jeez, I hope not. But you know one of the precipitating factors of the French Revolution was that ninety-eight percent of the wealth was held by two percent of the population."

"That was a different time and a different situation."

"Like I said, it's worst case. Maybe I'm around the seamy side too much."

Neidrich finally understood why people never took the middle ground with Randori. Some of his own ideas were extreme, and he didn't mind sharing them. But had he gone beyond mere preparation to act upon his beliefs? Had he concluded that those who opposed him must be eliminated? "You see yourself as a crusader?"

"A crusader? You think too much of me, Nick. It's just that I have to deal with people who put their pride, their egos, above what's right for kids. I'm not going to take that crap from anyone." The counselor abruptly stood and moved toward the kitchen. "But I am going to get more coffee."

Randori left the room, followed by Neidrich's glower. The trooper wanted to pursue the line of conversation that might determine his suspect's homicidal mindset; now the line was cut. *Had Randori realized he revealed too much then left to regain his composure?* Before Neidrich could answer his question, the counselor reappeared, holding out a carafe of coffee. He poured for both, keeping a steady hand as Neidrich said, "Who won't you take crap from?"

Randori scanned Neidrich's face then searched his eyes. "I think you used the word 'crusader' to pretty up your question, but it was *vigilante* you wanted to say."

Harking back to his conversation with Dr. Kaminsky at Farmcove, Neidrich had meant to plumb the depths of Randori's vigilantism, and the counselor had seen through his euphemism. He had underestimated the man's powers of perception. Of vigilance? Of paranoia? A lot to think about, but for the time being, the lesson to be learned was to be careful of every word, inflection, gesture, and expression when interrogating Randori. Neidrich broke away from his thoughts, realizing the counselor was smiling at him. Had these reflections lasted a millisecond or long moments? And what had they revealed?

"Yes," Randori said, "it's true, and it's all right, Nick; I won't waste time talking about the effect all this has on kids. We'll stick to who I don't like and who doesn't like me: which is just about any administrator and, of course, Tammy Eboli."

"What's your problem with Ms. Eboli?" Neidrich asked, forcing a flat affect.

"Good question; I'm not sure there's a good answer, though. If you interviewed her, you'd know there doesn't have to be provocation; if you haven't interviewed her, you should, because she and Bob were tight ever since the last negotiations. Big problem."

"Why's that?" The trooper knew the answer, but he wanted Randori's thoughts.

"Imagine the superintendent and the Association president ganging up on me. I wouldn't have a chance. Like when she and Leroy Dubcek used to double-team Kerry Wyatt. Those two are ruthless. Lucky for me their energy is directed at each other now."

"I guess attacks like that are hard to forgive, or forget." Again, Neidrich glanced at his watch. It was time to zero in, to find out how close to the surface the man's pride dwelled. "Like when Marburg suspended you."

"You know who I am, Nick. You checked on me back in my hometown. What have you concluded?"

"Your childhood was no day at the beach."

"I never much cared for the shore."

"Your family –"

"My family lives under this roof." Randori's voice lowered to an ominous purr, even in interrupting Neidrich. The easy smile was gone, the jaw set.

"Easy, Doc. I know your parents have passed on; no need to open old wounds. But I'm out to find a murderer, so it's aberrations I'm looking for." Neidrich peered intently into Randori's eyes and turned an imaginary doorknob with his hand. "The twists of mind that make a person a killer. What was it Nietzsche said? Something like: Whoever battles monsters had better make sure that in the process he doesn't become a monster. And if you gaze long into the abyss, the abyss will gaze back into you."

"And you think that deep down I might be a monster?"

"Let's just say I know inmates on death row who went through less as children."

Randori's glare amped up the passion in his response: "Those people are weak. They buckled. When life deals you stems and seeds, you overcome."

Neidrich gave a disarming smile. "I know you went through that, too."

The counselor's gaze softened, his eyes crinkled as he let out a small chuckle. "And I won't claim I never inhaled, but it was part of my journey. This prince has some warts left from the frog he once was."

"Yes, and they have names: Social Anxiety Disorder, Reactive Attachment Disorder, and Oppositional Defiant Disorder. I just wonder if they add up to murder."

"When you use psych-jargon, it sure sounds that way. And Lynn would probably add Obsessive Compulsive Disorder to your list. I prefer to think I'm not a real social, trusting guy, but I am a royal pain in the ass to anyone who tries to tell me what to do, all because I never had strong parental ties." Randori smiled. "Simply put, I'm your garden-variety shithead."

Neidrich showed no appreciation of the glib summary, and the counselor's smile dropped. "Look, Nick, you're not telling me anything I don't already know. And it's a good thing I have that awareness or I might've become the nasty bastard you're suggesting. But I've had a lot of years to work that stuff out." Randori pointed to his temple. "Sure, I have demons stomping around, but they're my demons; I embrace them as part of me, and, so, I control them." Randori sat back to allow his words to sink in and added, "And neither Bob nor Kass were able to make me lose that control."

"Samson and Marburg had a lot in common," Neidrich said, studying Randori. "For one thing, you had an uncanny knack for bringing out the worst in them."

"I know why Bob didn't like me, and it was right back at him." A wry grin crawled up one side of Randori's face. "But I can't understand why Kass hasn't been utterly captivated by my charm and good nature. You have to understand him, though; he has low self-esteem." The counselor lifted his mug as if offering a toast. "And it's richly earned. That's one thing those two didn't have in common: Bob had ego to spare, although I'm sure we could have a very boring discussion over whether arrogance and the need for power are symptoms of high or low self-esteem. Bottom line: The faces they showed the world were identical."

"They have another thing in common now. They're both dead."

Randori's eyes hooded. "Uh-huh, that's why you're here."

"You don't seem upset."

The counselor's stolid facade held firm as he responded in a soft voice: "Kass's death won't create a vacuum in my life."

"Where were you last night?"

"Home watching the kids. Again. Lynn was working. They went to bed around 8:30, and Lizzie never falls asleep right away. I check on them while they're awake."

"Any phone calls? Anyone stop by to fix your time?"

"I called Lynn before the kids went to bed—around 8:00. I couldn't find the TV remote. She didn't think that was a good reason to disturb her at work." Randori smiled.

"Anyone else beside you have bad blood with Marburg?"

At first, the counselor said nothing, and he squinted in thought. "Lots of people, but no one who could've done something like this."

"I need your help," Neidrich said through a skeptical frown. "People like a simple answer, and right now you're it. Now, I don't think you did in Samson or Marburg. It's too pat. Besides, your knowledge of Sun Tzu contradicts it."

"How's that?"

"After winning in battle, don't repeat your tactics in the next battle; prepare to attack in an infinite variety of ways." Neidrich cocked his head modestly to acknowledge Randori's approving nod. "But I still have to take care of business, and you have to give me something to go on."

"I told you what I know."

"Not enough," Neidrich summed up, disapprovingly. "What about Virgil Davis?"

Randori shook his head dismissively. "I don't see it. Virge is loyal beyond any rational basis. Kass could slap his face and Virge would do his bidding a minute later. Besides, I think he enjoys the suffering just so he has something to complain about."

The phone rang, and Randori glanced at the receiver. "It's Kerry Wyatt." He picked up. "Kerry, what's up?" ... "Uh-huh, Trooper Neidrich told me." ... "He's here." ... Randori flicked a suspicious glance at Neidrich. "No, he didn't say anything about Justin." ... "Let me ask." Holding the receiver away from his face, Randori raised his chin toward Neidrich. "You see any reason I can't go in to work?"

"No," the trooper said, "in fact it would be good." He knew that refusing the request would open the door for people at Freedom Con to assume Randori's guilt.

Randori spoke into the receiver: "I'll be in as soon as I can, but it'll be come as you are." ... "All right. Later." As he disconnected the call, he looked back to the trooper and grinned. "You didn't tell me about Justin."

"That's Ed Knepp's case."

"Yeah, well, Ed has that a little confused, doesn't he? He's been checking on me. The night of the fight at the game, remember? Ed showed up, saying he heard it on the scanner. Think about it. It happened; we responded. There were no calls." Randori noticed

Neidrich check his watch again. "The clocks don't change for another month."

Neidrich sighed. "A team is coming to search your home. Sorry, I have to cover the bases." He started to reach into his pocket. "You want to see the warrant?"

"No, I just hope they're low profile—the neighbors, you know. And I'd like you to stay and oversee things."

"I planned on it." Neidrich stood and picked up his cup to take it to the kitchen.

The men arrived at the front door in time to see a white van pull into a space in front of Neidrich's sedan. Stenciled on the side were the words *Acme Carpet Cleaners*. Men in work clothes emerged and began to tote carpet scrubbers and briefcases up the sidewalk to Randori's door. The counselor let out a choked-off laugh and said, "If a coyote gets out of that van, I'm sticking around." He bowed his head in a quick salute of respect to the trooper. "Thanks for doing this while my kids are at school."

"I'm just treating you as I'd like to be treated. I kind of like you, Doc."

"Well then, let me give you some free counseling. You *kind of* like Cat Blanchard, and she *kind of* likes you." Randori paused to parry Neidrich's quizzical frown with a cagey smile. "Come on, you two have been flirting ever since you met at the football game. Ask her to dinner. I can recommend some good Italian restaurants. Nothing like red sauce and cabernet to fan the flames."

Ed Knepp waited while a secretary called Brad Prusster to the office. The two activities that dominated his time were writing reports and waiting. He often thought that any young person aspiring to a career in law enforcement should shadow him on his job before committing. Presenting the DARE program convinced him that he might have become a great teacher and coach, maybe even a counselor. Those jobs were interesting every day—exciting, too, if one's adrenaline flowed at the prospect of influencing young people's lives. Maybe not the fodder for action movies, but it was the drama of real life. And if he needed more, he could always perform the high school equivalent of law enforcement and become an assistant principal. In a school the size of Freedom Con, though, the work rate was nonstop. Knepp concluded that the continuous, low-level stress would wear on a person. People need down time. He had learned to handle the waiting part of his job in a positive way, by recharging his emotional batteries and reflecting on the case at hand.

His thoughts drifted toward stemming the tide of drugs in the county. If Justin's fatal overdose were to have any meaning, it would be to drive the lesson home that drugs aren't a way of life; they're a way of death.

Earlier, he had stopped by the hospital and learned that the chief medical examiner had been called out on another case—Kass Marburg, as it turned out. He was in luck. The physician examining Justin's body was an old acquaintance and had no problem sharing information with Knepp:

"Lungs filled with fluid. The kid literally drowned in bed while he was sleeping. In fact, he was dead at his home; they were just more comfortable pronouncing him dead at the hospital. I can't say with one hundred percent certainty what killed him just yet, but if you'll settle for ninety-nine, tests showed a high level of heroin. His pupils were pinpricks, and he had vomited. I saw a lot of this back when I was doing my internship in Boston at St. Eligius, but it's my first one here. I didn't find track marks, but there's significant deterioration of the nasal passages, like coke would produce. My guess: he was a multiple drug user, and he used both coke and heroin."

The chill brought on by his conversation with little Brandon Prusster had returned, and Knepp barely choked out his question to the physician. *"Did you ever run into heroin that's snorted?"*

"Not around here. I'd be very concerned if that stuff hit town big time. There's no high like heroin, but historically its use was kept down because of the taboo against using a needle. Take that away, and we have a problem. It's not a real expensive high. And people think it's safer since they're not mainlining, so it'll cross socio-economic boundaries; the whole community will be at-risk. But what kids don't realize is that snorting it is just as addicting. Is that why I didn't find track marks?"

"No, I just heard about it, is all. I was curious. Is it possible he shot up under his tongue or something?"

"Could have. Junkies shoot up anywhere. I heard about a guy that shot up in his eye. Don't worry, I'll find out what happened."

"Have you told the city police?"

"No, I want to complete my exam. You're the first to know even this much."

Upon hearing that, Knepp's mind had begun scrambling. When it came to drugs, he knew he was better informed than the Freedom City police were, but they had an arrogant attitude toward the law officers in the surrounding boroughs. If they knew there was a heroin problem, they would call in the State Police and make it a regional effort. It would be out of his hands. Knepp decided to call in an account. He had once hushed up a DUI involving the physician's son, a charge that would have been difficult to explain to Freedom Con's National Honor Society selection committee. In the end, Knepp took a risk that would either make his career or end it:

"Give me a copy of the tox report when you're done. I'll tell Justin's dad and handle the media. Don't talk to anyone. This is pertinent information to a criminal case and it's important no one knows we're dealing with heroin until I say so. That includes other police; I don't want them blowing my case."

Dorrie's voice brought Knepp back to the present. "We can't find Brad. He's not on the absentee list, but he's not in class, either. He must've gone AWOL."

"May I see that list?" Knepp said with a canny glance.

The secretary fetched the paper and escorted Knepp to the attendance office. "Flora here can help you. Anyone who was missed earlier or came in late would be updated on her records. You need anything more, give me a holler."

Knepp thanked Dorrie then asked Flora, "Any updates on Brad Prusster?"

"I have skip slips every period on him. I was about to let Cat Blanchard know."

"Has Brad been a problem in the past?"

"Brad's a good kid," Flora said, wagging her head for emphasis. "Some of his friends, though, oh boy!"

"Any of them absent?"

The woman ran her finger down the sheet. "Looks like they're all here, but considering the circumstances they would show up." Knepp's creased brow prompted Flora to add, "Come on, Officer, those guys know if they're absent today, people will think they know something about Justin's overdose."

"Word's out?" Knepp cleared his throat to cover a surprised crack in his delivery.

"So it *was* an overdose," the woman said, a gleam of revelation in her eyes. "I heard the rumor, but I didn't know if kids started it or if it was just an educated guess by people who knew Justin." She leaned forward and whispered, "Everyone suspected he was a user. We kept an eye on him."

Knepp's pride in his newfound discretion took a wallop as the realization hit that he may never overcome this particular weakness. Sweat beaded on his brow and cheeks, and he took a self-conscious swipe with an open hand to erase the vestiges of his humiliation. "Don't say anything to anyone, OK?"

Flora crossed herself and kissed her thumb. "Promise," she said with dubious sincerity. Quickly recalling his attention to the attendance sheet, she flipped it over. "On this side are the odd absences: kids on homebound instruction, field trips, suspensions."

Knepp examined the list. First was the in-school suspension roster. There were seven names on the list, some familiar to him, and one name on the out-of-school suspension list: Paul Roberge. "Is Paul still out because of the drug situation?"

Flora nodded. "Ten days."

"Can we call his home?"

"Sure." She picked up the phone. "I should have him on speed-dial."

"Are kids on out-of-school suspension supposed to stay home?"

"If their parents have any control over them, yes, but that kid does pretty much what he wants. "It's ringing. ... Nope. You want to leave a message?"

Knepp shook his head. "No thanks."

As soon as the attendance officer hung up, the phone rang. She answered as Knepp mouthed another thanks and began to move off, but she beckoned him back.

"Hold on." She cradled the receiver against her shoulder and glanced up at Knepp. "One of our teachers has his class on a field trip. When their bus left campus, he saw a boy getting into a car outside the library exit. That's a favorite escape route."

"Ask what the kid looked like and what kind of a car he got into."

Flora repeated the message and paused. "Thanks, Gary. And next time, could you call right away instead of waiting till lunch? Virgil likes to know these things ay-sap."

Hanging up, she said, "Gary's description fits Brad; he couldn't see the driver, though. He said the car was a white Pontiac, maybe a GT."

The attendance officer pulled several stapled sheets of paper out of the top drawer of her desk. She searched the pages and shook her head. "Nope, not on the student parking list. Do you want me to check the faculty list?"

Feigning nonchalance, Knepp said, "Yeah, just out of curiosity." He had a suspicion but was not about to let the cat out of the bag again.

Flora frowned as she ran a finger down the page. "No Pontiac, GT or otherwise."

Knepp thanked her and backed out of the office after requesting that she contact him if she got any word on Brad. He decided to swing by Davis's office before leaving.

The assistant principal was on the phone. When he looked up and saw the officer in the doorway, he said, "Got to go, someone's here. Love you."

Knepp entered and sat without waiting for an invitation. "You ought to have that receiver surgically implanted on your ear, Virgil. You're always on the phone."

Davis did not acknowledge Knepp's joke. "What's up, Ed?"

"I'm looking into Justin Frederickson's death. I came to see Brad Prusster, but he's absent. Well, he was here, but he left."

"Walked out, huh; doesn't sound like Brad." Davis grabbed the attendance sheet.

"Don't waste your time. Someone in a white Pontiac picked up someone that fit Brad's description down by the library. Know who it might've been?"

"Doesn't ring a bell."

"I'm for thinking he left with Paul Roberge. He wasn't home when we called."

"No surprise there. Both parents work. Putting that kid on out-of-school suspension is like giving him a vacation."

"Don't you send anyone out to check on these kids?"

"You mean like a Home and School Visitor? If you recall, I wanted to hire one and Bob nixed it. And believe it or not, the counselors don't have time to do it. That was Bob's dumb-ass idea." Davis took a deep breath and patted his pockets as if searching for something then glanced up with a melancholic wince before ratcheting back his ire. Crossing himself, he added, "God rest his dumb-ass soul. … Actually, the parents should take responsibility for Paul. I know both of them work, but they could tell him they're going to call home, and he'd best answer or he'll be grounded longer. Or they could have him stay with relatives or go to work with one of them. Aw shit, that'll never happen."

Knepp smiled with sympathy. "I'll check Brad's house. I'll look in on Roberge, too, and let you know what I find." He bowed his head and twirled his hat between his index fingers. "How are things here? Bet everyone's pretty shaken up about Kass."

"The counselors are busy with kids. Leroy Dubcek is handling the faculty. I don't think he's real busy, though; the teachers don't have time to mourn. They have to be strong for the kids. Besides, only Leroy's cronies would go to him, and none of them are feeling grief over Kass. He had been coming down on their god, Leroy, a lot, lately."

"Sometimes a manager has to step on toes. Like Big Bob did. I wish Harley and Nick would've just nailed that coward Randori. Then Kass would be alive today."

Davis rose to signal an end to Knepp's visit. "Ed, that's something you and I will just have to disagree on."

Knepp rocked back then pitched forward, counting on momentum and a hefty push on his knees to jack himself out of the chair. "You and Randori are pretty tight, aren't you? And neither of you liked Bob or Kass. It doesn't pay to be close to Randori; you know that, Virgil? Someone might think you were in on those murders together."

Ed Knepp drove to Brad Prusster's house. He thought the boy was too smart to go home until after school was dismissed, but it was worth the trip, if only to see the old neighborhood. Returning to Avalon induced a spasm of nostalgia in Knepp, like visiting an aging parent. The neighborhood that had sheltered his youth wore the potholed-macadam, cracked-concrete stamp of municipal neglect, and the dingy, paint-chipped, weed-overgrown badge of derelict homeowners.

Avalon, the enchanted Arthurian isle. Knepp chuckled at the comparison as he slammed his car door and trudged up the steps to the Prusster home. He looked at Avalonians as losers whose pride was little more than a shell of bravado recalling glory days that never were. From the time Avalon rose like a pimple out of the mill grime of East Freedom, neighborhood kids bred with other neighborhood kids. That, along with air pollution, lead paint, drugs, alcohol, and a low priority set on education made each successive generation of Avalonians a bigger group of losers than the one before. Rare were the success stories of Avalon—stories like Ed Knepp.

He raised his hand to knock, but Ronnie Prusster beat him to the punch, swinging the door open just enough for the dank odor of alcohol and cigarettes to hit Knepp's face like a fist with the letters *s-t-i-n-k* written on it. Unshaven and unkempt, Prusster's hollow cheeks and sunken eyes bore testimony to years of self-abuse. It had been awhile since the deputy had seen him, and he stepped back, as much in shock at the man's appearance as from the stench that issued forth.

Prusster's lip curled into a snarl. "Got a warrant, Ed?"

"Got something to hide, Ronnie?" Knepp shot back. "I'm just looking for Brad."

"Brad's a good kid," Prusster hitched himself to full height, which was shorter than Knepp remembered. "He's at school."

"He walked out, left with someone in a white Pontiac. Know who that'd be?"

"No, what do you want with him?"

"Justin Frederickson's dead."

"I heard. Brad had nothing to do with that."

"Didn't say he did, but he might know something. They were best friends."

"Brad doesn't know anything."

"I'm glad you know your son so well," Knepp said. He wanted to end the exchange before the almost visible smell made him retch. "Call me as soon as you hear from him. If you don't, I'll be back. And next time—"

"Yeah, yeah, I'll call." Prusster scowled before shutting the door on Knepp.

"Ass," Knepp said, turning to leave.

"I heard that," came a voice on the other side of the door.

"You are that," Knepp hollered over his shoulder. He knew Ronnie Prusster wanted nothing less than another visit from a cop, so his compliance would be assured, if not enthusiastic.

Next stop: Paul Roberge's house. After passing through Campton, the small crossroads community where he and Molly lived, Knepp's spirits rose along with the terrain as he entered the groves of Culver Pond, and he smiled in the faith that someday they would have a home there.

Developed in the 1920s as a getaway for the wealthy, it was a rare community founded for the sole purpose of recreation. Its rustic charm attracted artists, and by the late 1930s, a small colony had taken up residence in Culver Pond proper. In the surrounding hills, wealthy professional families, some from as far away as Philadelphia, built "cottages" more elaborate than many people's homes. The wooded hills afforded a serene retreat from summer humidity, as residents and visitors swam in the natural lake and picnicked and hiked along clearings and trails that webbed the forest. A band shell and a theater housed local productions, hosting once-famous entertainers whose faded stardust carried them to smaller venues.

Driving along the shaded streets, Knepp imagined himself on his way home from work. Narrow lanes meandered in a lackadaisical effort to link the driveways of homes that had sprung up on the hillside following only the tectonic logic of terrain. The oldest cottages, immaculately kept Victorian-style clapboards; the newer homes, earth-tone stucco and stone that blended into the surrounding hills.

On the way to Roberge's house, Knepp's car rambled along the road that linked the post office, the theater, and several small restaurants. Passing by the roller rink and the soda shop—popular teen hangouts—he found no white Pontiac, no boys. He downshifted and climbed away from what he called the artsy-fartsy community into the residential area, where land and homes often required two incomes to afford. He crossed roads named Whitman and Thoreau (no "Avenue" or "Boulevard" attached to the wooden street signs) until he came to Dickinson.

Knepp pulled into the Roberges' driveway and got out of the car. Passing along the front of the house, he peered into each window, spying neither movement nor light. No one answered the door, so he returned to the driveway, along the way peering into the empty two-bay garage; reasonable, he thought, as both parents worked. Culver Pond was isolated; a vehicle was required to get anywhere outside the village.

On his way back to the car, he thought about the white Pontiac and remembered that, except for in-season athletes, only seniors had parking privileges; the cars of most underclassmen would not show up on the list. Knepp grimaced, knowing he had to call in to the station. He always felt guilty lying to the Chief, but he had to check in to avoid arousing suspicion and concern—and he had to find out who owned that car. To Knepp's relief, Phyllis said Snitz was out of the office, and she was too busy fending off the media to ask questions, offering only mild complaint when he asked her to run a make on the car, starting with GTs and the older Grand Ams, and then move to all white Pontiacs.

After hanging up, Knepp jotted notes in his private logbook, the one that he had bought that morning to record information he wanted no one else to know. On occasion, the Chief wanted to review his cases with him. At those times, Knepp had to produce his official logbook from its ever-present location in his hip pocket so Snitz could check it himself in an effort to divine patterns or clues. Knepp's official logbook made no mention of heroin or Paul Roberge, although Brad Prusster's name, along with several other friends of Justin Frederickson, did appear. Reviewing those names in his mind, Knepp decided to return to the school to question students. He shoved the private logbook under the driver's seat and headed out.

Interviewing students at Freedom Con was no piece of cake. Knepp asked Cat Blanchard for help, but she balked at allowing the sergeant to question students; she felt that, having just lost a friend, they would be too distraught. With less than two hours remaining in the school day, he convinced her to check with Virgil Davis. The more experienced administrator told Blanchard to get the boys, reasoning that they all knew "Officer Ed" from the DARE program, and the police had questioned most of them at one time or another, anyway. Blanchard just had to inform the parents beforehand.

All the conference rooms were being used for grief counseling, so Blanchard led the sergeant to the administrative break room for his interrogations. The assistant principal left to make phone calls, and Knepp watched her until she rounded the corner out of sight before asking an administrative assistant for a key to Marburg's office.

With one eye on the door, Knepp tugged on the top drawer of the principal's desk. It was unlocked, left open after the earlier sweep of the office by Neidrich's State Police investigative team. The contents consisted mostly of bureaucratic memos, directives, and procedures—*administrivia* was the term he had heard to describe it. One memo, though, stood out. It had been sent from Bob Samson three years ago, labeled "Confidential" and carried the superintendent's directive that it be destroyed after reading. Knepp realized the note held circumstantial evidence against Randori. He quickly pocketed it and shut the drawer.

Although Knepp and Marburg had never been close, they had known each other since their days as football teammates. As adults, they attended parties at Bob Samson's home when he celebrated football championships. On those occasions, Marburg avoided the deputy, preferring to rub elbows with administrators and prominent citizens. Those memories buffered Knepp's grief. What did bother him was evidence of a life interrupted: an appointment book with meetings Marburg had scheduled, never realizing he would be dead by the time they convened. The last day of his life had only two entries: "Randori," then "Roberge MDE."

For the most part, those entries yielded as much information as Justin's friends did. During the questioning, every boy seemed fearful, but when pressed, each one claimed he was just upset about his friend's death. No one saw Justin, no one knew whom he was with, and no one heard anything. Knepp thought some even got snippy with him. Zack Boyer, a boy with whom he always enjoyed a good relationship, had pounded the table and yelled, "Do you want me to end up like Justin?" Knepp recalled Virgil Davis questioning Justin at the football game and getting a similar reaction.

Boyer was the last student Knepp interrogated, and up to that point, his efforts had proved fruitless. Frustrated, he decided to take a wild stab. Still, though, he hesitated. If he were wrong, the answer would have no benefit; if he were right, Zack might alert the object of his fear. In the end, curiosity won out. "Was Justin with Paul Roberge?"

The color drained from the boy's face. He stammered; his voice became dry, raspy. "What? Where did you ...? We don't hang with Culver Pond guys."

"Come on, Zack, this is me you're talking to. Don't give me that crap."

"Paul wasn't with Justin. And if you tell anyone I said he was, I'll say it's a lie."

Knepp had the boy where he wanted him. "I thought you didn't know who was with Justin. If that's true, how do you know Paul was *not* with him? Look Zack, I already have enough to put Paul on probation for a year."

A frantic cackle erupted high in the boy's throat, but his face was a mask of Greek tragedy. " 'Probation?' If that's all you got, you got nothing."

"Then give me more."

"No way! That dude is sick!"

"OK, but I don't want Paul to know I'm checking on him. If he finds out, he'll wonder who told me." Knepp pointed at the boy. "That'll be you, Zack; you're the only one I asked about him. So, if I were you, I'd keep my mouth shut. I'll get to Paul when I'm ready." Knepp paused to allow his words to sink in. "OK, you can go."

Zack rose and shuffled out of the room, shoulders slumped in dejection. Seconds later, he returned and closed the door behind him. "I really don't know if Justin was with Paul. He could've been. Just watch your back, Officer Ed; I always liked you, and you always been straight with me. Be careful."

Justin Frederickson had few friends, and he had not been involved in school activities. Only the Avalon boys and some students from the vo-tech school talked to him; others steered clear, mostly out of fear.

Still, whenever a teenager dies suddenly, grief spreads beyond the circle of friends, at times reaching near-epidemic proportions. There are sensitive students who remember the deceased as an acquaintance; others who are awakened to proof of their own mortality; some who suffer from a combination of factors, including fear of where their own drug use might lead; finally, there are those for whom the demise of a fellow student provides a stage upon which to play the role of angst-ridden adolescent.

Even with triage to determine each grieving student's needs, the fallout was enough to keep the counselors busy all day. The number was not that high, but many of Justin's friends fell into the "educationally and economically disadvantaged" category, the politically correct term for at-risk students, a particularly fragile group. Keeping occupied was a blessing for Randori; although his fellow counselors treated him the same as always, when he ventured into the halls, it seemed others gave him wide berth. He said as much to Virgil Davis.

His friend feigned innocence. "People just don't want to get on your bad side."

"Thanks Virge," Randori said. "Compassion like yours keeps me going." The glib response left unsaid the truth that the counselor was accustomed to that reaction from colleagues, even before these murders, even before Freedom Con. *You never fit in, Randori, and that's on you.*

Davis had gone on to review the Roberge MDE; later, Randori reflected on it. It was typical of Dubcek to take on pet causes, adding to the maddening inconsistency he displayed in identifying emotionally disturbed students. *But why a thug like Roberge?*

The workday was over. On the way to his car, Randori detoured past Dubcek's office on the chance that the psychologist was still around. Light seeped under the door from the interior. The counselor knocked; there was no answer, so he knocked a second time. As he turned to leave, he heard papers shuffling. He rapped louder. Dubcek's tremulous voice followed. "Who is it?"

Randori smiled, hoping it came through in his voice. "It's Doc. Got a minute?"

The door opened a crack, and Dubcek peeked out. Seeing his colleague's friendly mien, he opened the door wider and stood aside. "Doc, come in," he said, his smile flickering like a light bulb not fully engaged in its socket. "I heard you were back."

"Mind if I sit down a minute? It's been a rough couple days."

"No, of course not. Come in." Dubcek's words and his behavior were at odds. Keeping a distance from and an eye on the counselor, he felt for his chair and backed into it. Through palpable unease, he affected a wide smile, but his fingers whitened as they clamped onto the arms of his chair. "I was getting ready to leave. I just finished a write-up on a student I tested today. We can talk for a few minutes, though." As if to convince himself the psychologist added, "Certainly."

Randori peered into Dubcek's eyes. The man had lied for no apparent reason; he would have postponed testing on a day devoted to grief counseling. Forcing a disarming smile, Randori said, "How is everything?"

"I'm swamped, as usual. I'm nearly out of time for testing several students. You know what it's like. We're both busy. Kerry just dumps on us, and he doesn't realize how overworked high school people are."

Randori nodded sincerely. "You got that right. I fill in for him on so many out-of-district IEP meetings, it seems he doesn't realize I have my own job to do."

Relief washed over Dubcek, a tide that carried a genuine smile. "You are correct, sir. Then, when people say wonderful things about our special education department, he takes the credit while we do the work. We are greatly unappreciated."

"That's all right with me," Randori said, tempering the bonding experience so it took a more gradual rise, "I don't want the spotlight.

The thing that bothers me most is that you and I rarely get closure on things. There are always loose ends."

Dubcek's lips pursed and his head bobbed earnestly. "How many times have I said that? You and I are on an island. When you're good at what you do they pile more and more on you, but when things don't get done by the timelines, we hear about it."

"Look, I don't want to keep you," Randori said, standing, but maintaining eye contact. "We haven't touched base for a while. I just wanted to see how you're doing."

"Thanks for stopping by," Dubcek said, rising to see Randori to the door. "Tomorrow, when we're both rested, we can check our calendars and schedule a time to catch up on business, maybe talk a little."

"Sounds good." Randori flashed a broad, honest smile and extended his hand. "We need to talk about Paul Roberge. The more I look into his situation, the more I think he needs emotional support."

Dubcek beamed. "I'm glad we're seeing things the same way. It will make it an easier sell to the administration if you and I are on the same page."

"Our jobs are tough, getting tougher all the time. It's good to know I can count on you to be you." Randori reached for the door handle, turning in afterthought. "There aren't many people I feel I can trust right now. I want you to know, I trust you."

The dispatcher called Ed Knepp with the report on the white Pontiac: there were six in the area, but none seemed linked to Paul Roberge, Brad Prusster, or Doc Randori. In his commitment to thoroughness, Knepp made a mental note to check them out later. The immediate priority was the dispatcher's other message: Ronnie Prusster would drop his son off as long as Knepp would take him home after questioning. It meant he could interview Brad alone, a fair trade. One-to-one, it was more likely the boy would be candid, and Knepp would be spared Ronnie's posturing as a caring parent.

Knepp arrived at the station to find Brad, elbows on knees and head bowed so far his face was hidden from view, seated across from the second shift dispatcher.

Knepp patted the boy's arm. "Soda, Brad?"

Prusster jerked, as if awakened from a nightmare, and stammered, "OK." His gaze faltered after a fleeting glance into Knepp's eyes.

The sergeant's voice mellowed with concern. "Bet you haven't eaten all day. We have soft pretzels in the break room. How about I heat one for you?" He dropped a light hand on the boy's shoulder and pointed down the hall. "Go to my office and relax."

While Knepp was in the break room, he kept an eye on Brad. It was obvious he was grief-stricken, but otherwise seemed clear-headed, ready for interrogation. As he reentered his office, Knepp slammed the door, startling Brad, but flashed a disarming smile as he handed over the food.

"Where were you all day?"

"Walking around. I went to school, but everyone was asking questions so I left."

"Were you with anyone?"

"No, I went to the woods. I had to think."

Knepp paused long enough for the boy to twitch and shoot a nervous glance. "You're lying, Brad. You left school by the exit near the library and got into a car."

"Kids walk out all the time. How do you know it was me?"

"Everyone else was accounted for." Knepp decided to bluff. "Besides, a teacher on a field trip IDed you."

Brad ran his palms down the length of his face. "When I saw that bus, I knew."

"Who were you with?"

Eyes darted to the side. "Is the school calling the cops when we walk out now?"

"Come on, Brad. Don't stall me."

"I was with a guy from City."

"Give me a name."

"Jason. I don't know his last name. I met him at the Lanes."

Knepp stood, looming over the boy. "You're telling me you made plans with some guy—you don't know his last name—you met at the bowling alley to pick you up at a prearranged time. Tomorrow, I'll call City High's office to find out the *Jasons* who were absent. And if no one by that name, no one who drives a white Pontiac, was absent, I'll be coming after you. Then we'll talk real serious about why you misled me."

Brad cocked his head, and a flicker of perplexity crossed his face before he turned inward. His composure began to crumble; sobs rippled his body in choppy waves.

Knepp waited out the storm, and as the outburst subsided, he returned to his interrogation: "That's twice you've lied to me, and we've only been talking five minutes. Now, I'd never believe you could be mixed up in Justin's death, but the way you're covering for the guy who picked you up, I'm beginning to wonder."

Brad rocked back and forth, chanting, "Ed, I can't tell you! I can't."

Knepp hated seeing the boy suffer. He had lost his best friend and knew he was in real trouble. His emotional dam was about to burst; soon the truth would spill through.

That was good; it showed he was still a good kid, unskilled in the art of deception, not yet hardened by Avalon. "I'll make it easy on you. It was Paul Roberge, wasn't it?"

The color drained from Brad's face and he fell still. Knepp waited, knowing silence added pressure to respond, silence that reached ear-throbbing discomfort when the answer finally came: a soft, pleading "No."

Knepp hammered the wall, making the boy bolt upright. "Don't give me that crap. I'm tired. It's been a long day and I want to go home.

Now if you want to stay out of Juvie Hall tonight, you'd best be straight with me. It was Roberge, wasn't it?"

Brad looked up at his inquisitor, searching for an out, but Knepp's unyielding gaze left him no recourse. His response was more imploration than confession. "Yes. But he can't know I told you. You don't know him."

"What is it about Roberge? What are you afraid of? He's a punk."

"No, I've seen stuff."

"Like what?" Knepp thought a kid from Avalon, especially one of the Prusster kids, would have already seen as bad as it got.

A groan rose from deep in Brad's chest, as if he was trying to expel a demon. He started spitting phrases, spasms of wretched recollection. "One time Paul, Justin—a few of us—we were in the woods with some beer, shooting a .22 at the empties."

Knepp interrupted in a soothing murmur. "Take a breath, Brad, relax." The boy heaved a deep sigh, but his voice cracked as he began to speak again. "Paul shot this groundhog, but he only wounded it. He took a lace out of his boot, made, like, this noose, threw it around its neck." Another deep breath and more tears, and the sergeant placed a calming hand on the boy's forearm. After double-clutching another breath, Brad continued. "He threw the lace over a tree branch and pulled the groundhog up. Then he started shooting again. When it died, Paul swore at it, like he was mad it took away his fun, so he kept shooting." Brad stared to the side, focused back in time, and fell silent. Then, as if rising from a trance, he blinked and went on. "Justin tried to cut the groundhog down, but Paul put the gun at his head and said, 'I got another shoelace; and you're a bigger target.' He would've done it, too, would've shot Justin; we all knew it. Paul rubbed his hand on the groundhog and wiped its blood all over Justin's face. And he said, 'How would your daddy like to find you looking like this?' "

Knepp stared slack-jawed and shuddered involuntarily. He finally spoke. "Why didn't you just stay away from him after that?"

"I don't know. I mean I wanted to." Brad took on a puzzled frown. "There's something about Paul. His parents were always out. We'd party. He knows girls, too. Lots. There was always stuff too, you know? Things got wild sometimes. The thing is, Paul had money, had everything, and a lot of times he just gave it away."

"You're talking drugs. Pot? Coke?"

Brad measured the sergeant before responding. "Yeah, and pills—Ecstasy. I just did some weed and beer. Sorry, Ed, I know what you tried to teach us, but everybody does it. There's nothing else to do."

Few things riled Knepp more than these global statements, excuses masquerading as reasons, teens spouted whenever they had to explain their drug and alcohol use—excuses he himself had made as a teen. "No Brad, not *everyone* does it; fact is, most kids don't use. And there's plenty else to do; you just have to go do it." The tirade pushed Brad back into silence. Knepp pulled his chair close; he had to ease the boy across the threshold, through the door set ajar by Brad's nephew, little Brandon Prusster. "There's more, isn't there? You're into something, and you don't think you can get out."

"I can't tell you. You'll put me away."

"And I can't help you if you don't tell me what's going on. A lot of people think all Avalon kids are bad; if someone else gets you before I can work things out, you'll take the fall." Knepp thought some creative lying was appropriate: "The city police are involved now, and you know if they are, the 'Staties' will be, too."

"Justin was … I don't know where to start." Brad closed his eyes and grimaced.

"The beginning would be good," Knepp said with a soft voice and inviting smile.

Brad closed his eyes and rubbed the cool soda can across his brow. "Last summer, we were at the Lanes—Justin, Zack Boyer, the Wenners, and me. Paul and Marcus Wyncoat showed up. Paul asked if we wanted to go four-wheeling in the Southern Mountains. Justin and the Wenners went, but Zack and I didn't like Paul, so we went home. That's when they started hanging out. Justin kept asking me to go along; I figured if I wanted to see my friends I had to. At first, we just had some beers, then Paul started bringing girls to the house—cheerleaders, rich girls. We couldn't believe it; we thought it was because he was good-looking and had money, then I found out they got any drugs they wanted from him. Anyway, they used him and he used them."

Knepp slid the private logbook off his desk. "Mind if I take notes?" Brad went rigid. "Not my official logbook; this one is only for me."

With a defeated sigh, the boy said, "It doesn't matter. I just want it over."

Knepp was eager to get to the topic of heroin. *Patience*, he reminded himself; *everything will come out, by and by.* "OK, Paul gave girls drugs. How did he use them?"

"Dude, sometimes all he had to do was give them a free high; *E* got them going, but he'd slip stuff in drinks, too." Brad searched Knepp's eyes, as if to catch a glimmer of understanding. "He'd take them upstairs, and when he was done, he'd ask us if we wanted any. He did that so guys had a chance to catch up."

"Catch up?"

"They have this game—contest—they call 'Dozens.' The first one to do twelve girls is the winner. Paul's in the lead, so to make things fair, he'll set a girl up so all the guys get a shot. He even did it for Justin one night even though he wasn't really in the contest. Justin has … had trouble getting girls."

"Were you involved?"

"No, but they started getting on me, asking if I was gay. So, I said I would, but they had to let me lock the door and be alone. She was just lying there. I could've done whatever I wanted." Brad's face screwed into a mask of revulsion—Knepp wondered: for Roberge, himself, the game? "It wasn't right. I just left? Do you believe me?"

Knepp tried to hide his own disgust. Roberge was a lower life form than he had imagined. "Of course, I believe you. None of the victims reported this to anyone?"

"Paul picks on ninth grade girls, mostly, and guys watch them afterward. Like, in school, if a girl acts mad or stays away from them, Justin, Ace, or someone warns the girl she better keep her mouth shut. Last Friday, he roped in a girl from City. I broke it up."

A mournful tremor overtook Brad, making Knepp believe there was more to the tale, but it wasn't the story he was after. Besides, making those charges stick against Roberge and the others would be difficult. The embarrassment of the victims and the teen code of silence would conspire against prosecution. He thought, *Heck, some immoral morons would even say, 'boys will be boys.'* "Back to Justin."

"We started hanging out at Culver Pond all the time. It wasn't different cliques, like school; everybody was there—everyone but the Hispanic kids." Brad winced. "Well, they'd let Hispanic girls in, but never the guys. Paul was proud he could bring everyone together. But it wasn't him, really. Well, he organized everything, but it was the drugs and the beer and the house that got everyone there.

"One time, Paul was saying we could make a lot of money because he knew what kids wanted, and he could supply it. I thought he meant coke. But when I went to take a leak, Paul said he had to go, too. In the bathroom, he said he wanted to meet my brother, said he had ideas Bolt would like. I told him I'd set it up, but I didn't want to have any part of drug dealing. It could ruin my chances for college."

Knepp glanced up from his notebook and forced a smile. "Good for you, Brad."

Brad seemed to be telling the truth. Trying to keep up with these revelations, Knepp scribbled frantic notes in his private logbook until his hand stiffened, and he had to pause to shake off writer's cramp. Brad, by that time eager to get his story out, held off until the policeman was poised to write again.

"Paul said I'd make more money than I could ever make going to college. I took Paul to meet Bolt, and Paul laid the whole thing out. That's when I found out what he was talking about." Brad halted until Knepp's eyes rose to meet his. "Heroin. I didn't believe it; I never saw anyone using needles at the parties. Paul said that I saw kids using, but I probably thought it was coke because they were snorting it. He said, at first, he only gave it to a couple guys, kind of like guinea pigs."

"And one of them was Justin."

"Yeah, and Marcus Wyncoat. He knew they'd try anything, and they wouldn't be scared of heroin. First couple weeks, he only got them off once or twice."

"Did he use with them?"

"I don't know. The first time maybe, to make them think it was nothing to be afraid of. It got to the point that's all they wanted, 'cause you know how it is: you try to get that original high back, but you have to keep using more just to get off at all. Then, you need it just to feel normal. I was really pissed, uh, mad at Paul, not just because of what he did to Justin, but he used me, too, to get a meeting with my brother."

"What did Bolt think?"

"At first he wasn't interested. But then Paul said, since kids snort it or smoke it, they would compare it to weed or coke, but it's a better high, and, once they got hooked, they'd be customers for life, even work for it, help grow the business, kind of like Justin did. Paul said the best thing was the two of them could drive the Hispanic dealers out, or, at least, force them to stick to the needle pushers on the North Side.

"I could tell Bolt was thinking about it—you know Bolt; if he wasn't interested, he would've kicked Paul's ass. He doesn't trust anyone outside Avalon. That night, after Paul left, Bolt talked to me about it. First thing, he wanted to know, was I using? I told him this was the first I heard about it. I told Bolt I didn't trust Paul; he's crazy, and he'd never be loyal. So, Bolt didn't get involved."

"I can't believe I didn't get wind of any of this."

"Paul told everyone that he's in with the Mafia and if anyone talked he'd have people come up from Philly to get them."

"Do you believe that?"

"No, but everyone else does, or at least they want to. I guess it makes things more exciting to them if he is."

Knepp smiled broadly, thinking that if he and Molly were ever to have a boy, he would want him to be like Brad Prusster. "You're very perceptive, Brad. When you go to college, what are you planning to study?"

"I want to be a guidance counselor," Brad said, blushing gently at Knepp's compliment. His eyes narrowed, honing in on the sergeant's continued stare, and he changed the subject: "Paul's story made sense because he always had heroin, and he went down to Philly a lot. He lives what, two, three miles from the turnpike?"

"Who made the connection for him there?"

"I don't know, but it's getting big. A few weeks ago he made one trip in the morning, and sold it so quick that he had to go for more that night."

Knepp jotted in his private log. When he looked up, he measured Brad and felt the boy could handle returning to the topic of his friend. "What was Justin's role again?"

"Like I said, he kept kids quiet and made sure they paid up if they owed money. He was Paul's main man that way, but then Justin got in trouble with Dr. Randori at the football game, and that's when he got in trouble with Paul, too."

Knepp's pulse quickened. "Paul didn't like it when Justin attacked Dr. Randori?"

"Justin hated Dr. Randori. He's the one who puts kids in alternative school."

"How did that get Justin in trouble with Paul Roberge?"

"When you guys questioned him at the game, he gave Paul's name to the police."

"How do you know that?"

"I heard Paul and Justin talking out behind Paul's house last Friday. They didn't know I was listening. Paul told Justin he knew."

"Did he say how he found out?"

"Paul said that Dr. Randori told him, but –"

"OK, what happened to Justin?" Knepp asked before Brad could finish. His longstanding suspicions were confirmed; Bob Samson had been right all along. *This will be the bust of a lifetime. A school counselor involved in selling heroin to kids. I might even make national news.*

"Yesterday, Justin cut school—he was hung over from the weekend. Paul stopped me in the parking lot after school."

"I thought he was on suspension."

"He is, but that wouldn't keep him from making deliveries to his 'cutties'—customers. Paul said Justin left his snuff can at his house, and he wanted to return it but couldn't give it back because he was busy. I said I'd give it to him. Justin can't—couldn't—do without his snuff. I didn't think that he could've just bought another one.

"I called Justin—I've been trying to get him away from Paul—and he met me last night. I told him he ought to go into rehab. Ironic, huh? I didn't think about it at the time, but he was really interested in getting his snuff can, but when I gave it to him he didn't even take a pinch." Brad's voice began to crack again. "After that, it was like he was in a hurry to get away from me. He said he promised his dad he'd be home by 9:30." Great tears welled and rolled down his cheeks, streams of misery.

"Relax, Brad. Take your time. It'll be all right."

Brad wiped his eyes and buried his head in his hands. Through wrenching sobs, he continued. "Justin didn't come to school with us anymore. Marcus usually picked him up; they liked to get high before school. This morning when I got out of Zack's car, Paul drove up and told me to meet him outside the library at 9:00. I told him I couldn't.

He said he'd be there anyway. It wasn't till I got to homeroom that I heard about Justin."

"Who told you?"

"Everyone knew except Zack and me. I didn't know what to do; I just knew I couldn't be in school." Brad sucked in air. "So I met Paul. He said, 'Too bad about Justin; I always said tobacco would kill him.' Then he laughed. I started yelling at him, but he said I was the one that delivered the 'H' and I better keep my mouth shut, 'cause if the cops didn't get me, he would. And he said if I got Bolt involved, I'd lose a brother, too. Then he pulled this gun out from under the seat. It was, like, this nine millimeter, I think. I don't want to get shot, but I don't want to be blamed for Justin, either."

Knepp narrowed his eyes and gripped Brad's arm. "Listen Brad, do exactly what I tell you. If Paul finds out we talked, say you didn't tell me anything. And don't fall for it if he bluffs and says he knows you gave me information because there's absolutely no way he can know. It'll take a little while to make the case solid, and I'll make sure he can't trace anything back to you. If anyone gets hurt, Brad, it won't be you."

Cat Blanchard propped her chin on her fists and gazed with unflinching affection into Nick Neidrich's eyes. "I'm glad you kept our date. I thought with Kass's death, you'd have to postpone." As soon as the words escaped her lips, Blanchard covered her mouth, and then her eyes. "That was horribly shallow, wasn't it?"

"Not really," Nick Neidrich said, stifling a smile, "considering how some of the school people have reacted. Anyway, I wouldn't have missed this."

Neidrich's frank admission following Blanchard's embarrassing one shoved both dinner companions into an awkward silence. She shifted her gaze, surveying the room, while Neidrich stared into the glass of water the waiter had just poured. With exaggerated care, he lifted his glass and sipped, buying time, searching for inspiration in its glacial chill, desperate to find something to say that would set them both at ease.

It had been a long time since Neidrich had made the effort to engage in date-talk. After his wife's death, early forays onto the field of tender engagement were disastrous: two blind dates set up by wives of fellow troopers who hated seeing him suffer. He had felt at once guilty for betraying his wife and angry at the audacity of anyone who dared compete with a memory that approached myth. But here he sat, in a restaurant—on a date—with Cat Blanchard. With a clear conscience and no resentment. He was surprised, exuberant even, but the possibilities made him nervous.

For four years, he thought he was destined to go through life without another woman. For four years, it wasn't there, and then, a few weeks ago, Tammy Eboli clasped his hand and stared into his eyes, and long-dormant feelings stirred. But that arousal was primal, flowing from his loins. He was relieved to learn that those feelings had not been lost, merely suppressed like molten lava beneath a brittle crust, a crust Randori had picked through by confronting Neidrich's self-immolative grief. Then Randori—Randori again, how much he had manipulated events—introduced him to Cat. Since that night at the game, she dominated his thoughts, and even though he was in the middle of a stone whodunit, this was a lead of a different type—a personal type—Neidrich felt compelled to follow. He found excuses to drop by

Blanchard's office as a courtesy for small talk, each interlude ending in an "Uh, well … nice-talking-to-you-see-you-soon" way, but otherwise conversation was easy and breezy, if not Bogie and Bacall.

And now, Neidrich sat staring into his glass of water, his mind racing to find a topic of conversation unrelated to his murder. His face flushed in the silence.

Blanchard's words broke through Neidrich's mute panic. "Cat got your tongue?"

"Yeah—literally." *Hey, that was kind of funny.* That small boost of confidence prodded him to continue. "I'm glad we could get together, too. I had to get away from the case. It's all I've thought about." *God no!* "Not that I think you're just a diversion." Heat spread across his brow. As the words escaped his mouth, he wished he could snatch them out of the air and stuff them back in. He forced his eyes up, afraid of Cat's reaction but curious, like a person watching an impending train wreck.

Blanchard leaned forward, her smile ardent in the candlelight. "At least you didn't ask me out just to question me—although I don't mind answering questions. I know how first dates can be: lots of pressure on conversation. Right now, the only thing we know we have in common is your investigation in the place where I work. We don't know much about each other."

"Guess not." Neidrich's verbal brush with disaster brought caution to his words. He got a momentary reprieve from tension as the waiter arrived to take their order. "I'm sorry," he said, "I didn't even ask what you wanted."

She waved him off. "That's gallant of you, Nick, but I'm capable of ordering for myself." Turning to the waiter, she said, "I'll have the penne and salmon in vodka pepper cream sauce; arugula salad with white balsamic dressing."

Realizing that he had yet to look at the menu, Neidrich blurted out his favorite meal: "I'll have spaghetti and meatballs."

The waiter grimaced and, with a patronizing tilt of his head, said, "Perhaps the Tagliatelle Bolognese? It is the closest we can come to meeting your wishes."

"That'll do. Arugula salad, too." Neidrich didn't know what he had ordered, but his embarrassment had reached the point where he just wanted to get that business out of the way. Besides, his anger at the waiter's smugness made him bite off further dialogue.

"May I suggest separate wines? Something white for the lady and a dry red for the gentleman?"

Neidrich started to respond, but Blanchard put her hand on his and addressed the waiter. "Just bring us a carafe of the house Chianti. And leave the attitude at the bar." Her brow slanted into a menacing *V*. "Got that?"

"Very well, ma'am," the waiter said before turning on his heels to leave.

"My kind of woman."

"Hey, I may be a babe in the woods as far as school administration goes, but don't mess with me in social situations. Besides, I only said what you were thinking. I'm impressed, Nick. You showed restraint. Most guys' testosterone would have spiked, especially around a woman. My former husband's certainly would have." Blanchard beamed as she changed the subject. "Virgil told me you played football at Notre Dame."

"I'm sure he did," Neidrich said, biting off his words, surprised and embarrassed by how many conversation-stoppers he was stringing in a row. To him, discussion about his own life was dull; he preferred to learn more about Cat. "Sorry, it's just that I try to downplay that part of my life."

"What's wrong with your being a football player? I'm a big football fan—you have to be around here. Comes from my dad. He'd love to meet you."

"There's a certain image people have."

"You mean big lummoxes who have no respect for women? I have radar for that; if I'd gotten that impression, I wouldn't be here. But it would have nothing to do with your being a football player, Nick. I don't like stereotypes. For example, I don't like it that women have to act butch and work twice as hard as a man to advance in a job."

"Is that how school administration is?"

"Around here, anyway. You know whom I admire? Meryl Morgan. She's sharp, sharper than anyone else in the District." Blanchard pursed her lips and winced, measuring her words. "Except maybe Kerry Wyatt, but Meryl knows how to apply it. She knows her stuff as far as education goes. Meryl has style *and* substance; plus, she's a manager and a leader. Rare combinations."

Relieved that the focus had shifted from him, Neidrich eased back in his seat, settling into what he felt comfortable doing: interviewing. "You put Kerry Wyatt in her class. Compare them for me. I'm not sure how to take him."

Blanchard paused to contemplate. "Toughness, that's an edge Meryl has; she's true to her principles and will take a controversial stance. Kerry is a diplomat to a fault. But Meryl knows how to avoid flaunting her intelligence; she comes across as being just smart enough. Kerry turns some people off because most people are intellectual inferiors. He doesn't try to do that; he's just that brilliant." She blushed and fell silent.

"What's wrong?"

"God, I must sound awful, being critical of Kerry. I have the greatest respect for him, it's just—" She hesitated, searching for the right words.

"You said you're a babe in the woods," Neidrich jumped in, hoping to let her off the hook, "but I think you show a lot of insight. My job is sizing people up, and I'd agree with you completely. In fact, you've made me feel better about Mr. Wyatt."

Blanchard smiled into Neidrich's eyes. "That's good. I think he's an acquired taste, like Doc Randori."

"What's your take on Randori?"

"He's hard to describe. It seems his heart is in the right place, but he can be a little cut-throat." Blanchard's eyes widened. "God, I can't believe I just said that!"

Neidrich laughed for the first time, and with it, he shed all residual tension. "I know what you meant: the ends justify the means."

"You have a nice laugh," she said, gazing warmly at him, then, abashed, dropping her eyes to her goblet as she idly swished its contents. Candlelight glowed through the glass, reflecting the sanguine blush of the Chianti onto her face.

An unbidden smile of affection crept across Neidrich's face. He recognized its presence and, fearing that he was exposing too much too soon, tried to erase it, but it hung stubbornly. Rather than risk its transformation into an idiotic grin, he turned his attention away from himself and Cat. "You don't put Randori into the same class as Wyatt and Morgan?"

Blanchard tented her arms and placed her hands together, as if in prayer, in front of her mouth, clapping them silently as she pondered the question. "You know, he just might be the smartest of the bunch, but his intellect isn't focused, like Meryl's is on education, or Kerry's is on psychology."

"You mean it's undisciplined?"

"Mmm ... not exactly. From what Virgil says—and from what I've seen—Doc seems to know a little about a lot—a true liberal artist. His mind is ... unconventional. When there's a problem to solve, he throws open his mental filing cabinet and pulls out a note here, a folder there. Before you know it, he comes up with some novel—or bizarre—way of looking at things. People underestimate him, because he goes against accepted practice and gets off on these maddening tangents."

"I've experienced that," Neidrich said, chuckling.

Blanchard's eyes met Neidrich's squarely. "But he's loyal to Meryl and Kerry, to their goals, anyway, and you don't find hired guns like Doc every day, someone who hates the political twists that might unhinge the needle of his moral compass."

"I never picked you as a Doc Randori fan."

"I wasn't until recently. Virgil influenced me there. That's one of his strengths; he knows who the good guys are, and that's the side he's on."

"You respect Davis?"

"He's my administrative idol; I love him." Blanchard halted and grimaced; her eye contact fluttered. "You always know where Virgil's coming from. But his strength is also his weakness as far as administration goes. He faces head-on whatever comes up and doesn't think of the bigger picture. Because of that, he's a great assistant principal, but he's also shot himself in the foot when it comes to career advancement."

"How so?"

"I'll give you an example. There's this school board member who has a daughter at the high school. One day, she gets disrespectful to a cafeteria worker. Now, she's not a bad kid; Virgil could've just given her a firm talking-to, but he writes her up for two nights detention because that's what he'd give any kid, under those circumstances. The board member asks Virgil to take the detentions away. Virgil argues that if he lets her off, she'll get the message that whatever she does Daddy will get her out of trouble. Besides, two nights detention is a small price to pay for a life lesson that people deserve respect regardless of their station. This board member, who, ironically, is running for judge, calls Dr. Samson. The detentions disappear, plus Virgil gets a reprimand. The moral of the story? Don't tilt at windmills or you get blown away."

"I admire his integrity."

"Integrity hasn't gotten him a building principal position."

"Too bad; seems like he's loyal, hard working."

"Doc Randori told me once in so many words: don't be loyal to bosses because they can be self-serving; instead, be loyal to my own ideals and to the students."

"When the decisions of the king will lead to the defeat of the army, the general may disobey the king."

Blanchard snapped her fingers and pointed at Neidrich. "He said that, too."

"One of Randori's Sun Tzu quotes. He must particularly like that one. Thinking like that can make you unpopular with the bosses."

"Doc is unpopular with them—he's unpopular with a lot of people, me included, at first." Blanchard rolled her eyes heavenward. "He sounded like an anarchist nutcase to me, and I thought, I'd be as crazy as he is if I listened to him. It didn't help that some of the people I'd known before I came to Freedom Con put him down.

"But, I'm off on a birdwalk. You were asking about Virgil. The best I can figure, after they passed him over for promotion, he threw his lot in completely with Doc, Kerry, and Meryl. That's when his relationship with Dr. Samson and Kass went south."

Neidrich wondered if Cat realized how potentially damaging to Davis her words were. Realizing he was about to enter the realm of interrogation, he decided to jump tracks, a problem solved when Cat looked past him and waved.

"Well, speak of the devils and they shall appear. There's Kerry and Meryl."

Neidrich smiled, but his stomach rippled in torment. *What if they want to join us for dinner?* Before he could further consider his dilemma, they were upon him.

"Hello, Cat," Morgan said, smiling warmly. "Trooper Neidrich, good to see you again." Her smile cooled, but remained cordial, as she clasped the trooper's hand.

Wyatt flashed his Cheshire Cat grin, and he spread his hands outward, taking in the ambience. "You know, I would have held out on talking to you had I known an invitation to this fine trattoria was in the offing. Winking, he added, "Although I am certain you prefer Cat's company to that of an old fart like me."

A couple at the next table shot a disapproving glare at Wyatt. The wide grin remained. "I just said it, I didn't do it." He winked at Blanchard and Neidrich, patted his lips with his fingertips, and said, "Oh dear, I wasn't using my indoor voice."

Morgan elbowed him in the ribs. "Stop it. You're embarrassing these two."

"Right, I'm sure they'd rather be alone than consort with the likes of us." Wyatt rubbed his hands together. "Let's go take the starch out of these tight-assed waiters."

"Have fun, you two," Morgan said. "Sorry if we—or I should I say Kerry—embarrassed you. Now he can concentrate his efforts on humiliating me."

Blanchard and Neidrich watched the hostess lead the administrators to a table in the corner and observed with glee that the obnoxious waiter they had experienced earlier was casually sidling toward their table. He was about to meet Kerry Wyatt.

"I really like those two," Blanchard said. "I wonder if they have a future together."

Neidrich was thinking the same about Blanchard and himself. As she turned her gaze toward him, he averted his eyes and offered the breadbasket. "Ms. Morgan seems more career than marriage-oriented. I don't take her to be particularly warm."

"Warmth and passion are different things, don't you think? Take yourself, for example. I've seen you on the job. You're curt and businesslike, never even gave me so much as a glance. And yet, I bet you're passionate—in a romantic way."

"How can you tell?"

Morgan giggled. "Because neither of us has touched these wonderful meals."

"No, really."

"OK, because passion translates. You're passionate about your work, so that's the kind of guy you are. And passionate people feel deeply; they sense things. Look at us. You sensed enough about me to know I wanted to go out with you."

"Believe it or not, Doc Randori told me I should ask you out."

Blanchard's smile dropped as her brow simultaneously arched. "And honest, too. You could have allowed me some romantic illusions, you know. But it figures Doc told you. He's a freaking empath: *he* senses things about people."

"Why do you say that?"

"First, there's no way he could have known I had any interest in you."

"Maybe Davis said something."

Blanchard shook her head. "No one knew. Virgil told me to watch that with Doc. He can tell when a person approves or disapproves of him. He knows when a kid is using drugs. He makes accurate profiles on people after meeting them once. At first, I thought Doc was just judgmental and cynical, but it's incredible how his snap judgments stand the test of time. It's ... creepy."

"Now Randori, I don't see him as being passionate so much as zealous."

Blanchard cocked her head as though she were fine-tuning her perception. "Interesting distinction."

"I guess I chose the word *zealous* because it has a more negative connotation. He doesn't let people get close to him."

"That doesn't mean anything. He's always been passionate, or zealous—you fill in the blank—in his dislike for Dr. Samson and Kass." Blanchard bit off her words with a wince. "I mean, dislike for the way they did business." She buried her face in her hands. "Shit, I'm going be your prize witness, aren't I?"

Neidrich touched her hand. "It's all right, Randori's admitted as much to me."

Rolling her hand to return his caress, Blanchard said, "This is where your passion for your job compels you to ask about Doc's relationships with Dr. Samson and Kass."

"I'm sorry," Neidrich said, looking down at his plate. His mind searched for the right words, and the revelation arose that Tagliatelle Bolognese was simply wide, flat spaghetti with crumbled meatballs, red sauce, and a high-faluting name. Embarrassed that Cat had him pegged, he tried to withdraw his hand, but her grip became a gentle vise.

"Nick, you're cute. Ask me all the questions you want. Just do me a favor, OK? No bright light in my face; I'm getting to the age where it's not flattering."

Neidrich shot her a quick glance then looked away. He and Snitz had spared Blanchard anything more than cursory questioning because she was relatively new to the district, unaware of the dirt, but now he knew he had to cast a broader net. "OK, tell me."

Blanchard scanned the area to make sure no one was listening then leaned forward so Neidrich could hear her whisper. "There was a time I thought maybe Doc did, you know, kill Dr. Samson. I was getting mixed messages from people I work with. Virgil defended Doc, and the secretaries and the other counselors said he couldn't have done it. But Kass believed Doc was guilty, and people I knew before I came to Freedom Con think Doc probably did it."

"What people, from where?"

"There's a gym a lot of us belong to. That's where I met Tammy Eboli. She's the one who told me about the assistant principal job opening. She introduced me to Meryl, too. Meryl fences there. Long story short, knowing both the Association leader and the Director of Secondary Education, I got the job, and the rest is history."

"I have a feeling that you probably got it on your own merit. It doesn't seem like Ms. Morgan would hire someone based on personal feelings."

"I'd like to think you're right. I know I had good references, and, pardon my bragging, I even won a *Teacher of the Year* award." Blanchard's eyes narrowed. "But you'll have plenty of time to learn my history. Hopefully. Right now, you want to know who warned me about Doc."

"Tammy Eboli?"

"I bet she made that clear when you questioned her." She smiled at Neidrich's look of mild surprise. "Yes, Tammy told me about 'this hunk' who was with Harley Snitz. But yes, Tammy, and some other teachers, think Doc is aloof, snobbish."

"That's what I've heard, but he's talked freely with me."

"It figures. Like I said, he's eerie. You two are a lot alike, so he'd peg you as one of the good guys. You're both honest, and I'd guess tenacious, and pugnacious." Blanchard seasoned the end of her statement with a grin and a hand-on-hip attitude.

Neidrich returned the smile, but he was about to steer the conversation back to people who disliked Randori when the waiter arrived with the bill, holding off an immediate segue. He and Blanchard engaged in flirtatious small talk while he settled the tab and helped her with her light wrap. After they hit the warm air and the empty sidewalk, he asked, "These people who are so willing to condemn Randori, any of them vindictive?"

Blanchard leaned into him, her eyes sparkling, eager to see a conspiracy. "Now I get it. You think someone set Doc up."

"You think you're a pretty good detective, huh?"

"You have to have a little Sherlock Holmes in you to be an assistant principal. And right now, I deduce that you aren't answering because I'm right." She snuggled his arm and said in a breathy whisper, "Come on, Nick, let me help you with your case."

"I don't have any real suspicions that way," Neidrich said, falling back to his predisposition to discretion. He unlocked the car and supported Blanchard's elbow as she slid into the passenger seat. "But you were saying there are people who have it in for Randori."

After waiting for Neidrich to slide behind the wheel, Blanchard said, "The people at the gym: Tammy, but especially Leroy Dubcek. I thought, why would they lie?"

"The psychologist? He doesn't seem to fit the gym-rat mold."

"He does to a degree—he's a rat." Blanchard bit her lip and winced. "I'm sorry, that was terribly hostile. It's just that Leroy is so self-righteous, so devious, so—"

"So I've gathered," Neidrich said, smiling. "But go on. Please."

"Leroy's in the fencing class with Meryl, but she does aerobics and weightlifting, too. He just fences. Anyway, he was sneaky, the way he undercut Doc. Fooled me, anyway, which I guess is why it makes me so angry. He played Doc up as being pleasant enough, but misguided. I think his exact words were something like 'Doc is in over his head with Pupil Services, so he compensates by acting as intelligent as I am.' "

"No problem with Dubcek's self-concept."

"I wouldn't put it quite so delicately. But I think his feelings are fueled by jealousy, too. Leroy wants to run Pupil Services at the high school, but Doc's in charge. The only people loyal to Leroy are the school nurse and the SAP members."

"Must've been some power struggle."

"I don't think there was a struggle at all. Doc doesn't try to be a boss, doesn't want power. Leroy, on the other hand, constantly tries to get the upper hand, to take control, but he ends up losing power by trying to grasp it. Ironic, isn't it?"

"You're saying Randori rules with an ironic fist?"

"Is that called a punaphor or a metapun?"

"It's cornball. Where does Ms. Eboli fit in?"

"She's the big reason for the jealousy. Leroy and Tammy knew each other from work; at the gym they, well, got together."

"I assumed Dubcek is married."

"He is, but that wouldn't stop either of them. Anyway, I believe Tammy had kind of a thing for Doc, too, back when he first came to the District."

"Unrequited, I hope."

"I believe so, yes, but Leroy judges everyone by his own standards, so he saw Doc as a threat, to his control of the department and his affair with Tammy, so he took every opportunity to put Doc down and Tammy bought it. He influenced me, too. The way it turned out, though, all Leroy's maneuverings were for naught." Neidrich started to speak, but Blanchard put up a palm to stave off the obvious question so she could give the obvious answer. "Tammy found out there's too much to dislike about Leroy himself, so she moved on. Believe it or not, Tammy isn't a bad person; she's just mixed up."

"Where was Dubcek's wife all this time?"

"She's some kind of business consultant. Travels a lot. Her job must be lucrative, too, judging from Leroy's tastes. He buys only the best of everything."

"So, Ms. Eboli looked for greener pastures. Where did she decide to graze?"

"I'm not sure; Tammy's pretty secretive in that respect. I knew about her and Leroy because of him, not her; in fact, she used to get ticked whenever he tried to be affectionate in public. Meryl and I might be the only people in the District who know about them.

"I had this weird feeling recently, though, the day Kass suspended Doc." Blanchard was silent for a long moment before tenuously continuing. "At first, Kass came on very strong, but Virgil questioned his rationale for suspending Doc, then Kass looked at Doc, and Doc had this cold, dead expression—" Blanchard bit her lip and frowned pensively. "Kass suddenly backed off, saying he was carrying out Phil Olson's orders. When he said that, Tammy gave him this disappointed—no, disheartened—look."

Neidrich pursed his lips. "I don't see what you're getting at."

"As I'm saying it out loud, it's making less sense, but at the time I thought Tammy seemed especially hurt, like Kass lost face with her."

"Like their relationship was more than professional?"

Blanchard dropped her eyes and shook her head. "Forget it, it's stupid. Kass isn't her type. Tammy prefers married men; no strings attached, no long-term commitment. I try to go easy on her, though, because her marriage was a lie, just like mine."

Neidrich thought the connection between Eboli and Marburg was flimsy, and even if something was going on between them, there was no reason to believe a jealous Dubcek even knew about it, but the trooper tucked the nugget away, nonetheless. Dubcek was an unsavory character, and Neidrich had learned long ago that unsavory characters bear watching.

Arriving at Blanchard's home allowed Neidrich the opportunity to file that bit of information away for later consideration and segue to matters of more immediate import. Three hours had passed in a flash, and Neidrich wanted it to last longer; he wanted to know everything he could about Blanchard.

Walking her to her front door, he asked, "How was it a lie?"

"From what I gather, Tammy was—"

Neidrich chuckled. "I don't mean hers. How was *your* marriage a lie?"

Blanchard caressed his face, her delicate palm settling on his solid jaw and she smiled, her eyes glistening in the afterglow of the wine. "I'd rather look forward than back." She kissed his cheek and stepped across the threshold of her home. "Call me."

"How about next time you meet my kids?" Neidrich asked.

Before closing the door, Blanchard answered his question with a smile.

Ed Knepp reached down, jerked the lever, and slid the driver's seat as far back as it would go as he settled in for the long vigil. A *Gargantulicious Chocolate-Peanut Butter Magnafreeze*—too large to fit in the car's cup holder—occupied his right hand. Instead of shifting it to his left hand, he reached across his body to open the cardboard box, grunting as he painstakingly separated the cheese on the slices of pizza he had bought at the Minit Mart. It was a difficult task but, once accomplished, one that brought a satisfied smile as he sat back to enjoy his meal and the surveillance of Randori's home.

He turned the first slice in his hand, inspecting it from all angles, like an art historian admiring a Ming vase. Finally taking a bite, Knepp's lower incisors knifed through the crust, but the uppers succeeded only in trapping the topping, and when he pulled the crust away from his mouth, the cheese stayed behind, keeping sauce with it. Before he realized what was happening, the elasticized slab slapped against his chin and clung tenaciously as the weight of the cheese finished the job his teeth had started. With the crust in his left hand and the *Gargantulicious Magnafreeze* in his right, Knepp sat helplessly as slowly, like an ancient tapestry whose threads could no longer bear its own weight, the triangle of mozzarella tore away from his mouth, lib-labbed down the front of his turtleneck, and settled on his continental shelf.

"Aw shit," Knepp whined, uttering in a rare curse, "Molly bought me this."

He refused to look down, afraid of discovering what the sauce had done to his favorite sweater but also intent on spotting any suspicious movement at Randori's house.

Since Wednesday, Knepp had been roaming Freedom County or staking out the counselor's home with little to show for his efforts, and he was superstitious enough to believe that as soon as he took his eyes away, something eventful would happen.

On Wednesday, he had asked the Chief if he could work overtime in his own car and log the mileage. He believed he had some solid leads and needed to work undercover. Snitz almost absentmindedly gave his permission. In a way, Kass's death was a lucky break for Knepp: Snitz and Neidrich had been so busy running around Freedom County all week, gathering evidence and information and trying to determine whether or not Marburg's and Samson's murders were related that they had not bothered to pay much attention to his investigation. Better still, the Chief had not even asked for developments on the cause of Justin Frederickson's death.

Knepp had spent Wednesday evening moving between Avalon and Culver Pond, ending the first night sitting at the turnpike entrance in the hope of catching Roberge or the white Pontiac on the way back from a Philly run. While he waited, he used the time to think, and plan. He concluded that his efforts would be fruitless if he broke up the drug ring and Randori got away and, therefore, his time would be better spent staking out the counselor's house until he had evidence to convict.

The next day he had followed Randori home from school. That night, Randori's wife had been at home. A light, steady rain fell all evening, and no one left the house.

On this, the third day of his stakeout, Knepp was becoming bored. As much as he hated tearing his eyes away from Randori's house, he felt compelled to assess the damage sustained by the pizza. The sauce was barely evident on the black sweater, but the cheese slab perched precariously close to a precipitous plunge from his paunch to his pants. He leaned to his right and, with the slow stealth of a mantis, lowered the *Magnafreeze*, allowing a relieved smile only when the heft of the shake displaced from his biceps to the passenger-side floor. His reprieve was short-lived. He felt a small pat on his right thigh. Had it been a woman's hand, the gentle caress would have brought delight. As it was, the pat echoed ominously, foreboding doom to a man who had to explain to his wife grease and sauce stains on a brand new pair of khakis. Knepp's head and shoulders slumped in despair. For a moment, he stared at the pallid slab before gently clamping the point between his thumb and index finger and lifting it back onto the crust.

While licking his fingers, Knepp caught a flash in the corner of his eye. Remembering where he was and why he was there, his eyes shot up to see the glint of sunlight reflect off a Honda's windshield as Randori's car rounded the corner and headed straight toward him. He ducked his head, peeking up as the car passed to see if he had been spotted, but the counselor seemed to remain focused on the road. Glancing into his rear view mirror, Knepp watched the Honda recede in the distance.

The deputy twisted the key in the ignition and almost simultaneously jammed the car into gear, accelerating to the intersection. He checked all directions for oncoming traffic and grinned at his luck that the road was clear for a U-turn. Bearing to the right then whipping the wheel back to the left, Knepp stomped on the gas and made the maneuver as fast as the laws of physics would allow. His smile quickly vanished, though, as that fickle bitch, centrifugal force, hurled the forgotten *Magnafreeze* across the floor with nearly enough force to separate cream. Through misty eyes, Knepp saw that Randori was nearly out of sight. The damage done, he stepped on the gas and shot ahead, leaving a trail of blue smoke. A half-mile later, he reached the first stoplight and saw that he was within manageable trailing distance of the counselor. He followed Randori to the nearby high school track and peeled off to a far corner of the parking lot.

Renewing his vigil, Knepp divided his attention between stints of scooping goo back into the cup and observing Randori. He finally settled back to watch his suspect jog for forty-five minutes then walk several laps. During that period, he stopped at intervals to do sets of pushups and later abdominal crunches, following each with a stretching exercise. After spending well over an hour at the track, Randori returned home.

Again, for the rest of the evening there was no action, so Knepp went home early, confident in the assumption that the counselor would do nothing while his wife was around. Besides, Knepp missed Molly. Maybe if he took home a couple subs and a mystery DVD, they could snuggle, and she might not be so angry about the turtleneck and the khakis.

Meryl Morgan trudged out of Kass Marburg's office with an armload of files. It seemed ghoulish to gather his work in progress before the funeral, but she reminded herself that the business of education goes on. Too busy with her own job during the week, she had decided to dedicate the weekend to Kass's work. She wished Phil Olson had appointed Virgil Davis as acting principal so the responsibilities would have fallen to him. Olson, however, following the tenets of management by tentativeness—he called it prudence—had to feel everyone out before making a decision. She flung the stack on the front seat and headed for the church.

A sardonic smile etched across her face at the notion that two men she scorned had been killed, and the bulk of their work had fallen to her. Davis had volunteered to help with the high school business, but Morgan rarely depended on others. Olson had stepped in as acting superintendent within days of Samson's death, and, although that had eased her burden to an extent, he was so ill-qualified that he still had to delegate to, or consult with, her constantly. Adding to the load, most District Office staff and building principals bypassed Olson in favor of Morgan to field their questions and concerns.

Phil Olson was de jure, Meryl Morgan was de facto, and now Kass Marburg was deceased. *Who the hell do they think I am, the Holy Trinity?*

It didn't help that Kerry Wyatt had gone to New York for the weekend. As he typically did when visiting his daughter, Wyatt had taken Friday afternoon off work, leaving early in order to spend an extra night and beat the rush hour traffic, so Morgan was not even able to benefit from their end-of-week "ain't it awful" session.

In truth, Wyatt also had to prepare for a special education hearing scheduled for Monday, one that could cost the District tens of thousands of dollars. "If it's any consolation, Meryl," he told her before he left, "I would rather attend a funeral than any special ed hearing. At least death is just and treats us all equally." Wyatt's words reverberated in her mind and off her lips, generating a wry snicker, easing the weight of a headache that neared starburst proportions.

The unconscious remnants of a smile remained as Morgan pulled into the church parking lot. At that precise moment, she encountered

Harley Snitz and Nick Neidrich standing on the sidewalk waiting for her to pass, both staring at her with identical furrowed brows, which puzzled her until she realized her own expression was inappropriate for the occasion. Checking her face in the rear-view mirror, Morgan forced sobriety—in lieu of true grief, she concentrated on her headache to elicit the appearance of proper gravity.

Entering the church, she walked up the center aisle, flitting furtive glances in search of someone with whom she might feel comfortable sitting. Near the front, behind family and closest friends, sat Marburg's administrative assistant. Morgan gave a subtle wave for attention, and the woman smiled and moved to make room.

The service was about to begin when Morgan felt a tap on her shoulder. Standing next to her was Doc Randori, the last person she needed to have around during a solemn rite. Glancing past him, she noticed Snitz and Neidrich posted at the front on the far side, where they could observe the behavior of the mourners. Morgan already had gotten off on the wrong foot with them, and she knew Randori was going to tear the reverential fabric of the occasion with his wise-ass, under-the-breath comments. She fired a warning shot across his bow in the form of a scowl before bumping down. "Not a word," she whispered just loud enough to be heard above the processional hymn.

"Gotcha."

Morgan's eyes threatened. In perfect timing with the end of the hymn, she said, "And wipe that shit-eating grin off your face."

Mourners from several rows around turned to her with chastising glowers. Regaining her signature composure, Morgan hitched her shoulders back, folded her hands in her lap, and stared ahead, straight-faced. Out of the corner of her eye, she caught a glimpse of Randori, the picture of beatific innocence, paging through the hymnal, giving no indication that she had been referring to him.

The congregation stood, and Randori leaned softly into her shoulder and said out of the side of his mouth, "Faux pas, Meryl. You should've said, 'Rid thyself of the excrement that bestaineth thy countenance.'"

Morgan massaged her temples. "What are you doing here, anyway?"

"I came to comfort any kids who didn't know Kass and are feeling grief."

"You mean anyone who *did* ... oh, I get it."

Caught up in their conversation, neither educator noticed the coffin being wheeled toward the altar. As the service began, their eyes finally were drawn to it.

"What is that?" Morgan asked.

"That, Meryl, is a checkered flag. Yes, I believe that's what it is."

"But what's it draped over? What an odd shape for a coffin."

"I heard it was a special order from out of state. They didn't have it in time for the viewing; that's why the funeral was held off. I heard it was custom-painted, too."

"Painted?" Morgan frowned. "They painted a coffin?"

"Shhh," Randori said, frowning and holding his fingers to his lips as the minister began to speak, an uncharacteristic adherence to decorum.

The service was poignant and blessedly brief, considering the minister's decision to structure his sermon around the "race of life." Exacerbating the situation for Morgan, Randori found it necessary to add his own whispered comments: "Kass *forded* streams of obstacles, *dodging* the shoals of doubt" drew a glare from Morgan. "Before we begin our *Caravan* to the cemetery, *Toyota* say a few words about the *Accord* he brought to union/administrative relations" brought a sharp elbow to his ribcage.

The service ended. Morgan sighed in relief and massaged her temples again. As they rose to leave, Randori offered his arm, and without looking up, she clasped it, her eyes downcast, her lips moving in a whisper. To an observer, Morgan might have been praying, but her words were those of an avenging archangel: "One word, Randori—one more pun, one more asinine statement—and I'm going to dig my claws into the veins of your wrist and watch you bleed out onto the ground."

Randori tested her immediately. Descending the steps of the church, they encountered Virgil Davis and his wife. "Say Virge, you going to the cemetery to see Kass's final hole-in-one?"

Morgan struck. She showed no change in demeanor as Randori stifled a wince.

Davis seemed in genuine grief. He glanced at his wife, who ignored him, choosing instead to scowl at Randori, deflecting any potential invitation for company.

Before Davis could respond, the counselor leered wickedly and said, "Race ya."

Morgan struck a second time. Again, Randori did well to hide the pain, and again she remained the picture of rigid stoicism.

"Stop, Meryl, I beseech thee," Randori said, checking the flesh-breaking wounds.

"I will when you stop being a goof. Until then, know thyself—biblically speaking."

She tugged his arm and moved aside to wait for the pallbearers to bring the casket from the church. "What's up with Lois?" Morgan whispered. "She doesn't like you."

"There's an understatement. She's the proverbial anchor dragging him to the depths of administrative depravity, and I'm the anti-administrator."

"Ah yes, she hates you because you encourage Virgil to go back to teaching."

"Lois wants to be a country-clubber, but she'll never get the invite with a grunt of an assistant principal for a husband, much less a teacher."

"I always got bad vibes from her."

"Bad vibes? Maybe you should go to San Francisco, just be sure to put a flower in your hair."

"Jerk!"

Randori grinned, but any pleasure he derived out of aggravating his friend was short-lived as the crowd suddenly hushed, magnifying the new sound, a cacophonous tap dance. "Jesus Moses, pick one theme, please!"

Morgan turned toward the sound: the click-clack of cleated golf shoes on concrete as two lines of men ascended the steps of the church where they queued up facing each other. They were dressed in black jackets and golf knickers. Atop their heads were Black Watch plaid tam-o'-shanters; below their knees they wore matching argyle socks. The casket emerged from the church, and the pallbearers hefted it off the dolly. Someone shouted, "Fore," and each man on the steps held a golf club aloft, crossing it with his counterpart in the opposite line to form an archway for the casket to pass through.

As the pallbearers marched down the steps, Morgan deadpanned, "Now that's class."

"There should be bagpipes playing *Wearin' of the Green*," Randori said, expecting painful incisions on his wrist.

Instead, Morgan smiled up at him. "You've got some grotesque tangle of dendrites in that skull, Randori. You should be studied." She tugged his arm in the direction of her car and hugged it close but said nothing more as they walked. He opened the door for her and held her arm as she slid into the driver's seat. It was only when she was seated that she looked up at him again. "Meet you at the cemetery?"

"Sure. I don't think anyone else will stand with me. You sure you want to?"

Morgan stared through her windshield. All around were grieving staff members, crying friends. "If I have to choose between your irreverence and their hyper-reverence," she paused and rubbed her temples again, "God help me; I'll take you. Just be good." She returned her eyes to his, imploring. "Please."

Randori closed Morgan's door and leaned his elbows on the open window as she turned the ignition key. "I'll be as good as I can be."

"That's what worries me."

The counselor started toward his own car, passing a clot of school board members huddled, speaking in hushed tones. Turning toward Morgan to see if she was paying attention, he announced: "Gentlemen, start your engines."

Morgan lost track of Randori when he cut away and headed down a side road. *Typical Doc: won't even follow a funeral procession.* She realized that her headache was gone, but checking herself in the mirror, she also discovered that the grin she wore was broad and unabashed. This troubled her. *You look like an idiot. Knock it off.*

Many who attended the service decided to go to the cemetery, and during the slow drive, Morgan had time to think. If the number of people attending the funeral determined the final measure of a person, then Kass Marburg's life had been a success. Of course, one way to guarantee a large attendance was to be an educator who dies while still on active duty. Another way was to have a coffin that aroused curiosity.

At the cemetery, Morgan began at once to look for Randori. She chose a spot beyond the burial plot to stand, a vantage point on high ground from which she would be able to observe the parking lot below and, thus, everyone who made their way up the hill.

"Hello, Ms. Morgan."

She jerked in surprise and turned to find Snitz beside her with Neidrich just beyond. The Chief grimaced apologetically. "Sorry, didn't mean to startle you."

Morgan managed a polite smile and wondered why, of all available areas, the two officers had chosen to stand next to her? Then she realized that they, too, would want a location from which they could observe the mourners.

"Hey, Meryl." Randori finally showed up.

She spun and beamed up at him. "Where did you come from?"

"I parked behind the rise," he said, hiking a thumb to the rear. "It's a longer walk, but I didn't have to put up with any pain-in-the-ass small talk about how great Kass was."

"Dr. Randori's pretty good at sneaking up on people," Neidrich said.

"Hey Nick, Harley. OK if I stand here, or do you want me to go across the way so you can observe me better?" Neidrich ignored the comment, but that did not deter the counselor, who looked down at the grave and added, "That's a hell of a divot."

Morgan flicked Randori's hand with her knuckles to get his attention and glared at him. It was one thing to kid around between themselves, quite another to make light of Marburg's death in front of the officers investigating it. Still, she felt the odd ambivalence: On the positive side, she realized that, with Randori on her left and the officers on her right, few, if any, people would want to engage in any "pain-in-the-ass small talk," as Doc put it. To the negative, standing between the murder investigators and their suspect was awkward. She didn't want the police putting her with Randori, although, strangely, she wanted more than anything to be with him in that moment.

Before she could further consider the matter, the rear doors of the hearse opened and the pallbearers—now outfitted as a racetrack pit crew—tugged the coffin out. They placed it on the web belts running from the winch that would lower Marburg's body to its final resting-place. Finally, the flag was removed.

A hush descended. For a long moment, the only sound was the breeze whispering through nearby saplings, a gentle shush reminding all that, despite the spectacle before them, reverence must be observed. Mouths gaped, eyebrows raised, and Morgan clasped Randori's arm, her fingernails poised for quick and painful incisions.

"Holy crap," Snitz muttered, the best a non-cursing man could do, given the circumstances.

Before them sat a replica of a racecar, complete except for wheels. Emblazoned on the side were flames and, in large black numerals, Marburg's age—40—at the time of his demise. His feet and legs extended into the engine area; a glass dome was at the rear, under which Marburg's head, topped with a crash helmet, was propped up.

The Chief's statement distracted Morgan, so she was unprepared for Randori's follow-up: "The road to hell is paved with good intentions."

Morgan was unflappable; neither Snitz's uncharacteristic response, nor Randori's typical one, not even the ghastly absurdity of Marburg's funeral arrangements could move her once she committed to self-discipline. Over the years, she had developed coping skills for such occasions. She sucked the insides of her cheeks between her upper and lower molars and bit down enough to produce slight but distracting pain. Then, she set her face to "pensive" and her eyes on a point in the distance, in this case, an ash tree near the parking area. Its branches and leaves were graceful, hypnotic—distracting.

Beneath its boughs, she noticed a man in a fedora rounding the front of a BMW. She squinted in vain to improve her vision. The man was in a hurry; understandable, as the graveside service was about to begin and he was almost a hundred yards away.

Randori leaned into Morgan and whispered out of the side of his mouth, "I have to hand it to Kass. Not many people could have brought this off with dignity."

Morgan, assured of maintaining her composure, forgot about the man in the hat and returned her attention to the service. She smiled into Randori's twinkling eyes and said, " 'Dignity,' that's the word for it, dignity ... and class."

As the service ended, Morgan glanced around, checking mourners' reactions. Some were solemn; others nudged friends and sneaked peeks back at the glass bubble and the helmeted corpse. It was then that she noticed Leroy Dubcek for the first time. After he passed the casket, the psychologist donned a hat, and, with a flourish, skimmed his index finger and thumb-tip along the edge of the brim. "Leroy wears a fedora."

"Oh, yeah," Randori said. "Did you check the move at the end? What a rakish knave." He wrapped his arm around Morgan's. "Say Meryl, why don't I walk you to your car? Along the way, we can follow Leroy and talk about how Harley and Nick are looking into shady characters—psychologists that dress like old-time Mafiosi."

"No thanks, Doc. I mean, I will take you up on the walk to the car, but as far as shady characters go, you'll fill the bill quite nicely, thanks. I'd rather avoid Leroy."

"I don't think it's a good idea, either," Neidrich said, his eyes flinty, bearing emphasis on an otherwise flat statement.

Randori turned full-face to Neidrich. He cocked his head, saying nothing, but measuring the trooper, a trace of a grin at the corners of his mouth.

Morgan and Randori waited for the crowd to move off before starting down the grassy hill. As the decline steepened, Morgan stopped. "Wait a minute." She slid her hand down his arm, clasping his hand for balance as she bent to pull off one high-heeled shoe, then the other. Still clasping the counselor's hand, she smiled and pulled him into motion. "That's better. I love walking barefoot through the grass, don't you?"

"Yeah, particularly in a cemetery."

"God, I wouldn't have picked you to be a fuddy-duddy like Kerry." When it was evident that he would not be shamed into taking his shoes off, she said, "Suit yourself."

They walked in silence; Randori pondered his brief exchange with Neidrich. Morgan, though, seemed at ease with the world. She tilted her face up, relishing the gentle wind and sunlight that caressed her face. Randori sneaked a sidelong glance at her and felt a tender pang. He always judged Morgan to be beautiful, but in the pastoral setting she was crushingly so: her contours lush, yet delicate, summer's rose blush pastel on olive tones, sultry splendor radiant from within. Her hand, no longer threatening incision, felt like a tiny dove. The brush of her arm against his was calming, and at this moment he wished more than anything to feel her silken skin against his rather than the wool-on-wool formality of their funeral attire. A sudden shortness of breath, and Randori closed his eyes to ward off the temptation that tested his very fiber.

"I love this time of year," Morgan said, a lilt in her tone.

"Yeah, something about the fall." And then he went silent.

"Tell me what you're feeling," she said, fixing an unrelenting gaze on him, "what you're really feeling."

Randori paused to breathe in the day and decide if he would grant Morgan's request. For some reason, he did: "I don't know; it's the angle of the light, the smell of the leaves, the cool air. And there's this ... melancholy—like nostalgia, but bittersweet at the edges. Maybe it's the end of growing and the beginning of dying, warm memory behind, cold mystery ahead ... standing at the edge of history. Fall is when I feel most in touch with life." He inhaled again, ending on a muted sigh. "I can't put it into words."

"I'd say you just did. I loved it," Morgan said, her tone delicate, an inflection Randori had never before heard in her voice. The grip on his hand tightened as she drew him to a halt and forced him to turn; her eyes locked onto his, burning away the camouflage protecting his thoughts. Her lower lip trembled, and she gave it a steadying bite before whispering, "And what mysteries would you reveal?"

"I want … what I really want …" Searching for words, he glanced up the hill, and a frozen fist of reality crushed his rising ardor. "Harley and Nick are watching." Randori pursed his lips, thinking; then, for the benefit of the officers, he raised his voice enough for them to hear, if they strained. "I want a Rolls-Canardly. I used to drive one, you know."

Taken aback by the cosmic shift in mood, Morgan dropped Randori's hand and said the only thing she could: "Shit, Phil Olson—over by his car."

"Phil doesn't drive a Rolls-Canardly."

"Huh?" Morgan shook her head, not comprehending. "What is a Rolls-Canardly?"

Randori grinned. "It rolls down one side of the hill and canardly get up the other."

Morgan's eyes ignited, but her voice remained steady, if menacing. "You are a creep! Phil's watching, too. I think he's waiting for me."

"He probably needs a consult on how to start his car."

"I'd better see what he wants." Morgan shifted embarrassed, pleading eyes to Randori. "Come with me. That'll keep whatever he has to say brief."

"My pleasure; I enjoy being a social pariah." A twisted grin spread across his face. "I have an idea. Come on." He strode purposefully toward Olson.

Hustling to keep up, Morgan said, "I don't like this. Doc, you're frightening me."

Never breaking stride, he muttered, "You'll thank me in a minute." He raised a finger as if hailing a cab. "Hey Phil, missed you at the service."

Olson pushed away from his car, snapping to attention. He stood uneasy, seemingly unable to decide what to do with his hands and arms: crooking one into an awkward wave, letting it fall, lifting the other straight forward in a half-assed, half-Heil Hitler salute, dropping both arms stiffly to his side for a moment before folding them across his chest. He finally settled on cupping his hands together in front of his groin and leaning back against his car in forced insouciance.

Randori peeked at Morgan out of the corner of his eyes. "What the hell was that, semaphore?" Returning his attention to Olson, he said, "You want to go to brunch with us? We have to hustle." He checked his watch. "They stop serving soon."

Olson began fumbling for his keys. "No, I, uh, have to get going. I just wanted to say hello to Meryl."

"Well, don't let me stop you." Randori stepped aside, giving a swooping wave toward Morgan like one of *The Price is Right* models showing off a new toaster-oven.

The acting superintendent cast a wary glance at the counselor before offering a nervous smile to Morgan. "Hello, Meryl. I wanted to ask you something, but it can wait. Will you be in tomorrow?"

"Monday?" Morgan corrected. "Yes, Phil, we can talk first thing Monday."

Olson struggled to find the button on the remote-entry to unlock his car, although he did open his trunk on the first try. "New car," he said, clearing his throat.

Randori whispered, "How much would you pay to see him set off the alarm?"

The car alarm went off.

Morgan's hand went to her mouth as she watched Olson's humiliation level shoot from mild anxiety to full-blown distress. "Oh my God, Doc. Look what you've done."

Olson finally got the alarm off and the door unlocked. Looking at Morgan as if he wanted to crawl under his oil pan then glaring at Randori as if he wanted to crawl back out and shove him under, he spluttered something about a defective electronic system and bade goodbye—only to Morgan. He atoned for his recent ill-fated maneuvers by successfully starting up and shoving into the correct gear, small and short-lived victories, as he ran over the curb on his first turn.

"And he's going to be appointed superintendent," Randori said.

"You really know how to make a bad situation worse."

"What? You didn't want to talk to him, and I made your wish come true. I wanted to see him set off his car alarm, and, well, Phil made my dream come true. Man, I have to remember to get a lottery ticket today and hit the trifecta."

"But telling him that you and I are going to brunch together? That won't play well back at the office."

"I'm more worried about Nick and Harley," Randori said, scanning the gravesite, then the hillside. The investigators were nowhere in sight. "But Phil? Think about it, Meryl. He saw us, and if he's at all perceptive—a leap, I know—he'd have to be suspicious. My asking him to join us for brunch showed we had nothing to hide. After the vaudeville show he just put on, he'll probably want to forget the whole episode." The counselor turned a sly leer on Morgan. "All of which makes me wonder: Why did Phil get so out of kilter? I certainly don't intimidate him that much."

Morgan looked away. "Phil is having some issues with me."

"Issues?" The dawn rose in Randori's eyes. "Kerry, Phil. Why Morgan, you vixen, you just turn everyone on, don't you?"

The fire in Morgan's stare scorched the grin off Randori's face, but as his expression sobered, hers softened to smoldering embers. She leaned in, her mouth close to his, and she whispered, "Everyone but the one I want." Trapping Randori in her gaze, her lips parted.

He shifted forward, the listing of a ship swept by an irresistible tide. He lingered a moment, then with a quick blink he righted himself. Morgan glanced around. The only people in sight were two cemetery workers at Marburg's grave at the top of the hill. Leveling her eyes on Randori, she said, "What about you? What do you think?"

Randori looked to the hillside. "You know I think you're great."

Her eyes flared. "Answer my question."

A hesitation, then: "You're the most beautiful woman I've ever known."

Morgan stood close, her dark eyes glistening. The breeze kicked up, tossing her raven hair. This was a Morgan that Randori had never seen, wildly sensual, enchanting, inviting him to live his desire. Silent, poised, her only movement was to brush wisps of hair from her eyes, revealing mists of promise and surrender. Her grip on his arm softened, and her hand slid up and across his shoulder to his jaw.

"Meryl ... I can't."

"Can't be unfaithful to Lynn," Morgan said, finishing his thought as her eyes dropped to his chest. "Too much honor."

"Not enough. The temptation is too great."

Ed Knepp followed Randori home from the funeral, and contemplated the suspect's relationship with Meryl Morgan. He had seen them together outside the church. Afterwards, he drove to a spot in the cemetery where he could remain hidden but observe them through binoculars. They were a little too close. He wondered what would happen if Kerry Wyatt and Randori's wife got anonymous calls from a "concerned friend" about their relationship? Shaking off the thought, he realized that if one or both of them confronted Randori, he would know he was being watched. A good investigator has to think two steps ahead, like a chess player. A grin lit up Knepp's face, and he began to bob his head and drum his fingers to some tune inside his head. After the case was wrapped up, maybe then he would add this insult to the injury of Randori's arrest.

A little before 1:00 PM, Randori piled his family into the car and headed to a farm market. Upon returning home, they took the dog for a walk. Knepp was tempted to go home himself, spend some time with Molly and maybe watch the Penn State game. Then he remembered Justin Frederickson and resolved to make the best use of what little time he had before news broke about the heroin overdose.

At 3:30 PM, Randori's wife got into the car and headed for her own job. Uneventful hours passed, and Knepp wished he had brought something to read. At 5:40, feeling as if his bladder was about to burst, he risked a trip to a nearby gas station. After relieving himself, he bought a football preview magazine and hustled to his post, hoping he hadn't missed something. His anxiety achieved the same relief as his bladder as the only change was that the lights had gone on in his suspect's living room. Using his flashlight for illumination, he read that the best strong safety since Nick Neidrich was going to make Notre Dame's defense invincible. *Ironic*, he thought.

At 9:30 PM, the basement lights went on. After considerable vacillation, Knepp's curiosity overcame his fear of getting caught. He crept out of his car and approached Randori's house, his eyes darting in all directions, checking if any neighbors spied him. Getting caught would be bad; if Harley found out he was on a stakeout outside his jurisdiction without first securing permission, he would get reamed out for sure. Several surrounding homes were already dark. The only sign of life was in an enclosed porch where elderly neighbors were engrossed in a game of cards. Knepp sneaked to the rear of Randori's home, checked around one more time, then crouched and twisted to peek into the basement window.

Randori was in the middle of a large room, wearing a black *gi*, moving slowly through his katas, every punch, kick, and block strenuously delivered. When he finished his forms, he alternated a set of pushups, a set of crunches, and a stretching exercise. Most striking was the counselor's demeanor: intensity edged with gloom, a soldier facing an unbeatable foe, realizing that defeat was inevitable but determined to go down fighting. When the time came for Randori's arrest, Knepp decided, he would draw his gun and keep his quarry at arm's length. And shoot without question if threatened.

Ed Knepp was becoming desperate. The truth about Justin's death would break at any time. That notion fled his mind as he recognized a break in Randori's routine. Every evening, the living room lights were on by 7:00 PM, but on this night, the room remained dark. Grasping at straws, but maybe ...

Although most of the neighbors were up and about, he left the safety of his car and headed for the rear of Randori's home. Edging around the garage of a neighbor's house, he saw lights in the counselor's basement and kitchen. He crept up to the house and peered into the basement, where Randori's children were playing video games. Straightening, he arched to peek into the kitchen. No sooner had his eyes risen over the sill than Randori passed, just inside the window. Startled, Knepp ducked so quickly that the bill of his baseball cap caught the window ledge, flipped back off his head, and tumbled down his back. As he spun to recover his lid, a light went on in the sunroom, illuminating the back yard like a magnificent Chinese lantern. Knepp froze for a moment in the glare. Gathering his senses and his hat, he lumbered to the side of the house. Once again in the safety of darkness, he sneaked a peak around the corner, breathing through his nose to silence the heaving wheeze brought on by fright and his unplanned sprint.

Randori had put the dog out and returned to the kitchen. The mutt nosed around the yard looking for a place to do its business, working in ever-widening circles, moving closer to Knepp. A shudder struck when he noticed that the dog was unchained. The animal stopped and perked her ears, and the deputy snapped his head back, praying she hadn't sensed his presence. Holding his breath until he thought his lungs would burst, he backpedaled along the side of the house, ducking as he passed windows, and slunk to the front yard before turning to a high-kneed sprint back to his car.

Sliding behind the wheel, Knepp wiped his brow and forced deep, slow breaths as he stared at the house. Lights went on in the bathroom and in rooms the officer assumed to be the children's bedrooms. He waited, regaining his breath and his composure and his belief that it was safe to go back onto Randori's property. After almost an hour, the rooms went dark, and still he waited, gathering the courage to step outside his car.

He pressed the door closed and moved from shadow to shadow until he could peer into the back yard. The home had gone dark. After surveying neighboring homes for prying eyes, he crossed between parked cars and onto Randori's property. Again, he prowled the perimeter, crouching, creeping with slow stealth, every muscle in his body coiled. Perspiration bloomed on his neck; the warm breeze rattled through the branches of the tall oaks, tickling the back of his head, chilling the sweat as it seeped from his pores. The icy sensation writhed down his spine, and he shuddered in the growing suspicion that someone was watching him.

Knepp should have trusted his senses. On the roof above, a black silhouette, blending into the indigo heaven, squatted and peered down at him, an animated gargoyle that moved in silence as Knepp moved, stopping only when the breeze died.

Knepp backed away from the window, shooting twitchy glances to every side. He skulked to the front of the house then picked up speed, bustling across the street with the awkward gait of a person trying at once to hasten yet remain silent. Back in the safety of his car, labored, fearful breaths wracked his chest. The case was making him goosey, he told himself as he gazed through the still darkness at Randori's house. Knepp tried to convince himself that his alarm was irrational. His mind finally set at ease, he pulled away from the curb, turning his headlights on only when he was a block away.

On his way home, Knepp decided to shift his stakeout to Paul Roberge's home. The boy was the one to follow if he was going to make a quick break in the case. In his zeal to get Randori, Knepp had forgotten that in the world of drugs the daily action occurred on the street. Roberge was the street level dealer. Once he got the boy, Randori's house of cards would fall.

Crossing the line into Freedom County, Knepp's thoughts clung to the counselor. The man was dangerous and smart. While he kept a safe distance, high school kids did his dirty work. And if any of them dared question his authority, he would be more than willing to show off his martial arts proficiency. Out of blind hatred and jealousy, Randori had ambushed and killed Big Bob. Then he murdered Kass, too, probably because Kass was hot on the trail of the heroin ring, maybe closing in on the counselor himself. That was it, all the proof Knepp needed; now all he needed was evidence.

Excited by his conclusion, he decided to detour on a sneak run to Roberge's home. He had seen little of Molly lately, but he was too close to breaking the case to stop now. Pulling off the road, he reached under the seat to retrieve his private logbook, flicked on the dome light, and scribbled in his latest ideas. When he finished, he headed to Culver Pond. In his eagerness, he leaned forward, like a jockey prodding his mount. Several times, he had to remind himself to ease up, and only when he reached Roberge's neighborhood did he slow to a prowl car pace.

Several days earlier, when he first checked out Roberge's home, he noticed a vacant house across the lane. Its tree-lined driveway provided good cover for a stakeout. Cutting his lights, he backed in between two stone pillars that guarded the driveway.

Knepp had not noticed the car that followed a distance behind him from the time he reached the outskirts of Culver Pond. It was only after he cut his engine that he saw its lights creep up the road. He turned off the dome light and eased out of his car. Sneaking to the end of the drive, he squatted beside a stone pillar and squinted to filter the headlights' glare. It was a light-colored, midsize car with a small split grill. His gut clenched. *The white Pontiac.* But as it passed by and pulled into the driveway two doors down from Roberge's house, he realized with disappointment that it was a BMW.

Returning to his vigil, Knepp saw the lights above Roberge's front door and garage filter through the foliage. The rest of the house was dark. He waited until the neighbor's front door closed, but as he rose out of his crouch to step forward, a shadow appeared, moving right to left past the garage and toward the front door. He recognized Paul Roberge's silhouette and guessed he had been in the BMW. A thought struck: *what if the teacher on the field trip had mistaken the BMW for a Pontiac?* He hustled to his car and jotted in his private log: "White BMW (500 series?) NOT Pontiac. Owner is neighbor of PR - brought him home." He put the logbook back under the driver's seat.

Again, he started across the lane and trudged up the rise toward the house. This would be a snap compared to spying on Randori: no nosy neighbors, heavy tree cover. The only problem was the noise he made shuffling through the underbrush. It occurred to him that he might have been better off walking right up the driveway.

Breaking into the clearing near the garage, he surveyed the surroundings. To his left, the long façade of the house dissolved into darkness; shrubbery and dense ground cover hugged the wall. To his right, a macadam driveway and a quick trip around the garage, he just had to hurry across the path of light, and he would be on his way to the rear of the house. Easy choice, Knepp bent at the hips and scurried to his right. Skipping to a halt at the corner of the garage, he peered around the side and saw a four-foot band of mulch, not ground cover, surrounded the mature shrubbery lining the side of the house, less chance of tangling his feet and stumbling.

Knepp worked his way from window to window, weaving and twisting to maneuver between shrubs in his effort to catch a glimpse of the interior. Cool fronds of arborvitae, supple and fragrant, caressed his sides on this muggy night, but the hollies and barberries pricked through his pant legs to his skin. Worst were the yews, whose ancient gnarled branches were like arthritic fingers jabbing his ribs. If only he hadn't left his leather bomber jacket in the car. He happily would endure the steamy Indian summer night in exchange for protection from those branches.

At the rear corner of the house a light flashed on, and Knepp flattened himself against the wall. Its glow flowed from a large picture window onto two yews, bringing a wintry glisten to their branches. He crept toward the light, sucking in his stomach to squeeze between shrubbery and the stucco wall. When he reached the window, he stooped and peeked in to see half of what must have been the family room: walnut paneling, fieldstone fireplace, pool table. Moving to the center of the window, he saw Roberge sitting at the edge of a leather ottoman, hunched over a glass table, working on something with both hands—rolling a joint, as Knepp came to realize.

Hoping to improve his view, Knepp kept his head low and moved to the right. To the left was a home theater system: a huge flat screen TV and more electronic gadgetry than he had ever seen. He watched Roberge pick up a video small game controller, and a game popped onto the screen as bass-laden rock music boomed from the speakers. The sudden blast of sound and electronic carnage startled Knepp.

He eased up out of his crouch, confident that the boy's concentration on the game and the music emanating from the speakers would cover his movements. As he stood, a thunderous grunt exploded up and out from the base of his lungs, escaping his mouth before he could catch it, and his body lunged forward. He thought he had backed into one of the sharp branches of a yew and reminded himself to be quiet, but his thoughts became a tangle of confusion, colliding and fracturing, giving way to pain that radiated out from an icy puncture at ground zero. It scorched through his chest and across his back, and his body heaved into a wracking cough, splattering saliva across the window. *Black spit? Or red? Be quiet!* Gasping for air, struggling to stand, messages to and from his brain garbled and slowed as his mind swam into shock. A vague notion arose that something had run him through. His legs caved in, betraying his will, and he pirouetted.

Another thrust, now into his gut, ripping upward and plowing him into the wall.

The blaring stereo had cloaked not only Knepp's movement, but also that of another. The garish light that spilled out from the family room window illuminated a familiar, merciless face that was now staring down at him. Ed Knepp smiled; he had solved the case and kept his mouth shut, but unless he acted fast, he would never be able to tell anyone. *Ironic.*

POSITIVELY APOCALYPTIC

Like a sentinel monitoring an approaching enemy host, Randori watched the swollen purple clouds charge forward from the horizon. In the field across from the high school, cows turned tail to the impending storm and moved as one toward a clump of trees on a far hillock. He sensed more than heard Virgil Davis approach from behind.

"Say, Doc," Davis's hearty voice rang out as he clapped the counselor on the back. "Ready to rock and roll?"

Randori's gaze remained on the field a quarter of a mile away. "I hope the boys make it."

Davis frowned in bewilderment. "What?"

"The cows." Randori motioned with his chin. "They always head to the foot of that hill when rain's coming."

"We have to go kick ass on Leroy, and you're worried about cows?"

Randori finally turned his solemn gaze on Davis. "A cow saved my life once."

Davis cocked his head, awaiting a punch line. With none forthcoming, he chuckled. "That's a story I have to hear sometime. Not now, though."

"Not ever, Virge."

"OK," Davis said cautiously. "You want to walk to the meeting together?"

"We'd best go in separately. I don't want Leroy to know we're in cahoots."

Davis shot a disbelieving look. "Don't you think it's a little late for that?"

"The timing is perfect," Randori said, a sneer punctuating his statement as he turned again to the ominous morning diorama. "It's positively apocalyptic out there."

Davis followed Randori's stare. Sure enough, the cows had gathered at the foot of the hillock, just as the counselor had predicted. "I never noticed that before."

Cat Blanchard swept through the office doors and into the vestibule, smiling a greeting at the two men. "Hi guys! Ready?"

"You look chipper today," Davis said, "but I've got to rain on your parade. Doc doesn't want to be seen with us. Which is all right with me; he's weirding me out."

"You two go in first and sit across from Leroy," Randori said. "I'll sit beside him, at the right hand of the father, as it were, so I'll be in eye contact with you. Don't acknowledge me. Cat, you keep thinking about Nick and smiling; it'll rattle Leroy."

Randori's mindreading display brought a blush to Blanchard's cheeks. "All right," she said. "Where's Kerry going to sit?"

"Don't worry about him. Wait till I move, then jump in whenever you like."

Davis disliked the idea of entering a meeting with no preparation or control over how events would unfold. Close observation of Randori when he arrived at Dubcek's office provided no insight. More revealing was the flinty stare Mrs. Roberge fixed on him, but she softened when the counselor smiled and shook her hand.

"Don't worry," Randori said, "we're going to get Paul the help he needs and deserves." Turning to Dubcek, he gave a surreptitious smile. "Right, Mr. Dubcek?" He pulled a chair to the psychologist's side, reached underneath, flicked a lever, and the seat shot to its highest position. "Kerry Wyatt won't be coming, so we can start."

The door opened, and a SAP member peeked in. "Do you need us?"

Dubcek shook his head. "Thanks, I think Dr. Randori and I can handle it."

Before the door closed, Tammy Eboli brushed through, prompting Davis to meet Blanchard's suspicious eyes. Eboli answered the administrators' unspoken question. "When I heard about Paul's career goals, I told Mr. Dubcek I could recommend classes for his post-school transition." She sat, tugging at her skirt in a futile attempt to cover her long, slender legs.

Dubcek stared at them, lingering, before he said, "At our last meeting, we were about to recommend a classification for Paul." He went on to repeat his findings on his various tests. At the end, he said, "My conclusion remains the same: Paul meets the criteria for Serious Emotional Disturbance."

"The point where we left the last meeting," Davis said, ignoring Randori's pre-meeting suggestion, "was that the Roberges were going to visit the County Alternative Education Program. Have you done that?" Davis already knew the answer. He had called the director of the program that morning.

"I ... no," Mr. Roberge stammered. "We haven't had time."

Mrs. Roberge placed a hand on her husband's arm. "We called several times, but there was no answer. We both work; our schedules are tight. Besides, they don't serve Special Education students."

Davis's game face appeared. He had heard the excuses before and was not content to wait for Randori's strategy to unfold. "That's—"

"Understandable," Randori said, cutting Davis off, though his tone was soft, soothing. "You're both busy with your jobs, and bringing up a teenager these days is difficult. You're looking to us for help."

Tammy Eboli shot a glance at Randori; her eyes went wide before curving into crescents of disappointment as she burned her gaze into the legal tablet on her lap. Davis scowled in confusion, both at Randori's words and the flicker of a smile the counselor flashed after seeing Eboli's reaction.

Randori continued: "We have to examine Paul from all angles and with prudence." He waited for nods and murmurs of assent. "Mr. Dubcek's report, I notice, uses information from SAP team members rather than from Paul's classroom teachers."

"That's because the teachers are prejudiced against Paul," said Mrs. Roberge.

Randori looked at Dubcek, who shifted in his seat, but still managed an uneasy smile. Returning his attention to Mrs. Roberge, he said, "Most of the teachers I talked to have compassion for him, although they do want to see his behavior improve."

"Well, I disagree," Mrs. Roberge said. "Ever since middle school, teachers and principals have harassed him. They say he's noncompliant, I say he's self-reliant."

"We can't just call the whole thing off," Randori said with a private smile. "We have to respect what his regular teachers report if we're going to understand and, therefore, help Paul. But for now please say more about Paul's self-reliance."

Mrs. Roberge proceeded to contradict her own statement from the previous meeting recorded by Dubcek on the rough draft report Theresa had provided Randori. "My husband and I have made sure that Paul has a good self-concept despite the school's efforts to destroy it. And he is independent; he resists unreasonable rules, as he should."

Dubcek was quick to interject: "I think what Mrs. Roberge means is—"

"This is important," Randori cut in, holding his hand up.

"Most of the time," Mrs. Roberge said, "Paul has no problems. He's very mature, but school is an intimidating place. Paul is just trying to take control."

Randori nodded. "You're saying that Paul manages his behavior. It's purposeful. Has he ever shown self-destructive tendencies?"

"No, never, although he is depressed because of what the school has done to him. Sometimes that depression—and frustration—makes him lash out."

Mr. Roberge added, "That's only natural."

Randori said, "He externalizes."

Davis scanned the room, trying to read faces. Blanchard still looked as concerned as he felt. For some reason, Eboli flashed a furtive grin at Randori before returning to her assiduous note taking. The counselor himself was sphinx-like. The Roberges sat forward, eager to discuss their son's merits and rationalize his deficits. Most perplexing was Dubcek: He sat back, legs crossed and arms folded across his chest, yet he maintained a self-confident smirk. The assistant principal concluded that Dubcek believed he had the votes to hold sway, and even if the parents made a few verbal gaffes, they would be droplets in a vast gray sea that determined emotional disturbance.

Smiling benignly from Mrs. Roberge to her husband, Randori opened a folder he had been using to support his legal tablet as he took his own notes. "You'll be happy to know that Paul's regular teachers back up your own views. Before I get into that, I'd like to ask Mr. Davis a question. Has Paul shown any remorse for his negative behaviors?"

"No, never."

Dubcek wagged an authoritative finger. "I find that—"

"And why should he?" Mrs. Roberge snapped, overlapping the psychologist. "He has emotional problems. Isn't that what this meeting is all about?"

"Yes, it is," Randori said. "And the good news is, Paul is not emotionally disturbed. The bad news is, he appears to be socially maladjusted."

Dubcek bolted upright and clasped the armrests of his chair. "You're splitting hairs. Who are you to make that differentiation?"

Randori soft voice became menacing. "Those are the hairs we need to split to decide if a student is best served through emotional support or alternative education."

"You are not a psychologist."

"Kerry Wyatt has been a school psychologist for 25 years. He reviewed the Achenbach you administered with input of the SAP team members and had Paul's regular teachers fill out the Behavior

Checklist. Their results differ significantly with those of your SAP people."

Dubcek's brow gained an officious arch. "The regular teachers have only taught Paul for a month. Of that time, he's been on suspension for two weeks."

"And your SAP people only worked with Paul a few days."

"But I personally trained them in what to look for."

"Precisely." Randori smiled through the sibilance, a cobra whose prideful prey had verbally backed himself into a corner. Continuing, he said, "I would submit that the classroom teachers' inexperience with the instrument makes them more objective observers, less likely to manipulate answers to arrive at the conclusions you want."

"If you are implying what I think you are, I intend to file a grievance."

Tammy Eboli sat up and raised her hand to make a point. She flashed a sympathetic smile at Dubcek. "Um, no. Dr. Randori is an Association member, not an administrator, so you can't file a grievance against him."

"Go, Doc," Blanchard whispered out of the side of her mouth to Davis.

The counselor shifted his eyes to the assistant principals and flashed an almost imperceptible wink before returning to business. "To get a complete picture, we had Paul's teachers from last year complete the checklist, as well. Those results also contradicted the ones your people came up with."

Dubcek reached for the phone. "Perhaps I should have the SAP Team join us."

"I don't think so." Randori's tone was a treacherous sheet of ice, daring the psychologist to venture forth. "They weren't invited to this soiree."

Dubcek's eyes flitted across the invitation letter. To Davis, it seemed the psychologist used the moment to marshal his wits, for when he lifted his eyes again he placed his palm on his chest and chortled. "Using last year's teachers flies in the face of test objectivity. What would they know about Paul's current emotional state?"

Randori cocked his head to the side and said, "Are you saying the onset of Paul's emotional problems came only this academic year? In the past five weeks? If that's the case, he hasn't met a prime criterion for services: the evidence of emotional disturbance over an extended period. So, what is it, do we admit the teacher reports, or do we dismiss them along with any argument that he's emotionally disturbed?"

Kerry Wyatt's sudden entrance brought an awkward silence to the room. "Sorry I'm late."

"Mr. Wyatt," Dubcek said, "Dr. Randori is being unprofessional."

Wyatt's mouth veered into a disapproving scowl. "You evaluated a student who was exhibiting antisocial behaviors without making an honest effort to differentiate between conduct and emotional problems? *That* is unprofessional."

"Kerry, that was a low blow," Dubcek complained.

"What does all this mean?" Mr. Roberge asked.

Dubcek began to answer, but Wyatt's voice overrode him. "What we're seeing, Mrs. Roberge is a conduct problem, which does not indicate emotional disturbance in and of itself. It is, however, associated with social maladjustment. And there is no supportable evidence to indicate that Paul suffers from depression."

"As I said earlier," Dubcek persisted, "this is splitting hairs. There is no definitive line that separates emotional disturbance from social maladjustment."

"That may be true in some cases," Randori bluffed, "but this isn't one of them. Even the statements of Paul's parents support the case for Conduct Disorder."

Poised on the precipice of defeat, Dubcek tried to get a toehold on one final defense. "Paul's behaviors may not be self-destructive, but behaviors that work to the detriment of the student are, by definition, self-defeating. And self-defeating behaviors are indicative of emotional disturbance as well as social maladjustment. Therein lies the gray area that supports my conclusions. I would wager that a hearing officer would choose to err on the side of the student rather than on that of the school administration."

In the past few minutes, Davis's optimism had inflated, only to burst on the acuity of Dubcek's conclusion. If special education law and case history proved anything, it was that the school is assumed guilty, if not downright sinister in its dealings with disabled children and their families. Still, he suspected the Roberges to be ignorant of this, and so he held out a shred of hope that Wyatt and Randori would prevail.

Randori turned to the parents. "Now, I don't want to put Paul—or you—through an expulsion hearing. We can accept him into our on-campus Alternative Program, as opposed to the county school. Even though he'll be separated from the regular population, he can benefit from close monitoring in a small, structured environment. It's really an opportunity for him to get a fresh start. We can work on a behavior support plan and his grades, so when he's reintegrated into the high school, he'll have all of us working toward his success."

"What is it you want?" Dubcek asked, offering a conciliatory smile. "A fulltime emotional support class here in the high school would accomplish the same thing."

"What I want isn't important," the counselor said. "The prime requisite is to develop the best plan to help Paul while protecting the student population as a whole."

"You just want to warehouse him," Dubcek shot back. "An alternative school placement is unacceptable. Furthermore, the student population, as a whole, is of no concern if its rights trample Paul's."

Mrs. Roberge's shrill voice tore through the exchange between the counselor and the psychologist: "I want my son to get help—emotionally and academically."

Wyatt smiled at the woman and said, in a soothing, yet insistent tone, "Mrs. Roberge, I must be frank. If Paul were to be placed in an emotional support class, we would be doing him a disservice and that placement would likely exacerbate his situation. In my opinion, true emotional support children tend to be victims, easy pickings for Paul. He would be in serious trouble if harm came to one of them.

"Our main goal for all of our students is that they become happy, productive citizens. We have the means to attain that for Paul, but we have to help him learn that in real life, negative consequences follow negative behaviors. Putting him back in the high school would teach him that if he has the right advocate, he can get away with anything." Wyatt leaned forward in his chair and looked from one parent to the other. "And if that happens, then I'm afraid we will lose any chance we have to help Paul become the young man we all want him to be."

As he watched Mrs. Roberge dissolve unto anguished tears, Davis mutely cursed Dubcek. The psychologist had done to the Roberges what he had done to so many: through mind games and manipulation he had used their weaknesses against them, convincing them that only he had their best interests at heart; therefore, as Wyatt spoke perfect sense to them, a cognitive disconnect set in, twisting both mind and emotion.

"Very well," Dubcek said, training his pen over the Evaluation Report sign-off page, "Mr. Wyatt is the Local Educational Agency representative. The recommendation is that we not identify Paul as a student with a disability and that we pursue a placement in our on-campus alternative school. In the MDE process, anyone may disagree with the recommendation. Sign as you wish, but I will dissent." He directed his attention toward Tammy Eboli. "I would hope that any right-thinking person would also disagree." After the sheet was signed and returned to him, Dubcek sent a piercing glance of disapproval at Eboli. "Mr. Wyatt, Mr. Davis, Ms. Blanchard, Dr. Randori, and Ms. Eboli agree with the recommendation; the Roberges join me in dissent. If they take my advice, they will get legal services and demand a hearing."

Sheets of rain lashed the window in Harley Snitz's office as he stared through the thin pane that separated him from infinity. Later, dry Canadian air would bring the first cold snap of the fall. He sensed that he, too, stood on the threshold of change, close to a break in his murder investigations.

Phyllis peeked in. She feigned geniality, but fatigue had drawn deeper the lines of her face; fear forced her blood to the core, leaving her skin sallow. "Ed's not in yet, and he hasn't called in sick." She turned to leave. "Just thought you should know."

A queasy squeeze in Snitz's stomach told him something was wrong. Knepp was scheduled to report at 7:30 AM, and he usually arrived early. Since joining the force almost twenty years before, he had generated his share of consternation, but on balance, Knepp was a good officer. He rarely missed a shift; even back when he was drinking, and whenever he was too sick to work—a rarity—he always gave advance notice. When he worked very late, he caught a nap at the station so he would be on time. Snitz occasionally gave him the day off, and no matter how tired he was Knepp took Molly on a day trip to Baltimore's Inner Harbor or shopping in Lancaster or King of Prussia.

Knepp still had his moments of unpredictability, so the Chief thought he was merely running late. But then the sergeant's wife called and Snitz went from annoyed to anxious. Snitz had always been impressed with Molly Knepp's ability to read the Riot Act to anyone who deserved it, and he received the full brunt for conspiring with her husband to keep her in the dark about Ed's all-nighter. But beneath the harsh words, a small trill of alarm rang up from the back of her throat. Molly wanted answers, but Snitz was at a loss for an explanation, and that raised her level of concern even further.

Knowing that Knepp often talked to her about cases, the Chief pressed for any information she might have. There was a pause, and then she muttered reluctantly that Ed had mentioned a high school connection in the drug ring he was investigating and that he thought it would be the biggest case of his career. After divulging information her husband had told her not to share, Molly flipped the game, demanding that Snitz confess the level of danger in the case. Despite his own gut-level fears, he felt no guilt assuaging hers based on the simple fact that

Freedom County had always been a peaceful place. Until recently. Through a forced chuckle, he told her Ed probably had fallen asleep in his car during a stakeout; it had happened to many an officer; Snitz reminded Molly that Ed himself had done the same. Finally, he assured her he would call when Ed showed up.

After hanging up the phone, Snitz stared at it as if waiting for good news. Recognizing the absurdity of wishful thinking, he moved with forced indifference to the dispatcher's desk and pressed Phyllis for any details she may have picked up when Knepp had checked in the day before.

"I wish I knew more," she said. "Ed's been on stakeout every night since last Wednesday. Only thing I know is he wanted us to check out white Pontiacs."

The door crashed open, and Neidrich entered with a smile and two cups of coffee. Shaking rain off his head and slicker like a young bloodhound, he struggled to keep the cups level, unaware that Phyllis had become the unwilling beneficiary of his spray.

"Every day you come in here with your own coffee!" Phyllis snapped. "Meanwhile, the stuff I make goes to waste."

Seeing Neidrich's expression turn from contentment to guilt, Snitz jumped into the fray. "Phyllis, you've been here as long as I have, and the next good pot of coffee you make will be your first." Both trooper and dispatcher gaped at the Chief who immediately realized that he was as shocked as his audience by his uncharacteristic outburst. "I'm sorry, I didn't mean that."

"I know," Phyllis said, recovering her own composure. "We're all worried about Ed. … And I know my coffee sucks."

Neidrich hooked a quick double take at Phyllis then asked. "What's up with Ed?"

Snitz scratched the back of his neck, an excuse for an abashed bow of the head. "He didn't go home last night or show up for work today; no one knows where he is."

Phyllis came around her desk and placed a hand on her boss's shoulder. "You know how he is; he probably had a snack and got woozy. He'll come rolling in here any minute all stinky and scruffy. You and Nick go solve your cases. When Ed gets in, I'll blutz him upside the head and tell him he has to give you a full report."

"Thanks, Phyl." Snitz gave a weak smile. Motioning with his head, he led Neidrich to his office. Before closing the door, he glanced back at the dispatcher, who was still smiling, but not with her eyes.

"Everything's going to hell," Snitz muttered.

"Could it be Ed just went on a bender? Or maybe he's shacked up somewhere."

"The bender's out; he quit the hooch years ago. And Ed wouldn't cheat on Molly." Snitz slumped into his chair. "I was so wrapped up in our work and so happy to get him out of our hair that I didn't even bother to keep tabs on him."

"You can't blame yourself for Ed's shortcomings. And you can't sit and stew."

"You're right," Snitz said, sitting up and hiking his shoulders back. "Back to Dr. Samson and Kass, I know we're stuck, but I have this sense that we're close to a break."

"Let's challenge our assumptions. First, we have to accept that we don't have enough to hypothesize whether or not Samson's and Marburg's deaths are connected." Neidrich sat forward, propping his elbows on his knees. "Second, we have to lose our fixation on Davis and Randori."

"Fine with me. Virgil has alibis for both nights, anyway, unless you're ready to believe his wife is in cahoots with him on Kass's death."

"She's not the most pleasant person," Neidrich said. "But her story puts Davis in the clear. And Randori? I don't buy him as a murderer." He held up a cautionary finger. "Although I'm not sure he's being completely up front with us."

"Seems like he's just riding it out, but who knows?" The Chief stood, stretched his back, and ambled to his window. "That guy thinks in convoluted ways."

Neidrich rose and stood beside Snitz. "We said before that we could be dealing with someone who doesn't like him, and if Randori is innocent, he's smart enough to come to the same conclusion."

"You think he's holding out because he wants to deal personally with his persecutor?"

Neidrich smiled and nodded. "We're thinking alike."

Snitz's brow crinkled studiously. "Folks who don't like Dr. Randori were mostly friends of Kass and Dr. Samson, though. You have anyone in mind?"

"The other night Cat mentioned this Dubcek guy, the psychologist at the high school. At first, I didn't think much of it—I'm still not sure it's anything—but it's been rattling around my brain for a couple days, and I want to talk it out with you: Dubcek makes a hobby of undermining Randori. Real devious. It's all based on power and control over Pupil Services—Randori has it, Dubcek wants it."

Snitz's eyes became slits. "Wait a minute." He reached for his notes. "Virgil mentioned his name when I talked to him and Mr. Wyatt on ..." He opened his log book and riffled through the pages, zeroing in with his index finger. "September 27, the day after Kass was killed. They said Kass had been butting heads with Dubcek. Seems Dubcek wielded a lot of power heading up the SAP and Crisis Teams. Kass broke all that up." Referring again to his log, Snitz added, "And Dubcek was upset with Kass over a special ed meeting the day before."

Neidrich said, "I know Marburg didn't like Randori, but it seems like they both were working toward the same ends. Dubcek and Eboli teamed up to go after Randori—Eboli for the in-your-face attacks while Dubcek stabbed him in the back."

"Happens all the time," Snitz said. "People's work lives get boring, so they pick on someone. It's bullying, adult-style, plain and simple. It's ugly, but that's about all. Is that why Ms. Eboli is so hostile toward Dr. Randori?"

"According to Cat, Dubcek and Eboli had a thing about a year or so ago. It's over now, but Dubcek's a jealous sort, and he didn't let go easily. Last Monday, Eboli got together with Marburg to dry-gulch Randori. Cat has a gut feeling maybe those two were involved, too."

The Chief gave a dismissive wave. "I didn't see Ms. Eboli at Kass's funeral, did you? And, if the two murders are connected, where does Dubcek fit with Dr. Samson? Still and all, I'm for thinking we ought to check him out."

"I agree. And here's another reason, although it's a long shot ..." The trooper dropped into contemplative silence, leaving the Chief on the hook, waiting for the thought to be completed. "Cat told me Dubcek takes fencing lessons at the gym where she works out. I wonder how good he is with a shorter blade."

Harley Snitz had dispatched an officer on a discreet search for Knepp almost two hours earlier. At the same time, Neidrich asked the State Police to follow up on the white Pontiac. Both investigators wishfully concluded that Knepp, in his effort to maintain secrecy, had yet to perfect the nuances of keeping a low profile, standing out when he should remain unseen and dropping out of sight when he ought to be checking in.

Meanwhile, they had spent the morning going over evidence in the Samson and Marburg cases, drawing lines and links on the old blackboard in Snitz's office. They kept Dubcek in mind but avoided forcing him into the prime suspect role if the evidence didn't warrant it, thus avoiding the time-wasting mistake they had with Randori.

Their goal instead was to gain new perspective. Instead of viewing the homicides as frontal assaults, they considered them acts of cowardice and avoided slotting Randori and Davis in as suspects. This outlook brought uncertainty as to whether or not the same perpetrators committed both murders. All the same, it was difficult to believe that two men so closely linked, killed one month apart, could have separate murderers—especially when the suspects came from a school system, hardly a hotbed of assassins.

Discovering the unsullied scene of Marburg's murder hours after his death at first had seemed a major opportunity, but it only added to existing questions. The murder had taken place in the driveway on the secluded wooded lot of his home, presumably as he was leaving his car. There was significant blood spatter, some of which must have hit the assailant. Because the attack took place in darkness, it would have been impossible to clean the area immediately, and the killer would not have risked returning in daylight. Also, despite going to the trouble of dumping the body in the quarry, the killer seemed not to care if the crime scene was discovered.

The Samson murder scene, on the other hand, was yet to be found. Indications were that his assailant—or assailants—wanted to conceal the site of the attack in the belief that the location might lead to the identity of the perpetrators.

There were, however, common links. In both cases, death resulted from efficient attacks with sharp, smooth-edged blades, the victims suffered facial battering, and their bodies had been removed from the crime scene and deposited in the quarry.

The officers did come to two conclusions with some degree of confidence. First, there were probably two attackers in each case. With Bob Samson, there were the simple facts that he was both clubbed on the head and stabbed, his hefty body was placed in the car, and his car was moved from the scene and steered into the quarry. For both Samson and Marburg, a second vehicle would have been desirable, if not necessary, to escape the isolated area, unless one well-conditioned person was willing to hike several miles through the woods at night or risk being seen walking the back roads of southern Freedom County. Marburg's murder was murkier. The cause of death was attributed to a deep laceration to the right side of the neck that severed the carotid artery. This led to the initial belief that an assailant holding a knife in his left hand had attacked from the front with an outside-in swing of the blade. Randori's left-handedness lent itself to this theory. The left side of Marburg's jaw was also significantly bruised, which could have occurred if he were attacked from the front and hit by a right fist. Examination of both wounds suggested another scenario: The knife had been drawn along the throat from left to right, as it would if a right-hander were attacking from behind. The lodging of dirt and bits of macadam in the facial contusions, along with the blood spatter pattern, suggested at least some of the damage to the left side of his face occurred on impact with the driveway after he fell.

The investigators agreed that both Samson and Marburg probably knew their assailants. Samson would not permit an attacker near him without inflicting some damage of his own. But there was no evidence of a struggle or blood other than Samson's on the body or in his car, and no defensive wounds—not so much as a scraped knuckle. There was the sticky fact that Samson's wallet had been rifled, but that could have been an elementary cover-up. In Marburg's murder, the floodlight attached to the motion detector above his garage door had been broken. The resultant darkness would have cloaked the identity of a known attacker, had the murder been botched. In addition, nothing was stolen, indicating a personal vendetta.

The officers agreed that it was time to revisit some people.

On his way to see Virgil Davis, Neidrich peeked in to say hello to Blanchard, but her back was turned to him as she whispered information from her computer screen into the phone. She hung up and swiveled her chair to reveal her face, hooded with gloom. She brightened only slightly upon noticing the trooper in the doorway.

"Hi," he said, "I didn't mean to eavesdrop."

"Kids and drugs," she said, shaking off the remnants of her phone conversation. Leaning forward, she propped her chin on her hands. "I had a wonderful time last night."

Neidrich shifted a sidelong glance to the outer secretarial area. "Me too. You passed a major hurdle. My kids smiled when they talked about you, and Cam paid you the highest compliment: he said you're pretty cool for an assistant principal."

"I'll take it, considering the assistant principal is the modern version of the wicked stepmother. Say, is that a pistol you're packing, or are you just glad to see me?"

Neidrich pulled his raincoat aside to reveal his Smith and Wesson. "I came to talk to Virgil Davis. But I am happy to see you."

"You want to do something tonight?"

"Things have gotten … a little stickier."

"Tell you what, if you work late, I'll take the kids out for a movie and pizza."

"On a school night? Without me?"

"What better way to show them I'm a regular person?"

"Bribery, huh?" Neidrich said, rubbing his chin. "Good idea." Again, he glanced out to the secretarial stations and felt certain he saw eyes spin away, suddenly engrossed in computer screens. "I'd better go. People will talk."

Blanchard met him at the doorway. "They already are, Sherlock." She squeezed his arm once then shoved him gently. "Now go catch Moriarty."

With thoughts of Cat impressed on his face, Neidrich moved on to Davis's office, entering to find him in his athletic director role, poring over a pile of game contracts. He rapped on the door to get his attention.

Davis looked up and grinned. "Hey Smiley, how you doing?"

Neidrich wondered how idiotic his grin had looked to the secretaries as he left Blanchard's office. " I'm OK."

"Better than OK, from what I hear—and see." Neidrich's frosty stare prompted Davis to add quickly: "I didn't hear that from Cat. Kerry said he saw you two out on the town. Don't be upset. I'm glad some good things are happening. And for me, it's Christmas come early."

"Because Cat and I have been seeing each other?"

"Well, I am happy for you, but don't get carried away. No, Doc and Kerry absolutely kicked ass on Leroy Dubcek this morning. It's a long time coming, and Doc set him up beautifully."

The trooper silently blessed his good fortune. He had come to discuss Dubcek, and Davis had brought the man to the conversational doorstep. "How's that?"

"Leroy's our psychologist; did you know that?" Davis laughed as Neidrich nodded and gave a slow-motion blink. "You've heard about him. Well, whatever you heard, it was probably mild compared to the real thing."

"And how was Dubcek laid low?"

"We had a meeting on one of Leroy's pet projects: a sophomore—should be a junior—boy. Leroy wants to identify him as Emotionally Disturbed. The rest of us believe the kid is socially maladjusted. That's—"

Neidrich fended off Davis's explanation with a wave of his hand. "I get confused with all that special education stuff."

Davis chuckled. "Totally understandable. The important thing is, this kid is a criminal—sneaky, manipulative, totally without caring or compassion. To make matters worse, whenever he gets in trouble, his parents defend him to the hilt."

"Sounds like a budding sociopath, and the parents exacerbate the problem by absolving him of any accountability for his behaviors."

Davis pointed at Neidrich. "What you said. So, here's the issue. If Leroy succeeds in having this kid identified as Emotionally Disturbed, we lose most of our disciplinary leverage. And this is one kid I'd like to give a road map and an apple to."

"You'd think Dubcek would back away from a kid like that."

"If you ask me, he just wants to flex his muscles as the almighty psychologist. Every year, Leroy takes a few kids under his wing and champions their cause, right or wrong. This kid is the worst of the bunch. Doc and I believe he's dealing heroin."

"Heroin? Who's the kid?"

"Paul Roberge, the kid behind the trouble Justin Frederickson started at the game—you know, the night you were grilling me."

"Does Dubcek know this?"

"I would hope not. Doc and I don't tell him anything. Leroy knows there's been at least one case of heroin addiction, but I don't think he's connected the dots. He's on the SAP team, though, and that case was reported to them. But Leroy loses objectivity when he's on one of his crusades. He typically makes two arguments: innocent until proven guilty, and then, even if the kid is guilty, he's a victim of the system. Of course, he stands on those principles only when it suits him."

"Wouldn't the SAP team be privy to the same information you are?"

"It's a long story, but we don't trust those people with confidentiality. Doc and I have been gathering information and sharing it with Kerry. He wants to have a strong case before we go to the superintendent or the Board, because some jocks and the children of some influential parents are involved."

"How many?"

"Three confirmed, a couple dozen more we strongly suspect. Didn't Harley tell you?"

Neidrich believed Snitz would share any important information with him, but Ed Knepp was handling the drug investigation. And, although it wasn't like Ed to keep his mouth shut, it did fit his MO to cowboy the case. One thing he knew for sure: if Knepp were tracking heroin, he was in over his head. Not wanting to betray more ignorance than he already had, he changed the subject. "So, Dubcek doesn't care for Randori."

"To put it mildly," Davis guffawed. "But now you could say he hates Doc's guts. Listen to this; it's beautiful. We've had two meetings on Roberge. The first one, Leroy stacked the deck. He sneaked his SAP team cronies into the meeting. Had a vote been taken that day, Leroy would've moved from the MDE right into an IEP meeting, and Roberge would've gotten Emotional Support on the spot. But Kass and I threw a monkey wrench at them, so they weren't able to conclude the meeting until today.

"This time, Doc bushwhacked Leroy, a real dose of his own medicine. I have to tell you, Nick, it was one of the most satisfying moments of my career. I swear, if Kass were alive, even he would have wanted to hug Doc." Davis looked down and shook his head, then suddenly reared back, exploding in a spasm of laughter that startled Neidrich.

The trooper found himself smiling along with Davis's obvious joy. "So, Marburg and Dubcek had issues, too?"

" 'Issues.' I like the way you put things. Yeah, they had issues. But they grew over time. Leroy's an acquired dislike. At first, Kass actually got along with him, I think because he thought he could use Leroy against Doc. But Leroy was smarter than Kass—too smart for his own good. He tried to manipulate Kass to maintain control."

"What happened?"

"Leroy built himself up and tore Doc down, telling Kass exactly what he wanted to hear, thinking he'd gain influence. But Kass wasn't into sharing power. He just wanted loyal minions to do his bidding."

"And Dubcek wasn't into that," Neidrich concluded.

"Not Leroy's gig at all. He can't be second banana."

"Then why didn't he become an administrator?"

"Oh, he wants all the power but none of the responsibility. Leroy's real big into making recommendations. Then, if there's any glory in it, he volunteers right quick. But whenever there's dirty work, like handling hostile parents or breaking the news to a kid that he belongs in drug rehab, Leroy has a standard response: 'I think that's an administrator's responsibility.' Hard to believe he actually had things his way until Kass—and Doc—came along."

"Then things turned sour."

"At first, Leroy tried *professionally* to get his way—throw his weight around as the psychologist." Davis spat out the last word as though it made bile rise in his throat. "Don't get me wrong, Kass still trusted Leroy more than he ever trusted Doc. He wanted Leroy to be his advisor on pupil services issues. But the Roberge case was the last straw. There was no turning back after that."

"What did Marburg have to do with that?"

"It was Kass's shining hour. He was the reason Leroy couldn't force-feed us the Emotional Support label for Roberge at the first meeting. Kass overpowered Leroy and his lackeys. Good thing, too. I was worried, you know, after he suspended Doc, how that meeting was going to go. But Kass came through with flying colors." Davis leaned back in his chair. He tented his arms and pressed his hands together, matching fingertips as he raised his eyes pensively. "You know, Kass died that same night."

As soon as Harley Snitz entered the Pupil Services Suite, Lionda Knepp was upon him. "Hey Harley, what secret mission did you send Ed on? Molly's worried sick."

Through a forced grin, Snitz said, "Ed will show up soon. He's been handling a case by himself."

Doc Randori appeared in the doorway of Kerry Wyatt's conference room. "Would that be a case of twelve or sixteen-ouncers?"

"Old joke, Doc."

Randori clicked his teeth and cocked his head. "New audience, Harley."

Theresa Wagner had been transcribing psychological reports. Noticing Snitz, she took off her headphones and demanded, "Where's Ed? That's the question of the day. Molly's been calling all morning."

Wyatt's disembodied voice bellowed out. "Harley just told us Ed's on a bender."

"Stop it, you two," Lionda said, flinging a CD in the direction of Randori and Wyatt, who had joined the counselor in the doorway of the conference room. They watched with mild curiosity as the disk sailed by, missing them by several feet, its flight path arcing sharply toward Theresa, who ducked as it clattered against the window beside her desk.

"Watch it, Oddjob," Theresa said, her head bobbing up like a turtle emerging from its shell after a bobcat had passed.

"We do have e-mail now, Lionda," Wyatt said. "It takes longer than your method, but it's potentially less painful."

"Can you talk to me now, Mr. Wyatt?" Snitz said. "I'm a little pressed for time."

Wyatt's broad grin evaporated. He stepped aside to usher the Chief into his conference room. Randori, on his way out, passed Snitz, patted a tired shoulder, and offered a commiserating smile. "Ed will turn up, Harley. Try to get your mind off it."

Avoiding eye contact, Snitz made his way to a seat. He gazed out the window at a maple sapling straining at the tie-downs that kept its trunk erect as wind and driving rain buffeted it. Wyatt's voice seeped into his consciousness, a gentle awakening from his bittersweet musing of Nature's violent beauty and Man's violent nature.

"Very busy time for you, Harley," Wyatt said, more statement than question.

Snitz scrubbed an imaginary spot on his hat brim. "Too busy, Mr. Wyatt."

"I wish you would call me Kerry."

Snitz could not bring himself to respond. To do so would demand the use of Wyatt's first name, and for some reason he had difficulty doing that. He had always believed that the best way out of an awkward situation was to take command of it. "We're heading up some blind alleys on these homicides."

Wyatt clicked a grin on and off. "I hope you've eliminated Doc as a suspect. Some would have you arrest him and be done with it, but that would be a mistake."

"Have your suspicions raised anyone else since the last time we talked?"

"There are people I know who had a common dislike for both Bob and Kass, but the most obvious suspects are people who, in my opinion, are above reproach. Now if you ratchet the motivation down to simple disdain, you could add Meryl Morgan and me to the list. Meryl is of impeccable integrity." Wyatt paused while his Cheshire grin swept to full brilliance. "My own character falls short of that, but one always strives for perfection even if attainment is beyond the grasp."

Snitz fixed his gaze on Wyatt and spoke barely above a whisper. "Then forget the obvious suspects. Open things up; maybe even look at them as separate cases."

Wyatt shifted uneasily in his chair. "You're saying different killers?"

"I'm saying I don't want to take anything for granted. And I'm not necessarily looking for hatred, just motivation." Snitz paused, allowing Wyatt to ponder the distinction. "So far, only Dr. Randori versus Dr. Samson qualifies on both accounts."

"Interesting thought, Harley," Wyatt said, his face a brooding mask. "Especially when you consider that the animosity aroused among the principles in this case stems from football—a silly game. Do you ever wonder what it is about athletics that arouses such passion? I just think we're all ferhutzed, as Theresa would say. A good football team can be the source of the highest community pride, but we could have a record number of National Merit Scholars, and the most that would elicit would be a collective 'That's nice' from our constituents."

"I like football, Kerry." *There*. Snitz finally brought himself to use Wyatt's first name. "I'm proud of our academics, too, but it'll be a chilly day in Cuba before I go to any Quiz Bowls."

"Why is that?"

"I truly don't know." Snitz wanted to get back to his questioning, but he guessed Wyatt was heading somewhere. "I guess it's the same reason more people go to an action movie than an art film."

"Aha!" Wyatt said, slamming both palms onto the tabletop. "That was profound, Harley! We can't objectify it. It's our brain's need for excitement, stimulation, much the same as the biological drive to seek pleasure. And it satisfies our drive to power, too, however vicarious." He raised an eyebrow, as if to coax an epiphany from Snitz. "Don't you see, Harley? This might be what you're looking for."

"Are you saying those old football rivalries are the motivation for these crimes? Then you're pointing the finger right back at Dr. Randori."

"If that's the direction you wish to take. But the finger, as you so graphically describe it, can be flung in quite another direction. Think about drives." Again, Wyatt waited for the Chief to respond.

Snitz squinted, trying to squeeze an idea out of the concept. "You're talking about the drives for pleasure and power. Whoever committed these murders was trying to fulfill one of them?"

"Yes," Wyatt offered with a coy tilt of his head, "and no. The drives to pleasure and power are instinctual. They are mere pathways that distract us from our overarching goal: the will to meaning. For our purposes, though, pleasure and power will do."

Snitz chastised himself for allowing the discussion to go off on what seemed to be a fruitless tangent, but he decided to give it a minute more. "In the psychology courses I took, professors harped on Maslow's hierarchy—the needs for food, shelter, belonging, all that—and how unmet needs drive human behavior."

"Maslow's hierarchy has great merit, but let's not think about that right now; it will muddy the water. In the various schools of psychoanalysis, each has its own theory of motivation. Freud, for instance, asserted that man's life is centered on a will to pleasure; Adler argued that man seeks power. Victor Frankl's logotherapy makes the most sense to me. *Logos* is the Greek term meaning, well, *meaning*. Frankl argued that the search for meaning is the primary motivator, whether or not we recognize it. It is an existential search, a journey of mind and heart—or soul, if you will—while the will to pleasure and power are outgrowths of instinctual drives."

"And it's instinctual drives that lead to murder," Snitz said. A wry grin crept across his face. "That'd be my opinion, anyway. I don't recall too many murders driven by existential angst."

Wyatt reared back and clapped his hands in delight. "Right you are. So, where do we go from here?"

The Chief tilted his head upward, searching the ceiling for an answer. After a moment, he smiled again. "Pleasure isn't a good motive, either. Power is more likely. People who stood to gain power by getting Dr. Samson out of the way were Phil Olson and Ms. Morgan. Phil has a rock-solid alibi, Ms. Morgan didn't really have a shot at Dr. Samson's job, and besides, she doesn't really fit well as a suspect. Who was Kass fighting with for power at the high school? Dr. Randori. Maybe Virgil Davis."

Wyatt gave an emphatic shake of the head. "It runs counter to Doc's makeup to seek power. He's above that; he seeks meaning. Virgil lost out on the high school principal job to Kass, but he's a good soldier. That's his 'meaning.' He only wanted to be principal so he could serve students, not wield power."

"Virgil has alibis for the nights of both murders," Snitz said. "Not airtight, mind you, but decent. Funny thing: the two people most likely to do something rash for power or pleasure were Dr. Samson and Kass. God rest their souls."

"What are you saying, Harley?"

"I guess what I'm saying," the Chief said slowly, measuring his words, "is maybe we're looking for someone who had his own power or pleasure stripped by one or both of those men. *And someone who doesn't like Dr. Randori.* Kass saw everyone as a threat to his power." Snitz hoped his next question came across as innocent, not leading: "Is there anyone at the high school who stands out in your mind, Mr. Wyatt—sorry—Kerry?"

Wyatt sat back in his chair, crossing one hand across his chest, rubbing his chin with the other as he pondered the question. "Leroy

Dubcek. I'm not the most objective person, though, because he has undermined many people, including me."

"Nick and I were just talking about that kind of thing. Folks get into petty bickering because they're bored. And they jockey for a higher place on the totem pole just so they can feel better about themselves at the expense of others."

"Good observation." Wyatt nodded. "The brain's way of seeking interest, enacted by people of low character. That way they derive both power and pleasure, no matter how perverse, out of the mundane daily grind. It happens everywhere. But Leroy is an extreme example. His is a persistent quest—power, control. He had manipulated his way into being the most influential person in the building with regards to pupil services issues. Until Doc came along, that is."

"But he's a psychologist. Isn't he the house expert in those situations?"

"Don't overrate psychology. The knowledge is a tool, but it's not finely honed. And like any tool, it can be used as a skilled craft or a bludgeon. Allow me a metaphor. I have this hammer. I can drive a nail into oak with two or three firm, skilled strokes or I may need twenty strokes and bend three nails before I get it right. Leroy is competent, but, as he's wielding it, he calls everyone's attention to how marvelous he is, arguing that no one else should even hold the hammer. Worse, all the while he's diverting their attention from the fact that he's driving the nails into some innocent's skull."

Snitz cringed. "That's one vivid description."

"I told you, mine is hardly an unbiased opinion."

"But did Dubcek have a problem with Dr. Samson or Kass?"

"I don't know of any problem with Bob, but when Kass became high school principal, he trusted Leroy until he realized he was sabotaging his discipline policies. The best example is a recent special education case in which Leroy tried to get special education protections for the most promising sociopath in the high school." A sardonic smile betrayed Wyatt's self-satisfaction with his description. "Kass blocked it and, of course, that was more than Leroy could bear. He has great ego, great pride, and when crossed, he is absolutely ruthless in trying to regain the upper hand."

"Ruthless enough to commit murder?"

"It's hard to picture that; Leroy prefers character assassination. But you may get your answer soon. Doc just made him look bad at a meeting—coincidentally, a follow-up on the same case Kass was dealing with." Wyatt suddenly stopped and stared out the window, an uncomfortably long stare, before he blurted, "A thought just struck: Kass may have influenced today's meeting from beyond the grave. Today, inexplicably, Tammy Eboli ended up siding with us against Leroy."

"And that's pertinent because…?" Snitz said, frowning.

Wyatt's wide grin took an abashed turn. "I guess I should explain: A couple months ago, Shirley—Bob Sawyer's, and now Phil Olson's, administrative assistant—told me confidentially that Kass and Tammy were seeing each other."

Snitz reflected on the accuracy of Cat Blanchard's intuition. "Wow!"

"Well put, Harley. The Association president and the high school principal, a conflict of interest, to say the least."

"Are you sure about that?"

"As I said, Shirley told me, and as you know, she's not given to idle gossip."

Snitz raked his fingers across his scalp and let his hand come to rest on the back of his neck. "What did Dr. Samson have to say about that?"

"According to Shirley, he was angry at first. But Bob always had a soft spot for Kass, so all he did was demand that they treat it like an atomic secret."

"Whew, so you're thinking Ms. Eboli's love for Kass outweighed her hatred for Dr. Randori, and so she threw in with you and overthrew Mr. Dubcek?"

Wyatt nodded. "A fortunate and thoroughly satisfying experience. Leroy thought he was going to get his way yet again, but Doc, with Tammy's help, pulled the rug out from under that notion." Wyatt laughed and wagged a finger at Snitz. "So, if Doc shows up dead, look for Leroy first."

"That's not funny. I'd hate to see anything happen to Dr. Randori."

"Don't worry. After talking to you, I'll be certain to warn him. But I have the feeling he'd welcome an attack from Leroy, especially over this recent case."

"Can you tell me about it?"

"I can't talk about the special education aspects—confidentiality, you know. The student in question is Paul Roberge."

Snitz whistled. "That kid's a bad actor."

"The worst, according to Doc and Virgil. He's the main reason I've been thinking about Viktor Frankl recently. Doc feels logotherapy is the way to go in dealing with some of the victims of Roberge's particular brand of sickness."

"You're losing me, Kerry."

"Remember, I said that the pursuit of pleasure and power are instinctual drives? A person can satisfy them, and thus contribute to, but never truly satisfy, the deeper search, the one for meaning. Also, meaning is unique in that other people and things cannot fulfill it. It certainly can involve others, but the individual alone must bring it to fruition. It is in the search for meaning that our deepest questions exist. When we don't find it through positive outlets, we sometimes find negative ones."

"I still don't understand what all this has to do with Paul Roberge."

Wyatt held up a finger to beg patience and continued: "Whether or not they realize it, young people also search for meaning. Sadly, too many parents are absorbed in their own pursuit of pleasure and power, hollow substitutes for meaning. Their children are mere extensions of, or impedances to, that. School people try to give children direction, but the goals of developing empathy and self-esteem have been tabled, unfortunately; we're up to our ears in meeting government standards for reading, writing, and math. The government couldn't care less about helping children develop social skills or coping skills. Social agencies are understaffed and underfunded. Churches seem to be caught up in their political agenda. And our political leaders? They've let us all down.

"Many kids make it because they do have strong families or other experiences that lead them on the path toward meaning, but for an ever-growing number existential frustration has taken hold and they don't even know what it is—neither do we adults; we've mistakenly labeled it cynicism. So, peer social norms become the guiding light. And when a Paul Roberge becomes the lighthouse, these kids are headed for the reef. Because instead of enlightenment he brings oblivion."

Snitz found Wyatt's impassioned speech fascinating, but the Director of Pupil Services still had not answered the question. "Exactly what is Paul Roberge doing?"

Wyatt jabbed a finger into the tabletop hard enough to make Snitz wince for him. "Paul Roberge is a faulty organism. He's dealing heroin at the high school. Ed hasn't told you?"

"No," Snitz stammered, "I mean, are you sure Ed knows?"

"Of course. Justin Frederickson died of a heroin overdose. Ed questioned his friends at the high school."

Snitz's blood receded to his core. "Heroin? At the high school? I knew there was some on the North Side, but I never thought. And Paul Roberge?"

Wyatt hiked himself up in his chair. "We got our first inklings late last spring. A boy from Culver Pond, affluent family, went into residential treatment. Very hush-hush. We found out because the hospital requested school assignments. The parents wouldn't release information to us, so at first we thought it was cocaine. Then the boy's girlfriend told her counselor about the heroin and asked to refer him to SAP in the hope that he would get aftercare when he returned to school. Somehow word leaked that she had talked, and she was assaulted—hospitalized."

"Missy Glosser? I remember that. Ed questioned her after the assault, but she wouldn't talk." Snitz raked his fingers through his hair. *How could things have gotten so out of control?* Then: "Wait a minute. Missy's a good kid. Why would she talk to her counselor then clam up on Ed? That doesn't make sense."

"She felt betrayed by her counselor. And *that* doesn't make sense; her counselor was Frank Spikes. Frank wouldn't have talked to anybody but the SAP Team."

"Then Missy must've gabbed to friends, and then the grapevine took off."

Wyatt shook his head. "She swore the only person she spoke to was Frank, and none of her friends knew she went to him. She was afraid of reprisals. Seems she is an intuitive young lady."

"You're thinking someone on the SAP team leaked it to students?"

Wyatt leaned toward Snitz. "To Paul Roberge, specifically." His conspiratorial tone and impassive stare chilled Snitz as much as the words that accompanied them. "Virgil and Doc have been gathering information but keeping the SAP team out of the loop. When the school year started, another student was in rehab for heroin; a third went by mid-September. Parents haven't been much help; they're in denial or embarrassed, or both." Reaching out to clasp Snitz's arm, Wyatt continued. "I've stopped short of calling it an epidemic, but Virgil and Doc have close to thirty names, and you know how it works statistically: we may only be aware of a quarter to a third of those involved."

Snitz's head was on a swivel; maybe if he denied what he was hearing, it would not be true. "I can't believe that many kids are shooting up."

"That's the problem. They're not using needles. They're snorting it, typically."

Snitz dropped his head and shook it, muttering, "Philly's the East Coast hub for heroin. It was only a matter of time." Raising his eyes to meet Wyatt's, his voice gained strength through rising anger. "Why haven't Virgil or Dr. Randori—or you—told me?"

"They knew you were concentrating on the murder—now murders—and that Ed was investigating the drug situation. Need I say more? I told them to discuss the matter only with me for the time being. We didn't know whom we could trust inside the school either. And, as I said, we assumed Ed would've told you."

At last, a break, or at least a promising path. Leroy Dubcek was a serious suspect, and Neidrich had to rein in his investigative fervor—and his tendency to drive fast when he was excited; he had hydroplaned twice already on his way back to the station. The trooper had waited five weeks; he could wait a little longer. He needed something solid, and the knowledge that his suspicions barely stretched to circumstantial evidence tempered his exhilaration. And, although Dubcek's relationship with Marburg raised concern, no link between the psychologist and Samson had been established. Still, some things did fit; he had something to latch onto. Dubcek was a fencer; proficiency with a foil could translate to skill with a knife. Pride and power, vicious sirens whose call can lure a person onto the shoals of irrational acts, drove him. And Dubcek felt challenged by Randori.

As he pulled into the lot of the Newcastle Borough Municipal Building, Neidrich was disappointed to find Snitz's parking slot empty. Despite the downpour, he ambled up the steps to the main door, stopped, and turned to face the pelting rain, thinking about the unexpected turns life can take. The night before, Cat Blanchard had committed to their relationship, and feelings he had long since given up for dead were resurrected. And now, just as abruptly, the scent of the hunt returned. It was a vague sensation, something he could not quite put his finger on, but just as the chill at the edge of the storm told him the first cold snap of fall was coming on, it went beyond belief to conviction. The transition had already begun.

The roar of Snitz's cruiser entering the lot jolted Neidrich out of his reverie. As he watched the Chief twist out of the car he smiled, and, in return, Snitz brightened, but only a little.

"You're looking comfy in the catbird seat," the older man said.

Neidrich opened the door. "I think we have a lead."

As they entered the station, the Chief's disposition darkened again. Approaching Phyllis, who was on the phone, he leaned in close, whispering: "Any word on Ed?"

The dispatcher shook her head; her own gloomy expression bore mute testimony to her concern. She cupped a hand over the receiver and said, "Jim and a couple off-duty guys have been looking around on the QT; they've been keeping in touch."

Neidrich didn't like the news, or lack of it. He laid a gentle hand on the Chief's elbow, turning him toward his office and away from thoughts of his missing officer. "I have lots to tell you. I have a feeling about the psychologist, Dubcek."

"Me too," Snitz said, closing the door and moving to his desk.

"You first," Neidrich said, hoping to divert his colleague from impotent worry.

Snitz leaned back and tossed a glance out the window at a passing car. "There was no love lost between Dubcek and Kass. Same with him and Dr. Randori."

Snitz recited the words, but Neidrich knew his mind was elsewhere, his eyes focused somewhere far beyond. "Come on, Harley, we don't have the luxury to think about Ed right now. We have to concentrate on matters at hand."

"That's not the problem. … Well, that's part of it. Kerry Wyatt told me there's heroin going around the high school—lots of kids involved. Snorting it. The school people never notified me because they thought Ed was on top of it. If he is, he's in over his head."

Neidrich was relieved to learn that Snitz had not withheld information from him. He also resigned himself to the fact that his partner had to settle his thoughts on Knepp before moving on. "That coincides with information I got from Virgil Davis, but it doesn't jive that Ed would have—let alone could have—kept you in the dark."

"I understand what he was doing. Ed became a cop because he wanted to make a difference. Problem is, folks around here have always seen him as a clown. He dealt with it by talking up cases he was working on, to get respect, but everyone saw what he didn't: some things, you have to keep mum about; if you don't, you look unprofessional. But I want you to know, Nick, Ed's working on his weak points." Snitz's eyes glistened; he cleared his throat and looked away. "I told him, if I give him control of the drug angle, he has to keep quiet. Otherwise, he hurts his case and he hurts himself. So, Ed's showing he can keep quiet and solve the big case on his own. He's not incompetent, Nick; it's just, well, sometimes he doesn't have good judgment."

Neidrich hurt for Snitz and wanted to ease his anxiety. For one bizarre moment he thought of calling Randori, certain the counselor would know the right thing to say. He quickly realized it was a ridiculous notion, so he dealt with it by not dealing with it. "Looks like there's a high school kid behind the heroin: Paul Roberge."

Investigative instincts jerked Snitz's mind back to the case. "That's what Kerry Wyatt said. Virgil and Dr. Randori have been looking into it, but secretly—they even kept Dubcek and the SAP Team in the dark." Snitz shifted to the edge of his seat. "And Justin Frederickson, Mr. Wyatt—Kerry—said he died of a heroin overdose."

"The bigger question is, did Ed know all this?" A piercing glint brightened Neidrich's eyes. "And why didn't the doctor who did Justin's postmortem report it?"

Snitz matched the trooper's glare as he snatched up the phone receiver and punched in Phyllis's extension, telling her to drop everything and contact the hospital.

While the Chief was on the phone, Neidrich measured his thoughts then sifted them with care as Snitz hung up. "This isn't marijuana or beer were talking here. No one handles a hard drug bust on his own. From now on, I say Ed gets help from my people. He can always get the credit when all's said and done. Your call though, Harley."

Snitz knew that with the information he had, Neidrich could be on the phone to the State Police as they spoke. "I agree—and I appreciate your asking." Glancing out at the storm, his voice trailed off as though he were afraid to complete the thought. "But where is he so we can tell him?"

"Look, Harley, why don't you surprise Aggie and get home early? Ed's been steering clear of us for days. The only difference now is he pulled an all-nighter and didn't call his wife. He probably caught a lead and got excited, probably went to Philly to track down the heroin suppliers." Neidrich chuckled, letting his joke sink in, but when he saw the color drain from the Chief's face, he quickly added, "Lighten up, Harley. He wouldn't do anything that stupid. Would he?"

Stunned, Snitz stared blankly. "It's exactly the kind of thing Ed would do."

Neidrich placed a steadying hand on the Chief's shoulder. "I'll have people check heroin dealers with ties to the mid-state and put out a call from here to Philly to be on the lookout for Ed's car. But you need to relax." He spoke with a tone of finality, a determined segue to the Samson and Marburg murder cases. "Meanwhile, I'll get background on Dubcek so we can get after it tomorrow."

Offering weary nodding assent, Snitz said, "I do believe I will check in with Aggie, but then I'm going to track Ed. I know a couple places no one has looked yet. And I want to do some checking on this Roberge kid."

"OK," Neidrich said. He locked onto Snitz's eyes to drive home his follow-up. "We've been laying back on this, Harley, but if we don't hear from Ed real soon, we have to go to a full-scale search and not worry about keeping a low profile."

Snitz unconsciously recoiled and became defensive. "This weather hasn't helped. What with the rain all day, the low cloud cover, and, soon, darkness, we're pretty much stuck to driving the roads and using the phone." Looking away, his eyes misted again. "Who am I fooling? I didn't search because I didn't want to admit ..."

"I know," Neidrich said, saving Snitz the anguish of delving too deeply into the possibilities. He left unsaid the fact that, had a state trooper been missing overnight, the dogs would have been out since daybreak. But, between Ed's efforts to make himself scarce for the past week, the peaceful nature of Freedom County, and Snitz's reluctance to overreact, it seemed as though they were taking a reasonable course of action.

Snitz pulled his collar up, and a shiver rose from his core as he crushed his coffee cup and shot it into the wastebasket. "That coffee didn't do it for me. This weather makes me feel every single one of my years." He forced a smile. "God takes care of children and fools, right, Nick?"

Harley Snitz had been up most of the night, his fruitless search for Ed Knepp followed by an equally futile quest for rest. He had finally given up trying and, taking care not to disturb Aggie, dressed and left his house at 5:30 to check places he had gone the night before, some for the third time. Finally, reluctantly, he reported to the station and found Neidrich talking to Phyllis.

The trooper stood to greet him, eager to pick up the investigation but said nothing, as Snitz slumped toward his office, barely acknowledging his colleagues. Neidrich fell in alongside, calling over his shoulder, "Phyllis, please make sure no one disturbs us."

Ignoring Neidrich's request, Phyllis showed up at Snitz's office moments later, balancing a large mug filled to the brim, moving gingerly as she stared into the black pool in an almost successful attempt to prevent it from lapping over. "Nick bought us a coffee machine, Harley, and he got you this mug, too."

The uncharacteristic buoyancy in Phyllis's voice summoned a curious gaze from her boss. She smiled up at Snitz, but a glance at his face caused her to fire a sharp glance at Neidrich. "So much for your big idea for cheering up Mr. Doom and Gloom." Returning her attention to Snitz, she added, "I'm just as worried as you are, Harley, so snap out of it; you've got a job to do." She slammed the mug onto the desk with a blow that would have done Thor proud and stormed out of the office.

"Did you ever think about giving her SWAT training?"

Snitz turned to his window without reacting. He forced a puff of breath onto the glass and drew a heart in the cloud of steam; inside the heart, he drew Aggie's initials.

Neidrich smiled. "It's nice you do that."

Snitz spoke, barely above a whisper: "We have to search for Ed."

"My people have been at it since dawn," Neidrich said, quickly adding, "Don't worry, they're discreet."

"Thanks, Nick. I guess that's all we can do for now. Phyllis is right; I'd better stick to the knitting. I've been thinking about what we have—"

Again, Phyllis entered; she began speaking immediately. "I meant to tell you, Dr. Peters handled the Frederickson boy. He was out of town yesterday. They said they'd have him call us as soon as he gets in." The dispatcher held up a finger as she tilted her head back into the hallway. "There's a call at the front; it might be him," she added, hurrying out the door.

Snitz's eyes went wide. "Oh, what with all this about Ed and the heroin, I forgot to tell you: Ms Eboli, the union leader, and Kass—"

Before Snitz could continue, Phyllis returned, her face an ashen canvas of horror. Drawing a quivering hand to her mouth, she gasped, "Hikers found a body up on Ranger Road."

Snitz grabbed his hat and hustled to catch Neidrich, who was already halfway to the door. "Where abouts?" the Chief called out, striding to keep up with the trooper.

Shaken out of her shock by the swift response of the officers, Phyllis hustled behind them. "West of the tower. Behind Culver Pond. I'll tell Jim to meet you."

Kicked-up gravel beat a staccato rhythm on the undercarriage of Neidrich's cruiser as he pushed it to the limit. He followed the route to the tower, and Snitz directed him from that point to the rutted road that stretched the spine of the ridge. Muscling the steering wheel, Neidrich skimmed across mud and swerved around potholes until he saw three people huddled on the side of the road ahead.

A bent, elderly man waved his hat, and Neidrich spun to a stop in the tall grass beside them. The old man with the hat pointed into the woods. "Over there. It's terrible. It's ..." His voice trailed off as he wrapped his arm around one of two women that were hugging each other, shivering, beside him. The officers peered into the woods. Through the trees, another man beckoned. The officers trudged along a rough path of flattened brush until the outline of a car came into view. As they approached, Neidrich's pace quickened as Snitz's slowed. Then, as one, they stopped.

"We were on a stroll. The four of us," the man said, fidgeting, his words spilling out, as if his presence at the scene somehow made him complicit in the crime. "We walk every day. When the weather's good, anyway. We walk three miles then eat breakfast. Every day, except when it rains—like yesterday. We saw the car through the trees. You can see it clearer when you're coming up from Culver Pond. I called right away. Got my cell phone." He held it up to show the officers. "See here?"

Neidrich patted the man's shoulder and shepherded him toward his party to take their statements. As his questioning proceeded, he soon realized that the elderly quartet's knowledge began and ended with the discovery of the body. He took their names and gave them his card, in case they felt the need to contact him, but they remained frozen to the spot.

Another police car approached, spinning to a halt behind Neidrich's sedan. He recognized the driver as Snitz's man, Jim. The young officer leaped out of the car and called out, "Where's the Chief?"

Snitz seemed unaware of the young officer's arrival as he knelt down beside the body. He spoke as if to himself. "Stabbed. Back and abdomen. Wonder who he met here." After tilting his face up to the bronze and orange forest canopy, he continued his dismal soliloquy. "Hope he wasn't too cold dressed like that."

"Harley, why don't you go with Jim? Let me take care of this."

Neidrich turned to the young officer, who nodded and lightly clasped his boss's arm. "Come on, Harley, I have coffee in the car."

"Culver Pond," Snitz said, pointing west. "Ed came from that direction."

"Go with Jim, Harley," Neidrich said, his voice taking a stern tone. "I'll bring in some of my people."

Snitz shrugged away from Jim's grasp. "This is my man here."

"This is state land," Neidrich said, his jaw set. "My turf, my call. Go with Jim and get yourself together." His voice and face mellowed. "I'll call soon. I promise."

At first, Snitz's eyes flared, but reason slowly took hold, and he turned toward Jim's cruiser, with his deputy falling in tow. The two officers stumbled through the damp underbrush, their shuffling bearing the numb, zombie-walk of family leaving a loved one's funeral, one leaning on the other for support.

After they drove out of sight, Neidrich turned to Knepp's car to take a closer look. The rear door on the driver's side was not latched.

Left with only the image of his sergeant's pale, rain-sodden corpse, Snitz was slow to regain his senses, but he insisted that Jim drive him to Knepp's house. Molly opened the door and turned doe eyes up at the Chief. Stunned by the wordless truth his face revealed, she quickly looked away and stepped aside to let the officers enter. On the surface, she handled the news, although the Chief knew the surface shock would last only long enough for her brain to assimilate the crushing reality. She backed into the family room and sunk into the love seat where she and Ed had nestled on so many evenings to watch mystery shows and try to see who would be the first to solve the crime. Suddenly small and frail, she bowed her head and dumbly wrung her hands in her lap.

Snitz sat beside Molly, his arm draped over her shoulders, hugging her close while Jim called his wife to come and sit with her. She asked questions Snitz either could not answer or would not, in order to save her further torture. To the relief of both men, Jim's wife arrived and rushed to her side, nestling Molly's head against her neck. Snitz offered words he had said to other families at other times, words that now seemed inadequate.

As he turned for the door, Molly leapt up and stumbled into his arms. Wracking sobs wrenched her body and she fell to her knees, imploring, "Get Doc Randori, Harley; get him and make him pay! Make him pay!"

Leaving Knepp's home, a sense of desolation replaced the numbness he felt at the crime scene, and somehow Snitz thought it an improvement; at least it had shocked him out of his mental paralysis. He wanted to think, to occupy his mind with the case, but Aggie would want to talk, and, although her intentions would be right and good, she would force him onto emotional turf he needed to avoid for the time being, and so Snitz was relieved upon entering his home to find a note informing him that she had gone shopping at the Lancaster outlets with some friends. Soon, though, he entered a strange netherworld in which he was unable to think clearly and unwilling to reflect.

On this, the worst day of his career, Snitz forgot about Bob Samson and Kass Marburg. Ed's mask of death was branded on his mind. When he had covered his sergeant's body, he had the presence of mind to look for his logbook. It was not in its usual spot, Knepp's hip pocket, nor was it on the ground near his body. *Sometimes the best evidence is no evidence. If the logbook is missing, it must have information that would lead to the murderer. And since Ed was working on the drug case, it must be one of the suspects. Doc Randori?* Harley had no stomach to press Molly on her certainty that Randori had killed Ed. *Paul Roberge? Could a kid have done this? Not likely—at least not by himself. Randori and Roberge together? There was that rumor way back when Randori rewarded players with drugs when they won games. But Bob Samson started that rumor. Another victim. Big money in heroin—enough to make people do crazy things.*

Snitz paced the living room; his mind steeped with possibilities. His thoughts echoed off the walls of the big, quiet house; he needed to bounce them off a person, another officer. Strapping on his holster, he ran out the front door, his veins pulsing with urgency to finish Ed's business so he could rest in peace, if only in Snitz's mind.

Soon after Snitz arrived at the station, Phyllis received a call and told him to stay put. Neidrich was on his way; he had something. Snitz stood at his window, but his view was focused inward, so he returned to his desk and shuffled through papers and files until he realized he was only creating a mess. He walked to the door and looked out at Phyllis, who was busy taking calls. Other law enforcement agencies would already know about Ed, and it was only a matter of time until the media descended upon him—and his four unsolved murders. Phyllis, in fact, might already be shielding him. That possibility spiked his impatience to see Neidrich.

The doctor who had examined Justin Frederickson's body called. He apologized but maintained that Knepp had said he would pass the information along. Snitz told him to fax a report immediately.

The sound of a sedan thundering into the lot brought Snitz to his window where he watched Neidrich pull a looping circle before screeching to a halt in front of the main door. The big man loped toward the station, gripping a notebook in his hand. Snitz forced himself to wait, sinews tingling with agitation and anticipation.

Neidrich burst through the front door, down the hallway, and into the Chief's office. "We caught a break." He held the notebook aloft. "This was under the seat of Ed's car; it's a private log he kept."

While he had been driving to the station, Neidrich mentally sifted through the mass of information Ed Knepp had recorded. He decided to leave out the animal torture and the gang rapes and give Snitz only what he called the "*Reader's Digest* version," just the information they needed to act, and act quickly. "Ed found out that Paul Roberge *is* dealing heroin. A kid named Brad Prusster told him that Roberge sent a lethal dose to Justin Frederickson on purpose."

"Why would he want to kill Justin?

"This is where it gets sticky," Neidrich said, his eyes narrowing. "Roberge was angry because Justin gave us his—Roberge's—name after the trouble that night at the football game."

"How could Paul Roberge have known that? The only people there were—"

"Hang on," Neidrich interrupted. "Ed was convinced that Roberge was involved with a high school staff member, a person who keeps heat off him."

"Doc Randori?" This time, Snitz held his breath.

"That's what Prusster boy overheard Roberge say when he confronted Justin about his breach of trust."

The Chief's head dropped. His trust in his own judgment and his faith in his understanding of human nature were rocked.

"Wait," Neidrich cautioned. "Ed believed that. He was staking out Randori's place from Wednesday to Sunday, the night his log entries end. That night, he broke that stakeout and drove to Culver Pond to check out Roberge's house."

"That makes sense since we found his body on the ridge less than a mile from Culver Pond. So, are you saying Dr. Randori's *not* the man we're looking for?"

"Get this." Neidrich opened Knepp's log to a dog-eared page. "Ed's last entry: 'White BMW (500 series?) NOT Pontiac—neighbor of PR brought him home.' " Neidrich looked up from the private log. "This might take Randori off the hook."

"Why's that?"

"There is a note earlier: The morning after Marburg and Justin Frederickson died, a teacher reported that someone in a 'white Pontiac' picked the Prusster kid up at the high school. Ed wrote that Roberge was driving the car."

Snitz rubbed the back of his neck. " Pontiac and BMW, those cars look similar from the front—split grill and all. I suppose someone might confuse them. So?"

Neidrich's eyes narrowed. "Follow my thinking here. Roberge supposedly killed Frederickson because he gave us Roberge's name at the football game. Do you think he'd tell Justin the name of his adult accomplice and let the kid run around with that information for days, then kill him for a breach of trust?"

"You're saying Paul just used Dr. Randori's name; there's really someone else?"

"We have to follow that up with Brad Prusster, but after checking out the white BMW, I think we have a better candidate. There are three white 'Beamers' in the area. One belongs to a neighbor who lives a couple doors down from Roberge, and guess where that person works."

Phil Olson had arranged for an early dismissal; the president of Jordan College was to speak to staff in the middle school auditorium at 1:00. As Randori stared out the main entrance doors of the high school, he was thinking up an excuse to avoid it. He didn't want to skip out with no viable explanation; that would be unprofessional.

A bevy of young female teachers approached him on their way to the office to close out the day's business. Although he had caught the women in his peripheral vision, Randori ignored them, fixing his gaze at the farmer's field across the blue highway. As one, the teachers fell silent, like trick-or-treaters sneaking past the neighborhood house everyone believed to be haunted. Randori was tempted to turn slowly and give them his Bela Lugosi impression—"Ah, the children of the night!"—but decided that an urban legend best served its purpose when the air of mystery remained intact. The young women were well past him before one began talking again, this time in hushed tones. But Randori's eyes focused on the old tree on top of the hillock.

On the rise of a small hill, the thirteen-year-old boy sits in a lotus position under a pear tree, staring through a veil of tears at a dead autumn field crushed under a leaden sky. He flips up the collar of his pea coat; his chin shrinks into its warmth and he scrubs the sleeves against his cheeks, replacing sorrow with a cold mask of resolve.

He slides his hand into his coat pocket and pulls out a glossy black switchblade, rolls it into his left hand, then presses the button on the shaft, revealing its lethal perfection. For a moment, he studies his distorted reflection in the blade. Tears well again, his head drops, and he shivers. His fist closes on the knife, and he raises his eyes to heaven, but the hypnotic, rolling clouds smother any answer heaven might send, except, from above those clouds and beyond the horizon, the low, angry murmur of thunder.

The breeze kicks up and the boy brings the shiv down, swift and violent, and the keen blade does its job, sliding to the hilt with a sickening snick. Fist and jaw clenched in determination, the boy's knuckles blanch like desiccated ivory and the veins in his wrist and neck distend to violet ropes of anguish, and he pushes, pushes, pressing the knife into the earth, holding his breath until he can hold no more, and he heaves forward in a great expulsion of torment.

Spent, he drops his forehead onto his fist and the haft-end of the switchblade, his back rising and falling as he draws deep breaths. Slowly, stillness falls over him. He rises again and releases his grip on the knife, placidly contemplating his unholy plant, its steel taproot buried unseen beneath the sod.

The boy touches the bulge in the left coat pocket, a light tap as if testing a hot stovetop. A faltering hand slips inside and draws out the service pistol. Eyes riveted to the precision-tooled surface, he grips the knurled handle in his left palm, and his right hand quivers, fumbling with the safety, flicking it off. Tears again spill down his cheeks as he raises the barrel and looks up to survey the world one last time.

A cow appears, seemingly out of nowhere, her black and white bulk in sharp contrast to the tans and grays of the world. She meanders toward him, stops, cocks her head, and stares into his eyes. The boy's hand halts as he gazes back at the animal. The cow cranes her head into the breeze, turns again to the boy and moves forward, stopping mere feet from him. Bowing her massive head, she ponders a pear fallen from the branches overhead, lows softly, and nudges it toward the boy's feet.

Tears streaming down his cheeks, his hand falters and his arm weakens under the weight of the pistol. Glancing down at the gun as if seeing it for the first time, he heaves it across the field.

The cow's eyes follow its arching trajectory until the pistol hits the ground with a thud. She slowly drops her body to the earth.

The boy yanks the switchblade out of the ground and wipes the blade on his pants. He stands and closes the blade. Rain begins to fall, trickling through thirsty, fluttering leaves until it makes its way to his face, cleansing his tears. He raises his eyes and focuses on a pear dangling from a branch overhead. Reaching up, he plucks it and edges toward the cow, holding it in silent offertory. With a placid stare, the cow allows the boy to stroke her head. She blinks; her eyes leave his and fall to the pear she had nudged toward him when they first met. Following the cow's gaze, the boy picks it up and sits before her. He wipes his eyes and bites into the succulent fruit.

Virgil Davis bellowed, "Hello ladies. Let me get the door for you." The startled women giggled their thanks, and entered, voices again chattering in excited competition, their encounter with the Angel of Death safely passed.

Randori's eyes remained fixed on the meadow as Davis approached and clapped him on the back. "Good afternoon, Dr. Randori. And how was your day?"

The counselor returned a sliver of a smile. "Just peachy, *Principal* Davis."

Davis extravagantly hooked his thumbs through his belt loops. "So, you've heard about my ascent to the principalship?"

"Throngs rejoice, shepherds safely watch their flocks, and, if I'm not mistaken, three rather intelligent fellows just parked their dromedaries out front."

"Screw you, all right?"

"Well, you picked your poison." Randori studied Davis's eyes; finding a blank reflection, he added, "How about we have a cup of joe to celebrate the sudden softening of Phil's heart to match his mind. I'll buy."

"I heard that." The men turned in unison to see Cat Blanchard gliding toward them. "You have to go to the middle school, Doc; you'll be in trouble."

Davis eye-checked Randori. "Look at that: the shit-eating grin of a man who doesn't care."

Randori blinked and maintained an ingenuous smile as he started for his office. "Admonition noted, Cat. So what is it for you two, fill the cup or Phil Olson?"

Davis fell in with Randori. "I, for one, know the fill I want."

Blanchard shook her head at the decision she was about to make. "Doc, you're a bad influence, but your coffee is good."

Standing aside at his office doorway, the counselor said, "Abandon all hope."

Coffee poured, the three settled around Randori's table, and Blanchard held her mug aloft. "Since we're indulging in deadly sins, here's to Doc's kicking Leroy's ass."

Randori shrugged and cocked his head to the side. He stared silently into the black pool in his cup.

Davis barely prevented an explosive spit-take. "Come on, Doc, allow yourself a little vanity. Old Leroy was spitting purple nickels when he realized he was finally on the receiving end of some treachery." He shot a quizzical glance at Randori. "Whatever it was, it sure won Tammy over, though. She cast the vote that threw the decision our way. I never thought I'd see that."

"She was probably sick of Leroy's jealousy," Blanchard said. "My guess is he still thinks he owns her."

"What?" Randori asked, his face conceding innocence. "Leroy's married."

"Oh, come on," Blanchard said. "Everyone knows his wife is never around. She travels all over the country consulting, or whatever. Leroy was lonely. Tammy is beautiful. Leroy got the hots for Tammy. And you know Leroy, when he wants something, he doesn't worry about whose toes he steps on to get it."

"You said something about jealousy?" Davis asked.

Blanchard frowned, forgetting for the moment what she had said. Then, "They had an affair last year. Just a diversion for Tammy, I'm sure, but it was a lot more than that to Leroy. After they broke up, he followed her, checked her home at night. Darn near stalking. Leroy finally backed off, but he's still hung up on her; he can't take his eyes off her. You had to see that at the MDE, right?" After a clueless look from Davis and a noncommittal stare from Randori, Blanchard slapped her forehead. "Guys, sheesh! Anyway, that episode drove Tammy even more underground with her relationships."

Davis pursed his lips pensively. "Makes sense. She and Bob treated theirs like a state secret for obvious reasons."

"Bob, as in Dr. Samson?" Blanchard said, moving to the edge of her chair.

Randori honed in on Davis's eyes, a grin blunting his piercing stare. "The Bobster consorting with the enemy? I must be more out of it than I thought. I didn't know anything about that."

"No one did," Davis said, directing his words at Blanchard. "As far as anyone knew, they just worked on mending union-administration fences."

"And you know this to be true?" she demanded.

"I was Bob's right hand man back when he was head coach," Davis said, settling back and nestling his coffee mug between his palms. "When he moved into administration, we weren't as tight, but in that world there aren't many people you can trust—really trust. I'd seen him warts and all, though, and never told anyone anything. Bottom line, I guess he needed to talk, and he trusted me.

"Last spring, out of the blue he calls, asks me to go out for a few beers to discuss some athletic issues. I thought it was his stab at reconciliation—we hadn't really spoken since he named Kass high school principal. Turned out he wanted to talk about Tammy. Seems what started as a fling turned out to be, well, they were falling hard for each other. He was thinking about leaving Sarah."

A wry grin eased onto Randori's face. "Did you tell him he'd lost his mind?"

"I told him he'd destroy everything he worked for, what it would do to Sarah. When I convinced him of the scandal it would be, he came to his senses."

"When was all this?" Blanchard asked.

"Around the time of the state track meet, so last May, I guess. He must have broken up with her right after that because by graduation night things were noticeably chilly between them. I know; I started keeping my eye on things."

"Why didn't you tell the police?" Blanchard asked. She dropped her eyes. "I mean if you'd told someone, maybe Doc wouldn't be in such a stew."

"Anyway," Randori agreed as he sat back with an easy smile. "Why would you try to clear my name? It's not like we're friends or anything."

"It was old news by the time Bob died," Davis said, a touch defensively. "Why haul out dirty laundry and hurt Bob's family. Besides, Tammy's a lover, not a fighter. And she was already going out with someone else when Bob was killed."

"I'm talking about—" Blanchard abruptly lopped off her thought. Glancing at the clock, she leaped up. "I have to get to the middle school." She slammed her palm against the door handle and faced Davis. "See you there, Virgil?"

"I'll be right down." As Blanchard left, Davis slowly stood and faced Randori. "I better go. Look, Doc, I'm sorry I didn't say anything about Tammy and Bob. I'll call Harley this after."

"Not a problem, Virge. Sometimes the best use of information is no use, at least not until the right time."

Davis's brow shrunk in wary bewilderment. "Another cryptic Randori aphorism."

"Let me ask you something, Virge. Bob was a high profile guy; where could he take a date around here and avoid being noticed? To one of his vacant rental properties?"

"Maybe, but even that would be a risk. He could've been seen entering or leaving." Davis leaned close and spoke barely above a whisper. "Bob liked to get it on in his Mercedes, said the women liked it, too."

"He took them parking?" Randori said with a small sneer. "Did they head out for malts and burgers afterward?"

Davis chuckled. "Yeah, feature that." He checked his watch. "We really should get to the in-service. So many people have been cutting Phil's programs that he's going to surprise us with a sign-in sheet."

"So I heard. Save me a seat in the back. I've got something that can't wait."

Randori listened at his office door as Davis bade goodbye to Jennie, the counselors' administrative assistant, and waited until the door to the Counseling Center shut in a final echoing click. With forced nonchalance, he ambled out. "Say Jen, did you see which way Cat went?"

Jennie pointed to the conference room, "She said she had to make a call."

"I'll just catch her later." Randori started back the hallway then stopped and turned. "I almost forgot, I have to get a report that Frank was working on for me."

The secretary picked up a stack of envelopes. "I'm off to the mail room, then I guess I have to go to the middle school."

Randori smiled. "OK, see you tomorrow."

"Doc, you shouldn't cut the meeting. If Mr. Olson finds out, you'll be in trouble."

"Yeah, Phil just shivers my freakin' timbers."

Like a mother who expected disappointment from her child and got it, Jennie bowed her head and slowly shook it as she walked out. Randori watched her leave before slipping his master key into the door of the office next to the conference room.

Minutes before, Blanchard had stopped short on a statement that Randori believed would have let slip her suspicions of Leroy Dubcek. She then beat a hasty retreat, the counselor again guessed, to share her newfound information about the Eboli-Samson affair with Neidrich.

After slipping into the office and easing the door shut, he edged as close as he could to where he guessed the phone would be on the other side of the wall, hoping that Blanchard chose the land line over her cell phone. He closed his eyes and took shallow breaths but heard no sound. Then he remembered that Blanchard had a habit of speaking softly when discussing sensitive issues. Picking up a coffee cup and carefully placing its open end against the wall, he pressed his ear to the cup's base and caught a faint voice: "Maybe now you won't question woman's intuition. ... Jealous isn't the word for it. ... Last year, late winter, could've been seeing both at the same time, I guess. ... Virgil said it ended in the spring. That's why he didn't mention it before. He said he wanted to protect Dr. Samson's family, too. ... Whatever, that links him to both Kass and Dr. Samson. … White BMW? I think so. … I can see if he's in his office. … All right, I won't. I promise! … I'll go straight to the middle school and call your cell if he's there. My guess is he skipped, though. … All right. Be careful! … Love you!"

The conference room door slammed, and Randori waited, giving Blanchard time to clear the area. *Well, Leroy, I guess you're as good as anyone to take the fall.*

Randori wondered how long it would be before Neidrich and Snitz arrived. *Ten minutes, fifteen tops.* He flung the door open and stepped directly into Tammy Eboli.

She smiled uncertainly. "There you are; I knew you'd bag Phil's program."

"Jeez, did anyone go to the middle school?"

"Can we talk?"

"I'd love to, Tam, but can it wait?"

Eboli held her hands up to Randori's chest, but her eyes remained downcast. "I know we've had our problems and—" Her voice faltered; she looked in both directions. "God, this is so hard to say. I understand if you don't want to talk to me, but it's taken me days to get up the courage, so listen." She took in a deep breath. "I realize now you were never the enemy. Leroy played us against each other, and I fell for it."

Randori nodded. "I knew Leroy was doing a *Yojimbo* number on us." Eboli frowned in incomprehension, and he smiled. "Listen, it's all right, Tammy—really. But I don't have time now. I'm on my way to take care of Leroy."

The counselor stepped away, but she joined him in stride. "I'm going with you."

"No, you're not," he said, quickening his step.

The teacher grabbed his arm with both hands and yanked hard, her surprising strength stopping him in his tracks. This time she met his eyes. "I think he had something to do with Kass's death. If I'm with you, he might not try anything." Her imploring eyes awaited a response, and Randori nodded to reassure her, but as he tried to move, her grip on his arm tightened. "Be careful. Leroy's an expert with a knife."

Randori leveled his gaze on Eboli. "I never underestimate anyone." He flashed a disarming smile. "And be quiet. You sound like the Seventh Cavalry."

She kicked off her heels, skipping to keep pace. As they entered the hallway leading to Dubcek's office, both slowed to a stealthy crawl.

The *Testing: Privacy Please* sign hung on the door. Randori quietly sucked in air as he tested the knob. It was locked. He rubbed his chin, pensive but tense. Eboli put a finger to her lips and gave Randori a firm shove to the side. He flattened his back against the wall beside the doorway.

Eboli knocked. No answer. Biting her lip, she glanced uncertainly at Randori before an idea abruptly manifested itself in a quick wink. "Leroy, it's me. Open up."

Still nothing. She frowned and knocked once more.

Then, a voice: "I'm fighting a timeline on a report, Tam. Can we talk later?"

Eboli bit her lip again. "Leroy, I made a terrible mistake. I'm sorry I sided with Randori at the MDE. I was angry, hurt, but I miss you. I miss us. Open up. Please."

There was no response at first, but then the door budged open a few inches, and Dubcek muttered a saccharine, "Tammy."

Eboli's eyes suddenly darkened; a storm of fury blotted out her fawnlike seductiveness. "Bastard! Murderer!"

Struck immobile by the shocking change in Eboli's demeanor, Randori could only watch as, simultaneous with her words, she launched a creditable right jab in the direction of Dubcek's unseen face. A growl from Dubcek and Eboli was yanked into the office.

By the time Randori spun into the room, he saw blood trickling from the teacher's nose and an angry welt on her cheek; Dubcek's hands were clamped on her throat. The enraged psychologist was unaware of Randori's presence, and the counselor knew he had to act quickly before more harm came to Eboli.

"Hey!" Randori commanded. His left arm cocked, hand open and flexed, and he whipped his palm—aimed and timed perfectly to reach the intercept point of Dubcek's face when his head turned. The shot landed squarely, sending the psychologist backward against his desk. Maneuvering his body to shield the teacher, Randori checked Dubcek, whose hands gripped the desktop to maintain his balance as he stared dumbfounded, blood gushing from his nose. The counselor grasped Eboli's shoulders and led her toward the doorway, trying to get her out of the room before the stunned Dubcek regained his senses. In the moment he had taken his eyes away from the psychologist, Eboli's eyes shifted toward the man.

"Doc!" she shrieked in horror

A blade had materialized in Dubcek's hand, and Eboli's warning was all that stood between Randori and a mortal wound. The counselor shoved Eboli out the door and quick-stepped to the side as the blade ripped through the skin that housed his ribcage. Dubcek was already starting another pass. Randori leaned back, balling his hands into fists to protect his fingers, gathering himself against the onslaught, feinting and shuffling to avoid the expert slashes and thrusts of Dubcek's blade, but he was unable to get into a fighting stance as deft maneuvers forced him into a corner of the room.

A wicked grin widened across Dubcek's face. One more onset and the counselor would be backed against the wall. The psychologist began another outside-in pass and Randori pulled his guard in close, but not close enough, as the blade notched his forearm.

As the knife arced to his right, Randori shot forward. Dubcek tried to compensate with a rapid pass back along the same path, but the counselor caught the wrist of the knife-wielding hand with his own right hand. He slammed his left hand against Dubcek's neck, pushing forward, and turned, pulling his attacker's arm clockwise, hoping to use the psychologist's own momentum to spin him face-first onto the floor so he could disarm him. Pain coursed down Randori's wounded forearm, weakening his hold on Dubcek's wrist. Halfway through the turn his grip loosened, and he hurled the psychologist into an awkward lunge toward the hallway.

Deftly regaining his balance, Dubcek eyed Eboli, who stood only a few feet from him, but yards away from Randori. Fearing the psychologist might take her hostage, Randori yelled for her to back off, and she responded with graceful speed. At the same time, he closed the gap, again positioning himself between Eboli and Dubcek.

Continuing the fight in the hallway presented new problems. The passage was wide enough to allow Dubcek his full array of attacks, but too narrow for Randori to call on more than a few parrying tactics. The psychologist's first move would demand a decisive counterattack. Dubcek's broad grin returned, prelude to an exultant "En garde, mon ami" as he swished his blade in an X-pattern through the air.

"Duc in altum, dipshit," Randori said, his voice little more than a whisper as he eased into a left-lead fighting stance. "Go for it."

Dubcek lunged forward with a lightning thrust.

Randori invited the blade perilous inches from his ribs to bring the psychologist within reach, then he stepped left and forward, clamping Dubcek's right hand in his own as he had moments earlier. Dubcek, expecting the same move as before from Randori, pulled back, straightening his arm. This time, Randori smashed his left palm into Dubcek's elbow, hyperextending it with an audible crack followed by the sickening grind of shredding sinew, and Dubcek's knife clattered to the floor. That damage should have thrown the psychologist into shock, but Randori left nothing to chance. On the follow-through of his palm smash, his left arm was positioned in front of Dubcek's face. He crooked the arm and whipped his elbow into the psychologist's already broken nose, jolting his head backward and arching his body forward.

Still gripping Dubcek's limp wrist in his own right hand, Randori threaded his own left arm underneath the man's armpit from the front, twining it behind and across the shoulder blades until his left hand pressed against the base of Dubcek's neck. He used that hand to press the psychologist's head forward and down, forcing him to bend at the waist, then brought his left knee up into Dubcek's ribcage. On the downstroke, he smashed his left heel onto the top of the psychologist's foot. As a finishing touch, Randori pivoted to his left and launched his right knee into Dubcek's face. The psychologist's body snapped up and back for a moment before his legs crumpled.

Within seconds, the counselor had rained five blows upon Dubcek; each meant to deliver devastating pain. The release of pent-up hostility had brought Randori to a state of rage in which he was inflicting more damage than necessary and left him unaware of his surroundings. He was about to bring a chop down to break Dubcek's collarbone when a shout broke through his concentration. "Stop, scumbag!"

Paul Roberge stood fifteen feet away. He had sneaked up behind Tammy Eboli and locked an arm around her throat. With his free hand, he tried to level the aim of a handgun on Randori, but Dubcek, on his knees and semiconscious, provided a partial shield for the crouching counselor, and the squirming teacher made the boy's aim waver.

"Get away from Mr. Dubcek."

"I'm not sure that's a good idea," said Randori, squatting deeper as he held the psychologist erect.

"If that's the way you want it." Roberge trained the barrel on Eboli's temple.

"Wait." Randori released Dubcek and stood up as the psychologist's body slapped onto the linoleum like a side of beef falling off a meat hook. "Let Ms. Eboli go, Paul," he added in a strong, direct tone. "You want me, not her."

"Shut the hell up!" the boy insisted in an odd, hushed shriek, again bringing his aim to bear on Randori's head. "You keep talking that loud and, someone will –"

A slight smile turned up the corners of Randori's mouth as he shifted a glance over the boy's shoulder. With a sly grin, Roberge said, "I'm not going to fall for that."

"I'd never try to trick you, Paul," Randori said in a voice loud enough to cover the last steps of the onrushing Nick Neidrich as he launched into a full flush clothesline tackle, separating Roberge from both his senses and Tammy Eboli.

Eboli spun awkwardly toward Randori, who rushed forward and wrapped her in his arms, bringing her quickly but gently to the floor and shielding her body with his. Meanwhile, Neidrich's hit whiplashed Roberge's body parallel to the floor. The trooper reached for the gun in the boy's hand as they both hurtled to the linoleum. Neidrich's aim was true, but as his grip closed on the weapon, Roberge pulled the trigger and a report echoed off the walls. Harley Snitz, who had been standing with his own sidearm trained on Roberge, emitted a guttural groan and collapsed, cut down by the wayward shot.

Neidrich looked in horror at his partner, and Roberge, regaining his senses, took advantage of the distraction to slip a punch at the trooper's jaw with his free hand. The blow snapped Neidrich's attention back to the grinning boy who was cocking his fist for another strike. The trooper snarled and launched his own crushing blow into Roberge's face, unhinging his jaw and erasing the vulpine grin as his eyes rolled into unconsciousness.

"Nice hit, 'Night Train,' " Randori said.

Neidrich ignored Randori, instead casting a desperate glance at Snitz's crumpled body. "We need an ambulance, pronto."

June is a fickle month: gorgeous, clear, heart-throbbing days followed by periods when the haze magnifies the sun's rays to blast furnace intensity. On a day too hot even to consider a steaming Italian meal, the Della Regina was less than half full, and Doc and Lynn Randori had no trouble spotting Nick Neidrich and Cat Blanchard.

As the Randoris approached the table, Blanchard said, "Doc Randori actually socializing. Amazing!"

"Why Cat," Randori said, "what a sultry glow you have. Is it the candlelight, or is something mystical at work?"

Blanchard raised a suspicious brow toward Neidrich. "Did you tell him?"

The trooper raised his hands, palms out, in protest. "I haven't seen Doc in months."

"I forgot," Blanchard said, "Randori senses all." She turned to Lynn. "You know, it was Doc who enlightened Inspector Clouseau here about my interest in him."

"So, your revenge is to invite us to dinner and stick me with the tab?" Randori said, inviting a sharp elbow to the ribs from his wife. "Ouch! That's where Leroy cut me, Lynn."

"You've been milking that since October," Lynn said. "It was just a scratch."

"A scratch? He attacked me with an assegai."

"Assegai, my assegai," Randori's wife said with a sneer. "Every time you tell the story that knife gets bigger; now it's a spear. It was probably a letter opener."

"A pointy letter opener," Neidrich said. "A pointy *little* letter opener." He measured an inch between his thumb and index finger.

Blanchard waved both hands to get everyone's attention. "Please. Without further ado, I have an announcement: Nick and I are getting married. Tah-dah!"

Lynn Randori clapped her hands with joy and embraced Blanchard, while her husband smiled and shook Neidrich's hand. The trooper, as ill at ease as Randori was at being the center of attention, breathed a sigh of relief with the arrival of the waiter—temporary relief.

"Our friends here just got engaged," Randori said. "Bring us a bottle of your best swill, please. And could you round up the rest of the waiters and have them sing a little ditty? Something romantic. How about *Return to Sorrento*?"

The waiter offered a small smile. "I'm sorry sir, we don't sing, but what type of 'swill' will you be having?"

"How about a bag of your best cabernet? And I'll be smelling the cap, so don't try to fool me with any of that lower shelf stuff, all right?"

"Fine, sir, I'll return shortly to take your order."

"No, stay the same height," Randori said. "I can stand up if it bothers you."

The waiter's lips bowed upward in mild amusement before he turned on his heels to depart. Lynn Randori buried her face in her hands.

Blanchard patted her arm. "It's all right, Lynn, Doc embarrasses us all."

"I can get him scheduled for an MRI," Neidrich offered, "and we can find out what area of his brain is responsible for this behavior."

"I'm just setting the guy at ease," Randori said. "He doesn't get to wait on high rollers like us too often, I bet. Besides, his sense of humor helps gauge how much I tip."

"Right," Lynn groaned, "and he knows he has to humor you, so he goes along, reinforcing your belief that you're funny. Meanwhile, I have to endure you."

Neidrich waved the sign of the cross at her. "God bless you."

"What, like I'm some kind of vampire?" Randori said.

"You'd have to be to drink this," the waiter said, returning with the wine. He displayed the label. "The vintage is October."

"My favorite month," Randori said. "Pour away."

He offered a toast to the couple then raised his glass to Neidrich. "I haven't properly thanked you for giving me the benefit of the doubt."

"Something told me you were OK from the start," Neidrich said, shifting to face Randori. "Although I have to admit, you're weird. I like to think we're friends, though."

"Maybe the only one I have outside my family."

That statement, unique as it was to Randori's lips, caught Blanchard's attention. "Wait a minute, Doc. What about Virgil, or Kerry and Meryl? What about me?"

Randori cocked his head and peered deeply into Blanchard's eyes. "One question, Cat: who told Kass about the phony announcements I posted? The ox roast?" A friendly smile brought an unsettling emotional dissonance to his query.

"I don't know," Blanchard said, taken aback. "Kass shocked the heck out of me with that one."

Randori stared at Blanchard for an uncomfortable moment before Lynn broke the silence. "Jeez, Brian, you are weird."

"Sure settled it in my mind," Neidrich said.

Lynn shot a piercing glance at her husband and clasped Cat's hand to pull her into a quietly animated conversation. They would talk about plans for the wedding—and afterward—and then discuss a detailed history of the relationship, including, of course, a loving recollection of Neidrich's merits and foibles.

Shaking off the counselor's exchange with his fiancée, Neidrich said, "Once I got to know you and the people around you, it was easy to tell the good guys from the bad."

Randori stared toward the restaurant entrance. "Not all that easy sometimes."

Meryl Morgan and Kerry Wyatt had just walked through the door. Morgan made eye contact with Randori and tugged Wyatt's arm in the direction of the foursome.

"Déjà vu," Wyatt said as he arrived at the table, "only better. Doc and Lynn enter the picture." He leaned over to hug Lynn and properly shook hands with the other three.

Randori was cordial, but not warm. Neidrich took it as a hint that theirs was a private party—a relief. He did want to be polite, though. "Congratulations on your new job, Ms. Morgan. And good luck in your retirement, Mr. Wyatt."

"Thank you, Trooper Neidrich." Morgan shot another quick glance at Randori. "It's sad to be leaving Freedom Con, but this is the opportunity I've been waiting for."

Wyatt smiled at Morgan. "I'm sure you will prove yourself in short order, Meryl, just as I am certain that I will prove to be an excellent retiree." Placing his hand on Randori's shoulder, he added, "That leaves you, Doc. To bastardize Sartre, you remain condemned to Freedom—capital 'f', that is."

"Nick and Cat have good news," Lynn said, refusing to allow anything to cast a pall over the gathering.

"We're getting married," Blanchard blurted, adding the clarifying, "Nick and I."

"That's wonderful," Morgan said.

Wyatt broke into a broad grin. "Well, this is a night to celebrate. Congratulations, Nick. Good luck, Cat." After a round of congratulatory hugs and handshakes, Wyatt said, "We'll be off, then, and allow the four of you to enjoy this momentous occasion."

Watching Morgan and Wyatt leave, Blanchard attached prophecy to the meeting. "Here we are, same as our first date, seeing Kerry and Meryl again. It's a good sign."

"You make your own breaks," Randori said.

"Thank you, *Coach* Randori," Lynn said, staring dagger-eyed at her husband. "How about a little belief in magic."

"Magic is big portions and fast service. Speaking of which, here comes the grub."

The couples settled into their meals and the conversations as they were before Morgan and Wyatt had arrived.

"What's Harley been up to since he retired?" Randori asked.

"Spends time with Aggie, mostly." Neidrich chuckled. "He doesn't even stop by the station. He says Phyllis keeps trying to get him to show his scar."

"He's a lucky man," Randori said, shaking his head. "The bullet split the distance between his femoral artery and his cojones. Talk about a rock and a hard place—bleed to death or join the Vienna Boys' Choir."

"Harley surely went out on a high note," Neidrich said without a hint of irony, "solving the biggest murder cases in Freedom County history. But it was also a very low note—Ed's death. He always said, when the view from his office window lost its beauty ... Anyway, he had his fill of action last fall."

"Me, too. You know, you train in a martial art hoping never to use it."

"You were pretty enthusiastic with Dubcek."

Randori's face flushed, and he wiped his forehead with his napkin. "Leroy had to pay. It's amazing; the vicious things people do and say, knowing the victims of their persecution can't retaliate. And Roberge gets off with a hand slap. The justice system sucks."

Neidrich shrugged in resignation. "The DA needed Roberge's cooperation. Without his testimony, the case against Dubcek would've been a lot weaker. Besides, juries are reluctant to send a kid away for hard time. Still, he's in youth camp."

"He won't be there forever."

"That's what a good attorney will get you," Neidrich said. "Roberge was an 'innocent' who just happened to have a nine-millimeter semi-automatic and a boot knife in his bedroom along with hate-group propaganda on his computer. Then there was the Beretta he shot Harley with and, oh yes, the ingredients for a bomb."

Randori held up his hands and countered, "Ah, but having the ingredients doesn't mean you're going to build one. His attorney showed that those chemicals could be used in harmless ways, too."

Neidrich chuckled. "I liked your testimony: 'maybe he was going to enter the Pillsbury Bake-off.' "

"The judge had no sense of humor. He thought my answer indicated animosity toward the lad."

"When, in fact, all it shows is you're a wise-ass. Not everything is a joke, Doc."

"Yes, it is, 'cause if you don't laugh, you have to cry."

"At least you won't have to worry about Dubcek anymore. We got him and Roberge on all the murders except Justin Frederickson's, since we weren't willing to drag Brad Prusster into it and risk implicating him. Plus, they're taking the heroin rap."

Randori finished his wine and refilled his and Neidrich's glasses. "Funny thing, in the end they only admitted to killing Ed. Even then, they said they thought he was a prowler, breaking into the house, and they used deadly force because he had a gun."

A grin that matched Randori's spread across the trooper's face. In a throwaway line, he said, "As a friend of mine might say: maybe they just wanted to avoid the premeditation number for the Samson and Marburg raps."

"They could get those cases reopened."

"Right." Neidrich nodded and blinked in resignation. "Our case hinged on four things: First, all three murders occurred in a five week period; difficult to believe there was more than one group of homicidal school people out there. Second, the pathologist testified that the dagger we found hidden in Dubcek's home with traces of Ed's blood couldn't be ruled out as the weapon used on Samson and Marburg—same with that stiletto disguised as a letter opener he attacked you with. Third was the romantic link between Tammy Eboli and both Samson and Marburg combined with Dubcek's obsessive jealousy. But the clincher came when Kerry Wyatt revealed that he had kept both Samson and Marburg informed about Roberge's heroin operation and his ties to someone on the SAP team. Either Samson or Marburg—or both—must have shot their mouths off to the wrong person, unwittingly setting up their own murders."

Randori's eyes shifted down into his wine glass. "Yeah, seems like that's how it played out."

Neidrich's jaw clenched, and his stare became flinty, as he turned his back to the women and lowered his voice. "As a cop, it bothers me that they rationalized Roberge's actions. Don't get me wrong, it's important to understand why criminals do what they do so we can try to eliminate the causes. But they shouldn't be made into sympathetic characters. Lots of kids have it tough, but only a few become killers."

Randori smiled coolly as his friend became heated. "Yeah, whenever behavior falls outside the norm, it gets classified as a mental disorder, so the behavior becomes rationalized, if not justified, based on some childhood trauma. Jeffrey Dahmer had an eating disorder. Adolph Hitler had Viennese envy."

"Between that and the sense of entitlement some people have, it's no wonder civility has become an endangered social grace. And why it's so difficult to enforce the law, let alone get people to take responsibility for their actions."

Randori sipped his wine, quietly smacked his lips, and blinked. "Laws are words, written and interpreted by men, so they're open to corruption. That's why honor transcends law, and so does the honorable man."

Smiling uneasily, Neidrich said, "Are you justifying the 'honorable' vigilante?"

Randori cast a wistful glance. It passed so quickly it might have been a shadow in the flicker of the candle. He drained his wine glass and looked off, pensive. In profile, the candlelight reflected a tear overflowing its well in the corner of his eye.

The counselor's silent reaction forced Neidrich to shift his own eyes away. "Why is it when women talk, they forget about drinking, but when men talk, we drink even more?" He sneaked a sidelong glance at Randori. "At least we have designated drivers."

Cat and Lynn took that as their cue to collect car keys from the men. Without breaking conversational stride, they moved to the door, while the trooper and the counselor stayed back to settle the tab.

"Why don't we head to the coffee shop next door?" Randori said. "I could use some espresso for the road."

"I never turn down a shot of good coffee."

At the door, Randori stopped short. "I want to say goodbye to Kerry and Meryl. You go ahead; I'll meet you in ten minutes."

Wyatt and Morgan looked up, surprised by Randori's sudden appearance. "Doc," Morgan said with an odd mix of affection and anxiety. "Sit down. We haven't seen you much since the infamous 'time of troubles.' "

"Just wanted to say goodbye. I won't be seeing you two anymore."

"I'll be coming back from Costa Rica to visit," Wyatt said. "I'll be tan, not to mention fat and satisfied, but I'll still be me."

"And I'll see you at conferences," Morgan said. "I hope so, anyway."

"I kind of thought you two would be getting together."

The pair exchanged smiles and Wyatt spoke for both. "Much as I tried to convince Meryl of my impeccable qualifications, the lure of the superintendency is more attractive than I am, even with a tropical paradise thrown in for temptation."

"Too bad. After all you've been through together." Randori flicked the back of his fingernails against his cheek as if brushing away an imaginary fly. He placed an elbow on the table and leaned forward so the softness of his voice carried to their ears only. "At least you'll have your freedom."

Wyatt frowned. "What do you mean by that, Doc?"

"The things we do for love or vengeance."

Wyatt's mouth drew down into its severe mask; his eyes narrowed, peering into Randori's mind. "Ah, I think I see what you're getting at. You're saying Meryl or I had something to do with one of those murders, and we're getting off scot-free."

"Nobody ever gets off scot-free. We live with the consequences of our actions."

Morgan's eyes fell, but Wyatt smiled and calmly said, "The patented Randori smokescreen. You knew the more we thought about it, the more we would realize the wrong people went to jail for Kass's murder. It was you, my friend, wasn't it?"

"No, Kerry, that particular assassin would be another friend of ours, one with a strong sense of duty and an even stronger sense of mission. And an opportunistic wife. A principal has status. Higher pay, too; the price of bragging rights at the country club."

"Virgil?" Wyatt chuckled. "He's loyal to a fault. He always says he would fall on his sword for the District. Besides, he has an alibi for the night Kass died."

"Come on, Kerry," Randori scowled, "Virge's alibi for the night Kass died is no better than yours or mine is for the night Bob died."

"You're saying Virgil and Lois were in on it together?"

"No, she's just being a loyal wife. I'm sure she thinks Virge is innocent, but she knew he didn't have an alibi. There she was, so close to having her dream come true, just a white lie away. After all, she said she met him at his office, not the stadium. That's why no witnesses could confirm she was there that night. And Virge? You don't think he could take a trek to Kass's house, do the deed, dump him in the quarry, and head home?"

"Through the woods? In the dark? That has to be three, maybe four, miles."

"He's trekked across Mesopotamia in the summer! You think a jaunt through the Newcastle woods would bother him?"

Morgan shook her head. "But we're talking Virgil here, Doc; I can't believe—"

Randori held up his hand to interrupt. "The day Dubcek and Roberge were arrested, Virge, Cat, and I were having coffee in my office. Virge just happened to reveal Tammy as the link between Leroy and Bob—Bob's affair with her and Leroy's obsession with her. When Cat asked why he hadn't told anyone about that, Virge said Bob and Tammy were old news by August; she had moved on to someone new. The way I figure, Virge knew that *someone new* was Kass, and he probably guessed Cat suspected it, too. All three of us were there the day Kass suspended me, and the way Tammy was looking at Kass and acting toward him told me she had strong feelings for him. So, without spoon-feeding Cat, Virge provided the link between the two murders. Then, he just sat back and watched the tumblers fall, knowing Cat would tell Nick."

"You're trying to clear yourself with assumptions," Wyatt said. "That's not the way we see it. Correct, Meryl?"

Before Morgan could respond, Randori said, "Wrong. Virge had his fill of both Kass and Leroy. And he was tired of freaking Lady Macbeth getting on him for dedicating his life to the District with nothing to show for it. He finally realized his highest duty was to his family. Virge is a smart guy; he was patient, and he withheld just enough information to keep the police running around while he waited for the right time to visit Kass. That right time came when Virgil maneuvered Kass into suspending me and taking my place at the MDE."

"Phil Olson ordered that," Morgan said.

"Phil's a punk; he could never make Kass do anything. No, Virge knew how to get Kass to move on me. He struck at his pride." Randori smiled and shook his head in appreciation of Davis's expert manipulation.

"How so?" Wyatt asked.

"I had been posting bogus memos from Kass on the faculty bulletin board, trying to get under his skin without getting nabbed for insubordination."

"Kass's TV offer," Morgan said, smiling despite the gravity of the conversation, "and the interviews to be his homecoming date. I should have known that was you."

"Yeah, well, Virge and Cat caught me with one inviting the faculty to Kass's house for an ox roast. Virge threw it away—so I wouldn't get into trouble," Randori added with silken sarcasm. "But on the day he suspended me, Kass couldn't resist bringing up the memos. And he specifically mentioned the ox roast. I bet Virge was hoping I didn't catch on to that."

"Cat could've been the one who told Kass," Wyatt said.

Morgan shook her head. "Cat doesn't have a treacherous bone in her body." She turned to Randori. "But one of them could have told a third party we don't know about."

The counselor cocked his head. "Maybe, but I doubt it. By that time, Cat was thinking I was OK, so she would've protected me. And Virgil is so anal-retentive he would never leave something like that to chance. It's a simple formula, really: Virge shows Kass my ox roast memo—to suck up and bring Kass's guard down. Kass suspends me and goes to the Roberge MDE in my place. Virge knows Kass will get confrontational, upstaging Leroy and threatening to expel Paul, thus setting up his own murder, with Leroy as the stooge.

"Next comes the execution. Virgil knows Kass's schedule: Whenever he takes the afternoon off to golf, he goes to the Miners' Café afterward. Since he's with the boys and not Tammy, and since it's a school night, Kass goes home alone. Virge waits for him, and, zip-zop: Sushi Marburg, commando-style."

"But Virgil set you up, too," Morgan said. "Kass suspends you in the morning, and that night he dies. Virgil doesn't know Leroy's schedule; he might've had an alibi."

"Don't forget, Virge and I knew Roberge was dealing heroin, and we thought he and Leroy might be in cahoots. Leroy's wife is usually on the road, so odds were good that he was moonlighting with Roberge. But, even if Leroy did have an alibi, Virge knew I probably didn't. Now, I don't think he wanted me to take the fall for Kass's death, but I was a great backup scapegoat. A good military man always has a contingency plan. In war there's collateral damage; innocent people sometimes go down."

"Interesting theory, Doc," Wyatt said, "but a roundabout route to a conclusion. Positing you as Kass's murderer is a direct line."

"There is one more thing. Do you remember Virge's tradition with funerals?"

Wyatt sighed with strained patience. "Back when he was in the army, Virgil and his men always saw the body onto the plane as it was being shipped home. After the war, whenever a man from his unit died, he always attended the funeral."

"Virge even traveled to Oklahoma once," Randori said. "He went whether he liked the man or not, out of respect for someone who shared the same cause."

"Yes," Wyatt said. "They pledged the survivors would throw dirt on the casket as a final send-off. Virgil carried on the custom with colleagues from work."

Randori smiled. "So, he went to Bob's funeral, and even though Bob stabbed him in the back and held him down professionally, Virge threw dirt on his casket."

"I watched him do that. Where are you headed with this, Doc?"

"Do you remember what Virge said about an exception to that custom?"

Wyatt sighed. "The soldier Virgil and the others were so prejudiced against. How did he put it?" Wyatt's eyes searched the ceiling and his memory banks. "Oh yes, they 'terminated the relationship.' When the man died, Virgil said they left his body in the sand. We thought it strange because we never knew Virgil to be prejudiced." He shifted in his seat. "Again, the relevance of all this?"

Randori smiled mildly and held up a hand, begging patience. "Did Virge just say prejudiced, or was there a degree of prejudice? Let me jog your memory. He told us the story at that School Board Appreciation Dinner you made me attend a few years ago."

"I remember, Meryl was mingling with the board members while you, Virgil, and I drank to anaesthetize ourselves against the entire experience. Virgil started telling war stories." He glanced off into the past, falling silent. Finally, it came to him. "I think he said he was extremely prejudiced. So?"

Randori nodded in approbation. "We were drinking single malt ether, as I recall. I'm glad it didn't blur your photographic memory. Virge said they 'terminated the relationship with extreme prejudice.' "

"That might have been what he said." Wyatt shrugged in perplexed assent.

Randori looked to Morgan and smiled. "Meryl, sweetheart, please tell our culturally-challenged paisan here what 'terminate with extreme prejudice' means."

Morgan's eyes narrowed pensively for a moment before they sprung wide in recognition. "It's from *Apocalypse Now*. It means: to assassinate someone. Oh, my God, Virgil must have killed that soldier! Now I see what you're getting at. Virgil was at the church for Kass's funeral, but he didn't go to the cemetery to throw dirt on the casket!" Her tone became cautionary: "I could've missed him, though."

"Not likely," Randori said. "You and I were standing beside Nick and Harley, in perfect position to observe everyone who passed the casket. That's why I went to the cemetery. I wanted to see if Virge would show—and to keep you company, of course. You don't honestly think I give a rip about seeing a corpse in a crash helmet. Virge had to show face at the church so he wouldn't raise suspicion. For him it was a matter of honor *not* to go to the cemetery, although killing someone isn't real honorable, either."

"But you're 'real honorable,' aren't you, Doc?" Wyatt said, lowering his voice to an ominous rumble. "If we're to believe the pap you're feeding us, you're letting Virgil off for Kass's murder, and, in your paranoid mind, you're letting me, or, I suppose, Meryl and me, go free for Bob's death."

"I never put myself up as a paragon of honor." Randori arched an eyebrow and glanced upward, as if balancing alternatives. "Leroy and Roberge did kill Ed; I don't mind seeing them take the fall for Kass's and Bob's murders, too. They're—how would you put it?—'faulty organisms.' That's what won out in the end for you, too. Right? Why else would you testify that you shared information about their heroin operation with Kass and Bob? Hell, you would never tell those buffoons anything, let alone something as sensitive as that. They would've blown the whole thing just to feed their egos."

"I still don't buy your theory on Virgil; it's based on assumptions. But let's hear your hypothesis about Meryl and/or me."

"Same as with Virge." Randori tapped his temple. "It's having the right information and putting it together."

"So you're smarter than both Nick Neidrich and Harley Snitz?"

"God, no, I just made a conscious decision not to share some information with them, information they would have no way of knowing unless they learned it by chance. Like Virge's custom of pitching dirt on caskets. Sometimes, they had partial information, and I withheld a key piece." Randori leaned across the table and smiled, raising and lowering his eyebrows, Groucho Marx-style. "Like the nunchucks. Then there were clues I received only tonight, but, of course, it's too late to enter new evidence, isn't it?"

Wyatt leaned back in his chair. "What about the nunchucks?"

"Interesting you should zero in on them. I would have found it more intriguing to learn what was revealed tonight. The clues keep trickling in."

"All right," Wyatt said with a sigh of exasperation, "what did you learn tonight?"

"Only a small piece in the big picture, really. When I came over and implied that you might've had something to do with the murders, you took the offensive by accusing me of Kass's murder. That's because you already know who offed the Bobster, right?"

"That's not a small piece in the big picture," Wyatt said. "It's another stone in the yellow brick psycho-path your mind is on. And stop it with the eyebrows!" The pitch of his voice, raised in frustration, caught the attention of a woman at the next table.

Randori ignored Wyatt's barb. "But of course you would be interested in the nunchucks—lacquered black with the gold-flake dragons that hit Bob so hard paint chips embedded in his skull. They should have pointed directly at me. Lots of witnesses saw mine when I gave my demonstration at the alternative school. But only one person left before the end of the demonstration—when I showed everyone that the nunchucks were rubber over a solid core. Relatively harmless." Randori raised his chin toward Wyatt. "You were the one who left. I kept that tidbit from Nick when he questioned me."

"Where would I get nunchucks?"

"Oh, I don't know. At any of the thousand martial arts retailers in New York?"

Morgan shot a piercing stare at Wyatt, and Randori shifted a smile toward her. "This is news to you, Meryl. The ninja-style stabbing was a nice touch, though. You learned to fence at the same place Leroy did. Right?"

"If you're implying that Meryl—" Wyatt said indignantly. "It's preposterous!"

"I'm not so sure Nick and Harley would've thought so. There's more. You have to know the nights Lynn works so you can avoid scheduling meetings for me after 3:00 on those days. You knew I'd be home alone with the kids. Through small talk, you even know when they go to bed. So, you scheduled a meeting with Bob to keep him around the office even later than usual. He always worked late in August, anyway—typical coach."

"Why would I do that to you?" Wyatt protested. "You're my friend."

"And who'd ever think a friend would frame me? But Meryl didn't know what the nunchucks were about, did she? The head bashing was just a sign of your devotion." Randori searched Morgan's eyes, and his gaze softened. "No, you didn't know. But you did know you got Bob's testosterone flowing. The way I figure, you told him you'd thought about it, and, what the hell, the opportunity to make love to Big Bob Samson was too great to resist. With his ego, he'd never think something was up.

"Where did he want to take you? Oh yes, to one of the parking spots he'd used since he was a kid growing up in Newcastle—in the woods near the quarry." Randori paused to bask in the heat of his friends' stares. "Meryl Morgan in the back seat of his Mercedes; hot damn. To make sure no one would see the two of you together, you said you'd meet him there, but he'd have to give you directions. Directions you passed along to Kerry so he could arrive early and hide out. The perfect set-up: no witnesses, no chance of finding the crime scene. I bet you really caught him off-guard, the way you caught me at the cemetery the day of Kass's funeral."

"That's not what that was about, Doc. If anything, it proved I'd never hurt you."

"I believe you, but I also know you covered for Kerry. When has he ever waited until Saturday to visit his daughter? When he's headed up there, he comes to work on Friday with his car packed and takes a half-day off. That way he can beat the New York rush hour traffic, get there for supper, and spend an extra evening with her. Why, on that particular weekend, would he change his routine?"

"It was the last weekend before the school year started," Wyatt said. "I couldn't afford the time away from the office."

"Maybe, but I like my scenario better. What I want to know is why did you have to drag me into it? Why not hit him with a golf club and blame it on Kass, or bludgeon him with a copy of the DSM and blame Leroy from the get-go?"

Morgan and Randori looked to Wyatt, who studied each of their faces in turn. His wide grin appeared, but no humor glowed in his dead, dark eyes. "I'm not admitting anything, but who would blame me if I wanted to get you out of the way? You and Meryl. I don't even want to know what happened at Kass's funeral, but I've known of your infatuation with each other for a long time. Don't be self-righteous, Doc, it's the only reason you haven't shared your theory with the police. You even bore the suspicion of murder for Meryl."

Morgan's head shot toward him. "Kerry, that's —"

"Did you really think you could fool me? I saw how you looked at him." Wyatt's voice caught; his eyes misted. "How you touch his hand but pull away when I offer mine."

Morgan leaned forward, her hand moving toward Wyatt's arm. "Kerry."

Wyatt lifted his fingers off the tabletop to wave off her caress. "And you, Doc, when you found out about Bob harassing Meryl, your outburst. It was proof."

Randori nodded. "And that's when you knew you had to do something."

Wyatt raised his eyes to the ceiling, in confession or frustration, or both. "True, I wanted Bob out of the way, no question about that, for the good of the District, but more importantly, for what he had done to Meryl. And I wanted you out of the way, too, although I have to admit, I felt a certain ambivalence about that."

"Kerry," Morgan said again, this time, her voice falling off in disappointment.

"So you pitched your scheme to Meryl," Randori continued, "conveniently leaving out your plans for me. You'd go on defending me, deflecting any suspicion that you might have framed me, but you set up the circumstantial number, almost perfectly, thinking your path to Meryl would be clear." He offered a tender glance to Morgan. "And Meryl wanted to believe the pipe dream rather than admit there's no way she could do anything really meaningful for needy kids. Not at the great Freedom Con."

Wyatt growled, "As proven by the Board's decision to appoint that … Phil Olson as superintendent."

"I wouldn't complain. If Meryl had gotten the job, don't you think you would've drawn a little more scrutiny, since you alibied for each other?"

Tears welled in Morgan's eyes; her lips quivered. She gripped Randori's hand and locked him into her soulful gaze. "And Kerry and I lost you. At least we know you didn't kill Kass. I'm so glad you're innocent."

"But I'm not free." Randori gently broke from her grasp and stood, casting a stony stare at Wyatt before returning his attention to Morgan. He bent and rubbed a tear from her cheek. "I guess that's the way it's supposed to end." Having said all there was to say, and having learned all there was to learn, Randori turned his back on Wyatt and Morgan for the last time and went to meet Neidrich.